*Also by Hanya Yanagihara*

A Little Life

# THE PEOPLE
# IN THE TREES

Hanya Yanagihara lives in
New York City.

'*The Peo*...                                                   st novels.
This is ...                                                    icle into
another ...                                                    nonstrous
confession, and a fascinating consideration of moral relativism.
Yanagihara's narrator is misanthropic and grotesque, yet simultaneously magnetic; her prose is dazzling; and her book is a triumph
of the imagination.' ANTHONY DOERR

'This is an engrossing, beautifully detailed, at times amazing (and
shocking) novel, and right up my alley: a far-off and beautiful place
in the Pacific, islanders living to their own drumbeat, earnest
meddling outsiders, and a sticky outcome – the Fall, with a lot of
science and passion behind it, and an impressive debut for Hanya
Yanagihara. I loved this book.' PAUL THEROUX

'An absorbing, intelligent and uncompromising novel which beguiles
and unnerves. The first memorable novel of 2014 is already here.'
*Independent*

'Told in the form of a memoir in the voice of the extremely unlike-
able Perina, it is impossible to resist being drawn into the mind of
this brilliant but depraved man. And to feel a little disturbed at
having enjoyed such a strange but brilliantly told story. The book is
packed with a symphony of complex themes made accessible by the
sheer poetry of the author's prose.' *Daily Mail*

'Power and its abuses are at the heart of this beautifully written
debut ... Striking and highly satisfying. Yanagihara's ambitious
debut is one to be lauded.' *Guardian*

'Feels like a *National Geographic* story by way of Conrad's *Heart of
Darkness* ... The world Yanagihara conjures up, full of dark pockets
of mystery, is magical.' *The Times*

'Suspenseful ... Thanks to Yanagihara's rich, masterly prose, it's
hard to turn away ... As for Yanagihara, she is a writer to marvel at.'
*New York Times*

# THE
# PEOPLE
# IN THE
# TREES

*Hanya Yanagihara*

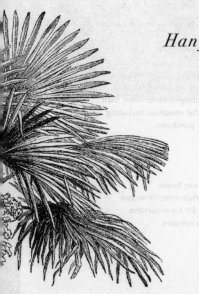

**PICADOR**

First published in the United States 2013 by Doubleday,
a division of Random House Inc., New York

First published in the UK 2014 by Atlantic Books

This edition first published 2018 by Picador
an imprint of Pan Macmillan
20 New Wharf Road, London N1 9RR
Associated companies throughout the world
www.panmacmillan.com

ISBN 978-1-5098-9298-3

9 8 7 6 5 4 3 2 1

A CIP catalogue record for this book is available from the British Library.

Printed and bound by CPI Group (UK) Ltd, Croydon, CR0 4YY

Visit **www.picador.com** to re͟
and to buy them. You will als͟
news of any author events, an͟
so that you're always first to h͟

PROSPERO:

A devil, a born devil, on whose nature
Nurture can never stick; on whom my pains,
Humanely taken, all, all lost, quite lost;
And as with age his body uglier grows,
So his mind cankers. I will plague them all,
Even to roaring.

*The Tempest*, ACT IV, Scene 1

# CONTENTS

To my father
*"Vom Vater... Lust zu fabulieren"*

# THE PEOPLE
# IN THE TREES

March 19, 1995
**Renowned Scientist Faces Charges of Sexual Abuse**
BY THE ASSOCIATED PRESS

*Bethesda, Md.—Dr. Abraham Norton Perina, the renowned
immunologist and director emeritus of the Center for Immunology
and Virology at the National Institutes of Health in Bethesda,
Maryland, was arrested yesterday on charges of sexual abuse.*

*Dr. Perina, 71, was charged with three counts of rape, three counts
of statutory rape, two counts of sexual assault, and two counts of
endangering a minor. The charges originated with one of Dr. Perina's
adopted sons.*

*"These charges are false," said Perina's attorney, Douglas
Hindley, in a statement yesterday. "Dr. Perina is a prominent and
highly respected member of the scientific community, and is eager to
resolve this situation as quickly as possible so that he may return to
work and his family."*

*Dr. Perina won the Nobel Prize in Medicine in 1974 for his
identification of Selene syndrome, a condition that retards aging. The
condition, in which the victim's body remains preserved in relative
youth even as his mind degrades, was found among the Opa'ivu'eke
people of Ivu'ivu, one of the three islands of the Micronesian
country of U'ivu. It was acquired through the consumption of a rare
turtle for which Dr. Perina named the tribe and whose flesh was
discovered to inactivate telomerase, the naturally occurring enzyme
that disintegrates telomeres and thereby limits each cell's number
of divisions. Individuals affected by Selene syndrome—named
for the immortal and eternally youthful moon goddess in Greek
mythology—were found to be able to live for centuries with the
condition. Perina, who first traveled to U'ivu as a young physician
with the noted anthropologist Paul Tallent in 1950, spent many years
in the islands conducting field research. It was also there that he
adopted his 43 children, many of them orphans or sons and daughters
of impoverished Opa'ivu'eke tribespeople. A number of the children
are currently under Perina's care.*

*"Norton is an exemplary father and a brilliant mind," said Dr.
Ronald Kubodera, a longtime research fellow in Perina's lab and*

*one of the scientist's closest friends. "I have every faith that these ridiculous charges will be dropped."*

*⁂*

### December 3, 1997
### Prominent Scientist, Nobel Laureate, Sentenced to Prison
BY REUTERS

*Bethesda, Md.—Dr. Abraham Norton Perina was sentenced today to 24 months at the Frederick Correctional Facility.*

*Dr. Perina was awarded the 1974 Nobel Prize in Medicine for proving that the ingestion of a now-extinct turtle from the Micronesian country of U'ivu would inactivate telomerase, which limits each cell's number of divisions. The condition, which is known as Selene syndrome, was found to be transferable in a variety of mammals, including humans.*

*Perina was among the only Westerners to be granted unlimited access to this most remote and secretive of islands, and in 1968 he adopted the first of what were to be 43 children from the country, all of whom were raised in his Bethesda home. Two years ago, Perina was charged with rape and endangerment of a child; his accuser is one of his adopted children.*

*"This is a great tragedy," says Dr. Louis Altschur, the director of the National Institutes of Health, where Dr. Perina was a scientist for many years. "Norton is a great mind and talent, and I fervently hope that he will be able to get the treatment and help he needs."*

*Neither Perina nor his lawyer could be reached for comment.*

# PREFACE

I am Ronald Kubodera—but only in academic journals. To everyone else, I am Ron. Yes, I am the Dr. Ronald Kubodera about whom you have no doubt read in the magazines and newspapers. No, not all the stories are true—they rarely are, of course.

But in my case, the most important ones are, and I am proud of them. I am proud, for example, to have any sort of relationship at all with Norton (and mind you, just eighteen months ago I would not have even needed to say this), whom I have known since 1970, when I began working in his lab in Bethesda, Maryland, at the National Institutes of Health. Norton had not then received his Nobel Prize, but already his work had revolutionized the medical community, forever changing the way scholars would perceive the fields of virology and immunology, as well as, it should be said, medical anthropology. I am proud too of the fact that after establishing a relationship as colleagues, we began an equally intense one as friends; indeed, my relationship with Norton is the most meaningful one I have ever known. Most important, though, I am proud of the fact that after the events of the previous two years, I am still his friend, and he is still mine.

Not, of course, that I have had the opportunity to speak or communicate with Norton as often as I'd—or, no doubt, he'd—like. It is a strange and lonely thing, not having him nearby. In fact, until I moved here[1] some sixteen months ago—a month after Norton's sen-

---

[1] To Palo Alto, California, where I hold the John M. Torrance Chair in the Immunology Department of Stanford University Medical School.

tence was handed down—I don't believe that, in the natural course of daily events and so forth, we'd spent more than two days not in each other's company. Maybe not even that long. (I am, of course, excluding special circumstances, such as the occasional vacation with my then-wife, or trips we made independent of each other to events such as funerals and weddings, etc. But even on those occasions, I would make an effort to communicate with him daily, either by phone or by fax.) The point is, talking to Norton, working with Norton, *being* with Norton, was simply a part of my quotidian life, in much the way some people watch television daily or read the newspaper daily: it is one of those forgettable yet not insignificant rituals, one that reassures you that life is progressing as expected. But when such a rhythm is suddenly interrupted, it is worse than unsettling, it is unmooring. It is how I have been feeling this past year and a half or so. In the mornings I wake and go through my day as always, but in the evenings I invariably delay bedtime, wander through my apartment, stare out into the night, wonder what it is I have forgotten. I tick down the dozens of tiny chores that I complete, thoughtlessly, in a typical day—letters opened and answered? deadlines met? doors locked?—until finally, regretfully, I climb into bed. It is only on the lip of sleep that I remember that the very *pattern* of my life has changed, and then I experience a brief moment of melancholy. You would think that I would be able by now to accept the changed circumstances of Norton's, and by extension my, life, but something in me resists; he was, after all, part of my routine for almost three decades.

But if life is lonely for me, it is far lonelier for Norton. When I think of him in that place, I am quite simply angry: Norton is no longer a young man, nor a healthy one, and imprisonment hardly seems an appropriate or reasonable punishment.

I know this belief is a minority opinion. I have lost count of the number of times I have tried to explain Norton—his humanity, his intelligence, his extraordinariness—to friends, colleagues, and reporters (and judges, juries, and lawyers). Indeed, there have been many times over these past sixteen months when I am reminded of Norton's former friends' treachery, how quickly they forgot and abandoned a man they claimed to love and respect. Some friends—people

Norton had known and worked with for decades—all but vanished as soon as charges were brought against him. Worse, though, were those who left him after he was found guilty. I was reminded then of how disloyal and duplicitous most people are.

But I am digressing. One of the primary difficulties of incarceration for Norton has been battling the intense monotony that has inevitably come to define his situation. I must admit, I was a little surprised when he began, less than a month into his term, to complain of crippling boredom. It had always been one of Norton's fondest dreams—the dream, I think, of many brilliant and over-extended men—that one month, or one year, he'd find himself in a warm place with absolutely no commitments. There would be no speeches to give, no articles to edit or write, no students to instruct, no children to look after, no research to conduct; only a blank, flat expanse of open time, which he would be free to clutter with whatever he wished. Norton had always spoken of time as a sea, a mirrorlike, endless stretch of emptiness, and indeed this dream—"sea time," he called it—became a sort of joke, a shorthand for talking about subjects he hoped one day to pursue but had no way of engaging in at the present moment. And so he would make vows: he would breed tropical ferns in sea time. He would read biographies in sea time. He would write his memoirs in sea time. No one, least of all Norton, ever thought he would actually ever *have* sea time, but now, of course, he does, minus the warm location and pleasant, lazy torpor that one associates with hard-earned idleness. But unfortunately, it appears that Norton is perhaps simply not equipped for leisure; indeed, it has been torturous for him (although of course I admit that a great deal of this may be attributable to the unfortunate circumstances under which this leisure was granted him). In a recent letter, he wrote:

> *There is little here to do, and, after a certain point, even less to think. I never considered that I might find myself in such a state, so exhausted, really, that I feel exsanguinated, not of blood but of thought. Boredom—I'd always thought, really, that I would treasure a period of unceasing emptiness, that I would easily fill it. But time, I've come to realize, is not for us to fill in such great,*

*blank slabs: we speak of managing time, but it is the opposite——*
*our lives are filled with busyness because those thin chinks of time*
*are all we can truly master.*[2]

It seems a wise insight.

But despite the obvious severity of the circumstances in which
Norton now finds himself, there are some who have had the temerity
to suggest that he should be grateful for what they consider the leni-
ency of his current condition, a suggestion that seems not only obtuse
but cruel. One of these people is a man named Herbert West (whose
name I have reluctantly changed), another of Norton's research fellows from the early '80s, who stopped by to visit Norton in Bethesda
while on the way to a conference in London. This was before the trial
but after the arraignment, when Norton was under what amounted
to house arrest and all of his children had been removed from his
care. West, whom I had always considered more tolerable than many
of Norton's previous fellows, visited with Norton for an hour or so
and then asked me if I wanted to have dinner at a restaurant with
him. I did not particularly want to (and thought it awfully rude that
he had invited me in front of Norton, who, after all, was not allowed
to leave the house), but Norton told me I should go, that he had some
work he wished to complete and would not mind the privacy.

So I was made to go to dinner with West, and although I found
it difficult not to think of Norton alone in his house, we did manage
to have a surprisingly pleasant talk about West's work and the paper
he would present at his conference, and about an article Norton and
I had published in the *New England Journal of Medicine* before he
was arrested, and about some mutual acquaintances, until West said,
as our desserts were set before us, "Norton's aged a great deal."

I said, "He is in a terrible situation."

"Yes, terrible," murmured West.

"It is grossly unfair," I said.

West said nothing.

"Grossly unfair," I repeated, giving him another chance.

West sighed and blotted the corners of his mouth with the point

[2] A. Norton Perina to Ronald Kubodera, M.D., April 24, 1998.

of his napkin, a gesture both contrived and effete, as well as ostentatiously, obnoxiously Anglophilic. (West had studied—decades ago, and for two years only—at Oxford University on a Marshall Fellowship, a fact he was unusually talented at alluding to in every social and business interaction.) He was eating blueberry cobbler, and it had stained his teeth the livid purple of bruises.

"Ron," he began.

"Yes?" I said.

"Do you think he did it?" asked West.

I had by that time learned to expect that question, and also what to say in response. "Do you?"

West looked at me and smiled, and then looked at the ceiling before looking at me again. "Yes," he said.

I said nothing.

"You don't," said West, a little wonderingly.

I had learned what to say to this as well. "It is not relevant whether he did or not," I said. "Norton is a great mind, and that is all that matters to me and I should say to history as well."

There was a silence.

At last West said sheepishly, "I'd better get back soon. I've got some reading to do before my flight tomorrow."

"All right," I said. And we finished our desserts in silence.

I had driven us to the restaurant, and after we paid for dinner (West tried to treat me, but I prevailed) I drove West back to his hotel. In the car he made some attempts at conversation, which infuriated me further.

In the hotel parking lot, after sitting in silence for a few minutes, West expectantly, me angrily, he at last extended his hand, and I shook it.

"Well," said West.

"Thank you for visiting," I told him crisply. "I know Norton appreciated it."

"Well," West said again. I could not tell if he had appreciated my sarcasm or not; I thought not. "I'll be thinking of him."

There was another silence.

"If he's found guilty——" West began.

"He will not be," I told him.

"But if he is," West continued, "will he go to prison?"

"I cannot imagine it," I answered.

"Well, if he does," West persisted, and I remembered how unattractively ambitious, how *grabby* West had been as a fellow, and how impatient he had been to leave Norton's lab and run his own, "that'll at least be a lot of sea time for him, won't it, Ron?" I was so appalled by this flippancy that I found myself unable to respond. As I sat there gaping, West smiled at me, said another goodbye, and got out of the car. I watched him enter the hotel through its double doors and walk into the brightly lit lobby, and then I started the car again to return to Norton's, where I spent most nights. In the months after, the trial began and ended, and then the sentencing began and ended, but needless to say, West never again came to visit Norton.

But as I was saying, no, people are not sympathetic to Norton's current situation. Indeed, people condemned and dismissed him before he was officially condemned and dismissed, legally, by a jury of his supposed peers—what must it feel like to be a man of Norton's intellect and have your character determined and your fate writ by twelve incompetents (one juror, as I recall, was a tollbooth clerk, another a dog-washer), whose decision renders virtually every one of your previous accomplishments insignificant, if not entirely meaningless? From that perspective, then, is it any mystery that Norton should now find himself depressed, bored, and unstimulated?

I should also like to say a few words about the media coverage surrounding Norton's trial, for it seems foolish to ignore both its tenor and its scope. I will first say that given the nature of the crimes of which Norton was accused, it has not surprised me in the least that the media has wasted pages and pages on stories that embroider, elaborately and with a shocking disregard for the truth, upon the few facts of Norton's personal life known to the public. (Admittedly, the stories did, rather begrudgingly, detail some of his considerable accomplishments, but only to throw into sharper relief his purported wickedness.)

I recall that in those days I stood vigil with Norton in his house while he awaited his trial (outside, a group of television reporters spent their days congregating on the curb at the edge of Norton's lawn, eating and chatting in the buzzy, insect-thick summer air as if at a picnic), of the many (unfulfilled, naturally) requests we received for interviews, only one—regrettably, *Playboy*—invited Norton to write his own defense instead of dispatching some salivating young writer to interpret his life and alleged misdeeds for the reading public. (I had originally thought the offer a good idea, despite the forum, but Norton was worried that whatever he wrote would be manipulated and used against him as a confession. He was correct, of course, and that was the end of that idea.) But I also knew that the realization that he must not allow himself to speak in his own defense infuriated and saddened him.

The ironic thing about this was that shortly before he had been arrested, Norton had in fact been planning to write his memoirs. By that time—1995—he was semiretired and no longer forced to contend with the various administrative duties and hassles of the lab. This is not to imply that he was not still the most vital and indispensable mind there—simply that he had begun to allow himself to organize his time in different ways.

However, Norton was not to have the opportunity to record his remarkable life, at least not under the conditions I know he would have preferred. But as I have always said, his is the sort of mind that can surmount any challenge. And so in April, two months after he began serving his sentence, I asked in my daily letter to him whether he might not consider writing his memoirs anyway. Not only, I told him, would they make a great contribution to the worlds of letters and science, but he would at last have a chance to prove to anyone interested that he was not what the world had been so eager to make him. I explained that I would be honored to type and, if he might let me, lightly edit his writing, as I had done before for various papers he had submitted to journals. It would be, I wrote, a fascinating project for me, and one that might keep him entertained.

A week later, Norton sent me a brief note:

*Although I can't say I wish to spend what may be the final years of my life trying to convince anyone that I am not guilty of the crimes they have decided I am, I have chosen to begin, as you say, the "story of my life." My trust [in you] is ... [very] great.*[3]

I had the first installment a month later.

❧

There are a few things I suppose I should say by means of introduction before I invite the reader to learn of Norton's extraordinary life. For it, after all, is a story with disease at its heart.

Norton, of course, will say it all better than I, but I will here give the reader some details about the man at hand. He once remarked to me that his life did not begin in any meaningful way until he left the country for U'ivu, where he would make discoveries that would transform modern medicine and lead to his receipt of the Nobel Prize. In 1950, when he was twenty-five, he made his first trip to the then obscure Micronesian country, a trip that would change his life—and revolutionize the scientific community—forever. While in U'ivu, he lived among a "lost tribe" that would come to be called the Opa'ivu'eke people on what was then known (among U'ivuans, at least) as the "Forbidden Island" of Ivu'ivu, the largest in the country's small formation. It was there that he discovered a condition—an undocumented condition, one never before studied—that was affecting the native population. The U'ivuans were known (and to some extent still are known) for the brevity of their lifespans. But while on Ivu'ivu, Norton encountered a group of islanders who were living far beyond a normal lifespan: twenty, fifty, even a hundred years longer. There were two other components that made this discovery even more remarkable: first, that while the affected persons did not physically age, they did mentally deteriorate; and second, that their condition was not congenital but acquired.

Never had men gotten closer to eternal life than they did with Norton's discovery. And yet never had such a wonderful promise slipped away so quickly: a secret found, a secret lost, all within the space of a decade.

❧

[3] A. Norton Perina to Ronald Kubodera, M.D., May 3, 1998.

But Norton's work among the Opa'ivu'eke reflected seismic shifts in fields beyond medicine: his nearly two decades spent among the tribe all but spawned a new field of modern medical anthropology, and his writings from his years there are now staples of many college curricula.

But it was also in U'ivu[4] that his troubles began. Of the many things that defined Norton's travels through U'ivu, one was the origins of what would become his enduring love for children. Ivu'ivu, for those readers who are unfamiliar with it, is a daunting landscape, as beautiful as it is intimidating. Everything there is larger and purer and more awesome than imaginable, and in every direction lies a vista more spectacular than the last: to one side, an endless stretch of water, so motionless and intensely colored that one is unable to look at it for any significant length of time; to the other, long, deep folds of mountain, its peaks disappearing into a froth of fog. From his initial visit to Ivu'ivu, Norton hired U'ivuans to be his guides, to lead him in search of sights and objects he had never before seen. Decades later, he would—at their pleading—take back with him to Maryland their children and grandchildren and raise them as his own, offering them the sort of upbringing they would have had no means of experiencing in U'ivu. He also brought back with him many orphans, toddlers and young children living in appalling conditions with no hope of ever changing their lives.

Before he knew it, he had accumulated a brood of over forty. Many of these children, adopted in three waves that spanned almost three decades, have returned to Micronesia, where they are now doctors, lawyers, professors, chiefs, teachers, and diplomats. Others have chosen to remain in the United States, where they have taken jobs or remain in school. And still others have, I regret to say, vanished into poverty and drugs and crime. (When one has forty-three children, one cannot expect all of them to be successes.) But now, of course, none of them are Norton's any longer. And Norton is, by their choice, no longer theirs: their near-mass abandonment of him during his recent hardships was nothing less than shocking. This was a man,

---

[4] When speaking here of U'ivu, I mean to refer to the country as a whole, not the individual island; as will become clear, the majority of Norton's time there was spent on Ivu'ivu.

after all, who had given them shelter, language, education—all the tools they needed to one day betray him, as indeed they did. Norton's children learned the message of the West, and America, all too well; somewhere they learned that accusations of perversity are an easy sell, accusations that not even a Nobel Prize, a respected mind, could successfully withstand. It is a great pity; I had once been fond of quite a few of them.

The second thing I suppose I should say is that despite my obvious interest in this narrative, this is not my story. For one, I am a quiet man. For another, I am not interested in telling my story anyway—after all, there are altogether too many stories nowadays.

And yet I would like to say a few words about the process of compiling and editing these pages. My tasks as an editor have actually been rather minimal. I should also say that each section (which I have titled myself) is in reality a series of discrete installments that I received from Norton while he was imprisoned. Each installment was also prefaced by a letter, but as those letters are mostly personal in nature, I have not seen fit to include them here. Because this text originated as installments, the reader will notice that it does at times have a spontaneous, casual quality, and that it assumes from the reader a familiarity with the author's life and work. Since I am the person who knows Norton best (and since the book was in effect written for me, at my request), I considered it my responsibility to add footnotes where I thought such additional information might help the reader's understanding of Norton's story. (Occasionally I have also added my notes as a way of augmenting Norton's chronicles. Also, I have cut—judiciously—passages that I felt did not enrich the narrative or were not otherwise of any particular relevance; such deletions will not detract from the overall portrait Norton has painted of himself here.)

Finally, I feel it is only fair to address a question that Norton posited in the letter preceding his initial installment, which is, what do I hope for from this project? The answer is not a complicated one: I want nothing less than to restore Norton's reputation, to remind the world that what preceded the last two years is immeasurably more important than what may or may not have happened for a few brief months. Perhaps this is naive of me. But I must try: to do anything less for a man who has given so much to the world of science and medicine would be, in short, unforgivable.

*Ronald Kubodera*
*Palo Alto, California*

{ The Memoirs of A. Norton Perina }

EDITED BY RONALD KUBODERA, M.D.

# PART I. THE CREEK

### I.

I was born in 1924 near Lindon, Indiana, the sort of small, unremarkable rural town that some twenty years before my birth had begun to duplicate itself, quietly but insistently, across the Midwest. By which I mean that the town, as I remember it, was exceptional only for its very lack of distinguishing details. There were silos, and red barns (most of the residents were farmers), and general stores, and churches, and ministers and doctors and teachers and men and women and children: an outline for an American society, but one with no flourishes, no decoration, no accessories. There were a few drunks, and a resident madman, and dogs and cats, and a county fair that was held in tandem with Locust, an incorporated town a few miles to the west that no longer exists. The townspeople—there were eighteen hundred of us—were born, and went to school, and did chores, and became farmers, and married Lindonites, and began families of their own. When you saw someone in the street, you'd nod to him or, if you were a man, pull down the brim of your hat a bit. The seasons changed, the tobacco and corn grew and were harvested. That was Lindon.

There were four of us in the family: my father, my mother, and Owen and me.[5] We lived on a hundred acres of land, in a sagging

---

[5] The Owen to whom Norton refers is Owen C. Perina, Norton's twin brother and one of the few significant adult relationships in his life. Unlike Norton, Owen was always interested in literature, and he is now a renowned poet and the Field-Patey Professor of Poetry at Bard College. He has also twice been awarded the National Book Award for poetry, once for *The Insect's Hand and Other Poems* (1984) and again for

house whose only notable characteristic was a massive, once-grand central staircase that long before had been transformed by generations of termites into a lacy ruin.

About a mile behind the house ran a curvy creek, too small and slow and behaviorally inconsistent to warrant a proper name. Every March and April, after the winter thaw, it would surpass its limitations and become a proper river, swollen and aggressive with gallons of melted snow and spring rain. During those months, the creek's very nature changed. It became merciless and purposeful, and seized from its outgrown banks tiny, starry bloodroot blossoms and wild thyme by their roots and whisked them downstream, where they were abandoned in the thicket of a dam someone unknown had built long ago. Minnows, the creek's year-round inhabitants, fought upstream and drowned. For that one season, the creek had a voice: an outraged roar of rushing water, of power, and that narrow tributary, normally so placid and characterless, became during those months something frightening and unpredictable, and we were warned to keep away.

But in the heat of the summer months, the creek—which didn't originate at our property but rather at the Muellers', who lived about five miles to the east—dried once again to a meek trickle, timorously creeping its way past our farm. The air above it would be noisy with clouds of buzzing mosquitoes and dragonflies, and leeches would suck along its soft silty bottom. We used to go fishing there, and swimming, and afterward would climb back up the low hill to our house, scratching at the mosquito welts on our arms and legs until they became furry with old skin and new blood.

My father never ventured down to the creek, but my mother used to like to sit on the grass and watch the water lick over her

---

*The Pillow Book of Philip Perina* (1995), as well as numerous other commendations. Owen is as famously taciturn as Norton is voluble, and I once witnessed a very amusing exchange between them when I visited Norton a few Christmases ago. There was Norton, fist full of chestnuts, spewing, chewing, gesticulating, holding forth on everything from the dying art of butterfly mounting to the strange appeal of a certain talk show, and across from him, his lumpish mirror image, grunting and murmuring his occasional assent or dissent, was Owen.

Sadly, Norton and his brother are now at irreconcilable odds. As these pages will reveal, their estrangement was abrupt and devastating, the result of a terrible betrayal, one from which Norton will never recover.

ankles. When we were very young, we would call out to her—*Look at us!*—and she would lift her head dreamily and wave, though she was just as likely to wave at us as she was to wave at, say, a nearby oak sapling. (Our mother's sight was fine, but she often behaved as a blind person would; she moved through the world as a sleepwalker.) By the time Owen and I were seven or eight or so (at any rate, too young to have become disenchanted with her), she had become an object of at first pity and, soon after, of fun. We'd wave at her, sitting on the bank, her arms crossed under her knees, and then, as she was waving back at us (with her whole arm rather than simply her hand, like a clump of seaweed listing underwater), we'd turn away, talk loudly to each other, pretend not to see her. Later, over dinner, when she'd ask what we'd done at the creek, we'd act astonished, perplexed. The creek? But we hadn't been there! We were playing in the fields all day.

"But I saw you there," she'd say.

No, we'd tell her in unison, shaking our heads. It must have been two other boys. Two other boys who looked just like us.

"But—" she'd begin, and her face would seize for a moment in confusion before clearing. "It must have been," she'd say uncertainly, and look down at her plate.

This exchange occurred several times a month. It was a game for us, but an unsettling one. Was our mother playing along? But the look that crossed her face—of real worry, of fear that she was, as we said back then, *not right*, that she was unable to trust or believe her sight or memory—seemed too real, too spontaneous. We chose to believe that she was acting, for the alternative, that she was mad or, worse, genuinely moronic, was too frightening to contemplate seriously. Later, in our room, Owen and I would imitate her (*"But— but—but—it was you!"*) and laugh, but afterward, lying in our beds, silent, considering the game's implications, we were troubled. We were young, but we both knew (from books, from our peers) what a mother was expected to do—to chastise, to teach, to instruct, to discipline if necessary—and furthermore, we both knew our mother was not fit for those tasks. What, we wondered, would we grow up to become under such a woman? Why was she so incapable? We treated her like most boys would treat small animals: kindly when we were feeling happy and generous, cruelly when we were not. It was intoxicating to know we had the power to make her shoulders relax, to make her lips part in an uncertain smile, and yet also to make her turn her face down, to make her rub her palm quickly against her leg, which she did when she was nervous or unhappy or confused. Despite our concerns, we never spoke of them aloud; the only discussions we had about her were tinged with derision or disgust. Worry pulled us closer to each other, made us ever bolder and more obnoxious. Surely, we thought, we would push her to a point where the real adult she'd kept cloaked so well would reveal itself. Like most children, we assumed all adults were naturally imbued with a sense of intimidation, of authority.

Besides her lack of substance, there were fundamental ways in which my mother might be considered a failure. She was a slipshod cook (her steamed broccoli was rubbery, its florets bristling with the crunchy carcasses of minuscule unseen beetles, her roasted chicken squeaky with blood) and an only occasional housekeeper—our father had bought her a vacuum cleaner, but it sat neglected in the coat closet until Owen and I one day dissected it for its parts. Nor did she seem to have any interests. We never saw her reading or writing or painting or gardening, all pastimes that we (even then) knew were of intrinsic worth and interest. On summer afternoons, we'd sometimes find her sitting in the living room, her legs tucked under her girlishly, a silly smile on her face, staring fixedly yet vacantly at a vast constellation of dust motes made visible by a stripe of sunlight.

Once I saw her praying. I went into the living room one afternoon after school and found her on her knees, her palms pressed together, her head lifted. Her lips were moving, but I couldn't hear what she was saying. She looked ridiculous, like an actress playing to an empty theater, and I was embarrassed for her. "What are you doing?" I asked, and she looked up, alarmed. "Nothing," she said, startled. But I knew what she was doing and knew too that she was lying.

What else can I say? I can say she was vague, drifty, probably even stupid. But here I must also say that she has remained an enigma to me, which is a difficult thing for any human to accomplish. And there are other things I remember of her as well: she was tall, and graceful, and although I am unable to recollect the specificities of her face, I know she was somewhat beautiful. An old, blurred sepia photograph Owen has hanging in his office confirms this. She was probably not considered as beautiful then as she would be now, for her face was ahead of her times—long, white, startled: a face that promised intelligence, mystery, depth. Today she would be called arresting. But my father must have considered her very beautiful, for I can think of no other reason that he might have married her. My father, when he spoke to women at all, enjoyed well-educated women, though he did not find them in any way sexually appealing. I assume this is because intelligent women reminded him of his sister, Sybil, who was a doctor in Rochester and whom he admired enormously. So he was left with beauty. It disappointed me when I discerned as an adolescent that my father had married my mother only for her beauty, but this was before I realized that parents disappoint us in many ways and it is best not to expect anything of them at all, for chances are that they won't be able to deliver it.

Mostly, though, she was unknowable. I don't even know where she came from exactly (somewhere in Nebraska, I believe), but I do know she was from a poor family, and my father, with his relative fortune and undemanding nature, had saved her. But curiously, for all her poverty, there was nothing work-worn or used about her; she did not appear to be depleted, nor hardened. Rather, she gave the impression of being one of those indulged women who floats from her father's home to the finishing school and into her husband's arms. (The glow that seems to surround her in Owen's photograph, her early, quiet death, her sleepy, slow movements, all make me remember her as luminous, protected, cosseted, even though I know otherwise.) As far as I know, she had no education (reading our report cards aloud to my father, she stumbled over words: "Ex-, ex-em-pu," she'd sound out before Owen or I would shout out the word—*Exemplary*—to her, smug and impatient and ashamed), and she was very young when she died.

But then too, she was young in all things. In my memories she is persistently childlike, not only in behavior but in appearance as well. Her hair, for example: no matter the occasion, she wore it loose, rippling down her back in a loose, snaking helix. Even when I was a child, this hairstyle of hers was troublesome to me; I saw it as further evidence of a rigorously, inappropriately maintained girlhood—the long hair, the distant, vacuous smile, the way her eyes would wander from yours the moment you began to speak to her, all things not admirable in a woman with her supposed responsibilities.

It is discomfiting to me now, as I list these few details of my mother's life, how little I know and how incurious I have remained about her. I suppose every child yearns to understand his parental origins, but I never found her an interesting enough person to consider. (Or should that reasoning be inverted?) But then, I have never believed in romancing the past—what good would it do me? Owen, however, later became much more interested in our mother, and even passed through a period as an undergraduate in which he attempted to trace her family and complete an informal biography of her. He abandoned the project months after its inception, however, and became very defensive about it when asked, so I can only assume he found our maternal relatives without much trouble, realized they were yokels, and gave the whole thing up in disgust (he was still enough of an avowed elitist back then to do exactly that).[6] She has always *mattered* to him in a way that I have never been able to understand. But then, Owen is a poet, and I believe he thought it important that he have these details available for future employment, however mediocre or ultimately disappointing they may have been.

At any rate. It was July of 1933. I hesitate to say "It was a day like any other," for it sounds so melodramatic and portentous, as well as wholly unbelievable. Yet it is also true. So: it was a day like any other. My father was off with his friend Lester Drew, a small-time farmer, doing whatever it was two small-time farmers did together. Owen and I were gathering a bucket of leeches that we planned to bake into a pie and then give to Ida, the part-time cook, a sour woman we both hated. My mother was dangling her feet in the stream.

For weeks afterward, Owen and I would be asked to try to remember—had anything seemed different about her that afternoon? Had she seemed listless, or ill, or particularly fatigued? Had she spoken to us of feeling dizzy or weak? But the answer was always

---

[6] Owen Perina has written a rather lovely poem about his mother and her death; it is the first poem in his third collection, *Moth and Honey* (1986).

no. Indeed, if I can tell you very little about my mother's actions or mood that day, it is probably because they so closely resembled what we had come to accept as her normal behavior. As exasperating as our mother was, we could never accuse her of inconsistency. Even her last day of life followed that same inscrutable rhythm that only she could decipher.

The next morning Owen and I slept late, as we usually did during the summer. When I woke—Owen was still asleep in the bed next to mine—the day was hot. Little was required of us. Unlike other children, we were not expected to complete any chores at all; the days were ours to fill however we chose. Consequently, our summer months were spent on frivolous pastimes—torturing the bullfrogs down by the stream, stealing apricots from Lester Drew's trees, creeping through the tall, scraping grasses after a family of groundhogs. In the mornings we'd wake whenever we wanted, eat whatever had been left for us in the kitchen, and leave to execute the day's plans. Sometimes my father would be there with Lester Drew, rolling a cigarette between his fingers, a plate of red sliced peaches between them glistening sickly like raw flesh. They would grunt at us, and we at them, and we'd sit at the table in silence.

They were there when I arrived that morning, but so were two other people: John Naples, the town doctor, and Reverend Cunningham, the town minister, all of them talking quietly. As I entered, their conversation ceased. My father was an impassive man, stoic and not given to emotionalism. (He had a large, square face and eyes the dull olive of caper berries.) Therefore, whenever he did evince some sort of emotion, it was cause for alarm, or at least curiosity. In fact, I remember his expression from that morning—a mix of surprise, consternation, and bewilderment—rather better than I do his actual face.

"Your mother's dead," said my father. He sounded calm and grave, and he spoke in normal tones, which belied his expression—indeed, his voice reassured me.

"Really, Joseph," said Reverend Cunningham.

"It's best he hear it this way, straightforward," said my father. He had looked directly at me to tell me the news. Now he looked away and spoke to somewhere over Reverend Cunningham's head. "I assume you'll take care of the body, Reverend. Do whatever ...

she wanted done." Then he slapped his hands together once, in a neat, conclusive gesture, and wandered out the back door into the yard. Lester, after giving me a long, dolorous look, trotted out after him, leaving me with Reverend Cunningham, who sighed, and John Naples, who scowled.

"You!" Naples said to me. "Don't you have a brother someplace?"

He knew I did. The previous summer, Owen and I had trapped a mess of green grass snakes and fed them, one slithery strand at a time, through Naples's clinic's letter box. It was a bit of childish fun, but he had been enraged and had never forgiven us. He was a bitter, angry man, made corrosive by his disappointment with the world, the sort of man who on the street kicked up puffs of dust in the direction of children simply because he knew they'd have few means of retaliation. "Aren't you interested to know how your mother expired?" he asked me.

"Naples!" said Reverend Cunningham.

Naples ignored Father Cunningham. "Those mosquitoes that crowd around your creek," he continued. "It's my medical opinion that they carry a strain of Chinese flu. Mosquitoes carry disease, and your mother wandered into a cesspool of teeming bacteria and caused her own demise." He leaned back against his chair, satisfied, and puffed on his pipe. "And if you and your brother don't avoid that creek, you'll meet with the same death."

Reverend Cunningham looked aghast. "Really, Naples," he said, and then, having exhausted his resources on that one rebuke, he left through the back door as well. I was not surprised, and had expected little from him—not simply because he was a minister, but because he looked so diminished. He had the sort of face that was memorable for its absences rather than its presences: cheeks so gaunt and cadaverous that it looked as if someone had reached in, scooped out the meat in two quick movements, and sent him on his way.

Naples shrugged. He, unlike the others, seemed to have no intention of leaving. Owen and I had noticed that when we talked to adults as if they were a bit slow, even inferior—as if they were nuisances we'd learned to tolerate—they were often shocked into giving us information and speaking to us in tones they would never normally use with a child. Such a technique, however, did not have the same effect on Naples; his arrogance had lent him a sort of immovability that proved very inconvenient.

"What the devil is the Chinese flu?" I began.

Naples puffed away. "You wouldn't understand," he said rudely.

"I think you made it up."

"And I think you're an insolent brat. You and your brother both."

"You *did* make it up, didn't you?"

"Watch yourself, boy."

"But what is it?"

There were a few more rounds of this—me asking, Naples threatening—until he finally sighed and yielded. "A kind of air-borne disease spread by mosquitoes. One bit your mother and she got sick and died." It seemed a logical explanation, and I was quiet. For a minute we sat in silence, each of us, I imagine, contemplating her somehow disappointing demise. But then Naples remembered how he had been manipulated into answering my question and recovered himself. "I'm surprised your mother hadn't killed herself," he said. "God knows I would have were I your parent." His eyes shone with triumph and anticipation.

It didn't bother me, what he said, but he must have mistaken my silence for hurt, and, satisfied, he knocked the ash out of his pipe into a tidy anthill on the table and left through our front door, banging it shut behind him. As he walked down the path, I could hear him whistling, until the sound grew faint and then disappeared alto-gether, leaving only the purr of a flock of summer insects. It was the first time I had been spoken to as an adult.

But it was also John Naples, this small-town, smug, fifth-rate doctor, who truly sparked my interest in disease. He did this inadvertently—I don't believe he told me about my mother's death in such blunt terms because he *intended* to speak to me as an adult; indeed, he was a petty, cruel man, and I am certain he was attempting to do nothing more than stun me into tears—but in his harsh and erroneous explanation, he offered me my first glimpse into the world of disease and its exacting, brilliant puzzle.

Even at that age, Owen was interested in words: he read dictionaries and all manner of books and loved any sort of wordplay—anagrams, puns, palindromes. He could amuse himself all day with strings of rhymes he had discovered or created. And although I too enjoyed reading, I never loved the sport of language the way Owen did. This was because to me, language had no native intelligence of its own—it was created by man and was given meaning by man, and therefore clever writing often seemed to me little more than a Chinese puzzle box of contrivances. Writers are praised for having a facility with something man-made, something that can be changed or manipulated at will; but why is augmenting a man-made construction considered an act of brilliance? But perhaps I am not making sense here, so let me put it another way: language has no inherent secrets.

But science, specifically the science of disease, was *all* delicious secrets, dark oily pockets of mystery. Language could be misinterpreted, misconstrued, its rules imposed or ignored at whim. There was no discipline to it. It seemed sometimes a sort of game made up by man to amuse himself with, much as Owen did. But a disease, a virus, a wiggling string of bacteria, existed with or without man, and it was up to us to fathom its secrets.

John Naples, of course, did not think about disease this way (a good sign of a weak mind is the doctor who insists that it's the patient, not the disease, on whom one's efforts should be concentrated), but I credit him for appearing in my life as a cautionary figure, the sort of person with whom I would now be interacting had I not chosen to pursue research medicine. Even then, I knew I would not be satisfied with imperfect explanations. I was simply too impatient.

Naples, thankfully, was not to have the last word. My father may have been a lazy man, but he wasn't foolish, and in this matter he proved surprisingly competent. Later that afternoon, after telephoning his sister in Rochester (he had overlooked the matter of informing Owen, which I had to do myself when he at last padded down to the kitchen, rubbing his eyes and grousing), he called a medical school classmate of Sybil's who lived in Indianapolis, who called a friend of *his* who lived in Crawfordsville, a town fifty miles to the east of us. This doctor—a Dr. Burns—arranged for my mother to be transported to his clinic for an autopsy.

The next week he sent us his report, which stated that my mother had died not of Chinese flu ("I myself am not familiar with the illness, though I must also admit that as a pathologist, I am perhaps not as well versed in local afflictions as my esteemed colleague Dr. John M. Naples," Burns wrote diplomatically in his letter) but of an aneurysm. An aneurysm! After Sybil explained it to me, I pictured it often, all but heard the soft explosion as the artery burst, saw the coil of soggy, flaccid tissue, the black blood staining the brain the shining, sticky red of pomegranates. (Later, as a teenager, seized in an odd moment of guilt, I would think, *How young! How unfair!* And later still, when I was an adult and old enough to give serious consideration to my own death and the circumstances I'd prefer, *How dramatic!* I'd picture shooting stars, fireworks, glorious drops of light falling from the sky like thousands of glittering gems, each shard no larger than a seedling, and almost envy my mother her last great experience.)

"She didn't feel any pain," Sybil wrote to me. "She had a good death. She was lucky."

A good death. I thought about that phrase often, until I became a doctor and saw for myself what Sybil meant. But as a child, the words were as mysterious as the concept of death itself. *A good death.* My mother was someone who was given a good death. A dreamer, a ghost, she was given the greatest gift nature can grant. That night, she slipped under her quilt as quietly as she slid her feet into the pale, murmuring stream and closed her eyes, unaware and unafraid of where she might go next.

For years afterward, I had dreams in which my mother appeared in strange forms, her features sewn onto other beings in combinations that seemed both grotesque and profound: as a slippery white fish at the end of my hook, with a trout's gaping, sorrowful mouth and her dark, shuttered eyes; as the elm tree at the edge of our property, its ragged clumps of tarnished gold leaves replaced by knotted skeins of her black hair; as the lame gray dog that lived on the Muellers' property, whose mouth, her mouth, opened and closed in yearning and who never made a sound. As I grew older, I came to realize that death had been easy for my mother; to fear death, you must first have something to tether you to life. But she had not. It was as if she had been preparing for her death the entire time I knew her. One day she was alive; the next, not.

And as Sybil said, she was lucky. For what more could we presume to ask from death—but kindness?

After that, it was Owen and me and our father. I have spoken briefly of my father, and while it would be inaccurate to say we liked him, he was certainly more tolerable than our mother, although they shared a similar maddening refusal to remain anchored in the world of practicalities. If my mother had found her share of luck in death, my father had long ago accepted luck as his birthright.

My father had been born and raised in a nearby town called Peet, another place of which you will have heard nothing. Today Peet is all but deserted, the sort of place that grows sadder and sparser with each passing year, as its children grow up and leave, never to return. When my father was young, though, Peet was something of an important town. It had its own railroad station, which had in turn spawned a small but healthy local economy. There was a hotel, for example, and a music hall, and a Main Street lined with two-story wood shops painted the colors of the sea and rock. Travelers heading west to California would stop in Peet for an egg salad sandwich and a celery soda from the general store near the station before reembarking. The townspeople thrived from these impermanent relationships, which were in their own way pure: the exchange of money for goods, a pleasant farewell, the assurance that neither party would see the other again. After all, what are most relationships in life but exactly this, though stretched flabbily over years and generations?

My father's parents, both of whose parents had immigrated from Hungary, were the owners of the general store. Unlike their son, they were hard workers, frugal, and made wise investments. In 1911, when my father was a senior in college, they died, one after the other, of the flu. My father and his sister inherited their parents' store, their house, and seventy acres of farmland they had bought in a town called Lindon, as well as their savings. As in the case of my mother's death, my father proved himself a capable and efficient administrator. He sold off the store and the house in Peet, paid the taxes, arranged for the burial, and established a savings account for his sister. Sybil, who was graduating from high school, used some of her money to pay for Wellesley. My father, lazier, made it through the rest of his term at Purdue, graduated, and moved to Lindon, where he built a house and every year added a few more acres to his land. While Sybil began medical school at Northwestern, my father grew soybeans, flat beans, and yellow beans. He fathered his sons. Eventually he began working for the local railroad as a timetable administrator. He had accomplished all he would in life.

My father proved as frustrating to me as my mother was elusive. He was, so far as I could determine, interested only in achieving a state of complete and total inertia. This was almost indescribably irritating to me. For one, we lived in a country in which a person's worth was measured by his industriousness. Not that either Owen or I particularly cared what the townspeople thought admirable; it was simply that we happened to feel the same way—that there was something shameful, and perhaps even obscene, in my father's behavior. It was, after all, the Depression. We heard stories of children abandoned by their parents, saw photos of defeated and exhausted-looking men waiting for a bowl of soup, a job, a loan. And yet my father, unambitious, placid, spectacularly unmotivated, somehow emerged utterly unharmed. I remember many nights sitting at our kitchen table, prickling with impatience for a father who would shout, berate me, beat me to do better, to work harder, whose ambitions for me would be greater than my own. Instead my father merely sat there, dreamily humming the latest popular song and rolling his cigarettes. Corn, the remnants of a hastily constructed meal, nested in his brushy mustache, and when I pointed it out to him, he would languorously poke his tongue out and sweep it around his mouth and nose in a serpentine and graceful movement, humming all the while. This careless, carefree gesture irritated me more than anything. It makes me laugh a little now, my self-righteous disapproval: I, of course, greatly benefited from my father's continual dumb luck, but back then it seemed to me that he was doing Owen and me something of a disservice. Growing up in our home, you would have assumed that fortune fell from the sky with a reassuring thump and that nothing, not even the prospect of amassing a great fortune, was worth aspiring to. My father did not in fact accumulate his money out of any sense of capitalist zeal—no, if it happened, it did, and the few times he made poor business decisions, he didn't seem to mind that either.

The entire situation enraged me, as indulged children yearn for nothing more than the romance of poverty. Often I found myself dreaming of parents who were hardworking immigrants, for whom I was the sole hope. I was very moved by sentimental children's stories such as *The Silver Skates* and rendered my own family as characters in a similar narrative. My father would be the lumpish stroke victim, helpless and slobbering, and Owen my crippled, idiot younger brother. I was the pioneer and the hero, ruthless and resourceful as well. Education would be my family's sole hope. My academic success would be a necessity; I would become a doctor and yank us all out of despair and filth and into tight, square houses. In my fantasy, my hands, made magical by years of American education, would cure my poor father, who would immediately set to work despite my protestations. My mother, strong and determined, her beauty restored, would smile for the first time in years, and my brother, once proper schooling was paid for, would gain language, learn to move like an athlete. How I yearned for such motivation! But as it was, I had to defy the burdens not of poverty but of a contentedly and determinedly unkinetic father and a comfortable childhood—one I might have enjoyed were I not so set upon denying it.

But then, I also had Sybil. As I have mentioned, my father greatly respected Sybil; I do not think it an exaggeration to say that he was even in awe of her. Certainly she was as much a puzzle to him as he was to me; how could someone so industrious, so intelligent, so active, have come from the same family as he?

Not everyone was so impressed by Sybil, though. In those days, people who were jealous or small used to say that it was a good thing that Sybil could support herself, because no man ever would. If confronted, they would explain that they meant only that she was too independent, too outspoken, but really, everyone knew what they meant: Sybil, with her bready roll of hair, was considered too ugly ever to marry, and indeed, she never did. She was four years younger than my father, but when she died of breast cancer in December of

1945, she looked older than I imagined a fifty-two-year-old could. People had considered Sybil strange all her life, and by the time she began her pediatric practice in Rochester, she had, I believe, resigned herself to occupying the position of a provincial town's sexless spinster.

This is a pity for a great many reasons, but largely because I have always believed my aunt would have made an excellent immunologist. She was endlessly, unflaggingly inquisitive and creative, confident but not arrogant. She had a wide-reaching mind, one that made the sorts of balletic leaps in reasoning and analysis of which only the true genius is capable. She seemed to know everything, and once I myself reached medical school, she admitted that she herself had wanted to be a "medical adventurer" (I wasn't sure, and neither was she, what exactly such a job might entail; we knew only that we both wanted to do it) but could never have done so.[7] Later she would admit to me in that same shy way that she had always wanted chil-

---

[7] One can only imagine what life would have been like for Sybil Maria Perina (1893–1945) if she had been born fifty years later. Indeed, the great medical professor and anatomist E. Isaiah Witkinson, under whom she studied while a student at Northwestern, even mentions her in a letter to a colleague in 1911:

> [A] student of many talents, as well as grace and skill. It is a great pity to the scientific community that she will not be able to pursue a career in medical research. I even urged [her] to consider moving abroad to work with Christian missionaries, which would, alas, offer her more independence and opportunity than she could acquire through any university. However, she refused, although whether out of a lingering desire to remain close to her family (a shortcoming in many female students) or from a fear of toiling in uncertain circumstances I cannot discern. Certainly she is capable of whatever she chooses, although I believe her native domestic conservatism will keep her mired in some unchallenging provincial practice. She will become bored; she will hate it. (Francis Clapp, ed., *A Doctor's Life: The Letters of E. Isaiah Witkinson* [New York: Columbia University Press, 1984])

Unfortunately, Sybil never progressed much further beyond Witkinson's gloomy but prescient predictions for her. Her obituary in the *Rochester Picayune* is insultingly brief and desperately sad: "Dr. Perina was a doctor in Rochester for more than thirty years . . . She was never married and has no immediate survivors." However, Sybil did leave behind a great legacy; as Norton himself has said more than once, she was responsible for introducing him to the wonders of scientific discovery and possibility. So Sybil, her thwarted dreams, can be said to live on in one of the world's greatest medical minds: he has more than accomplished for her what she could not.

dren and urged me, no matter what else I might choose to do in life, to have children of my own. She promised me that nothing would bring me greater joy. Naturally, this has been much on my mind lately, for obvious reasons. Sybil was correct and wise in so many ways; how could she have been so wrong about this?

As a child, I saw a great deal of Sybil. Until my mother's death—after which she came more frequently—she used to visit us for a few weeks every summer. She would refer her patients to the other local pediatrician and arrive with gifts for all of us. For my mother, whom she never quite understood, she would bring something frivolous and pretty, partly from a clumsy condescension and partly because she knew that beauty and frivolity would not be wasted on my mother—whatever it was, my mother would appreciate it, and her own beauty would only augment the gift's. One time, I recall, she brought her a silk dress printed with splashes of wildflowers. My mother immediately put it on and twirled around in it—I can still see her spinning in our living room, and the creamy, buttery blur the silk made. Sybil had never known quite what to say to our mother, whom I believe she both pitied and envied—pitied because my mother seemed so content with the simple, unambitious life she led, and envied because she *was* content, because she *did* have the life she did.

For my father she would bring something whimsical—a bird whistle one of her patients had carved, a container of maple syrup in its pebbly jug, a book on rock collecting. For Owen she brought books, puzzles, sheets of drawing paper so thick with cotton they were fibrous.

But as much as Sybil liked us all, I was clearly her favorite. Although Sybil loved Owen and he her, they never had the sort of relationship that my aunt and I enjoyed with each other. In fact, I have always suspected that Sybil regarded Owen as a bit facile, and although she highly praised all his artistic efforts (the epic poems, the abstract sketches of farm life), she did so with only a sort of diffused general enthusiasm; she could never offer him any specific criticism or praise. She did not have a disdain, exactly, for art, or artists, but neither did she make much of an attempt to understand either.

To be fair, I should here add that Owen never felt about Sybil as

I did, chiefly for two reasons. The first had nothing to do with Sybil herself, even. It was simply that Owen had always attributed a sort of mystique to my absent mother and torpid father—against the backdrop of an American culture he would eventually declare vulgar and excessively ambitious, he considered their lassitude radical and even rebellious. (To me, however, inertia does *not* constitute rebellion.) Of course, Owen too had phantom parents, but where mine were impaired, his were, for lack of a better word, countercultural. I have always thought that Owen's greatest regret was that he wasn't born thirty years later to a pair of Beatniks.

The other reason Owen never cared for Sybil as passionately as I did *did* have to do with Sybil. Although he respected her mind and was fond of her, he also considered her inelegant and untaught in all things cultural. But while that may have been essentially true, it doesn't negate the fact—as I have argued with Owen many times in the past—that she was still the most *vital* adult in our lives. Were it not for her, we would not have been given an alternative model of adult behavior and might have applied ourselves toward less challenging vocations.

At any rate, Sybil always saved the best presents for me: a small microscope; an old stethoscope; a hand-lettered resin model of the heart. She brought me cases of African dung beetles mounted on pieces of stiff white cardboard and encased in black leather frames. There was a ball and bat, which came with an early physics lesson; an old radio she lugged down from Rochester, only to show me how to disassemble it; a thick slab of magnifying glass and a lecture to go with it, after she discovered me crouched on the hard dust road, roasting ants to death.

Sybil's gift the year I turned eleven was a book that seemed initially something of a misstep. *The Lives of the Great Scientists* was unimaginatively written and childishly illustrated and the text insultingly cheery and simple, as if for a dull six-year-old. Really it was no more than a sort of "Who's Who" of the scientific canon, in which all the "top" scientists (their names, their important contributions, etc.; I half expected to see their height, weight, and extracurricular interests listed as well) were given a short entry, as if scientists, like baseball players, could be ranked in some sort of definitive fashion. I must say, though, that as absurd as this concept seemed at the time, it becomes more appealing by the year. (In fact, I was given my own entry in the most recent, 1994, edition. The text was of course extremely reductive, but no less inaccurate than many biographical sketches many times its length.[8] The entry also includes a picture of me with Philip,[9] who was around ten at the time. The photo's quality is so poor that Philip's face appears merely as a round dark circle with a gash of white for his smile. I myself appear hulking, awkward, a gently bumbling circus act.)

But to continue—the book, of course, was hardly my introduction to the possibilities and workings of the natural world, but it was, I suppose, my introduction to the personalities of science, with whom I found myself deeply fascinated. For it was then that I realized there is a certain sort of mind that turns to science, and this, I decided, was the sort of mind I admired.

---

[8] I'm afraid I must disagree with Norton here. But I will let the reader be the judge. The body of the entry reads in part as follows:

Abraham Norton Perina, b. 1924, Lindon, Indiana, USA

Currently lives: Bethesda, Maryland, USA

Significance: 7 [Ed. note: On a scale of one to ten. Perplexingly, Galileo is ranked a 10, as is Jonas Salk. But Copernicus is given only an 8.]

We're all told that nobody lives forever, but did you know that there is a group of people who actually do? It's true! Dr. Perina, who lives in Maryland with his more than 50 adopted children, discovered in the early 1950s a race of people who never aged—all thanks to eating a rare turtle! Dr. Perina's research won him a Nobel Prize in Medicine in 1974.

The book then goes on to give a flawed and simplistic description of Selene syndrome.

[9] Philip Tallent Perina (arrived 1969; ca. 1960–1975), an early adoptee of Norton's and one of his special pets. Philip was lean, childlike, and very dark-skinned. I never met him, but through various pictures Norton keeps, I imagine him as quick and spritely; in pictures, he always seems about to wiggle out of Norton's arms and straight out of the photograph itself. Although a lively child, Philip had suffered some brain damage at an early age, and his physical development too was retarded, possibly an effect of severe malnutrition in early life. He was an orphan, and something of the village mascot when Norton brought him back from U'ivu in 1969. (His name, until Norton's rescue, had been the equivalent of "Hey, you!") Philip was killed by a drunk driver in 1975; he was believed to be about fifteen years old at the time.

## II.

I have already mentioned the curving staircase that ran up the center of our house. It was incongruously fancy for such an architecturally modest place and always seemed to me something like a visitor, destined to return one day to its proper and glorious permanent state, joining two floors in a Fifth Avenue town house. This affectation had been installed by the previous owner (a fledgling architect who had attended Columbia and had never quite overcome the humiliation of having to leave the city to return to his family's property in Lindon), and although the construction was sound and the wood solid, the staircase had fallen into disrepair in the fifty years it had endured our family. My father spoke often and halfheartedly of tearing it down and replacing it with something simpler, but he never did, and so it was that by the time he died and I returned to the farm, the staircase had all but collapsed, and Owen and I were forced to use a ladder to access our old bedrooms on the second floor.

But in 1935 the staircase, while not especially aesthetically pleasing, was at least still functional, and at any rate quite suitable for my needs. I decided to begin my project from the top stair and paint my way down. The staircase's carpet had been removed some years before, and because the steps were so shaggy with dust and splinters, each one needed a few layers of paint before the grain of the wood was obscured. I made my way down the twenty steps, painting the front, bottom, and sides of each with varying colors in turn. After a few hours the paint dried and I once again began at the top of the stairs. Working my way down, I painted on the front and top of each step the name of a different scientist. By the time I had finished, the staircase was a blaze of color and words: Curie at the top, Galileo beneath her, Einstein beneath him, Gregor Mendel, James Clerk Maxwell, Marcello Malpighi, Carolus Linnaeus, Nicolaus Copernicus, and so forth. I had listed the names in no particular sequence, only as they occurred to me. But before I could complete my project, I was interrupted by Owen, who began yelling at me for not including him in it. Our ensuing fight brought my father and Lester ambling in from outside, and after gaping at the staircase for a long, silent moment (during which even Owen and I held our breath),

Lester began screaming that we needed to be beaten, the harder the better. And then, unexpectedly, my father began to laugh.

The three of us—Owen, Lester, and I—froze, all of us in mid-speech. Until that day, neither Owen nor I had ever heard our father laugh before. It was an unremarkable laugh, wheezy and rusty, and, I thought, irritatingly lacking in much enthusiasm or mirth or energy. The laugh lasted for only a few seconds, after which my father concluded this uncharacteristic expression of emotion by saying, "See, Lester, I can't destroy the staircase now—the boys have taken it over."

Lester scowled, disappointed that Owen and I hadn't received a proper punishment (he didn't think much of my father's parenting skills), and I too was angry, although for different reasons. Somehow my wonderful tribute to the mind of the scientist had been co-opted by my father to be employed as another justification for his idleness! But interestingly, the staircase—which my father left undisturbed not from any respect for my work but, as I have said, from his own laziness—would become much more significant than any of us then realized.

I have already noted that Owen and I returned to the house upon my father's death. In his last year, my father had, not surprisingly, taken to living in absolute squalor, and the house had transformed itself into a barn of sorts, with small rodents and untamed, unclaimed cats rummaging through the sticky kitchen cupboards. By the time we returned in 1946 (since leaving for college four years earlier, we had proved almost wholly successful in our resolve never to return to Indiana), the house had gone without cleaning for at least four years, and I do not embellish when I say that it was a disaster—peeling floorboards, rusted door hinges that screeched so gratingly we tried never to open them, furniture that choked out great vogs of dust when we sat upon them. And then there was the debris, which had been vomited throughout every room—papers, crumpled boxes and cracked bottles, various neglected gadgets. My father hadn't, presumably, been upstairs in some time, because the ladder, when Owen and I finally discovered it under the house, was rusty and unyielding after what must have been years of neglect. (Upstairs there was a mess of such proportions that contemplating it still exhausts me. We found a family of bats nesting in the beams above Owen's bed, whole dynasties of mice, balls of dust as big as human heads, replete with snarls of unidentifiable hair.) But it was the staircase, its crude, old-fashioned primary colors deadened from age and dirt and the canopies of glittering spiderwebs that covered it, that gave us both pause.

This was a massive staircase, and its collapse meant that my father was allowed only a small space—perhaps less than two hundred square feet—in which to live. It had bisected the living room, so that in order to enter the kitchen, one would first have to go outside and around the house to the kitchen door. In the summertime this was merely inconvenient, but in the winter, with its harsh winds and buffets of snow, such a trek would be arduous for even a young person. Because there was no makeshift bed in his small living quarters, and because my father had been discovered lying facedown in the grass some yards from the house early that March, we concluded that he must have been attempting to stagger to the kitchen—which was dismayingly ill-stocked: just a few tins of tomatoes and a can of mushroom soup—when he had his heart attack. (We later discovered a sad little bed constructed from some deteriorating quilts and an old sofa cushion in the little lean-to formed by the outside wall and the screened-in sunporch attached to the back of the living room.) It would therefore not be too great an exaggeration to say that the staircase was responsible for killing my father, although ultimately he killed himself with his own laziness. Even his suicide was an act of characteristic passivity.

I was torn between sympathy for and annoyance with my father's pathetic end. What can you say of a man who neglects his house until his house destroys him? Really, though, I was sorrier about my staircase, although it was purely a nostalgic reaction. As I had grown older, it had only irritated with its childishness in both conception and execution, and although I always said I would, I never did find the time to paint it over. Shades, I suppose, of my father yet.

Neither Owen nor I placed much value on funerals, but partly from a sort of guilt at the humiliating way in which our father had died, and partly out of guilt for not having attended our mother's funeral, we found a small church and convinced the local pastor, a man whose name I no longer remember (Reverend Cunningham having long since died), to perform the services.

Only a dozen or so people appeared at the funeral to mourn my father's death. Lester Drew had been institutionalized by his niece after he had had a severe stroke some years before, and so the only people in attendance were curious townsfolk, most of whom we didn't recognize, and some former employees of my father's, farmers and sharecroppers mostly, of whom we had dim recollections. I think some people were there simply to see how a rich man dies.[10] I imagine that the whole affair must have been a great disappointment to them—the shabby church, the pastor's vague and tentative sermon, the unenthusiastic expressions on my and Owen's faces, the scarcity of people and the absence of friends and family. If this was how one of the richest men in town was laid to rest, they must have thought, what bleak ceremony (if any at all) awaited them? Had we not been so young and callous, we would have thrown a more impressive and festive funeral, if only to reassure them. At the time, though, we were not in the habit of attempting to assuage others' insecurities.

After the punch and biscuits had been served at the pastor's house (we did not think it appropriate to invite mourners back to the scene of the death, where the long wisps of grass upon which our father's spread-eagled body had lain were still matted down in an unsettlingly distinguishable shape), and after we had shaken the hands of the dozen or so people present, we thanked him for his help.

"It was my honor," said the pastor, solemnly. He was a blandly handsome man with sad eyes who kept looking lasciviously at Owen when he thought Owen wasn't watching him. He was not much older than we but already had a defeated-looking wife and two squalling blond sons. "You poor boys—you have only each other now." (I wondered for a moment if he might have been pitying us not only for being left alone but for being in such poor company; it was clear he didn't much like us.) To me he said, "God be with you always."

---

[10] Although one would never have known it from his undignified death, Norton's father left behind a substantial fortune. The exact amount was never disclosed, but it has been assumed by Norton's biographers that it was enough to comfortably enable the purchase of his house in Bethesda and the maintenance and education of his children. Along with Owen, Norton would also have been Sybil's primary beneficiary.

To Owen he said, "Always watch out for your brother. You are his keeper."

"What for?" Owen asked. At the time, Owen was very interested in Truth and Justice and was beginning, tiresomely, to dabble in Marxism; he had always been very impressionable. "I shall treat my brother as I treat any of my fellow men, no better, no worse," he said grandly, and the pastor moved off, sighing and shaking his head.

Writing this makes me remember how much I miss Owen. I am a little surprised to see those words on paper,[11] but I would be lying if I did not admit it. Despite my many complaints and annoyances, it occurs to me (and not for the first time) that my childhood, while often tedious, was certainly much simpler than my life today. This is, I suppose, as many people remember their childhoods. But back then, I do believe I was familiar with a state that was reasonably close to contentment. I was not funny-looking, I was an adequately skilled athlete, I was rich but not extravagant, I was intelligent, I had interests, I was stronger and swifter than Owen. My school-mates left me alone: I was never beaten or teased, I never needed friends or anyone else—after all, I had Owen. Now I live a life in which I funnel great amounts of my savings to my lawyers from my barred-in quarters. I am fat and no longer stronger and swifter than Owen, and even if I had any hobbies, I would not be able to practice them. I am living a strange kind of life, a life in which I have no one. My children are gone and my colleagues are gone; everyone who has ever mattered to me has left me.

---

[11] I myself was surprised to read this admission. Greatly so, actually, for reasons that will become clear to the reader as Norton's narrative progresses. I shall say only that one of Norton's greatest fears has always been abandonment—that the people he loved and trusted would one day turn against him. (Unfortunately, it proved a prescient concern.) But as I have noted, it was not only his children's disloyalty that proved ultimately responsible for his current predicament—it was Owen's too.

Interestingly, it wasn't until four years into my relationship with Norton that I even learned of Owen's existence. When I asked him about this many years later, he merely chuckled and said that they must have been bickering about something at the time. These long silences and petty, frequent skirmishes defined Norton's relationship with Owen, who, as he notes, was his equal in depth and breadth of knowledge and opinions (though of course not the same knowledge and opinions). But he proved a good foil for Norton—perhaps the only person who has ever matched him in brilliance, eccentricities, and passions. I had once liked him very much.

Even Owen. Or should I say, especially Owen. We have not, of course, had either the easiest or the most consistent of relationships, but at one time Owen and I were very close, and even when we were not, even when he was passing through one of his childishly enthusiastic phases in which he adopted and abandoned idealisms and philosophies like other boys did girls, he was amusing, and witty, and bright. He was my ambassador to the world outside my own. Not that I myself was immune to romanticism. I remember as a young man once telling Owen that he should fashion himself after me. Look at me, I told him (he rolled his eyes)—I am going to be a scientist. That is all I care about. You are too scattered, I told him. I warned him that he would become a dilettante if he did not become more disciplined. But now I almost admire Owen's indecisiveness; it was almost as if he, to make up for my single-mindedness, was trying to be of as many minds as possible. I was impatient then, of course, but now I can recall fondly my brother's prickliness, his fierce idealism, his quickly burning passions. I remember Owen in those days as so vital, so indefatigable, so intellectually nimble in ways I was not. For such different-minded people, we were unusually and energetically competitive, but still—there were times when we agreed too, and during those moments we could argue anyone out of anything, bend them with our ferocity and righteousness. At any rate, we could always match passions, even when our passions were not directed toward the same subjects.

And it was with Owen that I shared my earliest, most fervent craving: that of leaving, of escape. I can't remember ever articulating this desire specifically, but I can remember my sense, from my very early years, that life was not Indiana, and certainly not Lindon, and possibly not even America. Life was elsewhere, and it was frightening and vast and mountainous and uncomfortable. I believe Owen knew this as well, the way some children know that they want to remain close to home, and it was this mutual determination—that where we were beginning would not be where we stayed, nor where we ended—that, more than interests or predilections, both united us and encouraged us to endure the obligations of childhood until we could leave it behind and pursue life in earnest.

Interestingly, the two years or so after my father's funeral were to be the happiest, most harmonious time in our relationship. In those years we were quite close, and for a brief, ambitious, honeyed period, I made an effort to write to him every week, something we had not done all through college. In the late spring of 1946, we embarked upon a vacation together, to Italy. A photo from this time shows us about to board the ship, the *Arcadia*, in New York. Both of us are wearing linen suits and derbies. It was our first trip to Europe—our first vacation together, in fact, and unfortunately our last, although we had no way of knowing that at the time—and when we returned, three months later, I remember promising one another that we'd reprise the trip annually, to places farther and farther afield.

I can remember only a few of the specifics from that trip—art we saw, meals we ate, conversations we had, ruins we admired, even places we stayed—but I can still recall, with a sort of odd, unpleasant clarity, that unfamiliar and inarticulable sensation I began experiencing, about halfway through the journey, whenever I gazed at Owen. I remember feeling something pressing against my chest at those times, substantial and insistent and yet not uncomfortable, not painful. After a few episodes, I deduced it was, for lack of a better word, love. Naturally, I never said anything to him (we did not have those sorts of conversations), but I remember quite clearly looking at him one evening as we stood at the prow of the ship, at his sharp nose that ended in a blobbish wodge of putty (*my* nose), listening to the dark waters slap against the side of the boat, and feeling almost overwhelmed. When Owen spoke to me, I was unable to answer, and had to pretend I felt ill, so I could go to bed and lie awake by myself and think about my new discovery.

The feeling did not last, of course. It came and went throughout our trip, and then over the years. And although it was never as intense as it was that day on the water, I grew to first accept and then long for that familiar ache, even though I knew that while experiencing it I was unable to accomplish, much less contemplate, anything else.

# PART II. MICE

## I.

After graduating from college, I began medical school[12] in the fall of 1946. I have little of interest to say about medical school itself; even its dullness and the unimaginativeness of my fellow students were not too great a surprise to me. I went to medical school because it was what one did back then if one was interested in anything even tangentially related to the biology of the human body. Were I an undergraduate today, I probably would bypass it in favor of a doctoral program in virology or microbiology or some such. It is not that medical school in itself is not an interesting or even stimulating environment; it is that the people who tend to matriculate there lean toward the self-righteous and sentimental, more interested in the romantic heroism of doctoring with which the profession has allowed itself to become suffused and associated than in the challenge of scientific inquiry.

This was perhaps even more true fifty years ago than it is today. My classmates—or at least those I came in contact with over my four years—were easily divided into two categories. Those in the first category, the less objectionable of the two, were dull and obedient and enjoyed memorization. Those in the second, more offensive group were grasping and dreamy, bewitched by their own future

---

[12] Hamilton College, summa cum laude, 1946; Harvard Medical School, cum laude, 1950. Both Norton and Owen received medical deferments from the armed forces in 1944, Norton on the grounds of his flat feet and mild but recurring sciatica and Owen for his asthma and extreme astigmatism.

status in the world. But they were all ambitious, competitive, and eager for their own bit of glory.

I was not a particularly distinguished student. Although I was probably one of the most intellectually curious and creative members of my class, or even the entire school, there were many, many others who were better, more diligent students than I: they went to every class, they took notes, they did each night's reading. But I was occupied with other things. At the time I was an avid beetle collector, a habit and interest I had maintained since childhood; naturally, the opportunities to find unusual beetles in Boston were somewhat limited, but during the spring months, I would take sometimes days at a time and ride a train down to Connecticut, where Owen was earning a doctorate in American literature at Yale. I would leave my bag at his place and then catch another, smaller, dozier train out to the countryside, where I would spend the day in one field or another with my net and my notebook and a pickle jar containing a bloom of cotton damp with formaldehyde. When the sky grew orange, I would hitchhike back to New Haven, where I would spend the evening in Owen's suite, eating whatever he had prepared and trying, with limited success, to engage him in conversation. Owen had grown more and more silent over the years (for which I must admit I was grateful, for his elaboration on his studies, which concerned Walt Whitman and the American imagination, sorely tested my claims of intellectual promiscuity), and watching him cut his omelet into small, fussy trapezoids, I had to stop myself thinking that he reminded me of our stolid, lumpen father.

Naturally, my professors were not enthusiastic about my skipping so many classes, but since I always did well on my tests and papers, there was little they could do to punish me but deliver lectures on how my lack of discipline would all but ensure mediocrity in my professional life. I didn't doubt their seriousness or their sincerity, but neither did I allow myself to worry about my own future; even then I knew that I was bound to have the sort of adventures for which I would not be best or usefully equipped by a perfect attendance record.

I do not wish, however, to idealize what was at least partially a fit of tiresome and immature disrespect for my professors and the institution. Now, in retrospect, with my career and legacy being what they are, I suppose it is all very easy to say that I knew everything would resolve itself in my favor in the end and that my lack of ambition was genuine. Though if I am to be honest, I suppose I should acknowledge too that I was even then so eager for a certain sort of greatness, the sort that seemed both possible and yet so distant, a blurry-edged dream on the periphery of my vision, that at the time it seemed easier to pretend to all and to myself that I did not care for a spectacular future at all, lest I come to think that my time in medical school—and my successes or failures there—might become a predictor for the rest of my life, something that might determine the chances of that shimmering image coalescing into something more vivid, or not.

But it was in my third year of medical school that things really changed for me, or rather, that I really changed things. This was the year that Gregory Smythe extended to me an invitation to work in his lab. You will now understand why this was so surprising, and indeed, for many years I was asked about my time there with some regularity.[13]

I would be lying if I said I was not initially flattered. Nowadays, a mention of Gregory Smythe is greeted (if it is answered with any sort of recognition at all) with ridicule, the sort of self-assured, self-satisfied smirk that is always girded with both relief and fear, the kind of response the mention of many of today's most highly regarded scientists' names will no doubt provoke a generation or two from now. But back when I was in school, Smythe was considered an important mind, a visionary, the sort of doctor and scientist it was expected one wanted to become.[14]

Smythe was also something of an unusual figure on the campus

[13] A well-known professor might pick one, or at the most two, of his most promising medical or undergraduate students to work in his lab for anything from one to four terms. These students are usually chosen on the basis of their grades, test scores, dedication, and diligence.

[14] It is difficult to overstate Gregory Smythe's influence and importance to the scientific community in the 1940s and '50s. Until his theories fell out of favor, Smythe was one of the rare scientists to gain popular appeal and acclaim; *Time* magazine even featured a drawing of him on the cover of its April 18, 1949, issue with the

and in the scientific community. For one, he was involved in what was widely acknowledged as some of the more interesting medical work at the time. Today it is very easy to laugh at the sorts of misguided notions and theories that were once considered groundbreaking, but there is no denying that the 1940s were, in their way, a period of great scientific expansion. As wrong (and there is no gentler way to state it) as many of Smythe's and his colleagues' theories were eventually revealed to be, his generation also possessed an admirable degree of curiosity, and their thirst—motivated by any number of things, but undeniably genuine—resulted in the foundation of what we recognize today as modern science. Without them, there would have been nothing for you or I to refute, nothing for us to dispel or debunk. I sometimes think, looking back at Smythe's work, that his most important legacy was identifying the *sorts* of questions that would occupy the scientific community for the next half-century, even if he was ultimately unable to provide the correct answers.

I knew of Smythe before I had even met him. One of the most popular theories in the mid-1940s was that cancer was caused by a viral infection. This theory had been proposed decades earlier, but it had been aggressively promoted by Smythe, who had spent much of the early part of the decade trying to prove that cancer (which, for all scientists knew back then, was caused by demons or sorcery) was not only tidily explainable but also eminently treatable: if, the thinking went, you could isolate the viruses that caused cancer, you would then be able to develop a vaccine to kill it, thus eradicating cancer forever. Like all the most pleasing theories, it was inspired but disciplined, as well as neat, logical, and satisfyingly plausible. It was also accessible, and Smythe's theory (which became known in the popular press as "Smythe's conceit," as if it were the Pythagorean theorem or the theory of evolution, or as if Smythe were the Aristotle-like author of some ancient, semimystical, heavily allegorical philosophy) soon made him a quite famous (and, inevitably, much envied) man in both academic and popular circles.[15]

---

headline "Harvard University's Gregory Smythe: 'We could see the end of cancer in our lifetime.'"

[15] Norton is being a little sarcastic here. Several cancers *are* in fact highly associated with viral infections (most notably, human papillomavirus and hepatitis B and C);

But I will return to him later, which seems fitting, as it was only after I had been working in his lab for several months that I actually met Smythe. Unsurprisingly, given my grades, my attitude, and my general unsuitability, I was rather a nonentity for almost the entire time I was there; my colleagues never spoke to me, and my tasks were the most menial. I felt no resentment, however—students such as myself were, it seemed, continually arriving and departing, there one day and vanished the next to someplace else, a presence as temporal as the monkeys we were responsible for feeding, the mice whose water bottles we changed, the dogs with terrified eyes we injected, until one day they too vanished from the lab, taking with them their sounds and smells.

There were usually around fifteen of us—and Smythe, of course—in the lab at any time, and although I had been somehow, romantically, anticipating a free and creative exchange of ideas and theories (I was that naive), it was in truth strictly hierarchical; although a controlled environment and peopled with only a very narrow sliver of society, it hewed slavishly to the formalities and distinctions of rank of the outside world. At the top was Smythe, and what he said—or what his immediate inferiors said he said, which was more often the case—had to be followed without questions or debate. But Smythe was a less and less frequent presence by the time I arrived, more interested, it seemed, in giving interviews to the *New York Times* and to Edward R. Murrow.

The next most important people in the office were the two chief residents, Walter Brassard and Monroe Fitch, both M.D.'s and both (as they managed to remind you every week or so) handpicked by Smythe to run his lab. It was their job to supervise the experiments, write first drafts of Smythe's research papers and handle them through their eventual publication, and administer the daily goings-on at the lab, which included the hiring of medical students and undergraduates. Both of them disliked me, Brassard more than Fitch, but I had been hired directly by Smythe, and so they were forced to tolerate me. Both of them—again, Brassard more than Fitch—were not unknown in their own right; at school I had heard

---

what he mocks here is Smythe's insistence that *all* cancers can be directly attributed to viral infections.

professors speak of their brilliance and promise. They were sometimes called "the Turks," and it was thought that they would be the
scientific minds who would succeed Smythe and in the meantime
carry his projects to fruition. The two of them rarely spoke to each
other and, I saw, were quite competitive. Each disdained the other
for the supposed inferiority of his education (a curious thing, as they
had been classmates from prep school through medical school), his
intellectual vivacity (again, both seemed equally unimaginative to
me), and, it became clear, for his relative favor with Smythe at any
moment.

Beneath Brassard and Fitch were four junior residents, also
M.D.'s, named Parton, Nesser, Ulliver, and Curtis. The four of them
were in their way even more insufferable than Brassard and Fitch,
who had chosen them (with Smythe's approval). All of them too
had gone to boarding school (though not Brassard and Fitch's), and
all of them walked about the lab with an expression that aspired
to solemnity—a gently furrowed brow underneath hair still cut
in a schoolboy style, their hands clasped behind their backs in an
approximation of greatness—but that was, despite its ambition and
seriousness of intent, unable to conceal the slight smiles they wore
when they thought others weren't looking, that admiring preen that
women affect upon encountering a mirrored surface. I was assigned
to work with Parton, whom I liked best of the bunch, for his smooth,
fat-cheeked face and messy shirt (for which he was always being
rebuked by the Turks, to whom these sorts of details mattered) and
for the fact that he left me alone, forgetting for days that I was assisting him with his experiments and that he was therefore responsible
for monitoring my movements and, as they called it, daily output of
activity.

After the junior residents came the two medical students: me
and a fellow named Julian Turnbull, who was a great favorite of
the Turks' and who never once spoke to me, as if my very inappro-
priateness were a condition he might be able to contract by even
the briefest communication. So he stayed away, and that suited me
fine; I knew he was in my year, and that he was from somewhere in
Connecticut, and that he had a fiancée at Wellesley, but I knew nothing of how he thought nor where his intelligence lay, for he never

spoke of those matters, almost as if they were incidental to his life at the lab.

Next came two undergraduates, both of them usually biology majors at the college (these turned over so quickly and were at any rate so interchangeable that none of us ever bothered to learn their names), both of them headed for medical school, both of them always looking rather frightened: to be working in Smythe's lab as an undergraduate was an almost kingly honor, and they wore on their faces expressions of fear and pride. Looking at them, I sometimes wondered what promises had been extracted from them to win them these slots, what tests they had had to pass with their advisers, what obligations they now carried.

After the undergraduates came a man named Dean O'Grady, who, in the humor of the day, was known as Fat Irish because he was fat and Irish. Fat Irish was the person in the lab whose work was the most visible and qualifiable: while the rest of us took notes and flicked our fingernails against air bubbles in syringes and extracted blood and took more notes, Fat Irish took care of the animals, and did the things we would not. He cleaned the monkeys' cages and fed them a slurry of browned bananas and oatmeal. He changed the mice's water and cleaned weeping scabs from the dogs' eyes. I was impressed by his impassivity: he was neither an animal lover nor a sentimentalist (the lab had once had one of those, I learned, and it had ended disastrously when Fitch had discovered him late one night trying to shoo the dogs from their cages and into his waiting truck), nor did he seem impressed by or interested in the lab itself. You sometimes had animal caretakers—as I would have myself one day—whose hatred for the people who ran the lab was visceral. It was not because they were animal lovers (a job application from anyone who admitted to loving animals was immediately thrown away) but because they abhorred science and the people who practiced science, all of us in our white coats and what they considered our despicable arrogance, though whether it was our education they hated or what we were doing *with* our education (they considered one excessive and the other self-indulgent) was difficult to say. They were not people capable of superior cognitive reasoning, and because they were unable to understand what it was we were doing and yet were equally unwilling to admit their limitations, they found it easier to call us names and detest us. (It is not only animal caretakers who behave like this, but also journalists, and animal activists, and priests, and politicians, and housewives, and artists—people, in other words, for whom every mystery must be attributed to human arrogance and evil.)

But to return to Fat Irish: he would arrive at four every afternoon and begin his work, and when we came back the next day, messes would be cleaned, water trays filled, and the labs would smell more intensely of their signature perfume, the eggy scent of detergent and the sweetish fragrance of stale feces. Sometimes, working late, you would see Fat Irish and nod at him, and he would nod back. He would not try to make conversation. If you asked him a question directly, he would answer in the most perfunctory way—not rudely, but not foisting on you the sort of chatter (about the weather, working hard, their various aching body parts) of which janitors and waiters and various service staff in general seem to have an endless supply. Instead it was "Good morning, Fat Irish." "Good morning." "Basset Four [meaning the basset hound in cage 4] croaked last night." "I'll take care of it." And that was all.

After Fat Irish we come to the bottom: the lab techs, David and Peter, the two of them granted neither last names nor desks, although they did have white coats. They went from station to station, cleaning flasks, cutting pieces of mesh, scrubbing spoiled biomatter from test tubes, delivering mugs of burned coffee, fetching mice from cages, returning mice to cages. I tried not to use them too frequently: first, it was faster to do the work myself, and second, they were both loquacious, fond of telling you about their women, or about the meal they were awaiting that night, or about how sick of their jobs they were. They were not needlessly cruel to the animals, but they were sloppy: they clutched the mice so tightly that they squealed and kicked their small feet in the air; they forgot which dog went into which cage; they knocked over Bunsen burners and swabbed up their ensuing mess imperfectly, so that you were for the rest of the day forced to pick your way around your own desk until the night janitor came to clean what they had missed.

The lab was located on the first floor of a building called Chase Hall, ten stories, red brick, ugly and utilitarian; it was destroyed some years ago. There was a main room, about twelve hundred square feet, a long rectangle with four windows looking out onto the green beyond. In the south corner, farthest from the roar of the building incinerator, which abutted our lab, was Smythe's office, a small, glassed-in square in which sat a burled desk (perfectly, suspiciously clean-surfaced), a metal filing cabinet, and a metal bookcase. Just outside his office, running along the east side of the room, beneath the windows, were front-to-front metal desks for each of the chief and junior residents and for the medical students and undergraduates. The remainder of the room was dominated by eight long metal countertops fitted with sinks and crowded with Bunsen burners and flasks. The floors were linoleum and the walls a pale butter that always made me crave bread or potatoes—something starchy and floury.

Behind the main room, running its length, were the two animal labs. The first, to the south side, was the mice lab, windowless, about three hundred square feet, and lined on three sides with cages stacked some seven feet high along the walls, which were here a shiny, curdled, charred orange color. The mice lab, like animal labs everywhere, stank of damp newspaper and feces and the moldy, algaeish stench of wet fur. Every night the floors were swabbed with disinfectant, but it seemed only to intensify the room's native odors, which were so impermeable they seemed to have been baked into the walls. Adjacent to the mice lab was the dog lab, almost twice as large but with the same smells, the same rust-colored walls, the same wire cages, although here they were stacked all the way to the ceiling. There were thirty-six or so cages, and they were all small, about two feet square, so that the dogs (usually hounds, for some reason) were unable to stand and spent their days on their sides or crouched, front legs spread open, in a way that made them appear drunk and unseemly. Then there were about ten or twelve taller cages, and these were reserved for monkeys, which we had with some regularity, but not frequently enough or in large enough numbers to merit their own lab. What I remember most about those labs is their silence—one heard the mice's frantic, shrill peeping, the dogs' futile, squealing whimpers, only when they were being removed from or replaced in their cages. The rest of the time they were silent, staring at their paws and waiting. Only the monkeys complained and chattered and screeched all day, shrieking at nothing. They were a bother for that reason, and for the enormous mess they made, and for the intensity of their odors, although they were of course more valuable specimens to work with.

I spent most of my time with the mice. One of Parton's ongoing experiments—the exact parameters of which I never did discover, because strangely, although I was trusted with much, I was apparently not seen as consequential enough to learn what it was I passed most of my days doing—involved infecting mice with various sorts of viruses in the hopes that they would provoke a cancer. You began with, say, a dozen mice, one mouse per each numbered cage. Then you would take a virus and inject it with a mix of saline into each mouse. And then you would wait. Every day you would weigh and measure and observe them. Did they seem torpid? Were they eating and drinking properly? Were they growing any strange nodules (you certainly hoped they would, but it never happened, not in any of the tests I conducted)? I recorded the results in my notebook, which Parton might have asked to see but never did. Boredom made me fanciful: "No. 12. White mouse," I would write (they were all white), "chalky in complexion. Nose and pawpads: rose pink from yesterday, when carnation pink. Personality: dull." (They were all dull. They were mice, after all. They spent their days doing mousy things.) After a certain point, around three months, you would kill them, autopsy them, and begin with a fresh group.

I rather enjoyed killing the mice. There were surprisingly few ways to do so: drugging them took too long and was too expensive; drowning them was messy and also tedious. (And at any rate, either method would compromise key tissues we would need to study.) It was Ulliver who taught me how to kill them. What you did was hold a mouse by its tail and twirl it in a circle like a lasso until it was dizzy, its head lolling sickly from side to side. Then you'd put it on the table and with one hand hold its head behind its ears and with the other hand pull it up by its tail. A little *crick!* and the neck would be broken. Sometimes Julian Turnbull and I would stand at either end of the long counter that ran down the middle of the mice lab, both of us whirling four or five mice in each hand, killing them in batches. It was a satisfying task, a small but real accomplishment to mark a day that, like so many other days, seemed devoid of structure, or progress, or meaning.

Then you'd take the mice to the main lab and spread them on one of the countertops, stomach up. You'd cut out each spleen—a tiny, savory-looking thing, richly, meatily brown and the size of a slender watermelon seed—and place each in its own Petri dish with a bit of saline. You'd have next to you a springy pile of fine wire mesh, cut into one-inch-square pieces, which you'd sterilize over a flame, and then you'd rub the spleen against it into another Petri dish to obtain a single cell suspension. Spleens, of course, are soft and pulpy, like foie gras, and you had to be careful to only brush them against the mesh; anything more vigorous and you'd find the organ smeared over your fingers, sticky and dark as fudge. You might do this a few times, or until the organ had turned liquidy; then you'd pipette some of the sauce into a tube, examine it under a microscope, and record how many cells there were per milliliter.

The main point of these experiments was, as I've noted before, not only to prove that cancers were caused by viruses (note that I have not said *whether* cancers were caused by viruses; Smythe, whether through his own arrogance or because he had decided to make the terrible error of believing what a science writer—always an oxymoron—had written about him, seemed to have convinced himself that his theory was impregnable. His lab was not interested in proving or disproving him; Fitch and Brassard and the rest were interested only in the specifics of his supposition rather than in its inherent veracity) but also how to establish a cell culture. If you could prove that, say, Cancer X was caused by Virus Y, then all you'd have to do was create a vaccine, which would eradicate the cancer. (I'm simplifying, but not by much; this is really how they thought at the time, not just in medicine but in all the sciences: you make a bomb; you drop it on a troublesome people; the troublesome people are no more.)

One experiment I was made to repeat involved kidneys, whose malformations were easy to identify—easier than spleens', for example. You'd take a mouse's kidney (a more fibrous organ than the spleen) and snip it into bits into a test tube. Then you'd take those pieces and pass them through layers of increasingly fine screens to try, again, to reduce it to a single cell layer, which would be distinguishable by its smeary quality. After that, you'd pulverize the tissue with saline and fetal calf serum nutrient—which of course helps promote growth—before placing this in a sterile bottle with a flat surface and incubating it at 37 degrees. The cells, in suspension, would then attach to the surface of the bottle, appearing in flat, starry clusters. Once you had a thriving monolayer of cells, you'd introduce a virus, inoculating the cells. After a few days, you'd then centrifuge the whole batch and remove the supernate—the noncellular part—as your vaccine.

That was the thinking, anyway. And I have to admit, at the time this method seemed sensible, logical. Perhaps, in retrospect, a bit *too* sensible, a bit *too* logical, but it was more plausible than many of the prevailing theories of the time, although as I would learn shortly after, what is most plausible is not necessarily the most correct or worthy of the most consideration. More often it is the outlandish theory, the one that seems so improbable, that you find yourself returning to again and again, paying it an outsized share of attention largely because you find yourself intrigued by the originality of thought behind it.

I was twenty-four; I was infecting dogs. I took syringes of various viruses and injected them into dogs' kidneys. They were very keen on organ transplantation in those days, and so soon I was doing real surgeries, albeit on dogs, and I was able to do them unsupervised, right there in the canine lab (sometimes Parton would walk in, gaze at me dolefully, as if he'd no idea who I was and it was not his right to ask, and then shuffle out without saying a word to me). I opened up the dog and tied off the artery to its kidney and stitched it closed again. A few days later, when the dog was in kidney failure—it moaned and whined; its urine was treacly and venomous in appearance and leaked out in fat, viscous, reluctant drops—I redrugged it, removed its dead kidney (now the bruised, sheeny blue of rotting meat), and tried to transplant into the dog a kidney I had infected in another dog. I sewed both dogs back up. The donor dog I had incinerated. The one that had received the transplant soon expired as well, although whether from the infected kidney or from my poor surgical skills I was never quite certain. I observed it and took notes on its decline in my notebook, and when it died, I harvested its organs of interest and preserved them for further analysis and then had its corpse incinerated too.

This is how day after day passed. I realize I sound bored recounting it now, and perhaps even a little dramatically fatalistic, but at the time it was interesting enough, both the work itself—for at times I truly did feel, as a good lab with a charismatic leader encourages its fellows to feel, that I, as much as anyone, perhaps more, was on the inevitable verge of a discovery of a small but important sort, something that might change science forever—and because I was learning from my days in the lab and the lives of those around me that it was not a life that I would choose. It is a funny thing, working for someone else in a lab: you are chosen because you are the best in your class or the most promising in your field or an interesting thinker, and you are put in a room full of others like yourself. In some of your colleagues you see your past, the student you once were, and in others you see your future, or at least a template for your future, although you yourself, you assume, will be better and brighter and more talented than they.

But what does it *mean* to be successful or talented in a lab? For your work there is not truly your own; you are chosen because of your mind and then asked, to varying degrees, to cease thinking for yourself and begin doing so for another. For some people this is easier than for others; they are the ones who remain. And so although you gain fraternity, you forsake your independence. But ambition is a difficult thing to quash completely, and so it is redirected—instead of working alone, you work in a room with others, but even as you do, you hope every day that *you* will be the one to make the key discovery, that *you* will be the one to find the answer, that *you* will present it, triumphant, to your director and that he will be generous and intellectually confident enough to give you your due credit. This is your hope, and it has motivated and kept alive men much more distinguished than I. But it is answered for only a very few of them, and they—the ones who one day are awarded their own labs, their own patented cell lines, their own papers—are the lucky ones. They are all of them patient, though; I, however, knew by the end of my first term with Smythe's lab that I could never be that patient, nor that pliable.

Part of this certainty was attributable to the discomfort I felt with the culture of the lab itself. Labs at that time were not like the ones today. Not that I cared a terrible amount about my colleagues' lives, the things they were interested in outside of the office, but there was at work a kind of conservatism, a fixation on neatness, that I found difficult and dispiriting. In those days science considered itself the realm of gentlemen. This was the era, after all, of Linus Pauling and J. Robert Oppenheimer, both of them exceptional, of course, but not exempt from having to dress a certain way, or from being able to perform at cocktail parties, or from pursuing romance. Genius was no excuse for social ineptitude, the way it is today, when a certain refusal to acquire the most basic social skills or an inability to dress properly or feed oneself is generously perceived as evidence of one's intellectual purity and commitment to the life of the mind.

But this was not how it always was. Then, it was difficult to ignore one's colleagues' extraoffice activities and interests because one was expected to be appropriate in one's own. People spoke of the Turks approvingly not only because they had done well in school and were, so it was said, quick-minded and obedient and thoughtful, but because they were so presentable. Both had wives who had gone to Radcliffe, both came from well-known East Coast families, both were handsome enough and well dressed. They were very earnest. They were convinced that what they were doing was serious and important work—and so was I—but they were the sort of men for whom humor was to be practiced only at the appropriate events (parties, dinners, etc.) and then only within a very limited range. Except to Europe with their parents (and, I suppose, with the army in wartime, which hardly counts), neither of them had traveled, and neither of them longed to. Their friends were people like themselves, and they hired people like themselves—Ulliver and Nesser compensated for their strange Scandinavian surnames with their nicknames, which were Skip and Trip—and their lives were the lab to their homes in Cambridge or Newton and then back. People like Fat Irish may never have thought beyond a life of emptying mice cages and swabbing urine from the lab floors, but in their own way the

Turks were as limited, as unimaginative: they assumed they would make a great contribution to mankind, and that is a faultless goal, I suppose, but the process itself never seemed as compelling to them as the outcome was, nor as the fantasy of having their name appended to whatever it is they dreamed of inventing or solving or fixing. I had gone into science for its adventure, but to them, adventure was something to be endured, not sought, on the road to inevitable greatness.

## II.

It was not until I had been working at the lab for six months that I finally had my chance to meet Smythe. I had seen him before, of course, but only in glimpses: in newspapers, in magazines, as he ran into the lab to talk with Brassard and Fitch or to grab a piece of paper or a journal from his otherwise worrisomely tidy desk before leaving again for the world outside his lab. A few of my professors would occasionally ask me about him, jealous: What did he have me doing in that lab? What was *he* doing? I always told the truth, and this was boring and opaque enough to stop their questions: I cut open mice; I didn't know. Had I known what I thought about him, had I admired him and wished to protect his work, I would have lied and made my own work sound more fascinating.

One day, however, Brassard stopped by my counter as I was grating mice spleens. "Smythe left this for you," he said, placing an envelope by my elbow. He was disapproving, but he was always disapproving. I took off my gloves and opened the envelope, a regular business-sized envelope with my name typed on the front. Inside was a letter on onionskin—also typed, so poorly I assumed Smythe had done so himself—inviting me to dinner that Friday, at 6:30 p.m. He had signed it with a black fountain pen and the ink had bled through the paper and blurred into a smudge. It's difficult now to remember precisely what I thought of this invitation. I suppose I was flattered—although Brassard, who had somehow figured out what the letter was, made sure to inform me later that day that Smythe made a practice of inviting over each medical student who worked in his lab *once* (he emphasized the word) during his tenure—but oddly, I don't recall being overly excited. Nor was I particularly worried. I had never quite understood how I had gotten the position in Smythe's lab in the first place, and I knew for certain by then that it was not a place I would stay; lack of interest has a kind way of eliminating all potential nervousness.

On Friday I arrived for dinner at Smythe's house, a tall, narrow brownstone on the edge of the medical school campus. In the front was a Japanese red maple, now bare (it was early March), a holly bush with glossy, sharp leaves, and a clump of veined crocuses peering through their halo of mulch. The rest of the garden was bare, just plain wood chips. There was no harmony or apparent order to the plants' arrangement; they just were. Inside, the house was very much the same way: in one corner of the entryway sat, incongruously, a Japanese tansu of blistering, puckered camphor. In another, just as incongruously, was an old-fashioned English secretary desk, the grain of the wood patterning its surface with satiny stripes. The rugs that covered the dusty floors were old Orientals, and I saw what looked like cracker crumbs speckling their tassels. The walls were hung with black shadowbox frames backed with black felt upon which were mounted lockets, their gold dull and whitish, and little scrimshaw carvings (a gnome, his crudely carved hands slapping together in a gesture of merriment; a ship, its sails pooching out unconvincingly), and cameos showing dreamy, loose-curled girls gazing off to the side, their expressions vacant. They were deeply idiosyncratic touches, and yet there was something furtive and unspecific about the house as well—it looked like the showroom for a second-rate auction house specializing in estate sales. There was nothing there that echoed who Smythe appeared to be, with his birchbark-colored hair and his lined face and his tall, upright walk and his magazine articles. Behind the frames, the walls were painted, each a different, strange color: puce and teal and that bright light green particular to unripened fruit. I had expected beiges and browns and perhaps some unobjectionable blues, everything neat and in order, not an eccentric's house, for Smythe was not an eccentric.

And yet everything around him that night seemed to argue that he was. Dinner, when it was at last served, was as ill-organized and haphazard as the house itself, as if assembled from whatever had been found in the refrigerator ten minutes before. There was tomato soup, thick as gravy and tasting strongly of ketchup; game hens, so undercooked that I could see the red arteries marbling the flesh; carrots and onions, so overcooked that they overflowed the tines of my fork with the gentlest press; another soup, this one seeming to consist purely of boiled onions and leeks and topped with a wet, suggestive coil of mustard; and for dessert what Smythe proudly told me were persimmons, sitting prim and Oriental on their blue-and-white chinoiserie plates but as hard as green plums—they tasted, when I was finally able to saw off a bite, like grass but sour, and it would be many years before I would be able to correct this impression.

It was only the two of us at the table. Smythe sat at the head, nearest the kitchen, and I sat to his right. With each new course, he popped to his feet, disappeared through the pocket doors behind him, and came back bearing two plates in triumph. It had occurred to me, walking up the path to his house with a bottle of wine I'd thought to buy at the last minute, that he might be interested in interrogating me, that this might be a test of some sort. I was not worried about passing, but the thought of sitting down with Smythe—and, I assumed, his family—and being interviewed about my thoughts on various scientific quandaries of the day did not exactly fill me with excitement. But these had been wasted worries, for Smythe spent the entire evening speaking, from the time I entered the door and he took my coat with one hand and handed me a juice cup of brandy with the other (I have never cared for the taste of brandy, so flannelly on the teeth, and I tossed it into the shedding ficus in the foyer when Smythe went to fetch himself another cupful), throughout dinner, and over the glass of sherry he placed before me afterward, which I drank although I was longing for something cakey to neutralize the persimmon. The sherry glass was cut crystal and heavy, and I rotated it slowly in my fingers, watching the spangles of light it made against the wall opposite, which was a sickly, parchmentlike yellow.

The evening began with small talk, which I was unaccustomed to and for which I had no talent. When I realized I had to say nothing, only to smile and nod from time to time, I was relieved. When we sat at the table—after standing for some time in the entryway, the two of us holding our plastic cups of brandy, while to my left lay a parlor, darkened and unused—he began to talk instead of his work. You would think, would you not, that in the more than two hours I listened to Smythe speak of his work I would learn something interesting, or that he would say something thoughtful, or at the very least provocative? But this was not to happen. He had the ability to talk at length on interesting subjects while somehow rendering them not only intensely uninteresting but completely opaque. "Sir," I'd interject as Smythe cut eagerly into his fowl—he ate the entire meal with vigor and apparent satisfaction, but failed to notice that I had left most of mine untouched—"will you tell me a little about your research into viral mutation?" This was, after all, the basis of his entire theory, his life's work. But he did not want to speak of his research; instead he spoke of the people who had impeded it. There was the dean, and the associate dean, and this colleague and that—he listed dozens of names, detailing to me what each had done and how now they had been humbled and made to look at him anew. The dean, he had heard, had rolled his eyes upon hearing about the *Time* magazine story. The associate dean had initially refused to give him the space he had wanted in Chase Hall, had tried to shunt him into a darker, inferior, smaller lab on the fifth floor. But he had prevailed, hadn't he? He was without rancor, even jolly, as he told me these stories, onion-and-leek soup dripping from his spoon. He was not interested in discussing science. Still talking, he excused himself to the kitchen and came back with more soup, this time a blend of the two, which he swirled together with the handle of his spoon until it achieved a strange pasty consistency, and then he tucked his napkin into the collar of his shirt to protect his tie. He held it flat against his shirt with one hand and spooned up the soup with the other, murmuring his appreciation.

Watching him, I wondered what the Turks would think of this display or if perhaps they already knew what Smythe was truly like, and if so, why did they remain with him, and how could they respect him? Had I underestimated the limits of their tolerance? Or was this an act that Smythe was performing only for me? Were the Turks and the junior residents crouched in the darkened parlor, their faces tight with held-back laughter, watching this bit of theater in which I was an unknowing and unwilling participant? Was this even Smythe's house? Where was his wife—I knew he had one, and on his left ring finger he wore a thin golden circle—and wasn't there something unnaturally still about these rooms? I kept thinking that if only I could find a reason to walk through the doors into the kitchen or cross the foyer into the living room, I would find the real house, one in which Smythe held forth articulately and behaved like the Great Man we all thought he was, and his pretty wife would serve a good meal, and his life would make sense to me and I would cease to feel like such an anthropologist in my own town, with the man who had hired me and invited me to dinner at his house.

After we had drunk our sherry, he was silent for a moment, and I was able to speak at last. "Sir," I asked, "why did you hire me?"

"Ah," he said, after a silence. "Why indeed." He sighed and spun his glass in his fingers, and the reflections it made moved across his face like firefly light. "You are not a good student—you are dreamy and arrogant. Your professors find you ungovernable." He said this all cheerfully, in the same pleasant tone in which he had recounted his enemies' many failed plots against him. "But when they told me about you"—and here he turned and looked at me, and I could see for the first time his eyes, the pleats of skin that hung beneath them, his scleras as pink as those of the mice whose organs I harvested and shaved through sieves every day—"I suppose I remembered myself when I was your age. How desperately I wanted to escape, how little I felt I belonged, how much I craved my freedom, how much I craved my fame. We are alike, the two of us."

"I'm not like that," I wanted to say, but I said nothing. He was drunk, I could now see. How long had he been like this? Had he been drunk when I first came in? I felt suddenly foolish, and childish, and embarrassed for myself. Why could I not see what was before me? What was the trick to understanding people that I alone seemed unable to possess? As I thought, Smythe was making strange noises, small gulping sounds. I thought he was choking, but when I hurried to him, I realized he was crying, his chin flat against the napkin still tucked into his shirt, his hands folded in his lap like a child's. "Oh god," he said. "Oh god." I did not know what to do. My coat was on the chair next to me, where Smythe had placed it. I picked it up and fled.

The following Monday I did not go into the lab. I did not go to any of my classes. Instead I stayed home and read, or looked at my atlas and made lists of places I wanted to see. I thought occasionally of what Smythe had said to me and decided he was wrong. I thought of him crying and felt pity for myself and disgust for him. For meals, I made my favorite snack, hot oatmeal into which I stirred raw eggs, until I realized that it was the sort of strange concoction Smythe might serve. I was terrified that I might become him, although it was not until some years later—about the time, in fact, I discovered what a persimmon should truly taste like—that I was able to define why: that worse than his poor science, the flimsy scholarship, was his small, inexplicable life alone in that strange house, with no one around to distract him from the meagerness of his own existence. It startled me to learn this about myself, that I had such petty, poor fears, that I had come to think in such trite and soft ways.

After a few days of my moping, the medical school secretary called, asking snippily if I was planning on returning to classes, followed by Brassard, who told me in his sniffing way that I had potentially ruined Parton's experiment and oughtn't bother returning. When I hung up, I was relieved, for in the space of my dinner with Smythe the lab had come to seem a sort of trap, a sort of place where I *would* become like him, holding my theory tightly to me, idealess, terrified of the inevitable day when I would be proved an imposter. Or at least this is what I told myself I feared. Now I had been not just released but told I was inappropriate, that I would never become one of them, and their words, their dismissal, left me shaky with joy. I was safe, I thought, and for some time, for a long time, I was.

The next day I returned to my classes. My professors—some of whom were quite close to the Turks—seemed to have heard that I was no longer with Smythe's lab and, surprisingly, treated me better than they had before, although I was still nobody exceptional. But I was careful not to feel resentful about this, as I might have before. I thought of Smythe—"But *now* they're coming back to me, *now* they're giving me what I want"—and cringed. For the next year I attended classes and sat silently in the lecture halls, determined not to make myself into something more significant than I really was. It was my first lesson in humility, in the lab or in life.[16]

---

[16] After his work was discredited, Smythe fell into disgrace, but it is difficult not to hold him at least partly responsible for his humiliation. Smythe had a reputation for arrogance and had many enemies within the academic world; when the tide began to turn against him, he fought back and insulted his critics instead of simply allowing himself to step into the more dignified shadows of obscurity. Because Smythe was a tenured professor, he remained at Harvard until his death in 1979 of—ironically—

## III.

One of the attractions of medical school for the unimaginative (or, if I am to be more charitable, to the less dreamily inclined) is certainly the lack of choices it offers. Of course, a doctor, whether he works with patients or alone, with tissues, must make dozens of decisions within a given day, but the larger questions—the ones about what you must do next in life—are answered for you. Indeed, you need never think about what the next year will bring, because for many years the path is laid before you, and it is only your duty to follow it. College leads to medical school, which leads to internships and residencies, which leads perhaps to fellowships, then to an appointment or a private practice or a job in a hospital or a group. It is this way now, and it was this way when I was in school as well.

By the January of my last year in medical school, I was feeling anxious. It was not a familiar sensation, and not a welcome one, either. I had no intention of working with patients, and so while my classmates interviewed for internships, I sat in my room like a hunk of wood, waiting for my future to resolve itself. It embarrasses me now, how inactive I was, how I allowed ignorance and naïveté to stymie me, but at the time it seemed a no more or less effective way of answering a future I could not even begin to imagine for myself.

A few months into this paralysis, probably in March or so—a year after my disastrous dinner with Smythe, in fact—one of my instructors, a man named Adolphus Sereny,[17] with whom I was com-

---

liver cancer, although he was less and less present and was placed on what amounted to permanent probation in 1968.

As Norton suspected, Smythe did in fact have a family—a wife and two daughters. Interestingly, it is they, not he, who remain well known today in countercultural circles for leading a small but influential Weather Underground–like feminist group that they founded in 1967. Norton probably had dinner at Smythe's house shortly after his wife, a poet named Alice Reeve, left him with their children to flee to Canada with her lover, a poetry professor at Radcliffe named Stella Janovic. But that is the stuff of another story.

[17] One of the great surgeons and biologists of his time, Adolphus Gustav Sereny (1896–1974) was among the more renowned scientists on the faculty at Harvard Medical School while Perina was a student there. He and Perina would go on to have a fruitful but ultimately contentious relationship, which is addressed later in this narrative.

pleting my surgical rotation, asked me to come see him in his office at the hospital one day.

"Well, Perina," said Sereny. "What do you plan to do when you graduate?"

"I don't know, sir," I told him.

Sereny looked at me for a long moment and then sighed. He was a large, cushiony man, with a fringe of pale, pebble-colored hair circling the back of his head. We had never spoken before outside of rounds, or much during them.

"Something has come up," he said, "and you have been suggested for it."

"What is it?" I asked.

He sighed again; not irritatedly, I think now, but because he was fat and puffy and it was in his nature to sigh. When he moved in his chair, air gusted from him. "Well, here it is," he began. "There's a man named Paul Tallent. An anthropologist from Stanford—young, well regarded. He claims to have evidence of some lost tribe on an island called U'ivu. Have you heard of it?" I hadn't. "Well, never mind. It's somewhere in Micronesia, I understand, though you'll have to look at an atlas to confirm exactly where. Small spot. At any rate, he has a private grant of some sort, reasonably substantial, I understand, to go there and study them—if he can find them, that is." Another sigh, though this one intentional, I believe. Doctors in those days did not think much of anthropologists, who were considered, often rightly, not truly scientists. "His team will include him, of course, and his assistant, and a doctor, who will be responsible for drawing blood, taking samples, recording, and"—he flapped a plump hand—"so on. He has connections here, and asked if a young doctor could be convinced to go with him. You were recommended. Are you interested?"

It may have been the first time in my life I felt giddy. "I am, sir."

"You understand, Perina," said Sereny with a sort of sternness I found dramatic and therefore thrilling, "that this is at least a four-month appointment, that there probably won't be money for you to come home during that period? And that nothing at all may come of this . . . expedition? That it could be many months of your life spent chasing down someone else's imaginings? That this island you'll be living on is, for all purposes, terra incognita? That it will almost assuredly be uncomfortable, in all likelihood intensely so? Do you understand that?"

"Yes, I do," I answered. He sighed once again, almost sadly, although that would have been impossible, as he neither knew me nor had any personal attachment to me. "When would I leave?"

"I've been informed that he wants to depart soon, very soon— probably late June. You'd barely have time to graduate."

"That's all right," I assured him. I would have left earlier; my diploma meant nothing to me. "But sir," I asked him, "why are you speaking to me about this? Why not Tallent's contact?"

"He's out of town, but he asked me to speak with you as soon as I was able."

"Who is Tallent's contact?" I asked. But I already knew the answer.

"Gregory Smythe," said Sereny.[18] He looked at me again, and this time he seemed puzzled himself. "He spoke very highly of you."

※

The fact that Smythe had suggested me for the job bothered me at the time, and it was not until I was much older and at my own lab that I realized his reasons for recommending me for such a job, one that would take me far away from him, one in which there would be no danger of encountering me on campus and becoming embarrassed upon seeing me—he had, after all, cried in front of me, and served me that strange meal—one in which the only people I could tell about his perplexing behavior would be Stone Age natives, their noses spliced with animal bones. By the time I had determined his motivations, though, there was nothing to forgive for such a self-serving act, and I had only pity for Smythe, his misshapen life and the even sadder turn it had taken. (It will perhaps say everything you need to know about the medical college, and Smythe too, when I tell you that my being offered this assignment was seen—by the Turks and their kind, at least—as a humiliating sort of punishment, and my acceptance as a sort of professional suicide, final proof of either my idiocy or my unacceptability, or both.)

---

[18] The contact was actually secondhand; one of Tallent's colleagues at Stanford, not Tallent himself, was friendly with Smythe.

The next few months passed quickly. I was not nervous; I was not anxious: I did my coursework and went home every afternoon feeling light and calm. I began packing weeks early, assembling in a canvas rucksack what were now to be the tools of my trade—a spirometer, a thermometer, a blood pressure cuff and stethoscope, a reflex hammer, and a small portable microscope. I had a cedar-wood container, a little larger than a cigar box, in which I stored various small items—buttons and screws, thumbtacks and rubber bands—and into which I now packed two dozen glass syringes, each wrapped in gauze, and an extra dozen steel needles, and a metal flask I filled with disinfectant from the labs. I had received a brief letter from Paul Tallent, welcoming me to the project and giving me my instructions: we would meet on June 20 (a day after my graduation, it turned out) in Hawaii and from there hitch a ride on a military transport plane, which would detour on its way to Australia to drop us off in the Gilbert Islands,[19] from which we would continue to U'ivu. Beyond these details, however, he had provided little useful information: nothing on what to pack, nothing on what I might expect, nothing more specific about the nature of his studies, nothing even about the island itself. Months later, in U'ivu, I would spread my gear before me, marveling at how misguided I had been, how thoroughly I had miscalculated, and before my time there was over I would have left most of it—books, jackets, shoes, even my butterfly net—scattered through the jungles of U'ivu, abandoned as things no more relevant to the islanders' lives than they would turn out to be to mine.

In part, though, I cannot blame myself too severely, for my ignorance of the situation I was to enter was almost entirely due to the fact that the world at large was ignorant of U'ivu. Directly after leaving Sereny's office, I went to the library to consult its atlas, and although I had the island's coordinates, it took me a few seconds to locate it, my finger skimming over pages of blue ocean. And then I found it: three small chips of light green arranged as three points in a ragged isoceles, its topography rendered unspecific and blurry, a little less than a thousand miles east of Tahiti. Further research yielded a small collection of facts, each interesting on its own but which once

---

[19] Now Kiribati.

combined somehow failed to illuminate one another in any helpful way. The country, I read, had never been colonized. Like the Hawaiians, its people were thought to have immigrated from Tahiti five thousand years ago on outrigger canoes. They were a hunting and fishing culture; all children, both boys and girls, were expected to kill (the encyclopedia did not specify how) a wild boar before their fourteenth birthday.[20] They had a king, Tuimai'ele, who had three wives and thirty children and who lived in a wooden palace in the capital, Tavaka. It was not a wealthy country, but the soil was rich and there was always food. But once its people had been notorious for their ferocity, and tales of their love of brutality and zest for cruelty had carried across the seas—so far, in fact, that theirs was the lone country that Captain James Cook purposefully bypassed in his 1787 travels through the Pacific. ("The fierceness of the Wevooans," he wrote in a letter to a friend the year prior, "makes the crew uneasy, and as it is difficult to sail, we shall not be anchoring there.")

I read this in the encyclopedia, but I could not believe all of it: the wooden palace, the king with thirty children, the wild boar killing—they all seemed somehow familiar, like something I had once read in, say, a Kipling story about some faraway, allegorical land. But although I had not enough experience in the world to prove this, I suspected even then that the strangest details were the most mundane, and that what we tell others to shock will only inure them to realizing what is truly remarkable. And in this perception I was not to be proven wrong.

---

[20] This popularly accepted myth is probably a conflation of two facts: first, all U'ivuan boys are given a spear upon their fourteenth birthday; second, the first king of the islands, King Ulolo the Powerful—who unified many of the various tribes scattered among the archipelago in approximately A.D. 1645; his work was eventually completed by King Vaka I more than a century later—was said to have killed a wild boar barehanded before his fourteenth birthday. Since then the boar has occupied a central place in U'ivuan life; although it is a treasured hunting companion and a symbol of the culture's ferocity to the outside world, killing or taming one is also considered a significant accomplishment and proof of the warrior's strength and bravery. The fundamentally paradoxical nature of the beast's place in society—both friend and challenge—is not a contradiction that seems ever to have troubled the U'ivuans.

# PART III. THE DREAMERS

## I.

June was a month unlike any I had experienced, and at the end of each of its days I would go to bed early, if only so I could think for a few minutes about all that I had seen and felt. As it happened, I had skipped my graduation and departed for Hawaii two weeks before I was to meet Tallent. My last night in Cambridge (which even before I left was vanishing from my memory, as cleanly and swiftly as salt in hot water), Owen had come up from New Haven to see me. Our goodbyes had been unsatisfying—he was brusque and seemed obscurely angry with me—but he did agree to keep for me some things (books, papers, my winter coat, heavy as a corpse) that I wouldn't need on my travels. We agreed to write to each other, but I could tell from his expression that he was as dubious about that ever happening as I was. It was only after we had shaken hands and he had left with a trunk packed with my things to catch the last train back that I thought about what my life would be like so far away from Owen; it was true that we spoke less and less as we grew older (a detachment that seemed as inevitable as it was mysterious), but he was the only one who knew me, who retained memories of me from each year of my life, because it had been half his life as well. But this regret too quickly dissipated, so eager was I to begin my new existence—it was easy then to believe that my life until this point had been only a long, tedious rehearsal, a thing to be impatiently endured and withstood: a simulacrum of a life, not a life itself.

I had a train ticket to California, and from there I took a ship to Hawaii. In those days, Honolulu was still very much a quiet colonial outpost, with all the attendant flourishes and clichés, and as the boat pulled into harbor, you could see on the dock groups of fat, jolly musicians plucking their plinky songs on their ukuleles, and barefooted boys, half Asian and half something else, smiling and begging for the disembarking passengers to throw them pennies.

It had been arranged that I would stay in a dormitory room at the local university, but because I had arrived earlier than anticipated, the building was fully occupied, and no bed was available until the next evening. And so that first night, after storing my luggage at the dormitory, I took a taxi to the edge of Waikiki, where I walked to Diamond Head on the sand, one beach giving way to the next. Beyond me I could sometimes hear the sounds of bars: groups of men laughing at something, the chingy-changy music. I stood periodically and listened to the dry palm fronds chattering against one another like bones, and to the ocean, its remorseless, lonely conversation with itself, a sound that—though I did not know it at the time—I would not hear again for months to come. I walked with the moon above me, which here seemed to glow whiter and rounder and brighter than it had in Boston, and when I grew tired, I lay under a tree and slept, as I had seen other shadowy forms doing as I made my slow way across the sand.

The next day I ventured to the city's downtown district, past its pretty colonial buildings. The grandest thing I saw, though, was not a structure, not even the humble, squat palace once occupied by the humble, squat queen, but instead the trees outside it: ancient shower trees, their leaves peachy petals that swirled about them in snowy, gentle cyclones. In Chinatown, I walked around the frayed shapes of sleeping men, the soles of their feet black and crisscrossed with channels and cuts, until I found a bar with an open door. It was not a good place, this Chinatown, with its sad saloon-shuttered buildings out of whose dark interiors poor jazz seeped like poison. But the sun was hotter than I had anticipated, and I was very thirsty.

The bartender was so flat-faced it appeared as if someone had held each of his ears and pulled in either direction, and so sun-darkened that his skin had become glossed and smooth, like a chicken that has been broiled in butter for too long. He was Chinese, I guessed, or at least some sort of Oriental, for his eyes were hooded and narrow, although his black hair was wavy and coarse. I ordered a glass of seltzer, and he watched as I gulped it down. "Where you from?" he asked finally.

"Boston," I said. I noticed he was missing his left thumb, although he was able to move the stump back and forth, which he did rather expressively, like a dog would its bobbed tail.

He was unimpressed by this information, but there was no one else in the bar for him to speak with, and when I finished my glass, he refilled it without my asking. "How long you here?" he asked.

"Not long," I said. Now that I had had something to drink, I was able to concentrate on the room, which was low-ceilinged and dark and lacquered, the wooden counter sticky from years of smoke and spilled liquor and cooking grease. "I'm on my way to U'ivu."

To my surprise, he nodded when I mentioned U'ivu, and when I asked him what he knew, he laughed and said, "Good hunters. Boars." He refilled my glass again. "Scary." It was unclear whether he meant the people or the boars. Then, almost gently, "They are very violent there." I waited for him to say more, but he had begun to hum a meandering, wistful tune, strangely moving in the ugliness of the bar, and when it became clear that he would say no more, I finished my drink and paid and walked back out into the sunshine.

I passed a few more days like this, taking taxis to various beaches on the island, marveling at how they first appeared to be uniformly, indistinguishably lovely but eventually revealed themselves particular and distinct: one had sand so fine that even after beating out my shirt and pants, I still found myself dusting it from my clothes and shaking it from my hair the next day; another was booby-trapped with tiny, unseen pinecones dropped by the fringe of gawky, shaggy ironwood trees that edged the beachfront, so that each step contained a small, unavoidable pain; another had sand the color and texture of wet, raw sugar, making it sludgy and sticky to the touch. One afternoon I went to the library downtown, where the librarian helped me find an old, cloth-covered book on U'ivu. It turned out to be a picture book, a Hawaiian-language primer published by the Honolulu Missionary Academy in 1871, each page containing a simple woodcut and a few lines of text. Because it was in Hawaiian, I could not read it, but the pictures—a boar, its eyes beady and black, its tusks as extravagantly curled as an old-fashioned handlebar mustache; the king, smiling and fat and shirtless, clutching what looked like a long feather duster; a knobby torpedo I took to be a sweet potato—made it seem once again more, not less, fantastic, a place that indeed existed only in children's stories.

And then finally it was the day I was to meet Tallent. He had sent a telegram to the hall where I was staying at the university, informing me of his arrival time and suggesting that we meet in the lounge area at six p.m.; we would leave the next morning at eight. The flight to the Gilbert Islands would take nine hours, followed by another three-hour-long transfer to U'ivu.

I was nervous before meeting Tallent, uncomfortably so; I was not usually anxious about meeting people, and after all, I had been requested, I was a doctor, I was (I told myself) essential to his operation. Yet this was a false sort of confidence, because as I was aware but unable to admit, it was Tallent who had allowed me to even dream of this adventure, and without him I would be back in Boston, jobless, grounded, scrabbling for a second-rate internship at a third-rate hospital. Shortly before six I got dressed (I had even brought a suit, one of the first things I would later discard) and went down to the lounge, which had cool cement floors and two orange-cushioned bamboo sofas separated by a dirty woven-palm mat.

There was already someone sitting there, bent over a book, and as I walked toward him, he looked up.

There is really no satisfying or new way to describe beauty, and besides, I find it embarrassing to do so. So I will say only that he was beautiful, and that I found myself suddenly shy, unsure even of how to address him—Paul? Tallent? Professor Tallent? (Surely not!) Beautiful people make even those of us who proudly consider ourselves unmoved by another's appearance dumb with admiration and fear and delight, and struck by the profound, enervating awareness of how inadequate we are, how nothing, not intelligence or education or money, can usurp or overpower or deny beauty. As the months I spent in Tallent's presence dragged by, I would alternately be tortured by and find solace in his beauty, and would find myself by turns surrendering to it, enjoying my proximity to it, and, less happily, trying to argue against it, as fruitless and pointless an activity as trying to convince yourself that sugar is sour.

"I'm Paul Tallent," said Tallent, unnecessarily, as I gaped at him. I mumbled a hello. We shook hands. "So you landed all right,

I see." I made a grunting noise. We were standing at the edge of the filthy mat, Tallent an inch or two taller than I. I stared at my shoes. "You're ready to go, then," he continued. I nodded. "Well, I'm very happy to have you on this mission," he said. He had a particular way of talking, I noticed—there were no question marks in his sentences, no exclamation points, and yet his voice was not toneless but rather shaded and rich and somehow substantial, something that conjured a dense forest of variegated trees, all lush and stately and grand. It was a voice that betrayed nothing—not approval, not happiness, not fear or anger—but that might make you crazy with its promise of mysteries. I wanted to hear him speak some more, but I was also afraid to ask him anything, was suddenly unable to say anything at all. "Well," said Tallent at last, no doubt worried by my monosyllabism, "I'll see you tomorrow morning."

At that moment I realized what I could have said to him— "Would you like to have some dinner?"—but he had already walked away, of course, and I was left standing there on my own.

I was able to study Tallent more closely on our flight.[21] The plane was a military vessel, so hugely bulky and bloated in its hangar that

[21] Of all the characters who have populated the last half century of anthropology, Paul Joseph Tallent (1916–?) is arguably both the most fascinating and the most unknowable. Thought to have been born to a mother of Sioux extraction, he was raised from a toddler at the St. Joseph's Orphanage for Boys in the town of Cloud Prairie, just outside of Pierre, South Dakota (the town's territory, if not its name, is now a suburb of the capital). St. Joseph's was a Catholic orphanage with a disproportionately large number of Indian boys; it was known for training its charges in various vocations, including plumbing and carpentry. Tallent, however, attracted the attention of one of his teachers, a Brother Peter (his lay name was Michael Tallent, and it is from him that Tallent undoubtedly took his surname, as all of the boys at St. Joseph's were automatically given the name of Joseph), who mentored him and secured him a scholarship to a Catholic boys' boarding school in Pierre, St. Francis's. Tallent excelled at St. Francis's and went on to win admittance to first Dartmouth (A.B., 1937) and then the University of Chicago, where he received his Ph.D. in 1941 (like Norton, Tallent was granted an exemption from service, although it's unknown on what grounds). He was indeed, as Norton notes, very handsome, a fact that contributed to the aura of heroic romance that later came to surround him.

Tallent was immediately considered something of a prodigy in his field, first at Chicago, where he stayed to lecture for three years after receiving his doctorate, and then at Stanford, which would become his permanent academic home. While

it seemed as unlikely as a dodo ever to fly. Tallent and I and our luggage shared room with crates and crates of supplies, but no other passengers; the engines were so loud that conversation was—I was relieved to discover—impossible, and so after smiling vaguely in my direction and writing in a notebook for an hour or so, he closed his eyes and napped.

I had never given much thought to my own appearance—my body was, until that point, a vehicle of utility, and not something I had ever even considered possible or in my ability to change or shape or perfect. But looking at Tallent—his hair and skin and eyes the same dark-gold, brandyish hue, his many teeth remarkably white and crowded, which gave his smiles a lupine affect—I was made unavoidably aware of my own flaws: my bunchy knees, my floury skin, my floaty puff of hair. It seemed both improbable and ludicrous then that Tallent and I should be of the same species, and cruel that he should be a mirror of human perfection against which I could only catalogue my deficiencies. I spent the rest of the flight staring at him, willing him to open his eyes and yet dreading it too, disgusted by the ache I felt and yet enjoying it too. When the plane at last

---

at Chicago he found a mentor in the renowned anthropologist Leo DuPlessix, who was at the time studying the reproductive rituals of the Hawawa people, a small tribe that lived in the jungles of Papua New Guinea; he was no doubt responsible for Tallent's intellectual leanings and fields of interest. It is thought that DuPlessix, who died in 1943, assisted Tallent in his first trip to U'ivu later that year, but this is not documented in DuPlessix's papers so cannot be definitively stated.

Chief among the many frustrations Tallent's later biographers and scholars would encounter was their subject's lack of journals or papers of his own. Indeed, most scholars find it difficult to believe that Tallent, who was so scrupulous about documenting every detail while in the field, should not have left behind a personal diary, or at the very least correspondence. This absence, along with his work and his still mysterious disappearance (which Norton will discuss later), has naturally only heightened the intrigue that surrounds Tallent, and several historians have been at work for many years now trying to compile definitive biographies of his life. (Norton, who is among the people who worked with him the most closely and at the most significant period of his scholarship, is often approached by them for interviews and insights.) In my opinion, however, it seems a job more suited for a novelist than for a historian: among the unknowns of Tallent's life are his sexual predilections, his parentage, the specifics of his childhood, his romantic life (if any), and, of course, the manner of his death. He has become fertile ground for conspiracy theorists of all make, and is even revered as something of a mystic among certain fringe elements of the liberal arts community.

landed and Tallent stirred, I was exhausted and exhilarated, abrim with a sweet, private sadness. "Next stop, U'ivu," said Tallent as we disembarked, and I thought he sounded happy; I was happy too.

From the Gilberts we were flown above U'ivu in a buzzing gnat of a plane, its loudly whisking propellers so vigorous that the trees, stalky clumps of date palms, blew backward as we descended. The plane dipped around a bend, over and along a long, curved stretch of mountain range, and for a second, suspended over the frayed, tender line where the ocean met the land, I looked toward the horizon and found myself unable to determine where the sky ended and the water began: it was all a dazzling, indistinct wash of blue, an audacious blue with no name, so insistent and unvaried I had to close my eyes.

U'ivu, as I have mentioned, is a group of three islands, but only two were officially inhabited. The first was U'ivu, the main island, baguette-shaped, about twenty miles long and half as wide, split lengthwise by a single, unbroken mountain range called Ta'imana. This was where the king lived, as well as the majority of the country's 35,000-odd occupants. Sixty miles to U'ivu's east was the second island, Iva'a'aka, the same approximate shape and size but whose entire northern side was made inviolable by a wall of cliffs; even from the sky I could see how the waves slapped against them into fat white plumes, like handfuls of feathers being tossed into the air, and see the haloes of broad-winged birds that circled their sharp lava-rock peaks. But the rest of Iva'a'aka was low green hills, and so it was here that the country did most of its large-scale farming: we flew over acres of neatly stepped fields, the soil freckled with barely distinguishable dots of green and gold.

"Taro," said Tallent, pointing at one and then, at another, "Sweet potato."

"How can you tell from here?" I asked him. The fields with their rows of vegetation looked the same to me.

He shrugged. "I can," he said, and I felt somehow ashamed of myself for having asked.

We passed over some huts, simple structures with what I could tell even from the air were palm-leaf roofs, and an occasional wooden house, but most of Iva'a'aka's farmers were seasonal, and the island had few full-time residents. Only the plantations' overseers—for all of these farms were owned by the king, and their produce was given to the government, which then distributed it to the U'ivuan citizens— lived here year-round, Tallent explained; the pickers and growers and gardeners worked on Iva'a'aka only for three-month shifts before returning by boat to their homes and families on the main island. The plane sank in the sky, and as I looked down again, I saw a blur of deep brown streak through one of the fields. "Boars," said Tallent, and I turned in my seat to look back and stare at them. There they were, the famous U'ivuan boars, and even from a distance one could tell they were monstrously large. There must have been a hundred of them in the pack, and I could see the dirt spraying up around them, an echo of the water breaking against the island's cliffs.

"And that is Ivu'ivu," Tallent shouted to me, and I followed where he was pointing. The angle was not ideal—I saw a slant of black mountain, its façade brushed with vegetation—and I crouched in my seat to try to get a closer look at the place where I would be spending the next few months of my life, at the Forbidden Island that would now be our home.

But then the plane turned again and descended once more, and we were above U'ivu. "This is the south side of the island," Tallent called over the noise of the propellers. "We'll land here." And so we did, bumpily, juddering over what I would later see were small hill-ocks of grass and soil; the runway was no runway at all, just a long stretch of plain earth—that was how few planes landed here.

As we were lifting our bags out of the plane, I saw a short, round figure walking toward us, and when it was about a hundred yards away, it hollered "Paul!" and I realized it was a woman.

"Esme!" Tallent called back, and I was upset and unnerved to see him smile, to see his face fall momentarily into happiness.

The woman came closer and the two all but flung themselves into each other's arms. Then there was a quick exchange in a lan-guage I couldn't understand but that sounded like pops of gunfire, followed by the two of them laughing, the first time I had heard Tallent laugh.

"Oh, I'm sorry, Norton," Tallent apologized (it seemed that he would call me Norton and I would call him Tallent, though neither of us had formally established this). "Esme Duff, this is our doctor, Norton Perina. Norton, this is Esme Duff, my research associate."

"Oh," said Esme, "Norton. Welcome! Welcome to U'ivu. Have you ever been to the Pacific?"

"No," I said.

"Well, you're in for a big surprise! Many big surprises, actually," she said, laughing.

"I'm sure," I said.

"Esme is the real U'ivu expert," said Tallent, while Esme smiled and preened. "She speaks the language much better than I do[22] and has arranged all our guides, everything. She'll be indispensable to you."

"I'm sure," I repeated. And in that moment I promised myself two things: first, that I would hate Esme Duff, and second, that within a few months it would be I, not Esme, whom Tallent would consider the expert.

⁂

I was very kind to allow myself such a generous timeline to usurp Esme in usefulness and knowledge, for the next few days were bewildering and dizzying. For one thing, it was soon revealed that there were no cars on U'ivu: from the field where we had landed (which, Esme informed me, had been kindly lent for our use by the king, who sometimes used it to practice boar hunting—a dozen boars would be rounded up and released, and the king would charge around on horseback, hurling spears at their ridged, humpy spines) we hoisted our bags onto horses, which had also been lent by the king and which had been tethered to palm trees at the far edge of the field. Even the horses—which were about a half foot shorter than the horses I knew, stumpy-legged and broad-shouldered, more like ponies—were unfamiliar.

As we made the half-hour ride toward town, I learned of all the things U'ivu did not have. There were no roads, for one—trails, yes, with patches of grass and struggling flowers tamped down by horses'

---

[22] This was actually untrue. While Duff, who was at the time a lecturer in the Anthropology Department at Stanford (her specialty was Micronesian village life), had accompanied Tallent on his previous two trips to the island, she had never been known among her colleagues as a linguist, and her understanding of the language was considered by later U'ivuan scholars to be rudimentary at best. However, she was certainly not quick to correct any misunderstandings regarding her fluency.

hooves—nor was there a hotel, or university, or grocery store, or hospital. There were, dismayingly, churches, quite a few of them, their white wooden spires the only thing taller than the palms, which cast stripes of black shadow against the dirt but offered no comfort from the sun, which washed the sky a hard, glaring white. I asked Tallent—who was managing to look graceful on his small horse—if there were many missionaries on the island, but it was Esme who answered, telling me that although a hundred or so had made their way to U'ivu in the early 1800s, most of them had died in a terrible tsunami that had destroyed the northern half of the island in 1873. The rest returned home soon after, and U'ivu was once again left to the U'ivuans, the way it had been for the thousands of years prior to the missionaries' arrival.

"The U'ivuans won't build their homes on the northern side by the sea—they consider it bad luck," she said. "But the missionaries wanted those views, and they paid the price."

I said I was surprised by the number of churches—I had counted four in about twenty minutes—which also seemed to suggest a high conversion rate. But this time it was Tallent who answered. "They weren't as successful as it appears," he said. "The U'ivuans enjoyed the novelty of the churches, and when the first one—St. Jude's, just beyond that crooked frangipani tree—was built, a great many of them came, including the king at the time, the current king's grandfather. They thought it was funny, I think. So the missionaries took this as a sign that they were ripe for conversion and built more. There are five—right, Esme?—on this side of the island, and there were an additional three on the north side, but the tsunami destroyed those."

"Did the U'ivuans help in the construction?" I asked.

"No. The missionaries had to do everything themselves. The king gave them the land and the wood—if you look at them, you'll realize it's all palm wood, a difficult and impractical material to build with, and the construction is poor—but he refused to let them employ any of his people. They were lucky to get even that."

"No one tells an U'ivuan what to do," Esme called out from the head of the line. "We know that well by now." She laughed, sounding smug.

"No one tells the *king* what to do," Tallent clarified. "Every privilege we have here—the mission we'll undertake, the guides we'll have—is with the king's permission. He is involved in everything that goes on here, and nothing can be done without his blessing."

But we would not meet the king this time, he said. A daughter was getting married, and His Highness was too busy with the preparations to see us. I would have liked to meet the king, to see his wooden palace, but I was happy for one thing, at least—Esme hadn't met the king either, and so was unable to inform me of all that I was missing: a mansion with dark floors that gleamed with oil, a bevy of silent wives seated on palm mats like a clutch of nesting doves, the king with his fierce, knowing smile.

My first night in U'ivu was spent in an arid, stifling hut whose ceiling was made of dried palm fronds plaited together so snugly that although I heard the rain clattering on a sheet of stray aluminum outside (what its eventual use might be, I had no idea), the only moisture inside came from my own sweat, which was intense and seemed to worsen as the sultry night crept by. I was on my own—it was unclear to me (and I did not wish to discover) whether Esme and Tallent were sharing a hut or slept separately—and all night my mind buzzed, and I worried and was unable to close my eyes without seeing the herringbone pattern of the ceiling floating behind my lids.

The next morning, the three of us hauled our supplies to a small launch with a diesel engine unconvincingly appended to the rear. A man, our captain, his skin a burnished walnut (although I think his shine was due not to superior health but to perspiration, a layer of which seemed to slick everything he touched), watched us climb in and then started the engine with a sharp tug and nosed the boat toward Ivu'ivu.

Had I known how long it would be until I would once again see the relative sophistication of U'ivu, I might have turned around and watched the land as I was dragged from it, but at the time I was too busy staring at Ivu'ivu, which seemed, curiously, not to draw any closer even as the water pleated away from beneath us. It was a dreary day, I remember, and the sea appeared as a flat disk of tin, storm-colored and dull. Above, the sky was the same sullen gray, and the spray on my tongue tasted of metal as well. I stared into the sea and once saw, or thought I saw, some swift shadows shimmering underneath the surface, but when I looked back down after having called Tallent's attention to them, they were gone.

Slowly, excruciatingly, the island came into view. We had approached it from its backside, which faced U'ivu's south and which made it appear as inhospitable in its physical reality as it was in my imaginings. This was the part we had seen from the air in our descent: a vast, sheer cliffside of, I was told, almost six thousand feet, rising assertively from the waters beneath it, which collected at its base in a thick, beery foam. It was so covered with layers of greenery—trees tiered upon layers of grasses, and mosses, and snaky snarls of succulents, all of them colored those improbable parroty shades of green you encounter only in jungles—that it was only when we drew closer that I could see the stone underneath, which was slate-black in some parts and the pale gray of wet newsprint in others and was revealed only in small gaps. If you looked directly up at the sun, it was possible to see, blurred against the white sky, a feathery skyline of trees at the island's peak. As the boat turned and headed eastward into the sun, the island sloped steeply downward and began to appear as a massive wedge of cake that had been tipped to its side. But perhaps in compensation for the physical dimensions of the land, which became more pregnable the farther down its length we traveled, the plant life grew wilder and denser, so that the forest pushed all the way to the very edge of its earth, and the water surrounding it was covered with a busily kaleidoscopic skin of its leavings—wind-tattered hibiscus flowers and sunburned mango leaves, hard little nuts of unripe guavas and scraps of ferns—so thick that you felt for a minute frightened of the jungle, its voracious appetite and ambition, its hunger to consume every surface it encountered.

A half hour later we had reached the far side of the island, and here, although there was no beach, land and water met on equal level. Our captain, who had not spoken a word to us throughout the journey, dropped a homemade anchor, a lidded tin pail full of jangling nails, about twenty feet from shore. The water was the complex green-of-many-colors of a dirty tourmaline, but so clear that I could see clouds of glassy minnows darting under the boat, casting pale smears of shadow onto the ocean's sandy floor. We could not pull closer to shore, not only because there was no shore to be had but because of a series of large boulders, their faces smooth and impassive, that punctuated the waters. As I waded toward the island, my supplies strapped to my back, I passed one that was pitted with small shallow pockets, each of which cupped a glossy, bristling black sea urchin. The last yard or so before land was fiercely pebbled with stones, the water's surface scummy with handfuls of vivid red seaweed, as if it were the ocean's last attempt to assert itself before the might and force of the jungle, which was here tauntingly dripping long tails of a peculiar, thick, three-sided cactus over the feeble waves.

There was a shivering in the bushes before us—rather as if in some castaway movie—and then, emerging from the thick of the forest (again, as if in a movie), three men, all U'ivuans. All of them were dressed in that inimitable blend of modern and native—a man's undershirt worn with what looked like a beaten-bark fabric sarong; a pair of drooping, sacklike pants worn by a man whose nose was, I was excited to see, actually punctured with a thin, reedlike bone; a limp cotton shirt atop nothing at all but a curious penis guard made of loops and loops of woven dried vines—that is particular to places whose relationship with civilization is a new or evolving one: I would see it in the Brazilian jungle, and later in Papua New Guinea, and again in Nagaland. After the boat captain, they were the second, third, and fourth U'ivuans I had met, and after all the stories of their ferocity, I was surprised by their size—the tallest came just to my shoulder—and by the flat ugliness of their faces, the way their noses sprawled sloppily across their cheeks, the way their skin shone like an old grease stain, the way their lower jaws seemed to punch forward from the rest of their features. They were neither fat nor thin, although their legs were corded with stringy muscle and their thighs were enormous, the thighs of people who had spent their lives climbing up and down steep mountainsides.[23]

The tallest of the three, the one wearing the cotton shirt,

---

[23] All three of the guides were boar hunters on U'ivu, where the hogs mostly keep to the forests on the Ta'imana range; they would have had great expertise not only scaling steep inclines but negotiating rough jungle terrain.

approached Tallent, and the two of them rubbed their noses against one another, hard, before beginning a low, staccato conversation in U'ivuan. The other two men stood staring at us fixedly—Esme, who'd been the last to struggle through the silty muck of sand, now stood a few feet from me, flapping a loafy hand at her face in a weak effort to cool herself—and although they did not appear to be hostile, something about the stillness of their attention made me not want to let my eyes stray from theirs, and I found myself staring back, dizzy in the heat, while little gnats busily orbited my head like planets.

We each had our own guide. Tallent's was the tall one, Fa'a, and Esme's the one in the sarong: his name was Tu. Mine was Uva, the man with the bone in the nose, and as he passed before me to hoist my rucksack onto his back, I caught a glimpse of what looked like carving on one end of it. My knapsack was very heavy, but when I reached out to help Uva adjust it on his back—his skin was as textured as rhinoceros hide—he sidestepped me slightly and rocked his shoulders until the bag centered itself between his blades before turning and following the others, who had disappeared between two large trees so thickly pelted with moss that it was impossible to see the bark beneath. He, like his fellow porters, had only a small soft cloth bundle of his own, about the size of a pillow, slung by a fragile rope across his chest.

We walked. There was no path, and so Fa'a, leading the way, pushed back saplings and bushes and leaves the size of frying pans, each of us catching and pushing them behind us in turn as we passed. I was unnerved at how quickly the jungle had swallowed us, at how insignificant our presence was within it; fifteen minutes or so into our journey, I turned around to look at how far we'd come, only to see that our path had already been obscured by armies of trees. Above and around us, the air was vivid with conversation—honks and clucks and shrieks and chirrups—and even after only a half hour, the sky had been all but blotted out by the treetops, the blobby swatches of blue growing tinier and more infrequent with each step. Uva and the other guides were barefoot, the bottoms of their feet crusted and puffy, but Tallent, Esme, and I wore heavy-soled boots, and with every footfall I could hear unseen creatures skitter on the ground beneath us. The trees' roots had braided themselves into a slippery latticework, and I had to concentrate on the floor below lest I tripped and fell; in my peripheral vision, all was richly dark green, and so close I felt as if I were walking through a narrowing, furred tunnel, an illusion enhanced by the sunlight, which became ever more inconsistent, dribbling through the dense treetops in trickles.

Our route, which had been uphill, grew suddenly steeper, and the air at once cooler and moister—so thick was the vegetation that there was no breeze, which only made the trees and bushes around me seem more unreal, more like statuary, although all around us was their smell, a complicated and insistent perfume of loam and rot and sugar that made the back of my throat ache—and still we did not stop. Above me, Esme swayed, and Tu grabbed her arm, swiftly and gently, and although she nodded and kept walking, when I passed her I felt and heard her breath, as hot and loud as a horse's after a long race. I was carrying nothing except for a small rucksack, but the air had begun to feel as substantive and thick as soup (I thought, ridiculously, of chowder, its pearly buttermilk sheen, its surface a wrinkled skin), and when Tallent announced, after we'd reached a shallow plateau at the top of a particularly steep passage, that we'd stop for the day, I wanted to cry with relief.

We dropped to the ground, the three of us, while Fa'a—after speaking with Tallent, who listened and then nodded—and the other two guides veered right off what I had come to think of as our path (although there was no path) and vanished into the forest. I drank the water in my canteen, which had become as warm as the air around me and therefore left me parched; Esme lay down and rested her head against her bag and closed her eyes. Around me the jungle hummed, a low, ceaseless buzz, as if the entire island were some sort of mysterious appliance plugged into an enormous yet invisible energy source.

I must have slept. When I woke, I couldn't tell how late it was—if such a thing mattered here—although the gloom did seem deeper, more urgently alive. Mats of woven palm had been laid out about three yards from each other, and our bags placed near them; between the first two, Esme and Tallent sat, talking quietly.

"Good evening," said Tallent, looking up as I walked over. "Have some dinner."

He, unlike Esme and I, had carried two bags, and from the

larger he drew a packet of crackers. On the ground, lying bright and disconcerting against the moss, was a can of Spam, its tin lid peeled back like a bedsheet and the meat beneath a slimy, nauseous, feminine pink.

"I'm not hungry," I told him.

"You should eat," he said. "You're hungrier than you know, and tomorrow's another long day. Besides, we should eat these crackers before they get too soggy—nothing stays crisp in this humidity."

"By the time I left U'ivu the last time, I was longing for crackers," Esme said, but her voice had lost its triumphant smugness. She seemed not yet to have recovered from the day's exertion; her face was still an unattractive, splotchy red that made it look stubbled.

So I accepted the crackers, which were floury and mild, and spread some cold meat on them. As I handed the empty plastic wrapper back to Tallent, who shoved it into an outside pocket of his bag, I listened to its lively crackle, which made me think of burning wood. "Shouldn't there be a campfire in cases like this?" I asked them. I even smiled at Esme, who was too busy hacking off pieces from the brick of Spam to notice.

In answer, Tallent took up a nearby branch and held it to the tip of the flame from his lighter. But the fire almost immediately fizzled, leaving behind a sulky curl of weak smoke. "Oh," was all I could say. Of course. The wood here was too wet.

"Don't worry," said Tallent. "Once we reach higher ground, Fa'a tells me, the forest will clear and everything will be much drier."

I walked a couple of minutes into the forest behind us, in the direction Tallent had pointed, where I found a thin stream, silvery as a snail's slime, creeping over the surfaces of a series of notched gray boulders. I relieved myself against a tree that disappeared, branchless and almost comically erect, into the canopy above us, and washed my face in and drank from the water, which was cool and tasted faintly salty, oceanic, as if it had been mixed with fistfuls of ground-up seashells. When I returned, Esme was asleep on her mat, another mat pulled over her, her boots lined up at her feet. Tallent, though, remained where I'd left him, his knees pressed against his chest, his head and neck pitched forward a bit, staring into the forest at something I couldn't see.

"How was it today?" he asked as I sat down.

"Fine," I said.

"I realize," he began, and then stopped, looking down at his hands. "I realize I haven't told you very much about what I'm— we're—doing here. You were very good to have come. Or very crazy. Or desperate."

I laughed, but he didn't.

"The truth is, I don't know, really, what we'll find," he continued. Another long silence, which I would come to know meant that he was thinking carefully about what he would say—not because he was afraid that I'd misinterpret him, but because he was the sort of person who never spoke unless he was certain; he was not interested in speculation or theoreticals; he never said anything unless he knew it to be true. Which is not to say he was incurious, or arrogant, or sloppy, or that he never doubted, or rethought things dozens, hundreds of times—nothing of the sort. But he did his wondering, his imagining, in silence; to engage someone in his uncertainties was, I think he felt, presumptuous, and perhaps even rude.

And yet he *was* uncertain; he *didn't* know what he'd find. He was not a man who operated on hunches and intuitions, and yet this time he had—he had guessed at what he might find, and he had asked me to follow him based on that guess.

This did not offend or alarm me. Science itself is guesses: lucky guesses, intuitive guesses, researched guesses. I had worked for people who were certain, and it had felt disquieting, and dangerous. And so I had been happy to come here (well, perhaps not happy, but certainly not worried; although Tallent had not been completely incorrect—I had been desperate as well) not knowing the full story. I suppose this sounds foolish now, unrealistic, but when you are young, planning seems less important, less essential, than it becomes when you have things to protect: money, research, a reputation.

And so I settled back to wait.

*

It took some time for him to begin.

"As a doctor," Tallent said, "what do you want the most? You want to cure diseases—you want to eradicate illnesses, you want to prolong life." (Actually, I had no interest in any of those, at least not in the way I believe Tallent meant it. But I did not contradict him.)

"But what I want—and this will sound childish, but it is ultimately why we are here, and it is an interest many of my colleagues share, even if they are too grand to admit it—is to find another society, another people, one not known to civilization, and, I should say, one that does not know civilization."

After this came a long disquisition about the discipline of anthropology and its various practitioners and heroes and miscreants and theories, which I mostly ignored, but which I listened to enough to learn that Tallent considered himself—though he did not use the word—something of a maverick, someone who would reshape the field entirely.

But then he said something that would intrigue me for those many months we were on the island together, and to which I would never find definitive answers. "I know what it's like to be studied," he said. "I know what it's like to be reduced to a thing, a series of behaviors and beliefs, for someone to find the exotic, the ritual, in every mundane action of mine, to see—" And then he stopped, so abruptly that I knew he had just revealed something he had not intended to, and that he, who was not an incautious man, was wondering why he had done so, and regretting it as well.

"What do you mean?" I asked, and I kept my voice as gentle as possible, so as not to startle him, so as to lull him into continuing.

But of course he was not a pet or a child, and it would take more persuasion or cleverness than merely a quiet voice to overcome his better instincts. "Nothing," he said, and fell silent, and I was at once aware of the loud, buggy air, and that I had been holding my breath.[24]

It was Tallent who spoke next. "I want to tell you a story," he said, and then paused.

---

[24] Later Norton would speculate that Tallent might have been referring to a series of experiments that were conducted at St. Joseph's around 1910 by a phrenologist named Murrow Upton, whose theories about skull size and proportion were considered quite fashionable at the turn of the century. Upton was particularly fond of saying that the Indians had been biologically ordained to lose their lands to the Europeans, which he was convinced could be proved by measuring their skulls, which he posited were both smaller and lighter than those of various European ethnicities.

I would grow accustomed to this as well, his way of beginning and then stopping, of great, paragraphs-long speeches that would end, abruptly, in silence, sometimes for minutes, occasionally for hours. But this time his silence was brief, and when he spoke again his voice was strong, and the story that emerged was delivered less as a speech and more as a recitation, as if he were a wandering story-teller whom I had encountered in a dark piney medieval forest, not a humid jungle, and I had given him a coin and a slab of black bread to bewitch me, for a moment to transport me from this world.

"Many years ago, many, many years, before the age of man, there was a great stone, a god, named Ivu'ivu, who ruled alone over a vast kingdom of water. He was very powerful, this god, and his dominion contained everything below the surface of the sea—his was a kingdom of tail-whipping, tooth-bared sharks and gigantic, blind-eyed whales and fleets of fish and fields of swaying sea grasses that brushed against his base like nymphs' hair.

"But Ivu'ivu was lonely. All around him he saw couplings, beasts that joined and bred and glided by him, trailed by their offspring. Even the loneliest, the most solitary of his subjects—the hermit crabs with their whorled, spotted shells and the creeping, prickly starfish—were surrounded by children. Being a god, Ivu'ivu was not worried about mortality, but he thought he would like someone to be with, with whom he could discuss the burdens and difficulties of being a god and a king, with whom he might give birth to his own race of children. But for this he would need another god, his equal.

"Ivu'ivu had a dear friend, a turtle named Opa'ivu'eke, who was almost as old as Ivu'ivu himself and who, because he could live both below and above water, had traveled far and wide and had many marvelous tales about places Ivu'ivu had never been. He regaled his friend with stories of the air and the land, where there were as many creatures as were underwater but who flew instead of swam— Ivu'ivu had to ask the turtle to explain flight to him many, many times before he was able even to begin understanding what it was— or who walked, or ran, or crept on two or four or a dozen legs.

"One day Opa'ivu'eke was telling Ivu'ivu about his latest jour-neys, and the god could not help but sigh. 'What is wrong, my friend?' asked Opa'ivu'eke.

"'Ah, friend,' replied Ivu'ivu, 'I am lonely. All around me I see happiness, companionship. I too would like a companion, some children. But I need another god, and there can be only one ruler of this world.'

"The turtle was silent for a long time. Then he bade his friend goodbye and swam away.

"Some time later the turtle returned, again with wondrous news, but this time even more wondrous than the god could have hoped. On his most recent trip above water, Opa'ivu'eke had talked to another friend, A'aka, the god of the sun, and explained to him Ivu'ivu's desire. A'aka, it emerged, would like to meet this powerful god of the water about whom he had heard so much. And so a romance began between the god of the water and the god of the sun, with the turtle their messenger. It was he who ferried comments and compliments and questions and chants, spiraling into the cold black depths of the water to deliver A'aka's words to Ivu'ivu and then, his flippers fanning through the currents—which Ivu'ivu calmed to make his friend's journey easier—up to the surface, where A'aka would pause in his course in the middle of each day to listen to the news from a world he could never visit.

"Within time, three children were born: the first a boy, named Ivu'ivu, after the god of the sea; the second a girl, named Iva'a'aka—the Daughter of Stone and Sun; and the third a boy, U'ivu, whose name means simply Of Stone. Half of all three children lived below water, like Ivu'ivu, and half of them lived above it, like A'aka. They floated in and were cooled by the watery kingdom of one father and warmed and nourished by the heat of the other. Always they were sustained by their parents' love and devotion. And so when they too grew up and became lonely, they turned to A'aka, who blessed them with their own children: mankind. And as long as the humans were kind to their parents, A'aka made sure that their crops would always grow, and Ivu'ivu promised that the sea would always be full of fish and that they would always be able to sail his waters, because men, after all, were his descendants as well and therefore his to cherish and protect.

"As for Opa'ivu'eke, he lived a long, long life, long enough to see his friends' grandchildren and great-grandchildren and great-great-grandchildren grow and prosper, long enough to give birth to his own children, who bore his name—Stone-backed Animal—and who on land preferred to live atop and in water around the turtle's favorite child, his godchild, Ivu'ivu. Opa'ivu'eke was not a god, of course, but he was, and is, always honored not only by his two friends but by all his friends' descendants—for his devotion and selflessness, of course, but also for his noble duties as a messenger. This is why, when a man is lucky enough to find an opa'ivu'eke, he must make a sacrifice to the gods and also eat some of its flesh himself. To do so is to send a message to the gods, a prayer for the one thing that A'aka withheld—with Ivu'ivu's approval—from his grandchildren: immortality. And maybe one day the gods might answer them."

⁂

Tallent stopped talking and we both sat for a moment without speaking. *I am sitting on the child of a god,* I thought. *Two gods.* It was preposterous, and yet I felt, despite myself, a tremor ripple through me.

"That is the first story a young U'ivuan learns," said Tallent quietly. "It is almost as old as these people are—thousands of years old, and it has never changed. They have no written language—or at least they didn't until the missionaries—but everyone knows it. This symbol"—he traced a circle on the ground with a stick, and through it a straight vertical line—"means *turtle,* and you find it on ceremonial stones and dishes from hundreds of years ago, from people who have made an offering of one of Opa'ivu'eke's children to Ivu'ivu and A'aka, hoping that they will be the one who will be granted the exception, who will finally be allowed to live as a god."

He was silent again.

"But there is another story now, one that is not old at all, one that has in fact emerged only in the past century or so. For many years the grandchildren of Ivu'ivu and A'aka made their grandparents and parents proud, and why not? The humans were brave and resourceful. They were excellent hunters, superior fishermen. They protected their parents against all invaders and properly respected both of their grandfathers. And although years, more than anyone could recall, had passed without anyone finding one of Opa'ivu'eke's children to sacrifice, neither god seemed to be offended, and all passed in harmony.

"But then, slowly, so slowly that no one noticed for many years, things began to go wrong. The people of U'ivu felled many trees and did not replant. They allowed people who did not belong on the islands—ho'oalas, or white people—to live among them. The ho'oalas brought with them great beasts made of iron that churned up the soft soil of Iva'a'aka, and great nets with which they scooped vast quantities of seafood from the ocean, more than could ever be consumed. They made waste, mountains of it, and what was not left on the land—on top of their parents!—the humans shoveled into the sea.

"From below and from above, Ivu'ivu and A'aka grew first alarmed and then angry. Ivu'ivu sent towering waves to batter his children, and A'aka wept to see him do so, for although Ivu'ivu intended only to scare the humans into respect, by destroying them he also destroyed part of the gods' children—chunks of all three of the islands crumbled into the sea. But still that did not change the humans' ways. And so A'aka sent blistering waves of sun, ceaseless, remorseless. During the months that he normally retired and left the skies to his sister, Pu'uaka, the goddess of rain, he instead stayed on, hurling sharp daggers of burning light to the ground. And now it was Ivu'ivu's turn to cry, for although A'aka's efforts caused the humans' crops to shrivel and many of them to die, he knew that his children were scalded and scorched and parched and that they longed for fresh water.

"The gods knew that not all of the humans had forsaken the old ways, and they felt sorrowful that they could not separate and save the good from the bad, the righteous from the disrespectful. But still the humans continued to ignore the gods and the agreement that they had made with their grandparents so long ago. And so the gods were forced to continue their punishments, the tidal waves, the fierce droughts. A'aka asked his sister to join his efforts, to subject the humans to torrential rains, rains so terrible that many-hundred-year-old trees were uprooted and slid groaning into the sea, and that waterfalls overspilled their canyons and turned creeks into barreling, angry rivers. With each attack, the gods watched their children grow weaker and smaller and more depleted, and with each attack, their sorrow grew.

"As did their anger. And so the gods decided that they had no choice. One day, after many years, a man named Manu'eke—Kindly

Animal—was fishing in a cool stream high atop Ivu'ivu when he saw swimming in the shallows, unbelievably, a turtle. Quickly he grabbed the creature and rushed home to his village. There he killed it, and in his eagerness and haste and perhaps poor manners, he ate the entire animal without sacrificing any to the gods, his forefathers.

"That night he dreamed that he had been turned into a god, that he was the first to be allowed to live forever. But oh! The gods were furious. They saw what Manu'eke had done, and they knew that if a human could forget to offer some of this sacred creature to them, as was their right, then man had fallen very far indeed. And so they decided to punish Manu'eke by giving him what he most desired, eternal life. But a horrible life. For after his sixtieth year—some say earlier, some say later—Manu'eke became less and less human. He forgot what it was to be a man. The people he had once known became strangers to him. He spoke in a voice no one recognized. He forgot to keep himself clean. He became a creature that was not quite an animal, not quite a man. He was driven from his people and never allowed to return.

"And so Manu'eke wanders the jungles still, not one thing and not another, a memory of a man, an example of the gods' wrath and their warning as well. He reminds us of Ivu'ivu's and A'aka's power, that life is theirs to give and theirs to take, and that they are always watching us, ready to take or give the gifts that men most desire."

Here Tallent stopped, and once again I felt that shiver. Around us the night seemed to have grown darker still, so dark that I could not even see Tallent seated right next to me, so dark that his voice seemed to become something tactile and textured, a curtain of deep-plum velvet hanging between us.

And then I felt yet another shiver, but this one more frightening and colder, because it was in this moment I realized: this story, this myth, memorized by Tallent from who knows whom and secreted and cultivated and petted and caressed until he was able to almost sing it, perfect in its pauses and rhythms, was why we were here. He meant to find Manu'eke; he meant to give meaning to a fable; he meant to hunt down a creature that loped through children's nightmares, that populated campfire tales, that existed in the same universe as stones who could mate with planets and father mountains and men. Suddenly my existence here seemed surreal, and the quest—even the word *quest* was something out of fictions and fantasies, in which an object, magical and imbued with improbable powers, is sought by a group of feckless heroes—we were to undertake seemed tinny and cheap.

And yet—and this was even more frightening still—I could also feel something within me come undone. Even today, all these decades later, I cannot explain it with any greater accuracy. I found myself suddenly imagining a long, fat, chalked line stretching across a flat burned earth. To one side was what I had known, a neat-bricked city of windowless structures, the stuff and facts I knew to be true (I thought, unbidden, of my staircase, its names of those wiser than I, and was at once embarrassed for myself, for finding myself in this situation, in speechless thrall to an anthropologist). And on the other side was Tallent's world, the shape of which I could not see, for it was obscured by a fog, one that thinned and thickened in unpredictable movements, so that I could discern, occasionally, glimpses of what lay behind it: nothing more than colors and movements, no real shapes; but there was something irresistible there, I knew it, and the fear of succumbing to it was finally less awful than never knowing what lay beyond that fog, never exploring what I might never again have the opportunity to explore.

And so I closed my eyes; I forgot my senses; and I stepped over the line.

"Is Manu'eke real?" I asked, and immediately berated myself for doing so. *You are forgetting yourself,* buzzed some high mosquito whine of a voice within me. *Be careful; you are forgetting yourself. Remember who you are. This is not how you think. Remember what you have been taught.*

But I couldn't. I tried, but I couldn't.

He sighed. "Nobody knows," he said at last. "Older U'ivuans, of course, swear he is. But no one knows where he was meant to live—U'ivuans say Ivu'ivu, not surprisingly—or what became of him. Or rather, there are many theories about what became of him. That he dove into the sea and never returned. That he vanished. That he grew shriveled and hairy and small and turned into a monkey. That he became a stone. The only thing that remains consistent is that he never dies in these stories—he may disappear, he may transform, but no one claims to have seen him die."

I thought about this. "Do they still sacrifice turtles?"

"Ah," said Tallent, and for the first time I heard approval in his voice. "Now that—*that* is a good question. *The* question, really. No. No, they don't. At least, not on U'ivu. Opa'ivu'ekes are very rare these days. You rarely see them in the water, much less on land. There is a subspecies of them, a smaller freshwater turtle that they seem to resemble, and you sometimes—once in a great while—will find them on Iva'a'aka or U'ivu. But the islanders are scared of them now and avoid them. They are prized, and it is good luck to see them, but no one dares touch them. No one except—"

"The Ivu'ivuans," I guessed.

"Allegedly. Yes."

He was silent again, this time for a very long period.

"There is a story," he began, and then stopped, began again. "It is said that there is a tribe of U'ivuans who live deep in the jungles of Ivu'ivu. It is said that they keep to the old ways, that they still sacrifice to the gods. It is said"—and here I could feel rather than see his head turn toward mine—"that they never die.

"I have never seen these people, this tribe, myself. But when I was last here, three years ago, studying the U'ivuan family structure—very interesting in and of itself—I met a man who said he had been to this island before, that he had seen a man who was not a man. Who looked like a man and moved like a man but who flailed and could not speak, who screeched like a monkey and, though he seemed strong and healthy, was without sense.

"This was distressing enough, but what was more upsetting still, he said, was that the man was followed by another, and another— a whole group of men and women, all normal in appearance but all incapable of making meaningful conversation. All they could do was jitter and babble and laugh at nothing, the neighing laughter of the brainless. The U'ivuans value conversation, you know, and to be without it is to be *mo'o kua'au*—I suppose the nearest translation is 'without throat,' although *kua'au* can also mean 'friends' or 'love.' So, without friends. Without love.

"The man, who was a hunter, left these strange people and hurried back to his home on U'ivu. For months, years, he tried to persuade his friends and family to return with him to the Forbidden Island and find these people, to see if he could help them and to learn who they were. But the U'ivuans, who are already wary of Ivu'ivu, as it is Opa'ivu'eke's children's favorite grounds and therefore sacred, refused to accompany him.

"But this man, this hunter, could not forget what he had seen, no more easily than he could explain what compelled him to return to the Forbidden Island, which in truth frightened him. These people haunted him. The man could think of nothing else.

"And so when this hunter learned that someone had finally believed him—albeit a ho'oala—and was planning to find these people, he asked to come along as translator and guide. He would bring two cousins of his whom he had, over many discussions, finally managed to convince."

"Fa'a," I realized. "He was the hunter. The storyteller."

"Yes," said Tallent, and again I felt rather than saw his face turn toward me in the dark. "We are going to find these people. If they exist, we'll find them."

"Immortals," I said, and I could hear my own skepticism.

But if Tallent heard it too—and he must have—he didn't remark on it. "Immortals," he agreed, his voice inscrutable once more. And then he fell silent for the last time, and I sensed the darkness drawing itself around me like a warm and heavy cloak.

❖

For the first week or so after that night, I tried to keep track of what time it was and whether it was night or day. (My watch stopped working the second day; moisture had crept in through its joints and laced the face over in cobwebby patterns.) But quite soon I realized that doing so was pointless—so thick was the foliage that the sun became unnuanced and unreliable. You could not say that it had vanished, really, or that the light had faded, because there was no direct light in the jungle. There was only darkness and the absence of darkness. One was night, the other day.

Looking back on it now, of course, I realize how extraordinary those first few days were, before I became immune to the awes of the jungle and even grew to despise them. One day—it must have been our third or fourth—I was trudging uphill as usual, looking around me, listening to the conversations of birds and animals and insects, feeling the floor beneath me gently buckling and heaving with unseen layers of worms and beetles as I placed my feet upon them; it could feel like treading on the wet innards of a large dozing beast. And then there was for a moment Uva at my side—he normally walked far ahead of me, in a pack with Fa'a and Tu, darting forward and back to assure Tallent that all was safe—holding his hand out before him, signaling me to stop. Then, quickly and gracefully, he sprang toward a nearby tree, indistinguishable from the others, thick and dark and branchless, and scrabbled up it quickly, turning his wide feet inward to cup its thorny bark. When he was about ten feet or so up, he looked down at me and held out his hand again, palm down—*wait*. I nodded. And then he continued to climb, vanishing into the canopy of the forest.

When he came down, he was slower, and clutching something in his hand. He leapt down the last five feet or so and came over to me, uncurling his fingers. In his palm was something trembling and silky and the bright, delicious pale gold of apples; in the gloom of the jungle it looked like light itself. Uva nudged the thing with a finger and it turned over, and I could see it was a monkey of some sort, though no monkey I had ever seen before; it was only a few inches larger than one of the mice I had once been tasked with killing, and its face was a wrinkled black heart, its features pinched together but its eyes large and as blankly blue as a blind kitten's. It had tiny, perfectly formed hands, one of which was gripping its tail, which it had wrapped around itself and which was flamboyantly furred, its hair hanging like fringe.

"Vuaka," said Uva, pointing at the creature.

"Vuaka," I repeated, and reached out to touch it. Under its fur I could feel its heart beating, so fast it was almost a purr.

"Vuaka," said Uva again, and then made as if to eat it, solemnly patting his stomach.

"No," I said, horrified, "no," and he tipped his head at me curiously and shook it at my poor taste, I suppose, and then walked off toward the tree again, where he tossed the monkey upward, and I watched it latch onto the bark and hurry up, a flashing pulse of sun.

Later, from Tallent, I learned that the vuaka was an early monkey, a sort of ur-monkey, and that they lived in enormous colonies in a certain kind of tree that was also endemic to U'ivu. The U'ivuans considered them a delicacy—they scalped and then roasted them by the dozen on long twigs and ate them like kebabs—but the tree, the kanava, grew only in thickly forested areas, the kind that no longer existed on Iva'a'aka or U'ivu. In fact, these days the kanava (and therefore the vuaka) could be found in great quantities only on Ivu'ivu, but nothing, not even the lure of fresh vuakas, could induce the U'ivuans to this island.

Tallent laughed. It was something he rarely did. "Fa'a may be here to find the lost tribe," he said, "but the others? I think they're only here for the vuaka." It was too wet to roast them, of course, but Tallent said the men would skin them and cure them with salt they'd brought from home for exactly this purpose.

I knew it was sentimental (not to mention pointless) to feel pity for the poor, pretty vuaka, and I didn't want Tallent to think I was weak, so I said nothing. But that night, lying on my mat, I thought of the vuaka, its huge, sad eyes, the glorious streak of gold it had made as it vanished into the dark above us, and felt for a moment a despair so profound that I was momentarily unable to breathe.

But soon even the forest—what I had initially seen as its diversions and newness, its unsullied perfection and possibility—became wearying. Where I had once seen mystery, I now saw instead only repetition: the constant damp, the constant half-light, the constant pattern of trees and trees and trees, an unbroken grove of them reaching into eternity. I longed to see the sky above me, blue and sticky with clouds, or the sea, its anxious, roiling energy. Here we knew it had been raining only because the trees—so incessantly thirsty I thought of them as stands of throats, greedily swallowing every drop they could—sweated water, which disappeared into the pelts of moss that clumped around their bases, and because the ground grew squelchy and spongy. At the shoreline, any seedling that had been dropped by birds could live—I had seen mango and guava trees, and others I could not name but recognized anyway—but this deep in the forest the plants were more ancient and native, and I knew none of them. This ought to have been exciting, but it was not; the total absence of familiarity can make a place seem alien and unconquerable, and you turn your attention and curiosity away from it to avoid growing frustrated.

Then there was the matter of the jungle's profligacy, which I began to resent, as if it were an overdressed woman parading her entire cache of sparkly jewels before me. I felt as if the jungle were constantly showing off to itself—every rock, every tree, every surface that would stay still was trimmed, bedecked, baroque with greenery: there were fistulas of bushes wrapped with creeping vines and spotted with moss and lichen and trees draped with great valances of hairy, hanging roots from some other unseen plant that lived, I imagined, high above the canopy. Things flew up from the floor and trickled down from the treetops. It was an exhausting performance that never ended, and for what? To prove the imperturbability of nature, I suppose—its unknowability, its fundamental lack of interest in humanity. Or at least that's what it seemed like at the time: a mockery. It was absurd, I knew, to wake each day and resent the jungle and my own insignificance in it. But I couldn't help it. I began to think I might be going a little—well, not crazy, I suppose, but that I might be *losing touch*, as they say now. And then I felt childish, and ashamed.

On and on the jungle went, so unceasing in its excesses that I eventually became numb to them. A creature, its malachite-dark back diamonded with scales, skittered across my feet, a wraith-like monkey shrieked from a tree, and I did not stop or ask Uva or Tallent what they were. There were so many shades and tones of green—serpent, aphid, pear, emerald, sea, grass, jade, spinach, bile, pine, caterpillar, cucumber, steeped tea, raw tea: how inadequate is our vocabulary for color!—that I feared I would lose my ability to distinguish anything else. Fa'a's loincloth, a bright crimson, burned my eyes, and yet I found myself staring at it as much and for as long as I could bear, as if trying to fix its redness in my mind before it too began to be interpreted by my eye as yet another shade of green. At night I dreamed of green, great floating blobs of it, morphing gently from one shade to the next, and in the mornings I woke feeling beaten and exhausted. During the day my thoughts returned to visions of deserts, of cities, of hard surfaces: of glass and concrete and chips of mica glinting from asphalted streets.

There was also, still, the problem of Tallent, whom I could barely look at and around whom I was trying to become more fluent and less stuttery. He stayed up late in the evenings, writing in his notebook, and from my mat I'd watch him as the darkness filled the air like bats. He was careful never to use the flashlight unless we really needed to—to relieve ourselves, for example—and so even after the light disappeared completely he would continue to write, and I would lie there, as still as I could, listening to his pen skritching across the page; for some reason this was a beautiful image to me, Tallent writing without any illumination to guide his way, and when we were walking, I would sometimes close my eyes and turn it over in my mind, savoring it like a candy. On those long hikes, I also tried to make—and sometimes succeeded in making—interesting observations to him, but whenever I managed to do so, there was Esme, ready to offer her own opinion on whatever the subject was.

Esme was a difficulty of a different sort, of course. Aside from her bossiness and smugness and general possessiveness of Tallent (which, frustratingly, I was still unable to determine whether he noticed or not, and if so, whether he cared), there was the simple fact that she was unpleasant to regard. With each day her hair grew wilder and less manageable, until it floated like a penumbra above her puffed face, and her skin, as I've mentioned, had taken on a more or less permanent rash. This ought not to have bothered me, but it did.

There were more serious problems with Esme as well. Late one night I walked to the stream—the same one I mentioned earlier; its source seemed to be high in the mountains, where we were headed—and saw a crumpled blossom on the jungle floor. Against the dark, it was gloriously, impossibly white, the white of fresh paper, and at its center was a splash of deep burgundy. Here the flowers were waxy and indistinguishable as flowers: where there should have been stamens there were grossly suggestive plasticky lips upon which bugs alighted to rest; where there should be leaves there were aggressive, thrusting planes. But in that white flower I was reminded of the blooms I had grown up with: sugary peonies, as frilled and shirred as ballet skirts, gauzy clumps of asters. It seemed the loveliest thing I had seen for many days, and I stood there staring at it.

But as I continued stumbling over to the creek, I saw that the flower was no flower at all but rather a crumple of tissue, at its heart a smear of blood. I felt a sort of fury—first, rightly, that Esme should be so careless with disposing of her own trash, and second (and I admit less defensibly), that she should have spoiled for me an image so soothing.

Back on our mats, I poked her awake. "You have to be more careful," I told her.

She was slit-eyed, wild-haired. "What are you talking about?" she asked.

"Your waste," I said. "I nearly stepped in it."

"Leave it alone, Perina," she said, and flopped back over onto her other side.

"Esme!" I hissed. "Esme!" But she was already feigning sleep, and I dared not speak louder for fear of waking Tallent. "Esme!" I shook her shoulder, and under her shirt her flesh was repulsive, a quaking blancmange, its surface pimpled with perspiration.

The next morning we ate breakfast (more Spam, scooped out of the tin with the splintery slices of a hard yellow papayalike fruit that Fa'a had found and cut for us) in silence, with Tallent writing in his notebook and even Esme, for once, wordless. I did not look at her, but around her seemed the sickening scent of menstrual blood, a tinnily feminine smell so oppressive that it was a relief finally to begin the day's climb and to find it vanishing slowly into the odors of the jungle. And from then on I was unable to look at her without thinking of oozing liquids, as thick and heavy as honey but rank and spoiled, seeping from her every hidden orifice.

After some days of walking (I am sorry, but the exact length of time eludes me now as it did then; it could have been five days or fifteen), we entered one afternoon a different sort of place. I cannot describe it any better than that, except to say that the very quality of the air seemed to change: one step behind us was the jungle we knew, sodden and creeping and thick with secrets, like something in a fairy tale, and in the next was someplace else. Suddenly the air was drier, the trees less assertive, the sun—the sun!—visible, actually casting shifting, fuzzy-edged parallelograms of light across the elaborately ferned and twigged forest floor. Above me I could see a crochet of spiderwebs stretched between two trees, glinting like a tangle of jeweled necklaces.

Fa'a said something quickly and excitedly to Tallent, who in turn told us that we were little more than a day's walk from the place where Fa'a had seen his people. He had marked the location by scratching a large $X$ with a stick in the bark of something called a manama tree. The manama's bark grew in scales, Tallent said, and when pierced it wept a jammy sap that dried in a crust of hard blemishes: we would know it when we saw it.

But now, he announced, we would rest, and we did at once, all six of us dropping our bags on the ground. It was good, and odd, to lie there, to have survived the jungle (even though later I would have to admit that the jungle was without any real dangers, that *then* was really the time to feel frightened), to feel the sun creeping over our faces, to hear the first faint birdcalls; their music seemed like fairy song, so strange and beautiful was it, so otherworldly.

We slept then, all of us, even the guides, and when I woke and saw the others' still bodies, I thought for a minute that they were dead and I was alone in this strange, sunlit place, surrounded by trees I did not know the names of and birds I could hear but could not see, and that no one would ever know I was here or remember I had ever existed or would ever find me. The sensation was fleeting, but what I would remember is how quickly, like a breath, I moved from despair to resignation, how well equipped the human mind is to readjust to its realities, to soothe oneself of one's deepest fears. And then I felt proud, I suppose, of my very humanness, and briefly invincible, and sure that I would be greeted with nothing in the next day that I could not bear.

I walked in the direction of the stream, which had become perversely wider and more powerful the farther uphill we climbed, a clear, quick channel of cold water, its taste, oddly, more intensely sealike than it had been at the lower elevation. I drank from it and then sat at its bank, watching it move over pebbles, admiring the small orange flowers that trimmed its edge. And it was then, sleepy, daydreaming of nothing, that I saw something move from beneath one of the boulders that lay across the river: a dark form, no more than that, like the shadow a cloud casts when it scuds over the sea. But as it grew closer it began to take shape, and I saw it was a turtle, the ridge of its peaked and bony back breaking through the skin of the water, and knew at once what it was.

"Opa'ivu'eke! Opa'ivu'eke!" I was shouting, and I could hear the others running toward me.

I say I knew it was an opa'ivu'eke, but it was only because we were on its land; otherwise the turtle, at first glance at least, was nothing remarkable. It was perhaps somewhat smaller than I'd imagined—about the circumference of a hubcap—and its feet, not surprisingly, more flipperlike, more like a sea turtle than I'd pictured.[25] Then I regarded it more closely—it had stopped its journey downstream to tread water, its legs paddling slowly against the current—and noticed its carapace, as humped as a dromedary's and a beetley, glossy green, so green it was almost black, and divided into neat squares, the border of each as well defined as if it had been wrought from metal by a chisel. But it was its head, a small, oddly shaped cashew of a thing on a long, telescoping neck, that made me consider it further. I had never to that point been in the habit of imbuing animals with human traits or human intelligence, but watching the opa'ivu'eke, I was discomfited by what I suppose can only be called its expressiveness. I looked in its bagged, drooping amber eyes and felt, if only briefly, that Tallent's story was true, that this was an animal possessed of wisdom and fortitude, and that we were its guests and certainly not its superiors. Behind me I could hear the three guides murmuring something in unison in U'ivuan, a low, chantlike hum like crickets' song, and after a few moments, in which we all remained perfectly silent, the turtle blinked its eyes at us and then, almost haughtily, continued its swim, head still held aloft, finlike feet parting the water in neat furrows.

We stayed and watched it leave, but once it was out of sight, the three guides began talking quickly, and I saw in their faces excitement and fear.

"This was the first opa'ivu'eke they've ever seen," Tallent told Esme and me in a quiet voice, and we observed the three men telling one another about the experience they'd just witnessed, all of them speaking so fast that it seemed they were trying to expunge themselves of the memory rather than cement it.

---

[25] The opa'ivu'eke remains the only turtle in recorded history that can live in both fresh water and saltwater for sustained periods of time.

We three—even Esme—said nothing, only watched them, and although at the moment I found their behavior, their near panic, curious, later I understood it: gods are for stories and heavens and other realms; they are not to be seen by men. But when we encroach on their world, when we see what we are not meant to see, how can anything but disaster follow?

The hours we walked following the turtle sighting were strange ones. I had never thought of our guides as particularly voluble—in fact, they were often so far ahead of us on our daily hikes that I, shamefully, thought of them rather little at all—but today they walked with us, near us almost, as if for comfort and protection (somewhat worrisome, as with the possible exception of Tallent, we were ill-equipped to protect them from anything), and their silence was not so much a quiet as it was a complete absence of noise. Unlike us, they did not pant as they trudged forward, they did not stop to wipe the slicks of sweat off their brows; they seemed in fact to need less breath than we did, to be immune to the jungle's heat. But this afternoon I was made to realize that the sounds they did make—little chirrups back at the unseen insects that peeped and scraped from the sky, the airy whistle they gave one another to announce their location—had been a part of the jungle's soundtrack after all.

It was in this silence that the thing fell from the sky, something wet and heavy that landed with a juicy, suggestive *thwack*, like one slab of raw meat falling smack against another from a very great height. This startled the guides into talk once more (I fear I may have shrieked a bit), and they clustered around the thing, which turned out to be a fruit, though not like any fruit I had seen before. It was disgustingly priapic, about eighteen inches long and fat as an eggplant, and that particular sugary newborn pink one finds only in tropical sunsets. But what really distinguished it was the fact that it was moving—something was forcing its thin, unspeckled skin to swell into small bulges before smoothing flat again, the ripples undulating up and down its length. The guides began their excited all-at-once chatter again, and Tallent, hurrying over, joined in their chorus.

"It's a manama fruit," he explained. "They only grow at this elevation. It means we're close." Then he took the thing from Fa'a's hand and with his penknife slit it down the middle. Out of the cut squirmed a large writhing mass of grubs the approximate size and color of baby mice, which fell from the fruit to the ground and began wriggling off; against the moss of the floor they looked like rivulets of suddenly animated ground beef, worming their way toward some sort of salvation. (Esme looked sick. I don't mind admitting I felt a little sick myself.) "They're hunono worms," Tallent continued, and for a moment I found his serene equanimity, his apparent inability to be repelled by anything nature might hurl at him, somehow inhuman and slightly suspicious. "They live in this fruit for their incubation period, and when they're mature they explode at once from it as butterflies, the most beautiful butterflies I've ever seen." He smiled at us. "They're a delicacy, if you can find them, but so is the fruit," and scraping the last of the grubs away with the blunt edge of his knife, he cut a slice of manama for us both. I wasn't looking forward to eating it, but what choice did I have? Esme was already bringing hers to her mouth. The insides were the same color as the skin, barely sweet and slightly fibrous, and had the meaty, elastic chewiness of tendon. When Tallent offered me another slice, I shook my head, and he shrugged and handed over the rest to the guides, who began tearing off hunks with their fingers. Against the dun of their skin, the fruit looked even more vulnerable and fleshy, and I felt a thrum of illogical fear.

And so we continued, the manama fruit falling with greater frequency the farther we climbed, each time landing with the same unnerving violence. I chanced looking overhead at one point and found I could see only their bottoms, so that the sky seemed punctuated with floating tumors, attached to nothing but suspended overhead like strange pink moons. Gradually too the other trees—like the kanava, which had heretofore been ubiquitous—began to be replaced by the manamas (whose bark really did grow in tiered, scalelike crusts), until eventually we seemed to be surrounded exclusively by them and the air seemed to smell faintly of something human and unclean.

But just as I was beginning to despair of Fa'a ever finding his tree, the one he had marked, Uva gave a call and pointed at a manama trunk upon which was a great swath of blood, a ragged and almost comical splatter-paint smear of it. As we moved closer, I saw that it was not blood but something living, so that it almost appeared a raw, exposed organ, as if the tree turned out to possess an anatomy of its own. *Oh god,* I thought, *can nothing in this jungle behave as it ought? Must fruits move and trees breathe and freshwater rivers taste of the ocean? Why must nothing obey the laws of nature? Why must everything point so heavily toward the existence of enchantment?* And so it was not until I—reluctantly, wearily—moved directly up to the manama that I saw that it really was just a tree, and that what I had taken for a thrusting heart, a heaving lung, was in fact a teem of butterflies, their crimson wings spattered with a pallid gold. These, of course, were what the grubs had become, and when Tallent chased them away with his hand—I watched a little sadly as they scattered and for a moment hovered around and above us in an assaultive cloud—I saw that they had returned to the tree that had once shel-tered them to feed on its sap, which, as Tallent had promised, had hardened into a mass of opaque, glassy bubbles.

We had made it. This was the tree, this was where Fa'a had seen his not-humans, this was what our days of walking had led us to. But this sense of accomplishment was diminished by what I very soon sensed was the lack of a real plan. Surely, I thought, slightly hysteri-cal, this had been better considered? Were we simply to wait by this tree, as if children in a fable, for these hypothetical half-humans to appear before us like walking dreams? I had a vision of us all turn-ing around, en masse, and heading back down through the thickets of the jungle, entering once again its wet, clammy embrace, until we reached the shore, and then—what? We would somehow return to U'ivu, and then Esme and Tallent to California, and I—to nothing. I found myself experiencing that same sense of dislocation I had had at Smythe's house, and wondered bitterly when in life I would be able to tell with certainty when the circumstances around me were a hoax and when they were simply unfortunate.

Finally, after conferring for a long time with Fa'a, Tallent announced that we would camp here for the night and continue the next day. Neither Esme nor I asked him for more details—I believe we were both afraid to, and besides, neither of us was in the habit of challenging him—but meekly laid down our things. He sounded defeated, I remember, which I found perversely satisfying, although really I should only have been alarmed: it was, as he had said himself, his hunch that had brought us here, and without him I was nothing more than a silly, directionless boy stuck in a forest populated wholly by madmen and myths.

That night I dreamed as usual, but perhaps because of the reintroduction of sunlight into my waking hours, or perhaps because I was still stubbornly clinging to the mistaken belief that I had reached some sort of significant threshold, or perhaps because of the strange manama fruit, whose ploppy cannonball drops broke the night in an irregular symphony, my visions were of earthbound things, a slideshow of all that was dear and typical and so mundane that I had never thought to miss them: a plain leather boot I had once owned, its sole flaky with dried sod; the elm that had grown outside our house, which seemed to represent all that was stately and dignified; a shirt that had once been my father's, its chambray faded to a blue so pale it was almost white—and Owen, his face floating planetlike against a rippling sheet of silky black, his expression unreadable but, I somehow intuited, full of pity.

But pity for whom? I wondered, even in my dream.

For me?

The next day we woke, ate, and sat. Or rather, Esme and Tallent and I sat, and the guides trundled off somewhere. It was becoming clear that in the absence of a plan, we were to sit and wait, like dogs, until some event chanced upon us.

Who knows how long we sat? Hours, of course, but how many? During all this time we occasionally heard the scuttle and slide of the guides, and in between furtively looking at Tallent (who was writing more furiously than ever—about what? I wanted to ask, since nothing of any anthropological interest had happened that I could discern) and avoiding looking at Esme, I lay on my back and tried to count the numbers of a particular vine (stringy, slightly dusty-looking) that had tangled itself into a snarl on one of the manama trees' branches above. Looking back on that day, I cannot—still—help but feel a bit embarrassed about this. Adventures really are wasted on the young, I'm afraid. I should have used that time for exploring, spelunking through the underbrush (now much more accessible and appealing than it had been a couple of days before), pawing through the forest floor for unidentified plant life (I physically ache now to remember how many grasses, ferns, flowers, trees I had never seen before and could have spent the afternoon recording), even attempting to follow the guides on their obscure and single-minded missions. Instead I remained supine and counted vines. Vines! All along I had prided myself on my curiosity, what I considered the unslakability of my intellectual thirst. And yet, once placed in a situation in which almost everything was foreign, I did nothing, saw nothing.

The problem with being young and in a singular place is that one assumes that one will inevitably find oneself in an equally foreign and exotic location at some later point in life. But this is very rarely true. For most of what we see in our immediate surroundings is in fact replicated elsewhere in the world with a sort of dull exactness: birds, animals, fruits, sky, people. They may look different from place to place, but their fundamental behaviors are essentially identical: birds tweet and flap, animals prowl and bleat, fruits are insensate and inanimate, the sky fills and empties of clouds and stars, people wear clothes and kill and eat and die. On Ivu'ivu, as I had observed multiple times, none of these things happened the way they were supposed to, and yet I was too inexperienced to fully comprehend how truly remarkable that was. (In retrospect, maybe Tallent did. Maybe that was what he was always logging in his book: not anthropological observations after all, but a documentation of the place's sheer oddity.) It is only the old who can look around them and marvel, for it is we who know how alike the world really is, how all of its problems and wonders have already been recognized and recorded.

I would like to be able to say that after waiting, the morning draining away from us, we were suddenly surrounded by Fa'a's people, who arrived as unexpectedly and dramatically as, say, the manama fruit had. But that is not what happened. Instead, finally, after conferring with a head-shaking Fa'a once more, Tallent announced that we would split up in different directions, each of us with our guide, to, as he vaguely put it, "explore the area and look for clues." He and Fa'a would go north, uphill, and Esme and I to the east and west respectively. We would meet back at the tree when the sun was directly overhead.

As I recount this story I am astonished anew by how patchy, how makeshift a solution this was. But again, at the time it seemed the most sensible, the most practical, the best thing to do. In illogical situations, one clings to any idea that seems at all logical, even if it is only a scrim, translucent and flimsy, that shields the lack of serious planning behind it.

And so we went off, all of us, I am certain, less than convinced that anything would actually happen. Fa'a's people, indeed! How did we know they even existed? *But you saw the opa'ivu'eke*, I reminded myself, while another voice inside me rebutted, *You saw a turtle, nothing more. A turtle, whom you have made into a god. You are as lost as the rest of them now.* And to that I had no response. The voice was right. I was.

## II.

It was Fa'a who saw it first.

This we learned later, much later, when the sun had almost set and the entire forest was awash, ghostlike, with an eerie reddish light, the air seeming to thicken with a bright haze of blood. We had been waiting, Esme and Tu and Uva and I, for Fa'a and Tallent to return, and as time passed Uva and Tu became increasingly anxious, taking turns running uphill while the other stayed behind to guard our things and us, as if we were prisoners, or children (which to them I suppose we were no better than).

And then finally they were before us, walking down the slope, Fa'a calling out frantically and rapidly to the others, Tallent behind him, and behind *him* someone else, a third person, and we stood, all of us, and watched them emerge from the trees. I saw fear on the guides' faces and knew it was echoed on my own. But I am getting ahead of myself.

After leaving us that morning, they walked, Tallent and Fa'a, past the butterfly tree (which, although none of us had said it aloud, we had begun to consider the demarcation line: below it was land we knew, above it terra incognita. Although this was of course nothing more than a contrived organizing principle, for the fact was it was *all* terra incognita—what lay past the tree was no more conquerable by us than what lay before it) and into the jungle beyond. A few hundred yards in, the copses of trees had thinned out further still, although their canopies had became more massive and umbrellalike in their reach, making the air increasingly dark and cool, muted in light and muffled of sound. I had been using the words interchangeably, but here was truly more a forest than a jungle, the bewitched forest of fairy tales, where huts made of glossy black licorice and lardy white frosting appear in clearings and talking wolves trot upright in old women's bonnets. Around them too the plants had changed: gone were the rapacious fly-eating orchids, the saucy, vulgar bromeliads, the squat cycads, and in their place were frilly wedges of sober-colored mushrooms and whorls of tightly closed ferns.

They had been walking for about an hour, they thought, when they heard a noise: nothing interesting, nothing large, just a crinkling like paper high above them. Two days before, they would have thought nothing of this; it would have been another family of vuakas gamboling across a kanava branch, or one of those vexing toucanlike birds whose aggressive, phosphorescent yellow feces streaked the tree trunks like oil paint. But here the animals were silent, furtive—they had seen enormous fleecy sloths the size of Labradors hanging sleepily from branches, and witnessed spiders, their backs daubed with glittery blue specks, picking their prim, careful way across spun-glass webs—and the sound here was of no sound, of a place holding its breath, an edgy, bitten-back quiet, as if it would at once explode with the color and noise of a great party. And so hearing this, they stopped, listened. Tallent found himself counting, nonsensically, as if once he reached a certain number, something would be revealed to them.

He had reached seventy-three when Fa'a grabbed his arm and pointed, and he saw it climbing down the trunk of a manama about fifty yards to their left. It was not a skillful climber, nor particularly graceful, and yet when it began to emerge, he mistook it for a sloth, not a human; unlike a human, who would have shimmied down feet first, this creature led with its arms, which encircled the tree in a tight grip, the rest of its body following limply and uselessly behind. The manama's branches are sturdy and level and grow from almost its base to its very top, but the animal did not take advantage of them, did not use them, as a human would, as a ladder. Rather, it continued to slither down, snakelike (although this was difficult, as the manama's bark made slithering all but impossible), and whenever it encountered a branch, it seemed to pause, confused, clearly unaware that the branch could be used to its benefit. At the bottom of the tree, when its head had touched the forest floor, it paused again, and then flipped over onto the ground and for a long moment simply lay there on its back, its arms and legs spread open, not making a sound. Fa'a held out his arm to keep Tallent from advancing (not, as Tallent said later, that he needed to; he was too spellbound to think of moving), and for a few minutes the two of them stood frozen, staring at the thing on the floor.

When it finally stood, it did so in stages, first moving to a sitting position—which it did without the use of its elbows, but at once, from the waist, as if attached to the end of an invisible pulley—and then, after another pause, abruptly to its feet. And then it began to walk, and Fa'a and Tallent stepped behind a tree to watch it.

It was a little shorter than Fa'a, maybe four feet or so, and a woman, with used, drooping teats and a hard-looking, rounded stomach and Fa'a's wide, flat feet, although hers seemed wider still, the ends of her toes pooling fleshily into the earth. She was very hairy—her pubic hair was a dense, rooty tangle, and the hair on her head appeared a solid block of black, so matted and snarled was it. Her legs too were dark with fuzz, and on her back was a fine pelt. Things clung to her hair: chips of leaves and smears of dirt and fruit and shit; Tallent saw a hunono worm nestled in the hair above her vulva like an extraneous organ. Her movements were human, he supposed—they watched as she bent (again, stiffly at the waist) to retrieve a fallen manama fruit, which she bit into violently, the hunonos oozing through her fingers and smearing into a pink paste around her mouth—but somehow poorly practiced, as if she had once, long ago, been taught how to behave as a human and was slowly, steadily forgetting. And then, in another of her abrupt gestures, she turned and stared directly at Fa'a and Tallent, and while Fa'a shrank behind the tree, making a low hissing noise of horror and repulsion, Tallent stepped from behind it and, ignoring Fa'a's scrabbling, beseeching hand, made his way toward the creature.

He was slow, careful, aware by now that her movements began

without preamble, and came within about ten yards of her before he stopped. All this time she had watched him approach, the wriggling manama fruit still in one hand, the worms still dropping from her mouth and palm, bouncing off her stomach and falling to the ground, her mouth stupidly, grotesquely open, her eyes not moving from his face.

Tallent walked a step closer. The creature watched him. He made another step. Still nothing. One more and he would almost be able to touch her. And so he made another.

And then she began to shriek, a noise that went up and down, up and down, moving in register from growl to keen to shrill to squeal, and then back again and up again. Behind him, he could hear Fa'a calling to him, "Come away! Come away!" but he did not, and remained there, a few feet from the thing, his arm still stretched toward her, her hand still squeezing the manama, the worms still dropping to her feet, her voice the only voice in that quiet, awful, haunted forest, going on and on, horrible and arrhythmic and ceaseless.

Then it was over. She closed her mouth and the sound stopped, the jungle seemed to echo with it, and then she was eating her manama fruit again, and all he could hear was the sound of her slurping and lapping at it, all he could see was her pink tongue thrusting into the cavity of the pink fruit, the pink worms listing from the corners of her mouth like cilia. She seemed to have forgotten he was before her, and he spoke to her, a few simple words in U'ivuan—*Hello. Who are you?*—and when she did not answer, he walked backward toward Fa'a, and she did not watch him go.

"Fa'a," he whispered, "give me one of the cans of Spam."

He prised the lid off with his fingers, slicing himself in his haste, and began digging out the meat with his nails, walking toward her again as he did so. When she was once again within his grasp (or, he fleetingly thought, he within hers), he laid down a chunk of the meat and took a step back in Fa'a's direction, leaving a hunk of pink flesh (the same color pink as the manama, he realized, although he had never made the connection before) every foot or so, until he backed into the tree behind which Fa'a stood, his eyes wide.

It took her some time to notice it. She had finished the manama fruit—she had been remarkably thorough with it, her broad, flat tongue sucking at the skin with such force that Tallent could see her cheeks pulling inward, like a purse—and stood for some time, breathing heavily as if she had just expended a great effort, her hard stomach puffing in and out.

When she turned, she stepped into the Spam, and Tallent watched it spread, slow and thick as lava, over the mud of her skin. For a while she seemed once again oblivious, a staring, panting statue, her tongue lolling out stupidly, her eyes fixed on nothing. And then she looked downward, very casually, as if admiring a new pair of shoes, and saw the meat, and quickly dropped to all fours and began sniffing the food avidly, her nostrils making wet, exaggerated snorts. She did this for some time, revolving around the pile on her palms and feet (like a pig) before settling onto her haunches (like a monkey) and conveying the soft meat to her mouth with the flats of her hands. After consuming the first installment, she rested and belched, and then, not standing from her squat, waddled to the next pile and began her ritual—stare, stare, sniff, sniff, eat, eat, belch—again, until she was close to the tree, so close that Fa'a and Tallent could smell her, a composty odor that was less noxious than one would have expected, and then Fa'a pounced upon her, grabbing her around her waist with both arms.

He had expected her to struggle, to fight, but she only turned and looked at him and drew her mouth back, her head tipping on its stem and her eyes widening, as if all three actions were connected, and although both Tallent and Fa'a waited for her to start screaming again, she never did. The moment passed. Her mouth snapped back into its normal dumb shape, her eyes regained their hoods, her head lolled forward; she was a marionette, her strings had been slackened, and she was ready to be returned to her box, where she would patiently await the next person to give her life.

Fa'a released her—she sat down, hard, not bending her knees—and he and Tallent stared at her again.

"This was what I saw," Fa'a told Tallent. "One of these. But there were many of them—men, women. But she is like them—they stood and stared and made noises at nothing. But where are the others? Why is she alone?" He was worried, although whether for the creature or for themselves, alone in a forest, perhaps surrounded by dozens of these not-humans, Tallent could not discern. He could sense, however, that Fa'a was exhausted and frightened; he had perhaps half thought, half hoped that he had conjured these people, and the proof that he had not—that yet another myth had come to life before him—was bewildering and terrifying.

"Let's go back," Tallent told him gently, although he knew he would be bringing this woman with them and that her very presence would unsettle poor Fa'a. But there was no undiscovering her now; Fa'a had led him here, and now he was tormented by his knowledge.

And so they began making their slow way downhill, Fa'a first, silent and jumpy, then Tallent, and following him—they had thought they would need to coax her with more Spam, but she followed quite naturally, her mouth held in its strange jack-o'-lantern grin, her teeth sharp and bony, like glints of flint—the creature. She sometimes wandered off, or stopped still to stare or scratch at herself, and then Tallent would walk close to her and beckon, which she seemed to understand, for she would resume walking.

In his desire to move far away from the creature and get back to his compatriots, Fa'a had bolted ahead, and so when he cried out, Tallent could at first not see him and stumbled after his voice, tripping over ridges of tree roots and slipping on floes of moss, until he saw what Fa'a was pointing at—a spear, about five feet long and slender, stuck into a manama tree, the sap frothing around it like foam. They pulled it out, the two of them grunting, fighting against the manama's grip, and saw how sharply its end had been carved, how it had pulled clean from the tree in one solid piece.

Fa'a had been uneasy before. Now, for the first time in all the time Tallent had known him, he looked petrified. The U'ivuans are master spear whittlers, and no adult man is without his spear: they are used to hunt boars, to hunt octopuses, and once, to hunt humans. But as any U'ivuan knows, spears are never, ever to be left behind. A U'ivuan's spear is his soul—*Ma'alamakina, ma'ama,* as the saying goes[26]—and if a warrior should die in battle, one of his comrades will rescue his spear from wherever it has fallen and return it to his family. It is the one possession about which U'ivuans are sentimental, although perhaps that is too weak, too cozy a word. So maybe

---

[26] Literally, "My spear, my self."

this: it is the one thing that they truly cherish. Everything else is *la*, meaningless.[27]

So it was no wonder that Fa'a was scared: an abandoned spear, one longer than he'd ever before encountered, left like an omen in this unearthly, unfriendly place. And it was even less of a wonder that Tallent was so excited, although he said nothing to Fa'a at the time: here was his proof, as much as the creature who stood beside him, making her wet sucking sounds again, that something lay above them, a different world. All he had to do was find it.

＊

We would call her, unimaginatively, Eve, the first woman of her kind, and while Tallent talked with the guides, their voices low and urgent, Esme and I led her to the river to wash her.

---

[27] This concept of *la*—which Norton here translates as "meaningless," though others have interpreted it as something closer to the Zen Buddhist concept of *mu*, or "nothingness"—is arguably the most important governing principle in traditional U'ivuan philosophy (not to be confused with their mythology, or their religion, which is largely animistic).

In *The Land of La* (New York: Farrar, Straus & Giroux, 1987), the theologian David Hohlt even argues that although Buddhism never reached U'ivuan shores, the core values of the belief system are "closer to early Buddhism than the way the religion is currently interpreted and adhered to throughout Asia today." In fact, Hohlt writes, we can see the U'ivuan philosophy as a sort of ur-Buddhism, an argument for the theory that the belief system—and, by extension, history's other major religions—was an inevitability, that its tenets are something man was destined to create for himself.

I myself have a *la* story, one I have always remembered from when I visited U'ivu, in 1972. It was very hot, and I was disoriented and groggy from the humidity, the bugs, the stenches. As I walked through the town's circle of poor, flimsy huts, I came upon a group of three little Ivu'ivuan girls, all half naked, holding hands and moving slowly in a circle, chanting. They had the sort of high, pretty voices only very small children have—sweet even in their tunelessness—and I watched them move round and round, singing their song.

Later, however, when I told Norton of what I had witnessed, he said he knew exactly what the girls had been chanting. A nursery rhyme, I guessed. But it wasn't; it was the first verses an U'ivuan child learns, a chant sung at both births and deaths:

| What is life? | *La.* |
| What is death? | *La.* |
| What is the sun, the water, the sky, the forest? | *La.* |
| What is my house, my pig, my beads, my friends? | *La.* |
| But what is life without my spear? | *O, la. La. La.* |

I will say this for Esme: she was good with the woman, more tender than I would have thought. Eve was scared of water—its coldness, its wetness—and when she felt it on her skin, she began to shriek and howl, and Tu came bounding over to make sure that Esme and I were safe.

We started with her back. Our washcloth was a white rag that I realized unhappily was one of Tallent's undershirts (how long had it been in Esme's possession?), and with every drag down Eve's spine it changed colors, from dust to dun to brown to black. I was careful not to scrub her too hard, but Esme was more aggressive, rubbing her skin as if its very pigmentation were a layer of debris that might be stripped away. Still, she was matter-of-fact in her duty, not cruel, and as she swabbed the cloth between the woman's breasts, under her arms, prising apart her crossed arms to reach her abdomen, she narrated what she was doing—"Now we'll just wash your elbows, and then your forearms. You're very strong, aren't you? And now your hands, and then we'll move on to your neck"—as if she did this every day, as if Eve were nothing more than another in a number of shivering half-human beings she had cleaned in a jungle, in a cool river that ribboned its way out of our sight.

As for Eve, she was more patient than I had expected, but when we started combing out her hair, picking apart the clumps with a manama twig, she began to growl, the noise burbling up from her throat, and showed us her sharp little fangs, and Esme stepped away from her, her palms held before her in surrender. So we led her, cleaner (but not much improved, appearance-wise), back to the others, and forced her into a sitting position.

Later we fed her—well, Esme and Tallent and I fed her; the guides would not. She took the slippery bits of Spam from our palms, sometimes with her mouth (her puckering lips, wet and vaguely vaginal, kissed against me) and sometimes with the flat of her hand; she seemed not to use her fingers—and waited until she fell asleep flat on her back, all of us watching her by Tallent's flashlight. There was some discussion about whether we should restrain her, and in the end we bound a long length of rope around her wrists and wound it around a nearby tree. We left her enough rope to be able to move her arms, but not so much that she'd be able to untie herself. While we were trussing her, she shat herself, licking her lips and sighing in her sleep, and in the dark her shit was an odd shade of magenta, like something fetal, sour and bilious from all the meat. And although the forest eventually became too black for any of us to do anything except lie down, I am certain that none of us except Eve slept that night; we could only hold ourselves flat and still, listening to her contented grunts and snuffles, her sighing groans, and waiting for the sky to brighten with sun.

The subsequent days were busy ones. I left the planning of next steps, the ventures up into the forest beyond and back, the gathering of food and the plotting of routes, to the others and instead concentrated on Eve. She was fifty-two inches tall, cobby and solid, and I guessed that she had had children, maybe quite a few: her breasts had been sucked dry, and the nipples were calcified warts, gray and tough as elephant skin. I could not do a vaginal exam—I tried, but she screamed and thrashed so violently, so extravagantly, that not even the guides and Tallent, each of whom was assigned to hold down a limb, could keep her still—but guessed she was postmenopausal, though I have to say I gathered this mostly from estimating her age, and from the amount and density of her body hair; I had no other U'ivuan women to compare her to, nothing to tell me whether they were all this hirsute or Eve was an exception. Her teeth, as I have mentioned, were pyramidal, spiky, but her gums seemed to be in good shape: when I pressed upon them, they were firm and dry, and her breath did not smell of rot. At the base of her skull, half obscured by her snarly hair and the rings of flesh around her neck, was a small, crude tattoo, smeared like an inkstain, of the symbol Tallent had once drawn in the dirt: the sign of the opa'ivu'eke. When I showed it to Tallent, he reached out to touch it but then stopped just before making contact, his fingers hovering above the mark, Eve's hair falling about his knuckles.

She was indiscriminate in what she ate, but she knew what was food and what was not; she would not eat the pile of grass we placed before her as a test (although she did spend a few minutes sniffing it, so intently that little shavings of it whisked up her nostrils, making her hack), but whatever we ate, she would eat too. She was hungry in the morning when she woke, and hungry again at midday, but otherwise undemanding; during the day she would forage for food, and when she found it, she would eat it right away. We always had something for her to eat upon waking, but one day we withheld it and watched as, after staring and panting for a while, she hoisted herself upright and began her search, moving her foot in sweeping arcs across the jungle floor, scraping leaves and moss and grubs into a pile that she would then sort through, eating the grubs and leaving the rest. But although she knew what was edible, she seemed unable to distinguish flavors: later we tried the grubs, which were plump and squirmy and a greasy, candle-wax white, and found them almost unbearably bitter, a taste that made you squinch your features and cough, your saliva deserting you in protest. Eve, however, could eat handfuls of them, chewing them with a sturdy, steady rhythm that seemed almost comically militaristic in its consistency, swallowing them in great noisy gulps. By observing her, we discovered that the jungle was much more edible than we'd thought; so distracted had we been by the manama that we had ignored the grubs, and the fragile, veined, lettucelike leaves that clustered sweetly at the trees' bases, and the pale, puddingy sacs of eggs some unknown insect had deposited in the shallow scoops where one thick tree root merged into the next. We didn't *enjoy* any of these new discoveries, necessarily—the leaves were crunchy like seaweed but tasteless and the eggs viscous, a thick silky clot of mucus—but we did marvel at Eve's ability to find them, especially because according to the guides, these were not things that a U'ivuan would normally think to eat, much less identify.

Temperamentally, she was placid enough until she was not. Sometimes I knew what might upset her (I had assumed my attempted vaginal exam would probably be a failure), but sometimes I did not—she would be agreeable, letting me examine her throat, her mouth, submitting to my tape measure, which I wrapped around her waist, her thighs, her skull, but then she would turn on me, baring her teeth and snarling, her eyes pricked open so wide that the irises seemed to be floating in a jellied egg of white. And then, just as suddenly, she would recede, return to her stupid, dreamy state, her tongue—an unnervingly bright, pretty peony pink—thrusting between her dark and scabrous lips. They never failed to alarm me, these abrupt turns of hers, although after the first few times I no longer saw malice in them, only boredom. She was restless in her own way, Eve; she woke each day without any apparent memory of the day before, and her patience for and with us was limited. Her curiosity was saved only for food and for the search for food.

At night, after we had fed and bound her—Tallent and Esme and I were in favor of letting her sleep unfettered, but Fa'a had protested strenuously, holding aloft the found spear as argument and speaking so rapidly that Tallent, mostly to appease him, had acquiesced—we talked, sharing the day's discoveries. The guides (who now slept near us) walked every day deeper and deeper into the jungle beyond, for hours at a time, looking for signs of other abandoned spears, of other Eves, but had so far found nothing. Their minuet with the jungle, their parries and retreats, were doing us no good, and we knew that soon we would have no choice but simply to enter it and move up the island until we found what Tallent hoped for and Fa'a feared.

I would recount my day's observations of Eve, and although I could sense Esme wanting to interrupt—her impatience, her need to interject, clogged the air like something living—she remained silent, letting Tallent ask for clarifications, letting him question me and react to the things I had seen and recorded.

"How old do you think she is?" Tallent asked one night.

I told him it was difficult to say with any authority, but I thought she was maybe around sixty,[28] given the gray in her hair, the condi-

---

[28] Among the many things that were unique to the U'ivuans was their way of measuring time. The U'ivuan o'ana, or year, is divided into four periods of one hundred days each. First comes the 'uaka, or wet season, when it rains literally every day, sometimes for hours at a stretch. Then comes the lili'uaka, or "small rain" season, when the air is still damp but the rainfall less frequent and the temperature warmer. The next season, lili'aka, or "small sun," is the most pleasant: there is rain in the morning, but it burns off quickly and the rest of the day is sunny and fairly arid, or as arid as a tropical climate can be. Last comes u'aka, the hottest season, when rain arrives only in unexpected, stingy splatters and even the trees seem to wilt under the relentless sun. (Although Norton does not specify, his journeys in Ivu'ivu probably began around the end of lili'uaka.)

Aside from these four seasons, the U'ivuans were remarkable for not measuring any increment of time: they had no sense of hours, minutes, weeks, or months; even their numeric system only went up to one thousand. A day began when the sun rose (or, in the case of 'uaka, when the sky lightened) and ended when the sun set (or the night descended). People's birthdays were marked by which day during the season they were born, so, for example, someone born on the seventeenth day of the small sun season would say that they had marked a year on lili'uaka oholole, or "small sun seventeen." This means that because of their four-hundred-day year, a sixty-year-old U'ivuan would actually be 65.7 by the Western calendar. But Norton has used the

tion of her teeth, the wrinkles that pulled her lower abdomen into a sorrowful, pleated dog's face, and the way she relied more on her sense of smell than on her sight, for it had begun to occur to me that her porcine behavior, the way she sniffed everything so deeply and at such close range, may have been a necessity, a skill learned to compensate for her impaired vision. Even in the dusk, when the grubs she so enjoyed glowed whitely like stars, she was unable to pluck them from the ground without first scraping them into a pile and then sorting through the pile, bringing her face close to each object. But of course it was impossible to say; I had no way to verify my hunch, and she had no way to communicate with me. But this nearness of vision seemed to be her only potentially serious disability—besides, obviously, her lack of language and general forgetfulness—and one commensurate with her age. In all other ways she was in good, even excellent health, especially for someone who by all evidence had been living on her own in the jungle for an unidentifiable length of time. She ate well and slept well and shat well. Her limbs were strong and her calves were complicated with muscle. Her hearing was remarkable: she could hear a manama fruit's windy whistle as it fell through the air, something I would never have thought to listen for myself. Each morning when I took her pulse, I was impressed anew by its steady thrum, like the faraway echo of some primitive drumbeat. (Later, when I was older, I would remember with awe and envy another quality as well—her apparent lack of loneliness, how she seemed to need no one and nothing except food, how our company seemed not to disrupt the unchangeable patterns of her everyday existence.)

"Sixty," murmured Tallent.

"I could be wrong," I added quickly.

---

U'ivuan calendar throughout this narrative to avoid confusion, as the majority of U'ivuan scholars have in subsequent studies and writings.

The past three decades have seen an erosion of many of the most compelling and distinct U'ivuan traditions, the result of a growing interest in the country— for which Norton always found himself to blame—and a great influx of Christian and Mormon missionaries, who were able, through their twentieth-century efforts, to gain a toehold that their nineteenth-century predecessors were not. Today the majority of U'ivuans adhere to the Western calendar and are fully conversant with (though do not necessarily abide by; U'ivuans are notoriously tardy) the civilized world's definition of time.

"No," said Tallent. "I think you're probably right. Sixty, though. That makes me wonder." But he said nothing more, and after waiting for a while for him to continue, Esme mumbled something about getting ready for bed, and I went with her to lay out our mats, leaving Tallent to sit and think his private thoughts, the nature of which I could only try and try to envision.

The average U'ivuan woman is fifty-three inches tall, the average U'ivuan man fifty-six. The average U'ivuan family has four children. U'ivuans are stocky and blocky. They have wide feet (which make them good swimmers), long thighs (which make them good trekkers), thick arms (which make them good throwers), and small, square hands. The women, like all women in tropical climates, begin menstruating early (as early as eight, though usually around ten) and are finished with menopause by forty. As a race, they are known for their excellent auditory sense and their exceptional sense of smell. They are prone to tooth decay. The primary cause of death among both men and women is dysentery, probably from their habit of drinking the same water in which they bathe. The average age of death is fifty-two.[29]

Of course, I did not know any of this when I examined Eve. So the next morning, when Tallent asked me to examine the three men as a sort of imperfect control group, I thought nothing of it. I suppose what was surprising to me was how similar—superficially, at least (though superficiality was all I had)—they were to Eve: the state of their gums, for example, their general flexibility, their good hearing and quick reflexes. They submitted to my exams tolerantly, opening their mouths obediently when I opened mine, taking deep breaths

---

[29] Of course, this is no longer true. Like everyone else on the planet, the U'ivuans have gotten taller, fatter, and longer-lived, themselves participants in that modern paradox in which we find ourselves becoming simultaneously healthier and less healthy. Today the average U'ivuan man lives to be sixty-three (women typically live a year or two longer), and although dysentery has been more or less eradicated with the introduction of plumbing, the primary cause of death for both men and women is currently heart disease—something once virtually unheard-of in the islands but now, given their new, tinned-food-heavy diet and love of alcohol, depressingly common.

as I pantomimed filling my own chest with air. I even improvised a vision test, in which I drew thick black marks on sheets of notebook paper and then stood about twenty feet away; the men showed me by holding up their fingers how many marks were on the page.

"How are the men?" Tallent asked me that night.

"In good health," I answered lamely.

"How old do you estimate them to be?" he asked mildly.

"Eve's age," I replied. I was very certain about this. "Sixty, give or take. Tu is perhaps a few years younger; his teeth are a little less worn, his vision a little sharper." I did not add that the vision test had surprised me; all three men's results were poor, poorer than I had anticipated. At first I thought that they had not understood the test, but when I stepped closer to them, it became clear that they knew what they were to do—they were simply incapable of doing it.

"Ah," said Tallent, and was silent for a bit. "You're right about Tu—he *is* younger than the others." He paused again. "Tu is forty, Uva just turned forty-one, and Fa'a is forty-two." He said this without triumph, only a sad kind of wonderment.

Then it was I who had nothing to say. "But . . . they can't be," I said uselessly.

Tallent smiled his brief, melancholy smile. "They're elders in this country," he said. "They are what forty-year-olds look like here. The question is"—and he nodded in Eve's direction—"why a sixty-year-old looks like a forty-year-old."

"Well," I admitted, "then there's a simple explanation. I'm wrong. She's not sixty. She must be closer to their age."

"I don't think so," said Tallent, and he called over to Fa'a, who, once he saw where Tallent was heading, came only reluctantly. All of the guides avoided Eve, but Fa'a perhaps most assiduously. He stopped a few feet short of her, and when Tallent pushed aside her fat beaver's tail of matted hair to show him the mark, he craned his neck forward, lifting his heels and lowering his torso like a crane rather than taking one step closer to her.

But when he saw the tattoo, his reaction was immediate. For a moment he froze in that strange stance, his hands still held behind his back in a parody of an English gentleman, and then slowly moved closer to her. As Tallent had that first time, he let his fingertips just hover over the mark and then jerked them away as if he'd been burned. His jabberings to Tallent sounded furious, and although I could not understand his words, I could guess at their meaning—*What is this? Is this a joke?*—and, through Tallent's soothing, low tones, his reply as well—*No, it's not a joke. Be calm. Be calm.* (Even all these days and conversations later, U'ivuan still sounded to me like a blur of glottal stops and aggressive *u*'s chopped up by the same three or four graceless consonants. Many years later, in Maryland, I would stand on a playground watching some of my newly arrived sons and daughters be taunted by the neighborhood children, who would scoop their hands under their arms, chasing after them and making noises like cartoon gorillas—"Oo-oo-ah-ah! Koo-oo-ka-ah!"—and would not be able to stop myself from agreeing with their interpretation.)

Fa'a stamped off; he and Tallent seemed not to have resolved their argument.

"Why is he so upset?" I asked.

Tallent sighed. "He recognized Eve's mark," he said, pointing at Eve, who was now lowering herself to the earth with a series of hoggy grunts, "as I knew he would. The mark of the opa'ivu'eke is given only to those who reach the age of sixty. It is given in a special ceremony, which is followed by a great feast." He was quiet. "I have never witnessed it myself."

I didn't understand. "But why would that agitate him?"

"Because U'ivuans don't live to be sixty."

"*Ever?*"

"Fa'a doesn't know of anyone. His great-grandmother, the longest-lived person in the known history of his village—that's what he kept repeating, over and over—was fifty-eight when she died. He has never heard of anyone who has lived to sixty. It is an impossible age, and a coveted one. So you're right, Norton. Eve is sixty—at least—and we need to figure out why, and how, she has lived this long."

Esme arrived then, back from the stream, and Tallent told her of what had happened. I sat near them, half listening, but really I was looking at Fa'a, who was standing slightly apart from his cousins (who, as Tallent had predicted, were greedily devouring their salted vuakas, moaning with delight and relish) and looking up into the forest beyond. And suddenly, watching these short-lived creatures eating another short-lived creature, all of them spending their days searching only for a taste of something delicious, the jungle seemed a very sad place to me, and I longed to urge Fa'a to enjoy his vuaka while he could; he was forty-two, after all, and would surely not return to this island. But instead I only watched the three of them as if they were figures in a diorama, while in low voices behind me Tallent and Esme puzzled over how an Ivu'ivuan could have possibly reached the ancient age of sixty.

The forest was as Tallent had described it—hushed and mossy and magical—and in it I could feel both its lull and its danger: it was dangerous *because* it lulled.

I knew the forest was having its effect because of the way the guides' behavior changed around Eve. They weren't exactly friendly or casual—I could still see their small fingers tighten almost imperceptibly around their spears when they drew closer to her—but they talked to her in U'ivuan, and sometimes even reached out to stroke her skin, a gentle skimming pet of a touch, never lingering, never with any pressure.

Only Fa'a remained aloof, his gaze upon her inscrutable, although it was also he who came to me one night after dinner and, pointing at Eve, said, "Iv" (that was how he and Tu and Uva pronounced her name).

"Yes," I said, "Eve."

"Iv," he repeated, and handed me a stick, mimed writing on the ground.

He was the only literate one of the three of them—Esme said his father had for a period attended one of the missionaries' schools—and he watched, curious, as I etched in the dirt her name in large capital letters.

"Ah," he said, "Eh-veh," saying it as a U'ivuan word.

"Eve," I corrected, but he smiled—the first time I had seen him smile; he and Eve had the same arrowheady teeth—and shook his head. "Eh-veh," he repeated, and from then on she was Eve to us, Eh-veh to the guides.

And so we worked through the days in a sort of not unpleasant half-truce, each of us taking turns leading Eve—she was so forgetful, her attention span so limited, that we kept the rope knotted loosely around her neck like a collar—laying out her food, waiting as she dropped to the ground and sniffed and snorted. One evening, after we had stopped for the day and were eating our own meal of manama fruit and Spam and shirs of velvety tree mushrooms that we knew, thanks to Eve, were edible, she suddenly heaved herself to her feet and began her flat-footed stomp into the woods beyond. Eve was capricious, her interest in things unpredictable and often perplexing, and there was always something both funny and irritating about how purposefully she would head off in one direction or another, one of us trotting dutifully behind, only to discover that the object of her fixation was nothing more exotic than a manama fruit trembling with hunonos or a steady drip of water pocking against a large flat leaf.

I was on Eve duty that night, and so I wearily had to leave my dinner and follow her, the long end of her leash trailing behind her like Rapunzel's braid. Her gait was so galumphing, so graceless, that I always found myself underestimating how quickly she really moved, and by the time she stopped at the edge of the clearing we'd chosen, I was panting and covered the last few yards slowly.

She was staring into the forest beyond, all blackness and shadows, but again, I thought nothing of this: she could spend literally hours staring at nothing, her mouth agape, her eyes dull as coins. "Come, Eve," I told her, and it was when I bent to retrieve the loose end of the rope and coil it around my hand that I saw it: a gleam of pale, fatty yellow about two feet beneath me.

I stepped back, and the yellow disappeared before winking once more into place. Time then seemed to yank into a long, zinging string, vibrating with a terrible, indiscernible significance as if it were itself alive, a witness to what I might do next.

I was terrified, of course. The others were not far behind me, maybe only a seven-minute walk, less if they moved quickly, but in that moment I was unable to think of them, unable to think even of Eve, although I could hear her loud, regular breathing, hear the saw of her fingers as she rubbed them over her scalp. The only thing I could concentrate on was that lozenge of yellow, which seemed to blink and tease like a firefly. I thought suddenly of Greek mythology, of Hades, and that beyond this clearing were not trees but the waters of Acheron, and that the yellow smear was Charon's flickering lantern.

But I had to know, I had to know. And so I stepped forward, my hands stretched before me like a blind man's, groping in the dark, certain that my foot would land in the river's cold, fudgy muck.

My fingers closed around the first thing they encountered, but so lost were my senses that it was another second or so before I was able to identify it as an arm, a disembodied arm that I could not see but that had somehow taken shape within my grasp, or so it seemed. And then I found my voice and screamed, and Eve screamed with me, and the arm screamed too, and from behind it came other screams, all of us so loud that I could hear the forest wake and rearrange itself: bird wings, bat wings, a chorus of flapping, of insects' patter, of colonies of unknown, hidden beasts being roused from their idyll and scuttling from one unseen tree branch to another, our noises an insult to the forest's perfect crystalline calm.

They were with me in what seemed no time at all: Tallent and Esme and Tu and Uva and Fa'a, all of them, and then they were pulling at me, working my hand loose from the arm and pulling the arm itself from the copse of trees beyond, and I saw it was a man, Eve's height, also naked, his face covered with a fantastic beard, his mouth still open in a scream, that yellow light his teeth, the brightest thing against the black of his face.

Behind him were arms, legs, hair, bone, and as Esme soothed Eve and Tallent the new man (but who would comfort me?), the guides were plucking from the darkness person after person, until there were seven of them standing before us, four men and three women, naked and creatively half clothed, clean and slovenly, talking and not.

Really, we realized later, when we had assembled them at our camp, there was little to distinguish them as a group, other than they were all Ivu'ivuans, and all (we checked) bore the mark of the opa'ivu'eke on the backs of their necks. They were also, as far as I could determine, all in good physical health; their pulses (after they had calmed themselves) rhythmic, their teeth and gums strong. None of the men had spears, and their absence made the guides cluck and chatter to one another; to them it was a fearful deformation, as if their hearts were beating outside their chests. It was a very long night, examining them, talking to them, with Eve, tied to a tree a few yards off, forgotten for the moment, although she seemed not to take offense.

They all knew Eve. The apparent leader of the group, the one I had grabbed, was named Mua, and like the others he appeared to be around Eve's age, a little older perhaps. But he—again like the others—was unlike Eve in one crucial way: he spoke. They all spoke, all coherently, some intelligently, others not so. But I will return to that in a moment. The important thing was that they had been looking for Eve (whose real name, it was revealed, was Pu'u, flower); she had wandered away from their group.

They seemed for the most part happy to let Mua represent them, but then some of them would start talking, their voices lapping over one another like waves, and then the guides—who until then had sat silent and staring and frightened, their fingers wrapped around their spears—would start answering them or talking among themselves, and poor Fa'a would be swiveling his head back and forth from one of us to the next, trying to follow the various scatters of conversation.

Finally, finally, we made them lie down, and soon everyone was asleep, even Tallent, and the forest resumed its impassive quiet. Only Fa'a and I stayed awake, the two of us on guard for the night, sitting across from each other while the others—eight now instead of one—sprawled in a misshapen ellipse between us. They were singularly ungraceful sleepers, their mouths yawning open, their hammy thighs twitching like a dog's, and in slumber they appeared a strange hybrid, their bodies those of sturdy children, their faces those of someone much older: a crone, a wizard, a sorcerer. Once I looked across the way toward Fa'a, who had not spoken a word since we had begun our watch. I could barely see him, so near total was the darkness, but he must have sensed that I was looking at him, for he bared his teeth at me in a gesture that felt reassuring, not malevolent, and I saw a flash of dingy white, proof that he was there with me and that we were seeing the same thing and living the same dream, however unlikely it seemed.

The next day belonged to me, and so while Tallent and Esme began, with Fa'a's help, to interview some of the subjects, I was left to give the rest of them basic neurological tests—simple, crude things, but no less interesting for that (and besides, they were the best I could manage). I had Tu, who spoke a trace of English, assemble three things I knew the names of, and placed them in turn before each subject.

"Name?" I asked, sitting on the peaty ground before one of these squatting dreamers with my notebook and ridiculous fountain pen (why, I thought, as the ink smeared and perspired across the damp pages, had I brought a *fountain* pen?).

"Ko'okina?" asked Tu.

"Mua."

They were Mua, Vanu, Ika'ana, Vi'iu (these were the men), and Ivaiva, Va'ana, and Ukavi (these were the women). Ivaiva and Va'ana were sisters, fraternal twins, I guessed. Ivaiva was plumper and her face jollier, and Va'ana somehow dignified, or as dignified as one could be in her state.

I presented them with an object. "What is it?"

"Eva?" Tu translated.[30]

"Manama."

The next one: "Eva?"

"Hunono."

---

[30] The U'ivuans and Ivu'ivuans spoke the same tongue, but Ivu'ivuans are now considered by linguists to speak "pure U'ivuan," the original version of the language, unsullied and unchanged by, say, Western influences. A good example of this can be found in the word for hut: in Ivu'ivu, a hut was known as a *male'e*, but in U'ivu it had become simply a *malé*, apparently changed after a protracted and heavily concerted effort by a pedant of a late nineteenth-century missionary named Daniel Makepeace, who decided he would rid the language of its distracting glottal stops and what he characterized as its "extraneous syllables." In the Ivu'ivuans' language was a record not only of a people without encounters with the rest of the world but of a people completely ignorant of technology, jobs, and even, largely, time. There were no words for doctor, for example (a village midwife and a village herb man administered to the pregnant and sick), or light (as in electric light), or of any country other than their own. Indeed, as isolated as U'ivu often seemed to visitors, its inhabitants at least had some idea of the peoples and innovations and cultures that existed outside their own, even if they showed remarkably little interest in encountering them in person.

The next one: the spear Fa'a had found. When I produced it, Tu recoiled for a moment, but then recovered and asked bravely, "Eva?"

"Ma'alamakina."

"E, ma'alamakina," Tu agreed. (Later I would learn that the name for spear was actually just *alamakina* but that both men had preceded the word with the honorific *ma*.)

And then I moved on to the next person. When I had interviewed all of them—Va'ana, despite her keen, intelligent eyes, misidentified the manama as something called a ponona (Tu drew a sharklike creature on the ground before me, jabbing at it and repeating "Ponona, ponona"), and both Vanu and Vi'iu were unable to name any of the objects—I sat again in front of Mua and asked him to name the objects I'd shown him (communicating to Uva what I needed required the help of both Tallent and Fa'a).

He remembered the hunono and the alamakina but not the manama. And it was the same with the others: they could not properly remember the objects that I'd shown them less than an hour before—only Ukavi got all three words correct, and recollecting them took her a full five minutes, most of which she spent staring at a tree, as if the items themselves might suddenly appear before her. Their results were so poor that I was forced once again to borrow Fa'a, whom I instructed to rerun the test. He had a low, gentle voice, Fa'a, and although I could not understand what he was saying, I imagined from his quiet, coaxing tone that he was offering them encouragement: *What did you see? You remember. Tell me.*

But his results were no better than Tu's, and indeed, I could see that some of the group were growing tired, their eyes slipping away from Fa'a's before he even began to speak.

There was so much I was unable to test. I could not ask them to read a sentence and repeat it back to me, for they did not know how to read. (Some U'ivuans, Tallent had told me, could still read ola'alu, their prehistoric hierogylphic alphabet, but when I had Tu trace some basic symbols on a piece of paper—man, woman, sea, sun— they stared at them uncomprehendingly.) I could not ask them what day it was, for, embarrassingly, I no longer knew myself. Besides, the difficulty wasn't simply that their memories were poor; it was that their attention spans were so brief.

But although they all suffered from mental impairment, their physical condition was, like Eve's, impressive, their reflexes sharp, their balance and coordination excellent. Without warning, I tossed the manama (its surface long broken and lively with worms after so much handling) to Mua, who reached out and caught it quite naturally before throwing it back to me in a lovely, clean arc. And like Eve, they all had impressive hearing: I stood two feet from Ukavi and rubbed my fingers near her right ear, only to have the other seven—and Tu—turn quickly in the direction of the sound, which seemed to me no more than a whisper. They were sensitive to smell, to touch—I traced a fern tip down the sole of their left foot, and they jerked it away as if I had cut them with a blade—but like the others, their vision was poor. As I widened the distance between Mua and myself for our game of catch, I noticed at one point that his eyes were closed, and I realized he was listening for the sound of the fruit parting the air, not watching for it at all. At the last second, he stretched out an arm, and the manama landed with a *thunk* in his palm, flesh striking flesh.

They also, not inconsequentially, *looked* very healthy, healthier in some ways than a sixty-year-old in the States. Yes, the women's teats were stretched and obviously depleted, but their faces were smooth, and the men's hair still mostly black—like the guides, they wore it twisted into a plush knot at the base of their skulls—and all of them had extravagant blooms of pubic hair, so thick that from a distance it was a bit of a shock, as if some volelike creature had grafted itself onto their skin. Like the guides, they were muscled and dexterous, if not necessarily quick: they had Eve's affectless, slump-shouldered stump, which made them appear curiously resigned; theirs was the shuffle of people leaving the factory after a long day of numbing work, or slouching down the aisle toward their prison cell.

It was an exhausting day, and it wasn't until the air once again grew blurred and thick with nightfall that we were able to talk with Mua. Anyone who saw him with the others would immediately have been able to single him out as the leader; he looked at you directly, unlike the others, whose gaze drifted from you uninterestedly almost instantly, and he was the cleanest and, though this ought not to have mattered, also the most competently and fully dressed. Ika'ana and

Ukavi and Ivaiva all had some semblance of clothing, though they seemed to interpret it more as decoration than as utility: all Ika'ana wore around his waist was a necklace woven from some vines, from which dangled five sharp teeth (human? I wondered), and Ukavi wore a short band of stiff, fibrous, frog-green cloth draped uselessly around her neck like a scarf. Ivaiva had some of that same cloth— later, when I felt it, I realized it was not as brittle as it appeared but instead had a soft, fawny texture—tied in a strange lump around her right upper thigh. But Mua wore his cloth fastened around his groin, and although it covered not much of anything (his pubic hair made a bristling hedge above it), it seemed the closest approximation to practicality.

"I'm going to ask him some questions," Tallent told me. "As he answers, I'll translate, and I need you to write down what I say as accurately as possible." He looked at me, his face unreadable. Tallent had chosen *me* to help him; Esme, along with the guides, would be watching over the others in the clearing uphill from us, and was already busy leading them to the stream for some water. "All right?"

"All right," I said. I felt, for some reason, frightened, both of what I would hear and of not rendering it correctly. It seemed—though Tallent had said nothing of the sort—that there was something crucial and irreproducible about this interview, this moment, and I had the sudden image of myself in the foggy, gray-haired future, standing before a rapt audience and telling them, "This is where it began. This is where I learned the great secret," though of course I had no idea what secret I was even supposed to be desiring to learn.

"Let's begin," said Tallent, and took a breath and turned to Mua, who tipped his head attentively, ready for what might follow. And so I raised my pen.

❋

"My family was not like the other families," said Mua. "Other families here on Ivu'ivu, they are born on Ivu'ivu and they die here, and it is the same with their parents and grandparents and everyone in their family. Ivu'ivu is their world, and there is nothing else.

"But my father was not from Ivu'ivu. He was from U'ivu, and there his family were planters. They planted makava trees—do you know what those are? They are like manamas, but the fruit is smaller and pinker and the flesh is sweeter. But they don't have hunonos, so people here don't care for them as much.

"One day, a day in the year the great king died, my father's mother grew very sick. She groaned and tossed from side to side. The pain seemed to come from her stomach, which was large and hard. For a day and a night she thrashed and screamed, and my father—he had twelve o'anas then—didn't know what to do. His father was away in the makava grove, where he spent every lili'aka harvesting the crops. The grove was not too far—my father could have reached it in a day if he hurried—but it would mean leaving behind his five younger brothers and sisters, and his mother, through her moans, had made him promise to watch over them. So what could he do? Nothing. He had to stay and watch his mother flop on her mat like a suffocating fish.

"On the second night, my father's mother's screams grew louder, and the neighbors who had come to hold her hand and slap her cheeks, calling her name so that she would come back to herself and rid herself of whatever was inside her, decided they had to have someone perform ka'aka'a. This was a very old practice that involved cutting away the flesh of whatever ailed you and burying it. My father's father's father was a ka'aka'a practitioner, and when I was a child, my father would tell me how he watched him once crack a woman's skull like a coconut with a blunt piece of wood held to one side of the woman's head, which he struck with a rock repeatedly. The woman's insides oozed out, and then my father's father's father stitched her back up with tava thread, and after that she had no more pains in her head ever again.

"At that time in my father's village there was only one remaining ka'aka'a practitioner. There had once been many, but then the ho'oalas arrived and there were fewer. The ka'aka'a practitioner came over and chanted to my father's mother, and the neighbor women held her down as she bucked and shouted. My father and his sisters and brothers were made to wait outside their hut, but there was a small window, and because my father was the tallest, he was just able to peer over the edge and watch as the ka'aka'a man took out a long stick, maybe from my father's father's makava grove, where he was harvesting crops because it was lili'aka, and which he had carved into a sharp point. And my father watched as he held it high above his head and then drove it into the stomach of my father's mother, who screamed so loudly that my father promised that the roof of the house shook and trembled.

"The ka'aka'a man carved a large wedge of flesh out of my father's mother's stomach and held it again above his head, chanting to A'aka and Ivu'ivu to save my father's mother, to heal her and comfort her. Then he wrapped the piece of flesh in some tava cloth that he would have pounded that morning and asked one of the neighbor women to bury it under a kanava tree. My father's mother was screaming and screaming.

"Just as the neighbor women were leaving the hut—and by this time the entire village had gathered outside, chanting for the sick woman, and some were preparing to leave and retrieve my father's father, whose groves were a day away if they hurried, and where he was harvesting makava fruit—my father's mother's screams became louder, so loud that the animals of the village, the pigs and chickens and horses, began screaming too, and my father said the whole world seemed made of sound and nothing else. He was tired from standing on his toes to look in the window, but he lifted himself up again in time to see the ka'aka'a man reach into my mother's stomach and lift something out of it. From my father's perspective, it looked like a great gleaming wodge of pale fat, the kind that the women would render from horses and cook with. But then it slipped from the ka'aka'a man's hands and fell to the ground, where, to my father's alarm, it cracked like a stone, shattering into many shards on the earth.

"Then there was a great uproar, and the ka'aka'a man was pointing at my father's mother and saying that she had had an opa'ivu'eke inside of her and that she had been carrying a god inside her all along. When the villagers heard this, they started rushing into the small hut to see proof of the opa'ivu'eke, and when they saw what remained of it, its shell broken in pieces, they started wailing, and the men rushed home to get their spears. It was unclear, my father said, what they meant to do. Was his mother a demon, as some said, for carrying the god, or was she to be worshipped for doing so? Why had she not said anything? What did it mean that she was carrying an opa'ivu'eke? Nothing like this had ever happened before, and so they did not know whether my father's mother was good fortune or bad, whether she must be slain or healed. Lost in all of this was the ka'aka'a man, who surely bore much of the blame for breaking the god but who had somehow managed to slip away, but not before convincing the others—for ka'aka'a men are known for their ability to persuade people, for their gifted tongues—that he deserved all of the glory and none of the blame for what had happened.

"But before the villagers could decide what to do with my father's mother, she died, and the people, who were angry at how she decided her fate before they could, set fire to my father's house and then ran after my father and his siblings, the women leaping out of trees, ululating in that fierce way women have, to scare my father and his sisters and brothers into running in one direction, then another, whereupon the women's husbands would leap out and stab them with their spears. But my father, because he was the oldest, was the fastest runner, and after he saw his second sister die, he ran as fast as he could toward his father's makava groves, where he was harvesting his crop.

"He ran and ran, and eventually he came upon a great hog lying dead on the side of the path. This was strange, because hogs normally kept to the jungles and always traveled in packs. Sometimes a sick hog might wander off by itself, but it was very rare.

"Even though the hog appeared dead, my father was wary. Many remarkable things had happened already, and the sight of the lone hog did not seem a good omen. He slowed his pace and walked carefully toward the hog. But as he grew close he cried out, because it was not a hog at all but his father, burned so black that my father had mistaken the little dried flakes of skin that were lifting in the breeze for a hog's sharp quills. My father said that later he would remember most vividly how his father lay, with his arms and legs bent and tucked into his body, how the fire had been so complete that his legs seemed to have fused into one large trunk. He knew that he must have been on his way home and attacked by some of the village men who had seen the turtle that was inside my father's mother.

"Now my father was an orphan, and alone. He had begun the day as the oldest child of six, with a father who had makava trees and a mother and sisters and brothers. But now he had nothing. He could not return to his village, and he knew no one else who might help him—his father's and mother's siblings had died long before, and there was no other person he knew in the world.

"My father crawled into a kanava tree not far from his father's charred body. That night he dreamed that Opa'ivu'eke came to him and told him that his mother was cursed for carrying one of his descendants in her womb, but that my father could reverse this curse—if, that is, he left behind everything he knew and traveled to Ivu'ivu, from which he could never return.

"The next morning my father awoke both frightened and determined. U'ivuans simply did not go to Ivu'ivu—Ivu'ivu was, my father said, a land inhabited solely by gods and spirits and monsters. Sometimes he had listened to the adults of the village tell stories at night about Ivu'ivu, about how in the dark the island came alive and roamed the seas, its huge bulk cleaving the waters and upsetting the tides before returning to its spot before dawn. He had heard stories of how trees there talked in whispery rushes, how stones slid silently across the ground, how there were plants that fed on flesh. Everyone had claimed to know some foolish person who had once gone there to explore and who had never returned.

"But my father knew he had no choice, and at any rate, he knew from what had happened to his father that while Ivu'ivu held the likelihood of danger and death, remaining on U'ivu guaranteed it.

"My father went down to the shore. He had nothing to trade, nothing to give, and even if he had, there were very few fishermen who would venture as far as Ivu'ivu—the trip would take almost a day, and that, and their fear, meant that convincing someone to carry him by boat would be impossible. *Oh*, my father thought, *if only I could fly! If only I could swim like a dolphin!* And then he thought of the turtle's dream and felt anger, and then despair. How could he fulfill such an impossible command?

"As my father stood near the shore, very sad, he suddenly saw something dark sliding beneath the water's surface. My father assumed it was a school of the skinny, silvery fish that anyone could scoop up with a bit of homemade net and then cook over an open fire, their bones so fine you could eat them whole. But then, to my father's great astonishment, the thing rose, and my father saw that it was an enormous turtle, the biggest he had ever seen, both taller and wider than he was, its feet as large as lawa'a ferns, paddling the water in brisk, forceful strokes and staring at my father with its slow yellow eyes. My father was so amazed he found himself unable to move, but then the turtle waddled the top half of his body onto land, and my father understood that he was to straddle the turtle's back and the turtle would take him to Ivu'ivu.

"My father had never felt exhilaration like the kind he experienced riding atop the turtle. The turtle swam gingerly through the shallows, careful not to scratch his feet on the great oceans of coral, but once they were in open water his swimming became swift and powerful, and they passed groups of sharks, pods of whales, and once a magnificent fleet of other opa'ivu'ekes, hundreds of them, each as big as the one he was riding, who lifted their heads from the water and stared at him as if in salute with a multiplicity of glowing eyes.

"In no time at all they were at Ivu'ivu, and as my father was climbing off the turtle's back, he was for a moment certain that the turtle, who had been watching him with his big eyes, as large and yellow as mangoes, was going to speak to him. But the turtle did not, only blinked at my father and turned and swam back to sea, while my father kept his head bowed in the turtle's direction, in respect, until he could no longer hear the turtle's strokes, only the sound of the waves.

"For the next many days, my father walked. Although he listened as hard as he could, he never heard the trees speak to one another, and although he stayed awake as long as he could, he never once felt the island make its nighttime perambulations. But he did see flocks of strange birds, their plumage bright blue and yellow and red against the forest, who swaggered through the trees in bustling, clucking groups, and branches so thick with chattering vuakas that they sagged under their weight, and makava groves so wild and tangled with fruit that his father would have wept to see them.

"After a very long time, my father reached a village, and there, although it was not easy—the people were suspicious and thought him a ghost—he was finally welcomed, and on his fourteenth birthday given his spear. And eventually he made a family.

"But even after all these years, no one ever believed my father was from another place. They did not believe in U'ivu. And why should they? They could not see it. My father's claim that this island was one of three that made a country called U'ivu was information they had never heard before and had no reason to believe. To us Ivu'ivuans, Ivu'ivu is the world, no more, no less. For many years I myself did not believe my father's stories—I thought they were tales he had made up to amuse us. But eventually I began to think he might be telling me the truth after all. Why? Well, first, my father is a very honest person. I have never known him to insist that something is true when it is not. And second, he has told this same story for so many years now, I can only believe in him, and because he is my father, I must."

You must remember that the entire time Mua was speaking, I was looking only at Tallent. I could not understand Mua's words, of course, so I tried to interpret how Tallent was reacting to them by watching his face. It was not very illuminating. I have to imagine that Tallent was changing some of the words as he went, making Mua's sentences lovelier and more complex, but I was unable to gauge his reaction—his voice only strode onward, his tone calm and unchanging, even when Mua's voice pitched up in excitement and then crested down. Later, when Tallent and Esme and I read over my notes and things were explained to me and put into their proper context, I would marvel at just how calm he had remained, how well he had been able to compose himself, when with each sentence Mua spoke he must have felt himself moving closer and closer to a discovery he had not even known to imagine for himself.

Only once did I hear Tallent's voice change, and much later I would wish that I had been watching him more closely at that moment, that I had thought to seize the image in my head and preserve it in wax, so that I might always be able to look upon it as one of those rare moments in which one senses the plates of the world shift beneath one and life is forever altered: on one side of the buckling earth is the past, and on the other side the present, and there is no soldering the two together ever again.

"I'm going to ask Mua when his father died," Tallent murmured to me, his eyes still on Mua. "Mua, e koa huata ku'oku make'e?"

Mua responded quickly, tossing his arm toward the group, and as he did, I saw Tallent grow absolutely still, and in that instant— as strange as it will sound—I had the sense that he was trying to shrink into himself, to pitch himself backward into the soft floor of the jungle, which might open like the mouth of a great beast and swallow him, gently, whole.

"He's still alive," said Tallent, and then he looked at me, and in the night—we had been interviewing Mua for at least an hour by then—his face, under the copper of his skin, was as pale as bone. "Vanu is his father. Mua says we can speak to him if we like."

It took an entire day of Esme and Tallent talking—to each other, to me—to make me fully comprehend the implications of Mua's story. By this time we were moving again, the dreamers (as I had come to think of them, for their somnambulists' drool, their dopey half-glaze of clarity, as if they were slogging through a thick sediment of sleep) separated into three groups, bound together by their wrists with a long string of vine which was fastened to the waist of one of the guides. We were headed—again—uphill, but in no particular direction, for Mua was unable, or perhaps unwilling, to explain to us where his village was. But uphill seemed the only possibility; to our left and right, the forest had once again closed in, the tree trunks nudged together so tightly that only the faintest ringlets of ferns could penetrate the millimeters between them.

Of course the first thing I had done after Tallent had finished translating was to pluck Vanu from the group (he had been sleeping and flicked away my hand several times, grouchily, before I was able to rouse him) and bring him over to Mua. I watched him as Tallent tried to negotiate a conversation between the three of them. Did he look—even as I was thinking it, I couldn't believe I was even entertaining the question—older than Mua? Maybe, I thought; if Mua looked sixty or thereabouts, Vanu appeared maybe five or six years older. And was there a resemblance? Perhaps—both had the same flat cheekbones, the same jutting lower jaw, the same low forehead carved up with horizontal grooves like a bit of bark. But on the other hand, they all looked the same to me, and had I brought over Ika'ana instead of Vanu, would I not have been able to see a similarity as well?

But later, when I was speaking with Tallent—or trying to, at any rate; Esme, who had been so slow throughout most of our ascent, was now trotting after us like a small white dog—and telling him of my observations, I was informed that I had missed the more important information, information that, as Esme seemed pleased to tell me, I could not have understood the significance of.

The first thing was, apparently, the matter of the king. "Do you remember when Mua said that his father was twelve in the year the king died?" asked Tallent.

"Of course," I said. "But that could be any king, right? The current king's father, perhaps?"

"It could have had he just said 'the king.' But he didn't. He used a particular honorific, *ma*, which is used only in association with one particular king—King Vaka I, the king to unite the islands. And when did King Vaka I die?"

I said nothing. Of course I didn't know.

"In 1831," chirped Esme from nowhere.

"Right," said Tallent. I had the distinct sense then that he and Esme had been practicing this call-and-response the night before, and I resolved right then that I would not participate in their little theater. "And do you remember, Norton, how Mua spoke of the ka'aka'a healer?"

"Yes," I said, and had again a vision of the healer holding the stone baby aloft in his hands, his chants and the women's cries filling the close, tiny hut.

"Well, ka'aka'a was outlawed by King Vaka I's son, King Maku, in 1850, upon penalty of death. So—"

"Actually, 1849," said Esme, all but panting with excitement.

"Sorry, 1849. So that means—"

"Yes, but surely there were people who disobeyed. If this was a tradition—"

"You don't understand, Norton," said Esme, and so intense was the effort I expended to keep from slapping her that I felt myself grow dizzy, "U'ivuans do not disobey the king. Ever."

"So what are you saying?" I hurried on, before Tallent could chime in with his agreement and the two could remind me how stupid I was. "That Vanu was born in 1831?"

"Actually, he'd have been born in 1819," said Tallent peaceably.

I stopped then and looked at them. "Please," I said. "Please don't tell me that you believe him."

"Why not?" asked Tallent in the same calm, reasonable tone.

For a moment I did not trust myself to speak. *Oh god,* I realized, *I have made a terrible mistake.* I thought of Sereny, his gusting, benign presence, the sad and resigned look he had fixed me with when I had told him—without any thought!—that I would be delighted to fly off to an island I'd never heard of, with an anthropologist I'd never heard of, for almost half a year. I felt myself gripped by an intense desire to get off the island, followed almost immediately with a dull sort of ache—I would never escape. I was aware then of how lonely I was, here with the dreamers and the guides and Tallent, who was frustratingly out of my reach, and ugly, charmless Esme, with her round, shiny face and her khaki shorts that bunched at her crotch.

"Well," I said, as calmly as I could, "the turtle, for one."

"Oh," said Tallent, waving his hand as if I were a waiter offering him a dish he did not care for. "Forget the turtle for a minute. What's important is—"

"The stone baby," I continued.

"But those do exist," Esme interrupted.

"And are *exceedingly* rare,"[31] I finished. "But Tallent," I pleaded—I needed to know, and I feared his answer—"you're not implying that you really believe Vanu to be *one hundred and thirty-one years old*, are you?"

Tallent looked at me for a long moment before answering, and when he spoke next, his voice was gentle again. "I know it seems improbable, even impossible, Norton," he said. "But I can find no other conclusion. And besides"—and here he swept his arm out, indicating everything that was around us: the trees with their microscopic monkeys and massive sloths, the stones bearded with green and the rocks stubbled with moss, and, ahead of us, Eve and her people, shuffling behind the guides in a slow, ragged line—"what about this place is *not* impossible?"

---

[31] A lithopedion, or stone baby, is a condition in which the fetus dies in utero and, being too large to be reabsorbed by the body (as the death usually occurs after the first trimester), instead calcifies to spare its host from infection. A woman can live perfectly normally for decades, even for her entire life, while carrying a stone baby; indeed, she can even bear other children. The phenomenon is, as Norton notes, extremely uncommon, a particularly ghoulish medical curiosity, and these days all but unheard of in the civilized world.

And to that I unfortunately had no answer. Even Esme was silent. After a while there was nothing left to do but continue walking, and for quite some time none of us spoke and the sounds of the jungle stepped in to supply the conversation we could not have.

So there I was, a scientist (presumably), a doctor (allegedly), and a colleague (regrettably) of two people who were convinced that a man who appeared to be 65 was actually 131.

I knew that they thought I was being rigid and intellectually incurious and boringly conservative, and I knew too that they knew I thought them ridiculous and undisciplined and dangerously fanciful. The difference was that only one of us was bothered by this. Esme, in fact, seemed overjoyed, cleaving to Tallent like a flake of fungus to a damp sapling.

It was difficult not to sulk. Even Tallent, whose ability to notice the everyday shifts of emotions normal people experienced was rather less than stellar, swung into step with me for a minute. "Don't worry, Norton," he said, handing me a manama fruit (bruised, bulging, busy with hunonos), which I by this time felt confident enough to admit I really didn't like.

It was also difficult to admit that in my desire to introduce some scientific rigor and logic into the process, I had unintentionally given Tallent and Esme even more fodder for their fairy tale. I had made us reinterview all of our foundlings in a process I had hoped would help us determine their true ages. This, however, had proved more challenging than I'd hoped, chiefly because it seemed that there were very few recorded events on Ivu'ivu: they had here no notion of the king, no notion of time, no notion of history. They had never seen a ho'oala before—they continued to stare at us, alone and in groups, in silence, the bolder ones plucking at our wrists and trying to peer up our shorts in an artless echo of our examinations of them—but this piece of ignorance was of no help, as no ho'oala had ever set foot on Ivu'ivu before. Indeed, one of the most memorable events of the past decades (I couldn't bring myself to say the word *century*) was Vanu's arrival, a day that Ika'ana and Vi'iu, Ivaiva and Va'ana all claimed to remember. Each told the story a little differently, embroidered and embellished in various ways (Vi'iu's rendering had Vanu arriving like a Micronesian Vishnu on the back of a monstrous, trudging opa'ivu'eke), but they all remembered it: skinny little Vanu, his funny, torn tava-cloth bloomers, too young even to have earned his first spear. The twins both claimed that they had been in the midst of their wedding ceremony when suddenly, disrupting the celebrations, there was Vanu, unable to move his eyes from the side of pork roasting over the fire for the feast that would follow.[32] Only Ukavi said that she had not yet been born to witness Vanu's entry into her life. But then she did remember being a young girl and watching Vanu get married. Like the others, her memories grew more complete and assured the deeper into the past she reached.

"He'd have been about seventeen when he was married," said Tallent later, his pen bobbing over his notebook. "So Ukavi was born shortly after he arrived, which means she's approximately—what? A hundred and nine? A hundred and eight? Around there."

But it was Ika'ana's story that really made him and Esme excited. For Ika'ana, it emerged, had been born five years before the great earthquake, the one event that everyone on Ivu'ivu seemed to remember. This was a terrible catastrophe for the islands, felt as far away as Fiji to the west and Hawaii to the north. U'ivuan mythology explained it as a passionate lovers' quarrel between Ivu'ivu and A'aka (over what, no one seemed to know), a war in which the gods, each determined to destroy the other, assaulted one another with all the weaponry they had, A'aka enlisting his siblings, the gods of the skies, to storm and rage on his behalf and Ivu'ivu riling the waters into towering waves, ones that reached so far into the sky they almost scraped the sun. After it was over, the two never fought again, in part (so the story went) because they realized their powers were evenly matched and one would never be able to overwhelm the other, and in part because their old and long-suffering friend Opa'ivu'eke had begged them to stop, and neither god could bear to see him made unhappy by them. In U'ivuan, the earthquake was known as Ka Weha: the Fight.

"I was a small child during Ka Weha," said Ika'ana to Tallent. "But I remember how the ground beneath me split and cracked

---

[32] Girls were usually married at age fourteen, so if Ivaiva and Va'ana's story was true, that would make them around 133 in 1950.

like a no'aka fruit,[33] and how my mother ran with me into a nest of lawa'a ferns and held me until the gods stopped their arguing. And I remember how when we made our way back to the village, the cooking fires had spread and the male'es were on fire, and how my mother said we were lucky it was the beginning of 'uaka because the rains would soon be coming and we would be safe. That night we prayed and danced to the gods and their happiness, and there has never been another fight since."

He said a great deal more, and although Tallent leaned forward, asking questions and writing and writing, he translated nothing else for me, and when I asked him what else Ika'ana had said, he only looked thoughtful and said he needed to think about it for a while.

"Think about what?" I asked, but he didn't answer.

But anyway, the important part: Ka Weha had taken place in 1779. Ika'ana was therefore about 176.

"He can't be," I protested, the panic rising up again, nearly choking me.

"It's 1950," said Tallent, calmly but with a slight edge to his voice; he was growing frustrated with me. "He was five during Ka Weha. Math doesn't lie, Norton."

Math didn't lie. But everything else did. Tallent was right about one thing, though: it was 1950. A few yards off, Ika'ana sat, slightly rheumy-eyed, eating his portion of Spam. Next to him sat Fa'a, his fingers fanning out and then closing again around his spear. And although I could have reached them in a few long strides, I still couldn't have told you simply by looking who was the younger and who was the older, who was the madman and who was on my side.

---

[33] A close relation of the coconut, no'akas are a round gourdlike fruit that grows on vines (like watermelons) and are about the size of a large honeydew melon. On U'ivu they're more commonly referred to as *uka moa*, or "hog food," for the resemblance the stiff black hair that covers their surface bears to a hog's bristles.

# PART IV: THE NINTH HUT

### I.

I have called it and would call it the village, but it wasn't a village really, just a large dirt-floored clearing with two-dozen-odd shaggy dried-palm huts ringing its perimeter, which appeared as abruptly as a mirage.

We had come across a particularly impassable-looking scrim of trees, and the guides grunted as they shouldered their way through them, the dreamers shuffling after them in their stumbling, disorganized way. Esme and Tallent and I followed, and although we began in the forest as we pushed our way through a clutch of manamas, we emerged at the edge of the village.

The first thing I saw were the bodies. They were everywhere: women lying flat on their backs, their children's heads thrust up into the furrows of their armpits; men, their legs spread wide apart, their mouths open; a passel of hogs, their forelegs tucked beneath them like a cat's, their bristles black and shiny as porcupine's quills. In the middle of the clearing a small fire snapped and spat to itself. Suspended over the fire was an unidentifiable skinned animal, smaller than the hogs and black where the flames had lapped it, its eyes still intact and staring wretchedly at us.

It was the scene of a massacre, a mass death, and it was only when I looked again, more carefully, that I saw that the women's chests were moving, and that the men's thumbs were dreamily stroking the spears they clutched even in their sleep, and that with each exhalation, the quiffs of stiff hair on the hogs' noses trembled and shifted.

Fa'a was the first of us to speak, and although I didn't understand what he said, I did understand that his tone was unsurprised.[34] Behind us clustered the dreamers, all of them uncharacteristically silent, and for a minute or so we all, as a group, simply stood and watched the village at sleep.

But then, and for no particular reason, Eve let out one of her echoing, pistoning shouts, and the sleepers burst into movement like

---

[34] The villagers were engaged in their lili'ika, or "small sleep," which traditionally begins directly after the midday meal and lasts well into the afternoon. The lili'ika was probably born as a matter of necessity; during the hot months, it was simply too difficult to get work done in the late sun. Second, Ivu'ivuans have traditionally stayed up very late at night, for it is then that the choicest hunting takes place (many of the Ivu'ivuans' favorite game animals are nocturnal).

Although the missionaries were, as Norton has noted, unable to win many converts, they *were* able, through the occasional envoy, to convince the king that lili'ika was somehow backward and would thwart the country's rise; King Tuima'ele therefore abolished lili'ika in 1930, in what was to be one of the missionaries' most significant legacies. However, the tradition persevered on Ivu'ivu because, as Norton notes, they had no knowledge of the king, much less of his kingdom.

Norton does not significantly address King Tuimai'ele in these pages, but he was by all accounts a fascinating man. Tuima'ele was as old as the twentieth century itself (so he would have been fifty when Norton arrived on the island) and had been ruling since he was twelve. His relationship with the encroaching West was a complicated one. On one hand, he had no doubt heard stories of how his grandfather King Maku had outlawed ka'aka'a as barbaric and backward, probably under direct pressure from the Protestant missionaries who still had a small stronghold on the northern side of U'ivu. And yet he had also heard stories of his own father, King Vake'ele, who as a child monarch had thrown out the last of the missionaries in 1875, shortly after the catastrophic tsunami that destroyed most of their nascent community.

Tuimai'ele's reign was marked by an intense curiosity about the West—for him, it was a forbidden place, and therefore exciting—equaled only by an intense suspicion of it. It is said (although there is no written record of it) that the reason the missionaries most upset Vake'ele was that they told him in order to become Christian, he must forsake his spear. And with that one command, the settlers' several-decades-long, stop-and-start inroads into U'ivu were halted: Vake'ele banished them, and Tuimai'ele grew up in an U'ivu completely without a white presence.

Before they were banished, however, Vake'ele had made friends with some of the missionaries, one of whom—his name is lost to time—gave him a series of picture books, which the king is said to have passed on to his son. Although Tuimai'ele was subliterate, the books were proof of a world outside his own, and it was he who would later try to establish diplomatic outposts in various South Pacific countries.

Unfortunately, he was not able to allow himself to commit to these overtures completely, and U'ivu spent the first part of the twentieth century in semiobscurity, falling in and out of notice in the West—until, that is, Tallent and Norton forced it into public consciousness.

a bundle of tinder catching fire, the men seeming to go from horizontal to vertical in one swift shift, the women adding their voices to Eve's in fear, the hogs grunting and running to the men's sides, their eyes small and mean and oily. Only the animal skewered above the fire remained where it was, the flames spitting to themselves. Later I would remember it as a repeat of the day the dreamers had encroached upon us, stepping out of the forest in a gang, and would think how this time we were the intruders, inserting ourselves rudely into a play in which we had no written part.

Later still I would remember this scene and the panic that had ensued when one day—many years after—I was watching one of my children watching television. On the screen was a cartoon: there was a hunter, a potatoey squirt of a man with a speech impediment, who bustled into a village populated by similarly tuberous people, although these people were black, and the only things distinguishable from the black of their bodies were their lips, fat and red and as ridged as an unsplit cacao pod, and the startled bright whites of their eyes. The hunter chased the black creatures, who ran about in frantic wobbling circles, waving their spears and shouting at nothing, while the hunter pranced around, the group of them making a crazy ballet.

And that was us then as well. The villagers ran and screamed, and we ran after and around and above them, probably screaming ourselves—anyone looking at us would have imagined we were playing a children's game. You can well imagine by this point how many hours it took Fa'a (poor Fa'a!) to reestablish something resembling order, for the men to cautiously lower their spears, for their snarling hogs to sink back to the earth, docile but alert. It took many, many hours, and by the end of it all—the women sitting on one side of the clearing, their children surrounding them, and all of them blinking at us like toads; the dreamers, guarded by Uva and Tu, at the edge of the clearing, somehow managing to drift off to sleep; most of the men sitting on the other side, their hogs beside them; and I, along with Tallent, Esme, and Fa'a, in the center of the village, where the creature[35] continued to roast above the fire, its whole backside so

---

[35] In previous renderings of this story, Norton has intimated that this beast might have been human. The *New York Times* reporter Milo Smoak quotes Norton at

burned now that its skin continually ashed off in little confetti that drifted through the air like flocks of moths—I was exhausted.

Across from us sat three of the villagers, all men, all robust in appearance, their hair dark and exuberant, their arms and legs stripey with tendon and muscle. For a moment the two groups stared at each other a bit shyly, as if one of our group was to be betrothed to one of the other and we were here to make introductions and discuss terms. The men held their spears upright in their right hands and, as I had seen Fa'a do, opened and closed their fingers around them in a gesture that seemed more rhythmic than nervous, so that at some points, when they were all fanning their fingers at the same moment, it appeared choreographed, and I half fancied they might break into song.

It was the man in the center who first spoke, and even were it not for this fact, nor that he sat in the center, I would have assumed he was the superior of the other two: he was slightly taller, even sitting down, and sat with his shoulders pulled back at an almost unnatural angle, and his hog was bigger than his friends', its coat marvelously shiny, as if it had recently been rubbed with oil.

I was mesmerized by the hogs, which were unlike any I had seen before, either in books or in person. The first thing that distinguished them was, of course, their size: they were as tall as foals and as fat as unshorn sheep, enormous, muscular beasts that might have been magnificent were they not so ugly. Standing, they had been scarcely shorter than their masters but looked much more substantial: their torsos were as round as barrels, and while I had seen that they were not particularly deft—they had a funny way of running, folding in both hind legs at once while flicking out their front quarters, which made them appear to be hopping rather than scurrying—their

<hr>

length in his book *The Lost Boys* (New York: HarperCollins, 1989), as saying, "The first thing we saw upon entering the village [of the Opa'ivu'eke people] was a fire, one that burned throughout the day and night. Suspended over it was a creature whose identity I couldn't quite discern—it was clearly some sort of mammal, for you could see, still edged along its crown, little bits of black threads that snapped like glass in the heat. But its head was too large to be a dog's, and its limbs too long to be a hog's. As I stared at it, I began to fancy that it might be a primate of some sort, although I had not until then seen any monkeys as substantial as the creature was, and I was scared to follow my line of thinking for fear of reaching the inevitable conclusion" (298).

hooves were as tough as horn and their legs thick and dense with hair. But I was most struck by their tusks, which curved out and up from either end of their wide, scythelike mouths and were chalky like stone and chipped and splintered at their tips. They sat prettily, like kittens, with their legs folded beneath them—all except for the leader's hog, who throughout our meeting kneaded with one front hoof a scrap of fur and blood that had once been some sort of living creature. I watched him worry it in the dirt, dragging it back and forth in a lazy arc that was somehow human in its insouciant cruelty, like a fat man in a pinstriped suit playing with a set of dice before his quavering victim. His eyes never left us, however, and as Fa'a and then Tallent spoke, he turned his great head slightly, moving between them, occasionally stopping to look up at his master, as if to gauge his reaction, which was the most unsettling thing of all.

Around me the conversation groaned on. There would be a long, bright spatter of talk from the village leader, then responses from Fa'a and Tallent. Were things going well? Not well? It was difficult to say. I could discern from the softness of Fa'a's and Tallent's voices that they were being willfully calm, possibly conciliatory, but was unable to determine whether this was costing them much effort. Next to me, I could hear Esme breathing adenoidally, but she often did that and so that too proved unhelpful. I saw from time to time the men, and then Fa'a and Tallent, turn to look at the dreamers, who did not look back at them, and when this happened, I heard Fa'a's and Tallent's voices dip lower, their speech become faster and somehow more beseeching.

Naturally, this interlude would prove to be another to which I wish I had paid more attention, that I had tried harder to fix in my memory every gesture and sigh, but in the actual moment I simply daydreamed. I studied the neatness of the boundary between the village and the forest, the abruptness with which the trees stopped and how they indeed seemed to ring the clearing like people themselves, as if the village were a theater in the round and we the actors. I wished I could turn my head and look at the women and children who were grouped behind us, but I didn't dare.

And so instead I watched a baby hog, which was about the size of a feral cat, play in the dirt behind the village council. He must have been very young, because his tusks had not begun to grow in and his eyes were still big and wet in his face. He was playing a game with himself in which he jumped back and forth over the line between the forest and the village: a little hop and he was in society; another hop and he was not. Hop, hop. Hop, hop. It was so easy. I couldn't take my eyes from him, not for a very long time.

※

Something about the village had been troubling me, but it wasn't until that night, when I was lying on my palm-frond mat and waiting for sleep, that I realized what it was.

The negotiations, or whatever they were, had taken time, so much that we all felt the light dim and the air grow cooler and heard the children behind us begin to mewl for their meal. At that point the conversation ended abruptly, and all of us, the three on their side and the four on ours, clambered to our feet, Fa'a and Tallent bowing their heads slightly to the others, who did not bow back. And then we rejoined our group—the dreamers—while the three village representatives went to speak to the other men and the women began to swat at the children and disappeared into various huts for dinner supplies.

It did not feel auspicious, the group of us sitting there, still at the forest's boundary, the guides passing around manama and kanava fruit to us all while just a few yards away the village went about its life as if we had never existed, but Tallent came over to Esme and me to briefly assure us that all was well. "We can stay, for now," he said. "I'll tell you about it once we've fed them."

It was a very grim meal, sitting there trying to swallow the manama fruit, whose squished, squirmy pulp seemed to clot and then expand in my throat. Some of the women had at last taken down the animal from the fire—it was now so charred that its entire back had been scattered to the wind—and replaced it with a large swaying apron of red meat, extravagantly quilted with white threads of fat. The smell of it cooking (indeed, the scent of the fire itself) made the fruit all the more unbearable, and I finally had to put it down so I could let my memory of eating flesh, real flesh, fill my mouth and mind and palate: the feel of meat's unyielding viscosity, how you could turn it in your mouth for minutes if you chose, how with every chew it seeped blood, so tannic and tart on your tongue.

The women did not cook the meat for very long—just until the red had begun to shade into brown—before two of them plucked it off the fire and laid it on a large lawa'a leaf, and the men and children hurried over to pull at it with their bare hands, stretching it until pieces smacked off into their palms. And then another, smaller curtain of meat was stretched over the flames, cooked, and eaten by the women.

In the end, it took us so long to get the dreamers settled for the night (they seemed oblivious to the smells of the fire) that we were all too exhausted to talk. But as I said, it was only when I was lying there, the dreamers and Esme snoring around me, Fa'a's back shadowed against the still-burning fire (a truce might have been made with the villagers, but I noticed that Tallent was not abandoning our nightly watch), that I was able to identify what I had noticed but was unable to articulate: there were no old people in the village. The three village representatives had appeared to be in their thirties or at the most their forties. But I had seen no one who looked older. It was a village of the young.

Of course, I had not had a chance to observe them closely, I reminded myself. Tomorrow I would pay more attention. But as I dropped off the edge into sleep, I could hear a small voice asking, *What does it mean?*

*Nothing*, I told it. I was tired.

But I knew even then that I was wrong.

⁂

"I'll have to explain later," Tallent told us. It was morning and the dreamers were agitated; Mua in particular was babbling away at Fa'a, who was holding his palms out placatingly. Sometime in the night, Fa'a and Tallent had moved them deeper into the forest, and I had to walk some two hundred feet or so into its darkened depths toward their voices to find them. "I have to find out what's bothering them." He turned to Esme. "Can you take the women to the stream and give them water?"

"What about me?" I asked.

He glanced at me wearily. "You can walk back into the village," he said. "They've given us permission."

"All right," I said. Part of me was miffed that I hadn't been asked to help sort out whatever was wrong with the dreamers. But the other part of me was bored with them and eager to explore.

"But, Norton—"

"What?"

"Don't antagonize them, all right?"

"Of course I won't," I assured him. I was serious about this.

He looked at me then, and was about to say something else when Fa'a called his name—"Po! Po!"—and he turned away again.

In the village, the people were moving around in the slow, muted, half-stagger of the recently roused, although it didn't seem to be particularly early: the huts were already throwing pale shadows against the ground, and the day was already warm. I had thought that my appearance would elicit some sort of reaction—panic, suspicion, fear, or at the very least curiosity—but no one looked up as I approached. They appeared, indeed, to have collectively decided to ignore my very presence, which I thought quite an accomplishment given the absurdity of my existence in their realm. One woman bustled past me with another sheet of meat, this one pinkish but again flounced with white fat like lace, and dropped it, blanketing the still-smoldering fire. Another dragged from a hut a woven basket piled with what looked like large pinecones and started snapping off their leaves as one might from an artichoke. A third woman took those leaves and placed them to soak in another basket, this one filled with water. On the other side of the village I saw the leader, across from whom I had sat yesterday, and raised my hand to him in greeting. But he looked past me, as if I were waving to him from across a busy street and he was pretending not to know me; the artifice of it made me smile.

There were thirteen huts in the first ring surrounding the fire and nine in the second, all of them about seven feet high and of a simple conical construction. In the center of each was a tall post of what looked like palm wood, and splayed out from it, like ribbons on a maypole, seven ropes of thickly braided palm frond that had been stretched taut like cables and staked into the earth. On top of this loose-knit infrastructure had been laid a large cape of tiered palm leaves. The cape overlapped in the front, so you could tie one edge of it back and make an entryway. The huts in the first ring were for sleeping; secured with more braid to the outside of the capes were woven-palm mats, each about five feet in length and three feet in width. Inside, though, the huts were empty and smelled of dried grass and dirt. They were sizable; I estimated perhaps two adults and two or three children could sleep in them comfortably.

The huts in the second ring—actually, it was more of a half-ring, a crescent that hugged the backs of half of the sleeping huts in a loose embrace—were of the same build and shape, but these, unlike those in the first ring, were used for storage. The first was the meathouse. After one of the women had left it, I walked in and saw that the entire floor had been hollowed out, maybe about ten feet down, and that its bottom was lined with parcels made from dark, glossy leaves. The villagers had carved from the dirt crude steps that led to the depths of the hole, and I climbed down them to scoop up one of the packets, which was cool and heavy with something dense but yielding. As I was lunging upward, however, my foot slipped and I caught myself against the leaves lining the floor's bottom. As I did so, I felt the ground shift under me, a gentle sway, and when I reached my hand under the leaves to investigate, I felt a cold slosh of water and realized that they had dug down to an underground stream, which they were using to refrigerate the meat.

The next three huts held dried things, many of them tied to braids that crisscrossed the interior of the space like strands of Christmas lights. I identified a string of vuakas hanging by their poor, hairless tails, their eyeballs sunken and clouded, and another heavy with dried manamas, their once-babyish skins leathered into wrinkled hides, and a third of mangoes, their scent still richly sugary. There were other things too, things I could not identify: something that resembled a flattened lizard, with a hideous death grin of burned-toffee fangs; plump cigars of dusty, silvery leaf sacs that appeared hollow but whose weight sagged their line until it almost brushed the floor; translucent amber triangles speckled with sprouty black hairs. In the baskets that lined the walls I found more of those pinecones (unexpectedly weighty, and fuzzed like mushrooms), seedpods of various lengths and widths, and fungi of different shapes and mustardy shades, and one, woven very tight, abrim with handfuls and handfuls of what looked like toenail clippings but that I eventually realized were hunonos.

The fifth hut was the only one occupied, but the three women within it, after looking up and seeing me, quickly returned to their silent work. Two of them were braiding fresh green palm into ropes, and the third was shredding the long leaves into strips. A braid demanded three pieces, each about four inches in width. The center section was taken from the center of the leaf itself, the part with the spine; the other two pieces were taken from its softer and more pliable wings. The leaves were quite long, about eight feet or so, and when the women were finished braiding the length of one leaf, they would hasp it to another braid with a short rolled rope of a curly, noodley plant that resembled Spanish moss. All around them, in neat coils stacked on the floor and hanging from the inside of the cape, were lassos of this rope in various stages of drying and in various lengths and thicknesses. The two huts adjacent to this held more rope and more capes for the huts, and other things made of the palm rope as well: nooses (for the hogs, I imagined) with long leashes, braided trebly thick, and a shoulder-high stack of palm-frond mats, and long, sawed-off pieces of palm, one end sharpened into a point so it could be driven into the earth and a hut staked around it.

There was no one sitting in the next hut, but it too was clearly some sort of workshop, for there was an indentation in the center of the floor where someone might sit and a large stone, its surface worn flat, that was clearly used as a table. Stacked in pyramids to the left and right of this were more lengths of palm, slenderer than the ones I had found in the previous hut, some of which had been polished and sharpened, and I realized that this was a place for making spears.[36]

---

[36] The villagers were vigilant about maintaining their stores; even later, when the outside world began to infiltrate their society more aggressively and there was less time and inclination to hunt, they made sure always to maintain a backup of food-stuffs and supplies that would last them at least an entire season. (No one person was responsible for overseeing this effort; rather, a person was assigned to each of the storage huts and charged with its upkeep; this duty rotated among the adults in the village every o'ana.) But although the work of keeping their supplies replenished was a constant one, to be practiced year-round, the majority of labor—harvesting, plucking, curing, sorting, foraging, hunting for game, etc.—actually took place during lili'uaka, or "small rain" season. Norton, of course, arrived at the end of this period, and what he saw would have been fresh stock, the results of the previous three months' work.

I found myself admiring the village, even its simplicity. Yes, it was a crude sort of life, but there was a cozy sense of bounty here, of everything having its place, of every need of life—food, shelter, weaponry—being well considered and provided for, of life stripped to its essence and yet comfortably fulfilled. How many societies can say this, that they have recognized all they need and have made provisions for it all? Here there was food and a source of water and the tools of self-defense, all of it not only available but of a surplus. This, I thought approvingly, was a place that had no needs, and therefore no wants.

So I was perplexed by the final hut, the ninth. Unlike the other structures, this was draped with not one but two capes, and inside the floor too was covered with a cape. Atop this cape was a woven-palm mat, but unlike the sleeping mats I had seen, this was wider, as if it were meant to accommodate two people instead of one. The hut was unlike the others for another reason as well: this was the only one that had any sort of decoration. Here, lashed to the supporting beam, was what I recognized as an opa'ivu'eke carapace, so beautifully polished that each of its bony plates glinted as if faceted, even in the gray nonlight of the hut. It was a mystery, this hut, especially after the straightforward utilitarianism of the others, and I even peeled back the edge of the carpet to see if some explanation might be hidden beneath: a secret bunker, perhaps, or a subterranean storage space. But there was nothing, only the ground, and after I left the hut and walked away, I could feel its presence, as if it existed only to remind me that in my tidy theories about the simplicity of life here I might after all be mistaken.

※

It was only after I had finished exploring all the huts that I realized I was hungry, and once again I was drawn to the fire.

I should interrupt myself here and explain that one of the reasons it was impossible to see the village as anything but benign—despite the omnipresence of the hogs, and the spears, and the fact that I was an intruder—was that it was so small. It took me only some eighty strides to walk from one side of the village to the other, and aside from the hogs, everything within it seemed miniature in scale: the huts were short, the people were short, even the flames spitting up from that ever-burning fire were short.

I stood quite near the fire and waited for someone to offer me some food. All around me was industry: there was a cluster of five women tenderizing a large misshapen side of unidentifiable meat with stones, and another group of six sorting through a small mountain of manama fruits—the bruised and inanimate ones they sawed lengthwise into thin rounds; the ones that pulsed with hunonos they placed in a separate stack. The trio I had seen with the pine-conelike vegetables had moved on to a pile of what looked like sausages, chubby little logs of young green, and I watched as they split them with a palm blade and flicked out the seeds within, which were kidney-shaped and the size of my thumb and a marbleized lilac and peach color. They talked among themselves, but not consistently, and only briefly: one would speak, and her companions would make a low, whistling grunt of agreement, so that it sounded in the moments between declarations as if a fug of wasps were hovering overhead.

To the right of the fire were the men, nineteen of them, including the village leader, who were using short, sturdy, sawtooth-edged leaves to polish and sharpen their spears. I stepped closer and saw that in the center of their circle were two bowls made of halved no'aka shells, each of which contained a little pudding of something jellied and the color of diluted milk. After they had addressed their spears' tips, the men would reach two fingertips into the bowl and stroke some of the substance down their weapons' shaft, repeating the gesture several times. Unlike the women, the men did maintain a steady sort of conversation, one that rolled and overlapped itself, an echoing monotone that sounded more like a chant than like speech.

I was wishing then, as I often would, that I spoke U'ivuan, when I heard my name and then saw Esme stamping into view. "Paul wants to talk to us," she said—*Paul*, I thought again, not *Tallent*; his name in her mouth seemed a taunt—and I turned to follow her back to the woods. I looked behind me as I left, but no one watched us go.

"Did you have an interesting morning?" Tallent asked me as we walked into view. He was tired, I could tell. The dreamers were nowhere in sight.

Was he being sarcastic? I didn't know. "Yes," I said. "I saw something strange," and I told him about the dish of strange ooze that the men had dipped their hands into, happy and hopeful that I might have discovered something new for him.

"Oh, that," said Tallent, kneading his forehead with his fingertips. "That was probably animal fat. The U'ivuans render it and polish their spears with it." He sighed. "Although it *is* interesting to hear that they do that here as well."

"Oh," I said. My discovery was no discovery at all. And of course that was what they were doing—how could I not have seen that? I didn't dare look at Esme, for I could not bear to see her triumph, her glee at witnessing yet another example of my naïveté.

"Sit down, you two," said Tallent, and we obediently did. "Are you hungry?" He pulled from behind him a club of yolk-yellow bananas. The entire stalk must have been three feet long, but each banana was only about three inches, though perfectly shaped and as gently curved as a sword. "Fa'a cut these down a little while ago," he said. "Taste them—they're delicious."

And they were: though clearly bananas, there was nothing mealy or starchy about them—they were juicier than I thought the fruit could be, and so sweet they left a burning singe on the tongue.

"I asked the guides to take the others down toward the stream so I could talk to you both," he continued. He ate a few bananas before he continued. "We're in a delicate situation here, one I need to explain to you as best I can." Esme adopted a serious expression, and I tried to as well. "Although we're welcome to stay—well, perhaps the better way of putting it is that we are to be hospitably tolerated—there are certain rules, and we must be careful to respect them at all times."

He listed them for us. We could observe the villagers, but should not initiate conversation unless the village chief permitted us to do so. We must never touch the hogs, nor the men's spears; nor should we feel entitled to their food, although of course if it was offered we could accept it. We must adhere to their schedule, which meant sleeping away most of the morning because we, like they, would be awake late at night (I didn't quite see the point of this rule). We would remain out of sight of the villagers, well into the forest, until told otherwise. And most important of all, we were not ever to bring the dreamers into the village. This was for their sake as well as the villagers'.

"But why not?" Esme asked.

"I'm not sure," Tallent admitted. "But I can tell you this—most of yesterday's negotiations involved the dreamers, and it was their presence that so distressed the villagers."

"But they *are* from here," I pressed.

"Yes," he said. "They knew them. Well, they knew Mua. And I think they knew Ukavi, and maybe Ivaiva and Va'ana and Vi'iu as well, just from the way they were trying not to look at them. Maybe. But regardless, they didn't want to see them. And Mua—last night, when you were asleep, I heard him say to Fa'a again and again, 'I must not go back there. I must not go back there.'"

We were all silent for a moment, trying to interpret what Mua could have meant.

"What did Fa'a think he was trying to say?" Esme asked.

"He didn't know. He only told me—and this I could see for myself—that Mua was frightened. But there was something else," said Tallent, who stretched his arms above his head, almost as if parodying a casual gesture—but unconvincingly, because he was worried too. "He wanted to be here, he wanted to set foot in the village, but he dared not." And we were all quiet again.

That night it was the same scene: the unbearable smells of cooking meat, the whine and chatter of the dreamers, the throbbing manama fruit, the darkness of the forest drawing shut around me like the throat of a drawstring purse. And once again, before I fell asleep I tried to seize the scattered thoughts that were flying through my head like bees: What was the significance of the villagers knowing some of the dreamers but not others? Why was Mua craving and fearing the village, both? Why would the villagers not allow them back in? There was something, some kind of connection. I knew it, knew it for certain.

But what?

## II.

Time compresses and conflates one's memories, but I think it accurate to say that soon after our unilluminating talk, things began to happen very fast indeed. In retrospect, I understood that several things were occurring simultaneously, although at the time they seemed semidiscrete events, related to but ultimately independent of one another.

The first thing that happened was that Tallent, Esme, and I were invited by the chief to explore the village and the villagers. I realize I am somewhat understating here the significance of our discovery of the tribe, and that is perhaps because that discovery was soon to be eclipsed, far eclipsed, by my own. But now, many decades later, I must say that even without my own revelation, the village's mere existence would have been sensational enough. In the moments of discovery, however, we were oddly muted. So many strange things had happened in the course of our journey that I believe all of us had, somewhere along our trek, begun to assume that something astonishing was awaiting us at the end of our walk, an assumption that made us take for granted what we had actually found: a lost people, a microsociety of sixty-six that had never been studied before.

Now, I know, both from listening to some of Tallent's and Esme's talk and from the many books and explorations that preceded and followed our own discovery, that many others have purported to have found a lost people as well. It is almost as if every generation or so, a new group of people is unearthed (which, if you look at it from a purely mathematical standpoint, is highly unlikely. The world is quite well explored by now, and yet every decade or so, like clockwork, a new claim is made and much time and money must be spent to disprove it). But if one discounts the fraudulent claims from that number, one is left with a very small population of potentially unknown peoples. And if one looks at *that* population, one sees that most of those "lost" tribes are actually lost only to the white man: just because civilized society stumbles upon a group of Amazonian people does not mean that those people are unknown to dozens of other, better-documented, neighboring tribes. One of the things that made our discovery so profound was that ours was of a group of people who had not only never been seen by a white man, but rarely by a U'ivuan either. For hundreds of years they had lived and hunted and bred and died while remaining nothing more than a myth, a dark fable, half human and half monster, to the very people from whom they had originated.

Given that, it was startling, almost unnerving, to witness the almost eerie equanimity with which the village accepted our presence. Of all the characteristics and temperamental quirks and oddities that were particular to them, it was this, their ability to readjust and recalibrate to almost anything that they encountered (or, in this case, that encountered them), that I found most compelling. In later years, of course, the village would be rediscovered multiple times by boatloads of civilized visitors, and although they came to learn the secrets of something else the villagers uniquely possessed, I would always think that they should have concentrated instead on isolating whatever gene endowed these people with such an expansive, unshakeable calm, with their ability to absorb (and in many cases simply ignore) whatever was new or disagreeable or even unfathomable.

During these early days, while Esme and Tallent were taking notes and conducting more fruitless interviews with the dreamers and then taking more notes, I explored the village in greater detail. Initially Esme and Tallent were reluctant to disrupt or contaminate the villagers' daily routines and so spent hours sitting like gargoyles on opposite edges of the village, watching its inhabitants toddle about their daily activities and filling entire notebooks with minute descriptions of the most mundane of activities. (Once, while Esme was bathing, I peeked inside one of her notebooks and found a six-page narrative of observing one woman's shit, down to a many-paragraphs-long detailing of the shit itself: its consistency, color, odor, tone, texture, etc.) I, however, was bound by no such ethics, real or otherwise, and was happy to step over the forest's boundary and into the circle of the village.

I liked to watch the children most. They were smaller than the children I had seen in America and, unexpectedly, more handsome: the features that looked odd on their parents—the squat, bricky legs, the inappropriate volume of hair, the large, batty ears, the coarsely chiseled messiness of their features, like something half melted—were charming on them, and they wore their nakedness well. They were bolder than American children too; the boys, even the toddlers, played with bits of stick sharpened into points, which they pretended were spears and with which they charged at one another, shrieking, and both boys and girls had the habit—which I initially found alarming—of running full speed toward their parents' hogs and then landing atop them with a *whump* (the hogs seemed accustomed to such treatment and merely flicked their tails, as at a fly, or twitched their ears).

Remarkable too was their almost total lack of supervision. There were twenty-six children in the village,[37] ranging from four infants to three who I knew were at least fourteen, for each—they happened to be boys—carried at all times his palm spear, which was about a foot and a half longer than he was tall. Unlike the case in other primitive societies, the children here were not made to do any work, not even the eldest among them; instead they seemed to spend their days simply playing. Sometimes the older ones would slip into the forest singly or in groups and return hours later with a whole clan of vuakas impaled on their spears and stacked one on top of the other like linens on a shelf, or with a palm leaf wriggling with harvested grubs. Sometimes I watched them play at the stream—the same stream we had followed uphill, although here it was wider and faster still, hurrying its way over rocks and twigs, ferrying briskly down-island the scraps of flowers and leaves the children tossed into it.[38] I knew from Tallent that they had been told to avoid the dreamers, and curiously—for this would certainly not be my experience with children later—they complied without challenge. There were days when I myself was told to avoid the dreamers, because Tallent or Esme was engaged in allegedly important interviews with them,

---

[37] In traditional Ivu'ivuan culture, all children were held in common. Although they slept with their families each night in their male'es, responsibility for feeding and disciplining them was shared among all the adults in the village. This is why many of Norton's earlier generation of children were from U'ivu; there, the old model of communal child-rearing had been abandoned for a more traditional Western approach (presumably a legacy of the missionaries), which meant that children with missing or inadequate parents were left on their own and not informally adopted or cared for by the other adults in the society. Therefore, no one in U'ivu posed any objection to Norton's claiming the unwanted children as his own.

[38] This stream, which was later discovered to run the entire length of Ivu'ivu, was the village's primary source of water and was used for drinking, bathing, and, as Norton witnessed, play. Many years later, the island was also discovered to be webbed with a series of underground rivers, which the villagers made good use of in the meat hut.

and on those days I felt myself drifting almost inexorably toward them despite Tallent's request to keep away.

The women spent their days sorting: beans, vuakas, manamas, palm leaves, palm wood, palm braids. Whenever I saw them, they were engaged in busy organizational work. They took pride and comfort in being well prepared: at the end of their day, as the air began to gray, they would heave their baskets back to the appropriate hut and place their supplies within and then stand in the doorways, making a satisfied clucking sound as they regarded the way the day's labor had added to their stores, which, given their steady work, seemed never to diminish. Unlike Esme, whom I overheard enthusing to Tallent one night that their efficiency must be attributable to some obscure and superior technique, I quickly realized that the reason they had so much time available to them was that they weren't wasting it doing things that women spend hours doing elsewhere in the world: they had no clothes, for example, and so did no laundry. Their hair, like the men's, was folded into a simple roll at the back of their heads, and I never saw them washing or brushing it. They never cleaned their huts or did repairs on their mats: when one was frayed, it was bent and snapped apart for kindling and placed on the fire, and a new mat was fetched from the hut. And they certainly, as I have mentioned, never minded the children.

I watched one morning as two of the women—one so fat that she could not even bring her hands to meet over the globe of her stomach—braided some palm leaves outside one of the palm-storage huts. A few feet away, an infant, a little girl, was pulling herself with her elbows toward a splinter of dried bean pod that had fallen from one of the baskets. Upon reaching it, she of course put it in her mouth, and when she did so, she of course began choking on it. I watched, fascinated, as her breaths grew shorter and wheezier, and then as she flipped onto her back, her stubby legs and arms pinwheeling, her face painting itself a radishy hue. Finally she gave a great cough, and the piece jumped out like a hiccup, and the girl began wailing. Neither woman moved the entire time. It is certainly possible that they hadn't seen her—they seemed quite focused on their palm braids—but even after she cried, they didn't look up. In the end, it didn't make a difference, as after a few minutes the girl rolled back onto her stomach and pulled herself off again, presumably in search of something else dangerous to gnaw on.[39]

The men hunted daily. Half the group would remain in the village, polishing their spears and talking to one another and stroking their hogs, and the other half would disappear, their hogs following them, between the trees. Watching them return with their catch—which was always disturbingly unidentifiable, as they skinned the animals on-site and returned with only the carcasses, already hacked into large ragged hunks—I always found it difficult to remember that we were on an island. Except for the stream, which was too shallow to support anything but the smallest slips of minnows, there was no sense of water, no sense of the sea. We were of course surrounded by it, but I had no concept of what the villagers knew of it: how and whether they conceived of it, or how much experience they had of it, or whether at any time in their village's history they had turned to it for food or exploration.[40]

The only animal they valued was the hog, and even those they did not fetishize. In later decades, after I had visited my share of remote and backward civilizations, I would come to recognize the animals and decorations and behaviors that mysteriously unite them, as if they had all outfitted their societies from some inner-jungle department store that catered exclusively to primitive peoples. They all had

---

[39] The vast majority of life in the village was lived outside. During lili'uaka, villagers carried about makeshift umbrellas consisting of lawa'a leaves lanced onto the sharpened ends of palm husks; every person had his or her own and carried it from place to place, sitting beneath it when the rain fell. Only during 'uaka, the "big rain" season, were the villagers forced inside their huts, which they hated—they spent most of their time during that season sitting at the mouths of their male'es, looking mournful and shouting to one another over the sound of thunder. Norton once told me he never understood why they didn't just erect one large canopy that they could all cluster beneath and unfurl when the rains began.

[40] Astonishingly, the villagers were not only not familiar with the sea, they had no notion of it at all. There is an account by Tallent of a villager being taken to see the sea for the first time and him mistaking it for "a sky without clouds." The poor man thought that the world had been tipped upside down and that he was entering the realm of Pu'uaka, goddess of the rains. See Paul Tallent, "The Island Without Water: Ivu'ivuan Mythology and Isolationism," *Journal of Micronesian Ethnology* (Summer 1958, vol. 30, 115–32).

beads of one sort or another, for example, which were either worn or traded, and they all had body decorations of one sort or another, and finally, they all had dogs: mangy, hungry, patchy creatures, some thin and some very thin, and every one of them dumb with exhaustion and neglect and a vague, persistent malnutrition that was never quite remedied. But there were no dogs in the village (or body decoration, for that matter), and when an animal was on occasion brought back to the village alive (usually because it was too big or there had been too many for the men to kill and dismember themselves), it was promptly attacked, killed, and cut up. Once they brought back a sloth, dangling by its paws from one of the men's spears. It was so large that the two men holding the ends of the spear had to rest the spear on their heads rather than on their shoulders, and even so the sloth's back dragged on the ground, its silvery fur tracing sad and graceful patterns in the dust. The men staggered to a spot behind the meat house, where the dirt was stained a permanent rust color, and began pummeling the creature with what seemed unnecessary avidity and force, thrusting their spear tips randomly into its pelt, while the reinforcements beat it with the blunt ends of their weapons. The sloth did not fight back but simply lay there on its side, its front and hind legs still bound to one another, and let out high, kittenish chirps that seemed to bother no one but me. After everyone had enjoyed beating the life out of it, the women joined the men and they collectively worked at peeling off the skin—which they tossed, its inside pearly and satiny with fat, to the hogs, who immediately set about slurping at it—and then hacking it into pieces, which were wrapped in fresh palm and banana leaves and stored in the meat pit. The whole thing was done very matter-of-factly, with something more than contentment but less than glee, and afterward they all cleaned their hands and the women began to prepare dinner.

But if they were unsentimental about animals, they *were* sentimental about their own existence. I was struck time and again by the smallness of the society, by what it must be like to live a life in which everyone you knew or had ever seen might be counted on your fingers. And yet although it was small, it was not in any way incomplete: every ritual that might have been practiced in a civilization a thousand times its size had been accounted for here as well. Indeed, it sometimes seemed as if there were a surplus of rituals and rules, as if to compensate for the number of people who would be able to participate in them. Life—a brief life, at that—unfolded as a series of bright-dazzled occasions, a drumbeat of celebrations marking events and milestones that would in a more crowded, busier society be considered everyday events, worthy of nothing more than a comment.

For example: There was a ceremony each month to mark the start of the women's menses, and another to mark their conclusion. There was recognition of sexual intercourse. The first time I saw a man and a woman disappear into a hut together, the rest of the village broke into wild ululating, and the children—it was very late—raised their bushy heads and looked around them with sleep-squinted eyes. The couple seemed not at all embarrassed, and when they were done, they came out of the hut to more ululating and then laid down their mats and went to sleep themselves. In the first few weeks in the village, I witnessed celebrations to mark a baby's first steps (in fact, the little girl I had seen with a craving for dangerous foodstuffs) and to celebrate a boy's receiving his first spear, and to celebrate a girl's birthday, and to mark the hunters' return to the village with what looked like a whole generation of vuakas, who wept and scritched from within a bulging, ad hoc palm-leaf sack that two men dragged behind them, and another, the purpose of which I was never able to decipher, in which four men and four women danced (jogged, really) arrhythmically around the fire, holding up to their foreheads one of the grinning lizardy things I had seen in the dried-goods hut before tossing them into the flames while everyone else watched solemnly.[41]

One evening I wandered back over to the village after my shift

---

[41] The four rituals that Norton glancingly mentions here are detailed in Tallent's landmark book about Ivu'ivu, *The People in the Trees: The Lost Tribe of Ivu'ivu* (New York: Simon and Schuster, 1959), one of the canonical titles of modern anthropology. The last ceremony—the one in which eight members of the village dance around the fire holding lizards to their heads—is a fairly obscure rite called tua'ina, which Norton was lucky to observe, as it is performed only during a partial eclipse. (The Ivu'ivuans had a complex system of tracking the moon's waxing and waning, which is also described in excellent detail in *People*.) In U'ivuan culture, the lizard—in this case, a rare reptile called an e'olu'eke—is considered a sign of the moon, and the moon is considered to have eight stages. During a partial eclipse, a specially elected village quorum pays tribute to the moon by urging him to return to his proper state; the lizards are held to the head as a sign of respect and then sacrificed to the fire

bathing the dreamers and saw that the entire population was standing around the ninth hut, and that they were collectively emanating a low, almost metallic hum, like the throb of a generator. In the opening to the hut stood the village chief, looking relatively tall and relatively stately and wearing a crown of pale fern leaves, whose tips bent and lifted in the limp breeze like a beetle's antennae. He said something, and one of the women gently pushed forward a young boy. It was still, at the time, very difficult for me to guess any U'ivuan's age, but later I would learn that he had just made maku o'ana, or eight o'anas, which meant that he was around ten by the Western calendar.

The boy and the chief turned to face each other, and the chief placed his hands on the boy's shoulders and said something to him, and the boy bent his head. The chief spoke again and then stepped to the side of the door, and the boy went in, followed by the chief.

The crowd began to move closer around the hut, and their humming grew louder. The woman who had plucked the boy from behind her sat directly in front of the entryway, facing in, and next to her sat a man—I assumed they were the boy's parents.

I drew closer as well, until I was crouching directly behind the parents, following their gaze into the hut, which had been lit by a small fire built directly under the turtle carapace. In the faint light, it looked waxen and somehow evil, like a trophy from a conquered beast that had been made talismanic over time.

Inside, the boy lay down on the mat on his back. His face was expressionless, but I saw his right hand, the hand that was visible from the door, opening and closing, the way the men's did around their spears, although of course the boy was clutching at nothing but air. The chief stepped over him so that he was straddling him and chanted a few words. The humming grew louder yet. And then the chief slowly lowered himself down, first onto his knees and then on top of the boy entirely, where he lay, quite still, for several minutes. He was not a big man, but the boy was very small, and the chief's body blanketed him so completely that I could see only the boy's hand, opening and closing against the palm mat.

---

so that the smoke will travel upward and its fragrance will appease the gods of the skies.

Did I know what was to happen next? I suppose. But the whole thing seemed so much the stuff of fever-dreams—the chanting, the weird light, the humming, the distant snorting of the hogs, the chief's naked, sweat-shined back and thighs—that when the chief finally said something brief and the boy turned onto his stomach, I was shocked by the violence with which it happened.

Although perhaps *violence* is not the correct word, because while it is true that the chief was assertive, he did not seem needlessly aggressive. I noticed before he began that there was a small no'aka-shell dish of fat by his side, with which he rubbed the boy, and his sodomizing of him, while thorough, did not appear to be in any way vicious. The boy, for his part, lay very still and utterly silent, his arms down by his sides, his hand opening and shutting, his face turned into the mat.

After the chief had finished, he stood and walked to the entry-way and bowed his head to the parents, who bowed back. And then he said something, and a group of eight men, among them two of the boys who had brought back those stacks of vuakas on their spears, joined him at the opening. The chief lifted the crown of ferns from his head and placed it on the head of one of the older men, whom I recognized from our arrival-day negotiations, who then went into the hut and repeated the chief's actions. When he was done, he bowed to the boy's parents (and they to him) and the crown was passed to the next man, and then the next, until all of them had visited the boy.

When everyone had had his turn, the chief spoke, and the boy moved onto his hands and knees and then stood, slowly, and walked to the entryway to join him, the two of them silhouetted by light from the fire. The chief brought the boy before him and turned him around in one slow revolution before his parents, and I could see that the insides of his legs were tattooed with dried blood. But otherwise he looked the same boy he had been when he went into the hut: the same solemn expression, the same perfect form, the same dark, inscrutable eyes. And then the chief spoke to him again, perched on his head the bushy fern crown, and placed his hands on the sides of the boy's head in a kind of benediction.

And then, abruptly, it was over. The humming stopped, the crowd, yawning and stretching, dispersed, the chief rejoined his cronies and wandered off toward the hogs, and the boy, his small head aflame with ferns, was swallowed by a group of his peers, who strode off toward the meat house as a pack. Besides the crown, the only thing that marked him as different was the slight bowleggedness of his walk. So anticlimactic was the denouement that I was left wondering for a minute whether I had hallucinated the entire thing.

✳

I know it is not a very popular thing to say, but I have always believed, even before this occasion, that certain ethnic groups are predisposed to certain types of behavior or, perhaps more accurately, naturally endowed with certain characteristics. The Germans and Japanese, for example (and I don't think it possible to dispute this), have an organic predilection for a particular brand of refined cruelty, the French for a kind of glamorous laziness that they have managed to pass off as languor, the Russians for alcoholism, the Koreans for surliness, the Chinese for parsimoniousness, the English for homosexuality. The Ivu'ivuans, for their part, had a special interest in and inclination toward sexual promiscuity. A week or so after that evening, I was walking deep in the woods, bored and a bit claustrophobic from the many hours spent in the village, and saw the boy from the hut with one of the spear-carrying adolescents. This time the older boy was leaning against a tree and the younger one was fellating him. Now, the natural assumption here (which was, predictably, the one Esme made when I later told her and Tallent about what I'd seen) was that the boy was some juvenile sex slave. But I do not believe that to be the case. Over the months we remained in the village, I witnessed a sort of pervasive sexual freedom and openness that I was surprised at not having noticed before: I saw couples (men and women, but other permutations as well) rutting in huts and in the woods, and children of all ages nuzzling other children, of course, but adults too. It had never occurred to me before Ivu'ivu that children might enjoy sexual relations, but in the village it seemed wholly natural, as indeed it was.

But to return to the ceremony. As soon as it was over, I trotted back to Tallent, who was reading by the precious glow of his flashlight over one of his notebooks, and tried quietly to tell him what I'd seen. As I have noted before, I often found it difficult to read Tallent's face, but this time, for once, it was easy: I saw shock, and disbelief, and disgust, and excitement, and envy, each emotion replacing the next as neatly and wholly as images in a slideshow.

Unfortunately, Esme awoke midway through my recitation and I was made to recount the entire incident again. Not surprisingly, she did not receive the information well, and essentially accused me of lying, her voice rising higher and higher until Tallent was forced to tell her to compose herself.

"I just don't believe it," she finally hissed (we were all speaking in whispers so as not to wake the dreamers). "There's been no indication of this type of behavior, there's been no mistreatment of the children, there's been—"

"But that's just it," I told her. "It's not mistreatment. The boy seemed completely fine afterward."

She scoffed. "You're going to tell me that a young boy who's just been raped by nine men—"

"You're not listening, goddammit," I snapped back at her. "He wasn't being raped. His parents were right there. It wasn't a violent occasion."

"It's by its very *nature* violent, Norton! I don't care if the parents were there or not!"

Anyway, it was a very tedious conversation, and round and round it went, and it might have gone on for much longer if Tallent, who had been watching us, had not put an end to it by promising he would talk to the village chief about it the next day.

And he did. According to the chief, what I had witnessed was a ritual called a'ina'ina, and it was bestowed upon each boy when he reached maku o'ana. The point of the ceremony was to instruct boys in the ways of lovemaking, and who better to teach a boy than another man? And what better way to help a boy relieve some of his preadolescent aggression and anxiety than to show him an outlet toward manhood? Girls, being less sexually charged, had no equivalent ritual, but they were thought to need less sexual instruction than the boys. The chief also invited us to witness the next a'ina'ina, which would take place in three nights. It was highly unusual, the chief said, to have two boys whose eighth o'anas were so close together, but that was what had happened this year.

I found the chief's explanation of a'ina'ina perfectly reasonable. Esme, of course, did not. I couldn't tell what Tallent thought. But three nights later we were all back at the ninth hut, watching as this time a different boy, a little more cushioned and somehow not as attractively alert as the boy I'd seen, was greeted by the chief at the entryway and taken in for his initiation. And even though everything was exactly as I'd described it—the humming, the chanting, the burning fire, the boy's acquiescence, the wreath of ferns—Esme adamantly refused to speak of it later. She marched back to our mats like a teenager in a fury, and if there had been a structure with a door available, she would have stomped into it and slammed it shut. As it was, she flung herself down and rolled onto her side and pretended to be asleep, even though she woke me twice in the night with her muffled sobbing.

Years later, when all of our lives were very different, Esme published a book about her time on Ivu'ivu[42] in which she neglected entirely to mention the ritual. I wanted to ask her why she hadn't addressed it at all, and even started a letter to her, but I was of course by that point very occupied with more urgent matters and so never completed it. However, I considered her omission the worst sort of intellectual hypocrisy: when documenting a culture, one cannot simply leave out details that one finds distasteful or shocking

---

[42] Esme Duff, *Life Among the Deathless: A Study of Ivu'ivu* (New York: Harper & Row, 1977), is a fairly sentimental memoir of Duff's excursions to the island. As Norton has noted, Duff was an excellent chronicler of the minutiae of village life— she provides exceedingly comprehensive accountings of the contents of the various storage huts—but there is something cloying about her renderings of the people: the children are described as "fattened cherubs," and women are singled out for their "gentle eyes." There is no mention of the a'ina'ina ceremony, nor of the sloth-beating exercises that Norton details. Of Norton, whose presence on the initial, 1950 trip she briefly acknowledges, there is only a single long paragraph, some lines of which I have excerpted here:

In later years, Perina would prove almost singlehandedly to be the source of the island's undoing . . . it is uncertain that he ever really cared anything for the Ivu'ivuan culture, much less its people, evidence of which can be found in his willful disregard for their most sacred of taboos. . . . Although he is credited, erroneously, with "discovering" immortality—as if such a thing can be discovered at all—he was, in my opinion, always more interested in achieving personal immortality, no matter the cost to the people he had to exploit in order to do so.

Unfortunately, Duff's book fell out of print in 1980, just three years after its publication.

or that do not fit into the tidy narrative one has constructed. But then, later still, I wondered if her reaction had not been born primarily from jealousy. After all, as far as such events went, the a'ina'ina was an anthropological treasure, and it had been I, not she, who had observed it first. That certainly was something I could understand and even sympathize with, especially considering the events that would follow, which would render her presence increasingly irrelevant.

As for me, I did not feel it was my position to pass judgment on the ritual. I had certainly found it a surprise, even a shock, but I cannot deny that it made me rethink certain assumptions I'd always had about childhood, and sex in general, and how there was no single correct attitude to either. This may sound very naive, but I suppose I had thought until that point that there were a few absolutes in the world—that certain behaviors or acts, like murder, were inherently wrong, and others inherently correct. But my time on Ivu'ivu taught me that all ethics or morals are culturally relative. And Esme's reaction taught me that while cultural relativism is an easy concept to process intellectually, it is not, for many, an easy one to remember.[43]

There was another unseen and not entirely pleasant consequence of bearing witness to these activities, which was that my dreams at night began increasingly to turn to Tallent. I am slightly ashamed to admit this, for it sounds so childish, but I was, after all, barely more than a child myself at the time. In the mornings I could not remember the specifics, only that he was in them and that I was happy, and that the days that followed often felt unbearably dreary and sad, a landscape bled of contentment, and I began to think of them as something to be withstood before I could return to the cosseting blank darkness of night.

---

[43] In a letter I wrote to Norton after receiving this chapter, I asked if *he* had ever submitted a paper to any anthropological journals describing the a'ina'ina. He replied that he had in fact done so several times, but that the revelation of the a'ina'ina seemed to contradict the idea of an idyllic and peaceful society that had been proposed by the post-Tallent generation of U'ivuan scholars and therefore the report was never accepted. One can only hope that this second, newer batch of U'ivuists are able to take a less romantic and more clear-eyed view of the island and revisit their long-held opinions about the culture, especially as regards children and sexuality.

### III.

Although it may seem otherwise, I do not mean to suggest that I, or any of us, had lost interest in the dreamers and the particular quandary they presented. I also don't want to give the impression that my haunts through the village were at their expense. Indeed, a significant amount of time was spent bathing them, feeding them, observing them, and interviewing them, all of which rapidly grew very dull. My disenchantment with them was partly because I now had something new—the village and its inhabitants—demanding my attention, but also partly because the dreamers were, by their nature and limitations, boring specimens to work with. They were in fact not dissimilar to those dim white mice I had spent all those mornings killing: necessary, but not engaging in the least. All of us knew there was something about them that was singular and important, but none of us could determine what that thing was, or even how to frame the question that might lead us to an answer. Here, however, I probably had an advantage over Esme and Tallent: I knew, simply knew, that there was some connection between the dreamers' advanced age and the youth of the villagers, between the villagers' refusal to see the dreamers and the dreamers' longing for the village, even as they refused to contemplate entering it; indeed, they would not even face in its direction and preferred to look into the gloom of the forest at all times. But I couldn't figure out what that connection was. It was always there, a sprite crouched in a sooty corner, beckoning me at the most unlikely, inconvenient times and then sprinting away, cackling, as soon as I began to creep toward it.

In the meantime, the dreamers remained mostly the same. We could get little more out of them about their lives than we already knew: Vanu's arrival, Ika'ana's memory of Ka Weha. We tried to interview them about their lives in the village and their lives in the forest, but their answers were patchy and vague: in Ika'ana's case because he seemed to have no memory of it; in Mua's case because of something else—a hesitation, a circumspection.

One morning, some ten weeks or so after our arrival, Tallent came to us as we sat eating our sad breakfast. (It was, however, less sad than before. As Tallent had promised those many weeks before, we were finally able to light our own fire and were holding over its flames long skewers of vuakas, which Fa'a had procured for us and which were shockingly tasty, like mammalian ortolans.) "We've been invited to another ceremony," he announced.

"Oh god," Esme muttered.

"Tonight," Tallent said. "It's the chief's birthday."

It had never occurred to me to think of the chief as an individual; he was simply the chief. I realized then that I didn't even know his name, or which of the women and children were his, or even why he was the chief. Was it because of an accident of birth or the rewards of accomplishment?[44]

"What's going to happen?" asked Esme sourly. She now assumed that any sort of ritual practiced in the village involved having sex with children, when in fact only two or three of them did.

"I'm not sure," said Tallent. "But I think there'll be a pretty significant feast of some sort—they're building an additional fire, and everyone's tidying up over there." I squinted toward the village and saw that indeed there were two fires smoking instead of one.

"How old is he turning?" I asked, more to make conversation than anything else.

But here Tallent turned to look at me and smiled. "Sixty," he said, saying the word as if he were giving me a gift.

*Sixty.* The word hung in the air like smoke, and I thought of what I wanted to say next, to separate the one question I knew I needed to ask from the tangle that filled my mind and mouth.

Naturally, Esme had to ruin the moment. "Sixty!" she yawped. "Eve's age!"

"Eve's approximate age based on Norton's physical examinations," Tallent reminded her gently.

It didn't matter, however, because Esme wasn't listening. And to be honest, neither was I. Tallent's revelation was demanding some recalibration on my part. No longer was this a village filled with young people; now it was a village with people who appeared to be

---

[44] Unlike on U'ivu, the position of village chief on Ivu'ivu was earned, not inherited. Typically, it was awarded to the first male to kill a wild hog before receiving his ma'alamakina. After receiving the honor, the boy would usually not actually assume his responsibilities until the current chief either died or abdicated in his favor.

young but might not be. What this might mean I could not determine, but I knew it meant *something*.

"He's the oldest person in the village," Tallent added, looking at me closely, as if he were giving me an essential clue that would make me remember where I'd hidden the answer.

But it didn't. I had to think, and to do that I had to be alone. I told Esme and Tallent that I was going for a walk. "The ceremony starts at dusk," Tallent called after me. "Be back by then."

I walked in widening circles around the circumference of the village, but by the time the light began to thicken into syrup, I was still no wiser. It was very frustrating, and in my frustration, everything about my surroundings—the damp, squishy forest floor, the far-off moans and bleats of the dreamers, the trees' continual droppings of various crackly dried plant matter onto my head and shoulders—chafed. I began, irrationally, to somewhat hate Tallent, who had brought me to this island and then dropped on me an enormous mystery that he seemed to expect me to solve.

By the time I crossed back into the village, I was in a very foul mood. But I walked over to the fires, where I saw Tallent and Esme sitting among the villagers, who had formed two long rows on either side of the flames. To my surprise, Fa'a was also there, seated next to Esme and staring straight ahead, his spear laid across his lap.

"Fa'a's here?" I asked Tallent, sitting down to his left.

"Yes," he whispered back (the villagers were again vibrating with their collective hum). "The chief invited all of the guides, but only Fa'a wanted to come."

Before I could think about what this might mean, the chief appeared, walking slowly toward the head of the rows. And although he, like the rest of the villagers, was wearing no clothes, he carried himself as if he were heavy with jewels and cloaks: his straight back might have supported a cape made of yards and yards of weighty crimson velvet; his long, thick neck might have been hung with twisted ropes of gold and slabs of diamond-studded metals. He did at least wear a crown, a double strand, about as thick as my thumb, of a gorgeous, shimmery marigold, in a soft material of such lambency that it gleamed even in the firelight. I had never thought of the chief as particularly handsome, but this night he was indisputably majestic: his skin had been oiled to the same mirrorlike gleam as his crown, and his hair had been brushed out somehow and oiled as well, so that it hung past his shoulder blades and flared around his face in an imitation of the fire; as he drew closer, I could smell the faint rancid odor of fat. His hog—and his hog was, not surprisingly, the biggest and cruelest and most dangerous-looking of the bunch—had been polished as well, and for once his mean little eyes, which were as shiny as lathed bullet shells, were outshone by his slicked, coarse hair and tusks, which seemed to have been honed and scrubbed especially for the occasion. On the chief's left were the men who had joined him for our negotiations, and on his right were three women, all of whom appeared to be in their thirties, and two boys, one of whom was one of the spear-carrying adolescents I had seen having sex with the boy during the a'ina'ina ceremony.

When he had almost reached the first of the fires, the chief sat down and began to chant, a rolling, rhythmic song without beginning or punctuation, which sometimes rose into a falsetto that was almost a wail and sometimes thickened into a groan that was almost a growl. After a few minutes of this, I sensed a movement at the other end of the rows and saw, staggering into sight, two men who were dragging behind them a boulder, atop which sat another stone of approximately the same size. As they came into view, I heard the crowd break from their humming to give a collective sigh—of pleasure or dismay, I couldn't tell—and as the men approached our end of the row, I saw that what I had mistaken for the second stone was actually an enormous turtle.

I had never seen, and would never again see, a turtle that large. Even now it is difficult for me to find something to which I might compare it. I can say only what it was bigger than: it was bigger than a truck tire, bigger than a washtub, bigger than a wolfhound. Because it wasn't particularly thick—only about two feet high or so—its size was almost completely attributable to its exceptional diameter. And although I knew it was an opa'ivu'eke from its distinctive, mountainous back, it otherwise seemed as unrelated to the creature I had seen all those weeks ago in the stream as it was to the chief's ferocious hog.

The men positioned the turtle in front of the fire closest to us—and the chief—and then stepped away, breathing hard with the exertion. The chief went on chanting, and just as I recognized the word *opa'ivu'eke* in his song, the turtle, as if on cue, slowly muscled his head out from his shell. He was facing me, and when he opened his eyes, he seemed to look in my direction, as if trying to communicate some message meant solely for me.

"What?" I whispered to him, ridiculously.

He raised his head then, that odd little beautiful head he had, his neck stretching out as he did so, his eyes never leaving mine, and I felt myself leaning toward him. But just as I was doing so, I heard the chief break from his song and give a great, gleeful, terrifying cry, and then bring his spear (which I hadn't even noticed him holding) down swiftly in front of him, and then the opa'ivu'eke's head was bouncing into my lap, its black eyes still staring at me, its blood weeping onto my shorts.

※

"What a bizarre ceremony," Esme grumbled as we walked back to our mats. Fa'a had left earlier, as soon as he politely could, and so it was only the three of us. "I can't believe that after all that, we weren't even offered anything to eat. It's very unusual, you know, to be invited to these kinds of events and then not be treated to some sort of feast. But I suppose I should just be grateful that no children were raped tonight."

Although I would never have agreed with her aloud, I did have to admit that it seemed a shoddy and somewhat pointless sort of event. And it did seem odd, given the participatory nature of many of the village's other ceremonies, that this was such a solo performance: a long and tedious night spent watching the chief dismember the opa'ivu'eke (which he did in a particularly bloody and laborious way, by ripping its carapace off—the sound was upsettingly juicy—and then spooning out the flesh with his hands) and scorch it in chunks over the fire while the rest of the village hummed and looked hungry. Having witnessed the chief's thoroughness with the boy, I suppose it should not have surprised me that he was also a thorough (though not very fast) eater: we sat there watching as he grilled and ate the soft meat of the turtle's body, but also sucked the cartilage and blood from its scaly feet and, having retrieved the head from me, crunched down on its eyes and, after heating it in its skull like a soup, greedily slurped down the slurry of its brain. Only one other man, one of the chief's advisers—one who had also been with the boy at the first a'ina'ina—was offered any of the turtle to eat; we all watched as he pinched out the liver, a glistening puce thing, and swallowed it as one would an oyster.

"What I don't understand is where they got the opa'ivu'eke to begin with," I said. Flies swirled around my groin, attracted by the turtle's sticky sweet blood. "That was far too large to have ever lived in the stream, but I haven't seen any other water source around here."

"It's a good question," Tallent said. "There must be somewhere around here—a lake, or a larger river—that they go to find these. But we've been asking and asking the dreamers, and they've never mentioned anything like that."

We were all quiet for a moment. And then suddenly I knew what I needed to do. "Mua," I told Tallent. "We need to talk to him."

"But he's asleep!" Esme protested. I ignored her.

"Tallent, please," I said to him. "I need to ask him some questions."

Tallent sighed. But what could he do? He had no answers, and if I thought I might be able to get him some, he had to defer to me. "All right," he said. "Esme, go tell Fa'a to wake him."

It had been a few weeks since I had last interviewed Mua, mostly because (I am now ashamed to admit) I had begun to find his perseverating exhausting. But now, seeing his sleep-puffed face come into view, I found myself convinced that it was he who had the answers, that if I asked just the right questions, everything would at once reveal itself.

I asked Tallent to translate. Fa'a was wearing his now permanent expression of wariness. For a few minutes I said nothing and thought carefully how to begin; it is difficult to choose a beginning when you don't know what you want or expect the ending to be. I felt like a prosecutor trying to make an accused man confess to a crime whose nature I had not been told. Mua sat there, patient and sleepy. Time seemed to mean nothing to him. "Mua," I said at last, "do you remember the celebration of your sixtieth birthday?"

"Oh yes," said Mua. "There was the vaka'ina."

"What is the vaka'ina?"

"A celebration."

"And what happens during the vaka'ina?"

"You go to the hut. You are rubbed in umaku"—sloth fat—"and your hog is rubbed in umaku. You go to the fires and you chant the vaka'ina chant."

"What else?"

"You eat the opa'ivu'eke."

I stopped to think. I felt like I was at the gates playing a game with the sphinx, but only she knew the rules.

"Do you like opa'ivu'eke?"

"Oh, yes."

"Do you—" I stopped again. I stepped one foot closer to the sprite. He tensed on the balls of his feet, ready to dart. "Does everyone like opa'ivu'eke?"

He hesitated, his mouth open in confusion. *Please*, I thought. *Please.* "I don't know," he said at last.

"Why don't you know?"

"Because not everyone eats the opa'ivu'eke."

"Why not?"

"Because you only get to eat the opa'ivu'eke at the vaka'ina."

"And why do you eat the opa'ivu'eke?"

"Because you are special."

"Why?"

"Because you are sixty o'anas. Because most people do not see that many o'anas."

"So you are special if you do?"

"Yes. And that is why you eat the opa'ivu'eke."

"Why?"

"Because if you eat the opa'ivu'eke, the gods are happy."

"What do you mean?"

"They will let you . . ." He was getting tired, I could tell; his face was growing long and ugly. "They will let you live forever. Like they promised."

No one spoke. Even Fa'a was leaning forward, his hand wrapped tightly around his spear.

"Mua," I said, very quietly, "how many o'anas do you have?"

His head nodded. "One hundred and four," he said. "Maybe."

*Think*, I commanded myself. "Mua, has everyone else you're with—Vi'iu, Ivaiva, Va'ana, all of them—eaten the opa'ivu'eke?"

"Oh, yes."

"And did they all eat it at their vaka'inas?"

"Of course."

We paused again. "I'm going to ask him when he left the village," Tallent whispered to me, and then put the question to Mua, who shook his head and replied briefly. Tallent turned back to me, apologetic. "He said he can't remember," he said.

"He kaka'a," said Mua. *I'm tired.*

"Wait," I told Tallent. "Mua, where do you get the opa'ivu'eke from?"

He looked at me directly then, a bit puzzled, as if I'd asked him how many hands he had. "The lake," he said.

"Which lake?" I asked him. "Where?"

"The lake where the forest ends," said Mua, after which, although we tried very hard, he would say nothing more.

"He kaka'a," he repeated.

"Take him to bed," Tallent said to Fa'a, and we watched the two of them go.

The next day it was abruptly hot, and the sunlight seemed to drool through the leaftops like honey. "U'aka," said Tallent, shrugging, when I looked over at him, my mouth dry. The hot season. We had been on Ivu'ivu a little more than four months.

I craved something cold and watery, something far from the fibrous fruits that the island seemed to specialize in, and was grateful to Fa'a when he brought me a gourd, about the size of a cucumber and covered with an unappetizing pelt of coarse brown hair. But when he cracked its tapered neck against a rock, I saw that it was hollow, and inside was a viscous clear liquid, as thick as oil but as coolly sweet as honeysuckle nectar. When he saw me drink it, he brought me four more and showed me how I could tear out the thin layer of meat with my fingers; it too was cool, and barely sugary, and seemed to dissolve on my tongue at once into a thousand little crystals.

After I'd finished my breakfast, I went over to where Esme and Tallent were sitting and announced that today we'd go find the lake.

Esme didn't want to go: as far as we knew, there was no lake; we didn't know where this lake was; Mua seemed exhausted; what did I expect to find at this lake, etc., etc. I found such skepticism and sudden embrace of practicality very ironic coming from a woman who had been willing to accept without question that Ika'ana was 176, but I knew enough by then to realize that her discomfort rose not from any philosophical differences but because the dynamic among the three of us had changed—*I* would be the one who would find what we sought (whatever that might be), not Tallent. He had recognized and accepted the inevitability of this; she had not.

"Fine," I told her. "You don't have to go." From her silence, I knew she would come anyway.

The next thing to do was to question Mua again, though I was dismayed to see that he looked no more alert than he had the previous night. It would be a trying day.

"Mua," I asked him, "where are we?" Tallent translated the question to him.

He laughed at the stupidity of the question. "Ivu'ivu."

"Yes," I said, "but where?" I handed him a stick. "Can you draw where we are on the island?" But he only looked at me in reply, his mouth open.

I thought for a minute. I could almost feel the smugness radiating off Esme. And then I knew what to try. "Mua," I said, "I need your help." He looked at me. "There's going to be another vaka'ina," I told him, "and we need to find an opa'ivu'eke. Can you help us find it?"

"Whose?" Mua asked, reasonably.

"His," I said, gesturing at Tallent.

"Ah," said Mua, nodding wisely. And then he stood and began striding in the direction of the village.

Was it to be that easy? Apparently it was. This, I reflected, was one of the difficulties of working with the dreamers and of being dependent on them for answers and direction: sometimes they grew mulish with a sort of stubbornly adhered-to logic understood and respected only by them, and sometimes they seemed wholly oblivious to the obvious. Tallent was clearly no more a sixty-year-old than I was, and yet here we were, off to find the lake of turtles like a jolly pack of travelers in a bardic tale. Or perhaps it wasn't that they were oblivious; perhaps they simply saw things differently than we did. Or perhaps it was that they saw nothing at all; if they were told someone was sixty, then he was sixty, and no more proof was demanded. It was exhausting, this quicksand logic of theirs, applied with an inconsistency that was all the more frustrating for being so unpredictable.

The five of us walked, concealed by trees, around one side of the village, Fa'a running back to tell Tu and Uva to watch the dreamers before joining us again, until we reached the back of the ninth hut, where Mua paused, frowning a bit, looking about him at the forest beyond. Then he gave a grunt, as if in recognition, and led us around a particularly thick manama trunk, behind which was hidden a rough sort of path, scarred with rock, that gradually, so slowly one barely sensed it, wound its way uphill.

It felt good to be walking again after being so long confined to the village. The air was warm, and the earth smelled cozy and biscuity, and we were none of us encumbered by anything but our notebooks and pens; I noticed Tallent sketching a rough, mostly gestural map in his book as we went.

The trek was not difficult, but we would never have been able to follow the path were it not for Mua. In some places it disappeared entirely, and in others it became an asphalted road of donkey-gray stone in which were embedded hundreds of chalky white fossils. I identified delicate insect carapaces, their legs as fine as threads, and the ridged backs of scorpions, and many other creatures that bore no resemblance in their stony state to anything I had seen before. Mua too seemed to enjoy the walk, and he hummed a vague, meandering tune through his nose as he went. Watching him bustle through the trees and sheafs of ferns, I was reminded anew of how superior his physical condition was, and how from the back he could have been no more than thirty.

Around us the foliage alternately thickened and thinned, so that sometimes we were in darkness, an utter cocoon of green and black, and sometimes we were in landscape that resembled a meadow, with vast, empyreal sweeps of feathery yellow bushes and only a few slender trees, their boughs extravagantly trimmed with ruffled drapes of leaves. In these meadows we could see the sky above us, a bright, aching blue, and feel all around us the clicks and whirs and mechanical ticks and tocks of whole societies of insects. I came to realize that we had been in a prison of trees, all of them our wardens, and recognized then all that they had kept from us: light, wind, air, sound, space—the things every living creature on earth craves.

So reveling in these familiar, long-lost sensations was I that I at first failed to notice that Mua had slowed, and that beside me Fa'a had stopped. We had entered, after another purgatory of trees, more meadowland—the fifth or sixth one—when I saw before me, about five hundred yards ahead, a shimmering lake. For a moment, I did not believe it existed. Not because it was particularly large (indeed, it was about the circumference of the village), or particularly lovely, or in fact particular in any sort of way at all, but because of its mere existence. Just as I had nearly forgotten what it was like to be in sunlight—true sunlight, not the inmate's portion that was meted out to us each day by the treetops—so too had I forgotten what it was like to see a contained body of water, one not in constant motion but simply being. My instinct was to run into it, to feel the sensation of breaking its surface, but of course I didn't.

"Opa'ivu'eke," said Mua matter-of-factly.

We looked. There was nothing around the lake: no reeds, no trees, no shrubbery. Its borders were as clean and precise as the borders of the village, and later I would wonder if the people had modeled their village on this lake. But as we walked closer (unconsciously, we moved together as one organism, as if that might protect us from something we didn't know to fear), I saw a cluster of tiny, clear eggs speckling the lake's surface: a group here, a group there, all of them as fragile and pretty as glass.

Drawing closer still, however, we realized that they weren't eggs at all but bubbles, and just as the first of us had begun to exclaim, the first turtle's head emerged from the waters, its mouth slightly open, its pleated throat stretching toward the sun, its eyes closed. This was followed by another and another, until we counted, dotted around the lake, seven opa'ivu'ekes. There was no sound, not even the sound of the water breaking, and when they submerged themselves again, they were replaced by another group, this one of six, including three that were clearly children, their heads no bigger than a walnut shell. Down and up they went, an uncomplicated and lovely synchronized performance, while we stood and gawped from just a few yards away. It was then that I noticed that the insects' buzz had been replaced by Fa'a's low chant, the same one (presumably) he had made when he had last seen a live opa'ivu'eke, the tiny one paddling its way downstream at the start of our journey.

"Hawana," observed Mua, squinting at the lake. *Many*. He said something else too, and Tallent translated: "Sometimes there are many, sometimes there are few."

Then he spoke to Tallent again, something longer, and I saw Tallent shake his head, and Mua insist, and Fa'a, despite himself, let out a faint cry.

Tallent looked at us, stricken. "He says I must go pick out the one I want, and that he will help me carry it."

Something was beginning to shape in my mind. "Ask him if I can pick one."

He did, and then turned back to me, shaking his head. "Only people who have reached sixty o'anas can touch an opa'ivu'eke, he says."

"So you can, because you're supposed to be sixty o'anas, and he can, because he already is." Beside me, Fa'a moved from one foot to the other, shifting his weight and gazing into the woods beyond the lake.

Tallent confirmed this with Mua and nodded.

"Ask him—ask him what would happen if you touched an opa'ivu'eke before you made sixty o'anas."

I saw the agitation in Mua's face immediately. His answer was long and seemed complicated, and Tallent frowned, so hard was he concentrating on what Mua was saying. A couple of times he stopped Mua and asked him for clarification, and Mua answered him rapidly, his hands fanning the air.

"He says," Tallent reported, and I could tell that he was excited by the way he was forcing himself to speak so slowly and deliberately, "I could be wrong, but—he says that anyone who touches an opa'ivu'eke brings a great curse upon his family. One of the wrong-doer's family *will* reach sixty o'anas and *will* get to eat the opa'ivu'eke, but after a period of time that person will slowly lose his ama and will become a mo'o kua'au."

And then, unexpectedly, he smiled at me, just at me, a brilliant, shining smile, and I knew what he was remembering: that first week on the island, when he had told me his story of the hunter and the myth of the mo'o kua'au, the creature who lived without love, without speech, whom Fa'a had seen prowling the woods of Ivu'ivu. Many decades later, I can reflect upon this and acknowledge that his triumph—our triumph—was premature (after all, we had no idea what any of this meant), but at the time it seemed a delirious relief, especially, I imagine, for him: he had not been foolish after all. He had followed a story and it had revealed itself to be—well, if not true, then certainly confirmed. In reality, of course, it was little better or more conclusive than rushing off to New Mexico because you had heard that aliens purportedly lived in some small town there, and then being independently told by the inhabitants of the town that they themselves had seen aliens, but in the moment, logic and its various demands were briefly abandoned.

"Ask him," I instructed, "what happens when you become a mo'o kua'au."

Tallent did. "You are banished," he reported.

"Ask him," I continued—and I will not lie, I was as excited as Tallent—"if he was banished."

He did, and for a long time, at least three minutes, Mua said nothing, only looked at the lake, where the opa'ivu'ekes were still performing their simple, avant-garde choreography. When he at last spoke, it was less his answer itself I noted than the sad, whistling sigh on which it rode, so that I knew what he would say even before I heard the word itself.

"E," he said. *Yes.*


Back in the village (which now seemed unbearably landlocked and airless and confined), I did my prisoner's walk through the woods, looping around the clearing again and again before going to my tree. The tree that I had begun to consider my own was a manama and distinguished only by the fact that it was relatively lonely; there were few other trees surrounding it, and I could sit, or even lie, on the thickly piled moss that surrounded it, protecting it from the forest floor. To get to it, I walked fifteen minutes to the west of our camp and then took a right at a particularly vicious-looking orchid, whose urinous blooms spat out two long, spiraling stamens the color of fresh blood.

At the tree I considered what I knew. First, I knew that the U'ivuans thought the opa'ivu'eke sacred. Second, I knew that it was forbidden to touch one unless you had reached sixty o'anas, in which case you were expected to eat one. Third, I knew that in the Ivu'ivuans' ceremony, only those sixty o'anas or older could join in the eating of the opa'ivu'eke. Fourth, I knew that it was relatively rare for people to reach this advanced age—witness the chief's vaka'ina, in which only his adviser had been able to join him. That meant that only two of sixty-six people in the village had reached that age. Fifth, I knew that Mua and his compatriots were all at least sixty o'anas (how much over sixty o'anas I couldn't trouble myself with at the moment), which meant they had all eaten the opa'ivu'eke. And sixth—sixth was Mua's story of the curse: if someone touches an opa'ivu'eke before his time, he dooms someone in his family to becoming a mo'o kua'au, which leads to banishment.

That much, naturally, was uncomplicated, a simple synthesizing of information. Esme and Tallent could have done it. Esme and Tallent probably *had* done it. "Obviously," I heard Esme's honking voice in my ear, "it's the opa'ivu'eke." But what did that mean? Did everyone who ate the opa'ivu'eke become, eventually, a mo'o kua'au? And what did being a mo'o kua'au *mean*? Tallent had translated the term as being "without voice," but with the exception of Eve, all of the dreamers could speak. Not very coherently always, or interestingly, certainly, but they all could. So why had they been banished? And if it *was* the opa'ivu'eke that was responsible, why did they keep eating it?

Back at camp, I shared with Tallent some of what I had concluded, although I couldn't share all my suspicions because Esme had approached us, breathing heavily and clomping through the undergrowth as she did. Tallent frowned, concentrating, and eventually it was agreed between us that I should interview the chief. Fa'a was dispatched and a meeting requested.

Later that night, after the villagers had eaten and a group of men had gone hunting for the screeching, red-eyed bats they liked to roast, we were summoned. Once again we were at the fire, the same group of four (though I had tried to suggest that Esme's presence wouldn't be necessary and might perhaps be detrimental; given her dislike of the chief since the a'ina'ina ceremony, might not she make her displeasure known and offend him? But she glared at me and announced that she was perfectly capable of keeping silent and would be accompanying us no matter what). Across from us sat the chief, alone but for his hog, who had reverted to his former dusty state, the chewed-bark tips of his tusks splashed with mud. He was masticating something I couldn't quite distinguish, but every now and again a piece of it—a little three-toed paw, as small as a thumbnail and speckled with a patchy fur—would emerge from between his teeth as he turned his snack around in his mouth.

I knew it was not logical, but I kept looking at the chief as if I might discern something transformed in his appearance. After all, I had seen him participate in two monumental rites of passage, and it seemed only natural that they should have left some sort of significant mark on him or his personality. And although they hadn't, I did notice that he was wearing something around his neck: a loop of woven vines, from the center of which hung a chipped shard of something hard and glazed, shining dully against his skin.

For a while we all sat in silence, polite and embarrassed yet again, neither side willing to begin. Finally Tallent spoke, and the chief nodded to him.

"I told him we were honored to be invited to join his vaka'ina," Tallent told us.

"Yes," said the chief.

There was another silence.

"Chief," I began, and watched as first his head and then his hog's moved slowly in my direction, "do you celebrate the vaka'ina often?"

"Oh, no," said the chief (naturally, this was all being translated by Tallent).

"When was the last one?"

"Three o'anas ago. It was Lawa'eke's vaka'ina." His voice was unexpectedly gentle. With one hand he held his spear, and with the other he stroked his hog's back in long, smooth sweeps, the hog making contented rumbling purrs as he did so. I saw Tallent scribble in his notebook: "Lawa'eke appx. 63 o'anas?"

"And Lawa'eke was the one who joined you in eating at your vaka'ina?"

"E."

"And at Lawa'eke's vaka'ina, did anyone eat the opa'ivu'eke with him?"

"E."

"Who?"

"Three others."

"May we speak to them?"

"They are not here any longer."

"They died?"

"No, they did not die."

I wasn't sure how to continue. "Where are they, then?"

"Away."

"Where away?"

He gestured with his free hand, lifting it from the hog's back and indicating the woods beyond. "Away."

"When did they go?"

He tilted his head to one side, thinking. "About one o'ana ago."

"And why did they go away?"

"Because they were becoming mo'o kua'aus."

I could feel Tallent tense beside me, could hear his breath change. "How did you know they were becoming mo'o kua'aus?"

"I could see them change. We could all see them change."

"What do the changes look like?"

"First they forgot to do things. They would go into the forest to hunt and not return. They would forget to take their spears with them. They would throw their spears at things and then return without them and we would have to look through the forest to retrieve them. Then they would tell the same story again and again. Their speech would sometimes lack sense. Then we knew that they were cursed and that soon they would be mo'o kua'aus."

"And so what happened?"

"Our best hunters took them very deep into the forest, farther than any of them had ever gone before, and left them there. It took the hunters many days to walk back to us. Before they left, we had to remind them that they were cursed and that they could not stay in the village because they were becoming mo'o kua'aus."

We were all quiet. "Did you ever see them again?"

He made a sudden sharp noise, like two wood clappers smacking against one another, which I later recognized as laughter, and jutted his chin in the direction of the dreamers. "E."

"The dreamers?" Esme asked in surprise, and the chief glanced over at her, and she flushed.

"Who?" I asked the chief.

"Mua," he said, and I could hear the distaste in his voice.

"So Mua was one of the people you led into the forest a year ago," I said.

"Not me. Others."

"All right. But do you recognize anyone else over there?" I asked. "The other two who had to go away?"

He peered over at them, though if his eyesight was as bad as Fa'a's and the others', I very much doubted he'd be able to make out their forms, much less their faces. "No," he said.

"No?" I asked him. "Not the others? Not Ivaiva or Va'ana? Not Ukavi or Vanu?"

He looked at me steadily. "No."

"No, they were not the ones who were led away, or no, you don't know them?"

He shifted on the ground. "They were not the ones we led away." *Ah*, I thought. *He* does *know them.*

"So," I continued, slowly now, "last o'ana, some of the hunters took Mua and two others who were becoming mo'o kua'aus into the forest, but the only one of those three you've seen recently is Mua, correct?"

He looked impatient. "E," he said.

"And what happened to the others?"

He tipped his head to the side, which I had begun to recognize was a sign that he was thinking but was also something of a shrug. "I don't know," he said.

"Your father," I began, and then stopped. The chief waited. "Your father," I said, "did he celebrate his vaka'ina?"

"No," he answered swiftly. "I am the first in our family. But Lawa'eke's father did."

"Where is he?"

"He is here."

"He is?" I looked around as if I would somehow recognize him, as if I might see him hefting himself out of the meat pit or strolling toward us. "Why wasn't he at your vaka'ina?"

"He is unwell."

"Unwell in what way?"

The chief sighed, and I thought—though it was difficult to tell—that I read sorrow in the flat, unknowable surfaces of his face, or perhaps regret. "He has become a mo'o kua'au."

"So—so will you have to take him away?"

"E."

"When did he become a mo'o kua'au?"

He tilted his head again. "Some time ago. At first it was slow. But now he really is a mo'o kua'au."

"But you kept him here?"

He made a strange gesture with his head, a sort of sideways wag. "He is Lawa'eke's father," he said, after a long pause. We were silent for a while.

"When did he celebrate his vaka'ina?"

He thought. "I was a child," he said finally. "It was shortly after my a'ina'ina." He smiled suddenly, and I saw that his teeth were the same discolored chips as Fa'a's. "He was my initiator." I could feel, if not see, Esme stiffen at his words.

I did not know how Tallent would feel about my next request, and indeed, when I asked, he paused before translating and looked at me quickly before he did so. "May we meet him?"

The chief was silent for such a long time now that I feared I had offended him, and for a moment the only sounds were his hog enthusiastically sucking on the remains of whatever poor creature he was enjoying and the background shrieking of the children and the guttural barking of the women. But then he grunted and climbed to his feet, and we followed him and his lumbering hog through the village and to the back of the ninth hut, to the exact manama tree behind which lay the secret path.

But this time there was, tied to the tree with some of that thick palm-leaf braid—a short, strong length of it, with a noose at one end that I'd assumed was for leading hogs—a man. Did he resemble Lawa'eke? I suppose, although I was having difficulty remembering what Lawa'eke looked like and what exactly distinguished him from, say, the chief (although I seemed to recall that he was shorter). This man certainly did not appear to be much older than the chief—perhaps his skin was slightly breadier in appearance, leavened somehow, although that could have been from the heat, or too much water, or lack of it, or a dozen other causes—and he too had his spear and his enormous shrub of hair and, like the chief, a leathery cord around his neck, from which dripped several stony splintery shapes.[45]

We all stood in a half-ring around Lawa'eke's father, watching him sleep. A fly circled above his open mouth, darting closer and closer as if playing a game with itself. Behind me, Tallent was quietly questioning the chief, and the chief was giving brief replies. If the chief was correct, then Lawa'eke's father was around 110 years old.

Back at our station, I considered this. (After some minutes of staring at Lawa'eke's father, there seemed to be nothing else to do—the chief had not wanted to wake him, and indeed, when I reached down to poke him, he said something in a tone even I could not ignore—and so we had gone back to our respective sides of the clearing.) I had asked Fa'a to fetch Mua for me, and he now appeared from within the darkness, pulling Mua by the arm, Mua yawning and staggering, Fa'a's normally unreadable face wearing an expression of great disapproval. Beside me, Tallent sighed. Esme was, thank god, at the river.

"Mua," I began, making my voice stern, even though I needn't have bothered, as he would compliantly answer any question posed to him, "this is very important. You once knew the chief, am I correct?"

He stared at me. "Don't be frightened," I told him. "The chief said you should tell me."

It was as if I had told him he would be eating nothing but Spam

---

[45] Norton does not say so explicitly, but aside from the tattoo, another indication that a villager had undergone the vaka'ina ceremony was his or her sudden ornamentation. Anyone who had reached sixty o'anas thereafter wore some sort of embellishment, whether a necklace or a cape or a length of fabric (of course, these were often lost or abandoned later, when their circumstances changed). This sartorial addition is not thought to hold any special symbolism or significance; rather, it simply seemed to be an easy way for the honored person to remind the rest of the village about his or her new status and remarkable achievement.

for the rest of his life, so quickly did his face transform itself into a mask of joy, and Tallent looked at me once, warningly, before translating his answer: "Did he?"

"Oh yes," I said blithely, unthinkingly cruel. "He said you should tell me everything."

He craned his neck upward then, as if directly behind me he'd see the chief, conferring upon him a blessing, but of course the light was gone by then and the chief was nowhere to be seen.

"We were friends," he said, his face sad again.

"The night you were led into the forest—do you remember that?"

He let out his breath. "Yes. They took us very, very far in and left us. They had to."

"When was this?"

He shook his head. "I don't know."

"It's all right." I thought. "The two people you were taken away with—were they men or women?"

"Men."

"Are they here? Are they part of your group?"

He exhaled again, noisily. I began to discern that he, like the chief, was growing impatient with my questions. But while I had sensed that the chief's impatience was born out of a sort of weariness with the subject—not to mention a wariness—Mua's felt different: he was waiting only for me to ask the correct question, after which he could and would tell me all that I wanted to know and all that he wanted to say. But "No" was all he replied.

This went on and on and on, me asking the (apparently) incorrect questions again and again, Mua giving up little smidges of answers with each, so that it was not until late that night, when I sat down with Tallent and we began to work through his notes, that the cumulative information revealed itself as a real story.

One night—Mua did not know when, as I have stated, but if we were to believe the chief, it would have been around one o'ana ago—Mua and two other men were led into the forest by the hunters. They had all known that this would happen, and indeed, they had been waiting for it. When Mua was younger, he had seen other men and women who were becoming mo'o kua'aus being led into the forest, always late at night, always by the village's best hunters. In fact, almost all of the people in his group, except for Ika'ana, Vi'iu, and Eve, were people he remembered being led away.

They walked into the forest for a night and a day and then another night, until on the second night Mua could feel the air around them become crisper and lighter and knew that it was dawn. Each of them had carried a palm-leaf package heavy with food that they had tied to their spears, and although they could keep the food, they had to surrender their spears to the hunters. They had known that their spears would be taken from them, for a mo'o kua'au is not a full human and therefore has no right to carry a spear. But when the moment came for them to sacrifice them, one of Mua's peers refused.

"He would not," Mua recalled. The hunters commanded the man, and threatened him with their own spears before simply attacking him, trying to seize it from his grasp. They were, after all, the best hunters in the village.

But the man, although becoming a mo'o kua'au, was still strong, and fought back. Years before, Mua said, this man had been one of the people elected to abandon the mo'o kua'aus in the forest. The hunters stabbed at the man, but he dodged their thrusts, springing from place to place, until finally, when even Mua could see him tiring, he turned and sprinted away into the forest, his spear still in his hand.

One of the hunters made to follow him, but he was stopped by another. "Leave him," he said. "He'll only get lost. He won't find his way back." And then, without another word, they left, with their spears and two extras.

"I was very sad," Mua said, "because these were my friends. I had fought with them and hunted with them, and they had all attended my vaka'ina, and now they were leaving me without saying goodbye. But I understood that this was the way it must be."

"Did they eat the opa'ivu'eke at your vaka'ina?" I asked.

He shook his head. "They had many fewer o'anas than I did," he said.

"Have you seen them in the village?" I asked.

"No. They are dead."

He said this with such fierce certainty that we were surprised.

"How do you know?"

He shrugged. "I know," was all he said. And then he began his chant: "He kaka'a, he kaka'a." *I'm tired, I'm tired.*

"Wait," I pleaded with him and with Fa'a, who was already standing, ready to take Mua back to the others. "Mua, what happened to you and the other mo'o kua'aus?"

He sighed. "We walked and walked. We ate the food. Sometimes we caught something to eat, but it was difficult without our spears. One day we came across a stream, very deep, very fast, and stayed there for a long time. There were plants that grew around the trees, and we ate those. The man I was with was becoming more and more of a mo'o kua'au by the day—he forgot and forgot, and I had to watch him like a child. I did more and more of the work. One day I came back from getting us something to eat and I saw that he was dead."

"How did he die?" Tallent asked gently.

"He was in the river," said Mua. He shook his head. "He forgot to ask permission to drink its waters, and the water choked him and he died." We were all quiet.

"So what did you do?" I asked.

"I left."

"And did you ever find the other man, the one who ran from the hunters?"

"No," he said. "But he was becoming more of a mo'o kua'au as well, so I think he is perhaps dead too."

"How would he have died?"

"Maybe he fell? Or maybe he too forgot to ask permission to take a drink and was cursed and killed."

"But how did you meet up with"—I gestured toward the group—"the others?"

"Ah," said Mua. "Well, I walked and walked, and some days I had food and some days I didn't, and then one day I met up with some of them, and then with others, and then we hunted as a group and ate as a group, and fought against the others when we needed to."

I felt Tallent look at me. "Which others?" I asked.

"The others," he said, a bit impatiently. "The others in the forest."

"Hunters?"

"No, no, not hunters—mo'o kua'aus."

"There are others?"

"Of course."

"How many? Where are they? Why don't you speak to them? Why were you fighting? Why—"

"He kaka'a, he kaka'a," he sang, almost mockingly, as if he knew how desperate I was for the answer, and Fa'a stood with a resolute air.

"Wait," I told him, but this time it was Fa'a who shook his head, Fa'a, who never contradicted any of us, and we all fell silent.

"Tallent," I hissed at him as we watched them go, "We need to sort this out right now."

"We need to figure this all out tomorrow," Esme interjected, a little too decisively for my taste (she had unfortunately returned from the creek just in time to insert herself into the proceedings).

"Tomorrow," Tallent agreed. "It's late." And although I hadn't noticed it before—we had quickly grown accustomed to the village's hours—in that moment I noticed that it was indeed very late, and that everything around us had grown so quiet that the only sound aside from our own voices and the nearby snores and grumblings of the dreamers was, as always, the fire, hissing to itself in the still air.

        ❋

I woke the next morning with my mouth dry with hate. My god, was I sick of the dreamers. I hated them, I hated their stingy, teasing way with information, I hated their stupid flat faces, their unintelligent eyes, their clumpy hair, their bulbous figures, their poor memories, their recycled conversation. I hated their village and their island and their weather (the heat was by this point so oppressive that we all spent most of the day sleeping, and I wished I had a tail like the hogs did to flap away the omnipresent flies and gnats and fleas and ticks and beetles and ants and wasps and bees and dragonflies that buzzed round us all day and night, never ceasing, never diminishing), and their fruit that moved and their endless supply of meat (of which we had not been offered one morsel), and their kin with their braying children and grunting women and taciturn men. I hated the way the breeze was so seldom that when it came it felt begrudging, that something that should have been consistent and plentiful had been made into something rare and capricious. I hated that Tallent would not let me walk alone up the path to the open field, that he would not give me an answer as to why I couldn't, that he wouldn't let me take Mua to show me the way. I hated the sloths who acquiesced so meekly to their deaths, their tiny, piteous voices, the way the hogs licked their skins clean as lazily as if they were lapping at ice cream. I hated Tallent, and I hated Esme, and I hated the guides, and I especially hated Mua and the chief, who I suspected could resolve the whole situation for us at once if they chose and yet for some reason—boredom? playfulness? who knew?—had chosen not to. But most of all I hated the smallness of life here, and how even though it was so small, I was unable to solve the mystery whose central question I could still not determine.

And yet here I was, trapped on this island (for I knew Tallent would never leave now, not when he was so close to unraveling something important), and my only way out was to resolve the problem.

I should add that there were other factors that were contributing to what must sound like petulance. I had begun, over the preceding week or so, to notice that the village was abuzz with what seemed like an oppressive amount of sexual activity. Whether this was in fact unusual or I had simply become alert to it I was unable to determine, but each day brought numerous examples of coupling, so many that I, to whom nothing human is foreign, began to feel somewhat assaulted. A walk through the village meant encountering a couple, their slabby bodies smacking against each other, tussling just a few inches from the fire, groaning like the hogs. Something had even been reawakened in the dreamers, and now when I tried to sleep, it was often to a chorus of moans, one evening so loud that I finally roused myself to investigate: there they were, their hideous loose flesh chafing against their partners', clawing and petting, their movements inexpert and inelegant. My presence, however, did not deter them in the least, and when, in a moment of desperation, I tossed a manama into their midst to startle them into silence, there was only the slightest of pauses before they resumed their activities, and I heard, faintly, the manama squish into the earth under the weight of someone's back.

Returning to my mat, however, I noticed something else amiss: both Tallent and Esme were gone. Their mats were there, but they were not. "Esme?" I called softly. "Tallent?" But no one answered.

My mind immediately filled with the worst of thoughts. I saw

Esme pressed against a tree, Tallent embracing her, her ugly mouth open like a greedy carp's, the messy excessiveness of her body—her sprawling hips, her bulging stomach, her puckered, dimpling thighs, her frizzed dandelion head of hair—a repulsive foil to the trim discipline of his own form.

I was, I am sorry to say, in a torment. Not knowing was unbearable, but so was knowing. Nevertheless, I found myself making concentric rings around the village, heading deeper into the forest with each lap, calling out their names in a low voice with every turn. Where could they have gone? I even, on the seventh lap, attempted to follow the path behind the ninth hut as far as I could, until it grew increasingly faint under a bloom of moss and I was forced to retreat downhill. The panic of discovering them was beginning to give way to new concerns. Where could they have gone, in our circumscribed world, that I could not find them? Was this a regular occurrence? And—this thought came to me last but was the most alarming— did not their disappearance mean that I was alone, with only Fa'a with whom to speak some semblance of English, and the dreamers my responsibility?

It was while I was contemplating these thoughts (only later would I realize that I had been running, my arms stretched in front of me like a zombie's to feel for unseen trees) that I encountered the boy. At this point I was quite deep into the forest, maybe nine rings or so in, and I first mistook him for a boar. He was turned away from me, after all, and standing near a tree, and when my fingers first touched his rough bundle of hair, I mistook it for a hide, giving a little shout of fear and surprise when I did.

He gave a shout as well, but I think it was just to echo mine, for when I knelt down beside him—there was a crack in the canopy above us, and a little moonlight leaked through, enough for me to see the outlines of his features—he seemed calm, and his eyes met mine without fear or suspicion.

It did not take me long to identify him as the boy from the first a'ina'ina. He was, as I have said, an exceptionally beautiful boy, slim and well assembled, with unusually good posture, although what was most striking about him was the steadiness of his gaze, which I could feel upon me, even if I could barely see it in the poor light.

But it was disconcerting to come across him here, so deep in the forest, holding himself so still, almost as if he had been waiting for me to find him, although that of course would have been impossible.

"What are you doing here?" I asked him gently, although he could not understand me and so said nothing.

"What is your name?" But still, naturally, there was no response.

I pointed to myself. "Norton." I pointed to him: *And you?* But he only cocked his head, the way the chief had, before righting it and looking at me again.

"It's late," I told him. "Shouldn't you be at home?"

But then, before I could keep speaking, he placed one of his hands on the side of my face. It was such a strange gesture, so shockingly intimate and adult—pitying, wise, maternal, even—that I found myself very close to tears. It seemed in that moment as if he were offering me a sympathy I had not even known I had been craving, but feeling his hot, dry palm on my cheek—a boy's palm, when I later examined it, sticky and faintly dirty and scuffed with small cuts, but underneath soft and somehow innocent—I felt the unhappiness and loneliness of the past few days, the past four months, the past twenty-five years, press upon me like a great, bony mass.

We stayed in that position for what felt like a long period, me in my painful crouch, he before me, my cheek tipped now into his hand. Above us the moon glided behind a cloud, and it was then, in the absence of light, that he reached down and lifted my hand and placed it solemnly on his genitals.

I immediately removed it. By now the darkness was so complete that the only part of him I could see were his eyes (and he mine), and in them I saw nothing that one might expect: nothing keen or conniving, nothing eager or lascivious, nothing hungry or fevered. I do not know how to explain it better; I do not wish to be sentimental and say that they had a wisdom, or any sort of special intelligence, but I do think it fair to say that they did contain, at the very least, a kind of gravity.

He took my hand again, very gently, like a seducer, and began to move it across his body. Once again I pulled it away, and once again he patiently replaced it.

*I am being bewitched*, I thought as we went back and forth, my hand now feeling almost disconnected from my body, a floating white bird moving on its own accord through the darkness. The boy shifted position then, to lie down against the base of the tree, and tugged at my other hand.

*Oh, Tallent*, I thought. *Oh, Esme, save me. I am being held captive. I am being spellbound.* I may even have said this aloud. But they didn't come, of course, and the forest remained quiet, the only sound the boy's breath, his face blurring in and out of focus as the moon revealed and concealed itself in an endless flirtation with some unseen lover.

## IV.

Something had been troubling me about my conversations with Mua, particularly my most recent one. *Why* was he a mo'o kua'au? What made him one? Yes, he was forgetful, and yes, he perseverated, and yes, he could quite often be very dull (I have not recounted here the numerous boring and repetitive conversations I had with Mua over these months), and yes, his short-term memory was very poor indeed (the day after our hike to see the opa'ivu'ekes, I asked him a question about it, and he had no memory of our trip; indeed, my insistence made him frightened and anxious), but his long-term memory was excellent, and his attention span, while by no means admirable, was no shorter than that of a child. Certainly all of these things combined to become very annoying, but was it really so bad? Was it worth abandoning someone simply because he was forgetful and repetitive?

I had been working on a list of the dreamers' approximate ages, and now I separated them into two smaller lists: one group that was apparently known to the village, the other that apparently was not.

| Known | Unknown |
|---|---|
| Mua (appx 104 years) | Eve (?) |
| Vanu (Mua's father; appx 131 years) | Vi'iu (?) |
| Ivaiva and Va'ana (sisters; appx 133 years) | Ika'ana (appx 176 years) |
| Ukavi (appx 108–109 years) | |

Except for Lawa'eke's father, the chief and Lawa'eke were the oldest people in the village. We had, in a subsequent conversation, gotten both of them to confirm unambiguously that they knew Mua,

Vanu, Ivaiva, Va'ana, and Ukavi and that they remembered them being taken into the forest. But as hard as we tried, we could not get them to recognize Eve, Vi'iu, or Ika'ana. Esme, being Esme, attributed their ignorance to willfulness. "Of *course* they know them," she insisted. She was, however, unable to explain what benefit to them there might be from denying knowledge of the others. "They have their reasons," she'd say—she saw conspiracy even in this simplest of civilizations, a civilization so guileless that its people didn't even bother to conceal the fact that they abandoned their elders once they began to stray from the obscure behavioral strictures that governed their society.

I, however, thought there was a much easier explanation: surely the reason that the three dreamers remained unknown to Lawa'eke and the chief was that they were so old they had been exiled when the two men were very young, too young to remember? This absolutely made sense in Ika'ana's case: if he was 176 now and he had begun becoming a mo'o kua'au at, say, 110, he would have been escorted away well before either of them had even been born.

That left the mystery of both Vi'iu and Eve. Vi'iu, I suspected, was younger than Ika'ana, though perhaps not by much. He had not, it seemed, been alive during Ka Weha, for example, but when Ika'ana spoke of it, he nodded wisely, in the way of someone who had heard about the event so often that he had almost forgotten that he had not experienced it. But he was very impaired, there was no doubt of that: I remembered how poorly he had performed on the basic neurological tests I had given him, how he was unable to identify any of the objects I had placed before him, how his attention drifted the moment I began to speak to him.

Last and least, then, there was Eve, who was her own special problem. Even in the company of the dreamers, she remained singular. There was so much she could not do! She could not speak, she did not listen, she could not interact with the others, she was without shame or manners or niceties or logic. Often when I regarded her from a distance, I felt as if I were watching something inanimate that had been unlawfully given breath—she staggered about and yelped when she felt like it, and crammed things into her mouth, and scrutinized the inconsequential, and ignored the fascinating. With her coloring and lumpy shape, she occasionally resembled nothing so much as a sweet potato, one set upon two legs and plopped amid us. It was not a life, but that she breathed and sighed and ate.

And then suddenly I realized: this was what being a mo'o kua'au must be. *This* was what they were afraid of; *this* was the end of the story. I flipped back in my notebook, looking for Tallent's definition of a mo'o kua'au, which I had written down after our conversation all those months ago—"all normal in appearance, but all incapable of making meaningful conversation. All they could do was jitter and babble and laugh at nothing, the neighing laughter of the brainless"—and knew: Eve was a fully transformed mo'o kua'au. She was what the others would become. All it took, it occurred to me, was time.

I flew back toward our camp. "Lawa'eke's father!" I screamed as I ran. All we had to do now was ask Lawa'eke's father to identify Ika'ana and Vi'iu, who would surely have been alive and been present in the village at the same time. We would also ask him to identify Eve; if he couldn't, it would confirm what I suspected—that Eve was so old that not even Ika'ana and Vi'iu knew her from the village. That would make her well over two hundred years old.

"Lawa'eke's father!" I shouted at Tallent, who was, with Fa'a, leading some of the dreamers back from the stream. When he saw me, he passed them to Fa'a and started walking toward me.

"Tallent," I gasped; I could feel myself grinning. "We need to talk to Lawa'eke's father *right now*."

He may have said my name, but I was talking too fast, and he stopped to listen to me and my theories, which I knew, knew for certain, were correct—I had never been more certain of anything, it seemed, and the feeling was exhilarating. Exhilarating and also somehow completely natural, as if such a feeling were my birthright. *This*, I caught myself thinking, was what my life should be like—*this* sensation, *this* breathless excitement.

"Norton," said Tallent finally, when I was at last able to calm myself, "Lawa'eke's father is gone. They took him into the forest last night."

I was of course devastated. I railed away at Tallent, demanding that he retrieve for me the chief (so I could what? Shout at him? Rebuke him?) or the hunters who had taken him (who had yet to return), and that we ask to borrow one of the hogs to sniff a path toward Lawa'eke's father (I had no idea if hogs were even capable of doing this). I was also struck by the unfairness of the entire situation. Here we were in a place where nothing—sometimes almost literally nothing—happened for days and days, and then, exactly when I needed things to remain the same, they suddenly changed.

But finally he was able to convince me that there was nothing to be done. "But we can still test your theory," he said sensibly (not that I was in any mood to be sensible). "If what you're saying is correct, Ika'ana should remember Eve."

"Why?" I asked sullenly.

"Because she can't be so old that she'd have left before Ika'ana was even born," he said. "That would make her, what? Almost three hundred years old? That's impossible."

He was so grave, so certain, that I wanted to laugh. Ah, how quickly we had grown accustomed to this absurdity, this world in which 300 years was an impossibility but 176 was not! Who knew—perhaps 300 years was not impossible at all. Perhaps Eve was 300, 400, 500, 1,000 years old. Perhaps she had been exiled long before Ka Weha, long before Ika'ana had been born, so long ago that monstrous opa'ivu'ekes roamed the land by the thousands, so long ago that the trees around us had been saplings, tender and girlish, and from where we stood, she would have been able to see in every direction the blue sky and the blue sea, stretching before her in endless planes.

As it turned out, however, Tallent was right: Ika'ana *did* remember Eve. She had been exiled when he was a young boy, after Ka Weha (when he was five o'anas) but shortly before, he thought, his a'ina'ina. He didn't know how old she was when she was taken, but Tallent and I had determined, based on the others, that people began exhibiting symptoms of mo'o kua'au-ness anywhere between, say, 90 and 105. Even if Eve had experienced an early onset, it would still make her today no younger than 250. How, I wanted to ask Tallent, was *that* possible?

She had had children, but none of them, according to Ika'ana, had lived to sixty o'anas, and neither had her husband. She had had grandchildren as well, but none of them had lived as long as their grandmother either. In the end there was only Eve, living in the forest alone for more than a century, trudging up and down its hills, eating her grubs and manama fruits and whatever else she could find, with only herself for comfort, her whole world at once oppressively narrow and oppressively huge. The forest was all colonies of like creatures: the families of vuakas, the trees dangling their bunches of manama fruits, the sloths and the spiders and the copses of orchids each with their companions. And then there would be Eve, an explorer searching for nothing, adrift in a sea without any memory of what she had once sought or of what she wished to return to.

"I was surprised when she found us," murmured Ika'ana, his eyes, as usual, focusing on nothing. "I had not thought of her in many years. Many, many years. But then I saw her, and I thought, *Oh, it is you.* And it was."

"Ika'ana," I said, struggling to keep the anger from my voice, because I knew it was unfair, and not productive anyway, "why did you not tell us this before?"

Then he did look at me. "You never asked," he said.

※

I may not have been discovering everything I needed to at the pace I had hoped, but (as I tried to reassure myself) each new revelation did lead to the next question I needed to answer. I now had some notion of how old Eve was and what a mo'o kua'au was. Further questioning of Ika'ana had revealed that Eve had not been born a mute, which meant that her silence, her antisocial behavior, were a result of brain damage or deterioration or lack of social interaction, not a congenital condition.

A theory was beginning to shape itself, a theory that now seems so obvious that I am embarrassed to call it a theory at all. I was working from the assumption that the opa'ivu'eke caused some sort of . . . what? A disease? A condition? A state that led to an unnaturally long life—an immortal life. But it was a parody of immortality, because while the afflicted did in fact remain physically frozen at the age at which she had eaten the turtle, her mind did not. Bit by bit, it disintegrated—first the memory, then the social nuances, then the senses, and then finally speech—until all that was left was the body. The mind was gone, worn down by the years, its fissures and byways exhausted by having to perform for far more decades than it was organically equipped to do. I had a fanciful vision of Eve's brain on its stem as a salt lick, its surfaces lapped clean and smooth into a pencil nub. Surely there must be an end to this life, for there is an end to every life. But it would not, it seemed, be from simple old age; it would end from disease, or accident, or murder.

It is a strange feeling to revisit this revelation as a seventy-four-year-old. When one is a twenty-five-year-old, such concepts can be experienced only academically. Age, then, is not something that can be understood; it is a preoccupation of the old, and the old is anyone older than oneself. It is a subject that has no relevance, a subject that seems a bore, an indulgence and lament of the weak-minded and feeble and querulous. As I have grown first older and now old, however, I have contemplated the dreamers' fate more and more, and today I see it very clearly for what it is—a curse. There is a point—for me, it arrived perhaps a few years ago—when, without even realizing it, you switch over from craving more life to being resigned to its end. It happens so abruptly that you cannot help but recall the moment itself, and yet so gently that it is as if it comes to you in a dream.

Back then, however, my thinking was uncluttered by such nuance, and I knew the two things I needed to do next, both of which were, unfortunately, highly complicated. The first thing was to get one of us—me or Tallent—to eat some of the opa'ivu'eke. This was not ideal, of course—I knew in advance what a production it would be and what a risk it presented—but it was necessary if I was to establish the opa'ivu'eke's central role in this affliction. For it was possible (unlikely, but possible) that the opa'ivu'eke was less to blame than I supposed; perhaps it was a genetic misfiring particular to the Ivu'ivuans—if they somehow were able to pass a certain threshold of age, they were guaranteed something close to eternal life. The second and more important thing I needed to do was to get at least two of the dreamers off the island and back to a proper lab so I could run tests and do some bloodwork. I had no idea how to begin doing this. But without that step, we—I—had wasted more than five months, which seemed an eternity (the irony of this thinking did not escape me). Without conclusive bloodwork, I was left with nothing more than a series of fairy tales, and I had never been interested in fictions.

I began with the slightly less difficult operation: securing an opa'ivu'eke for future experiments. Tallent and Esme were, predictably, horrified by my plan. A long and at times nasty debate began, in which Tallent, at least, recognized the purpose and indeed necessity of what I was asking but refused to participate on principle, which I found a rather weak and lazy excuse. Esme, however, refused even to acknowledge that such an action was the next logical step. I screamed at them for being intellectual cowards and sentimentalists. She screamed back that I was a monster, coldhearted and disrespectful, and that I was on the verge of ruining all that she and Tallent were trying to accomplish.

"What *are* you trying to accomplish, Esme?" I screeched back at her. "Recording the details of people's shit is hardly what I'd consider useful work." We were now shouting so loudly that a number of the villagers had ventured to the border of their property and were watching us with interest and some amusement, pointing back and forth among us and whispering and snickering to one another. Tallent made attempts to calm us both, but it was too late. In retrospect, it was somewhat ignominious.

"How dare you belittle me! I want to help them!"

"You don't want to help them at all! If you did, you'd do what's necessary!"

"*You* don't want to help them! To you they're nothing more than insects, and you don't care what you destroy in the process!"

"I didn't even want to come! I came because you needed me!"

"I never wanted you to come!"

Yes, the argument had soon reached those depths, and we would have gone deeper still had not Tallent—for the first time since I'd met him, truly furious—physically inserted himself between us. "Both of you are behaving reprehensibly," he said, and his voice was cold. "Esme, go take the dreamers to the river and get them something to drink. Norton"—he glared at me, and I realized suddenly how little he asked me to do with the dreamers, but instead of being relieved, I was wounded; did he too not trust me with them?—"go take a walk. Both of you stop this outrageous behavior at once."

"But what about the opa'ivu'eke?" I whispered, hating the whine, the pleading, in my voice.

"Norton," said Tallent, and he said my name as if he had spoken an entire page, "I understand why you want to carry out this . . . this . . . experiment. Wait," he said, raising his hand as I was about to interrupt. "But I'm afraid it's just not going to be possible. It's not possible logistically, and furthermore, it's simply not advisable. May I remind you that we are guests here? That we are here by the chief's grace? Don't forget this, Norton. Don't forget that those spears are used not only for killing sloths and spearing vuakas."

I was silent, and he was silent too, the two of us staring at each other.

"Promise me," he said, his voice regaining its plush tones, its bottomless calm. "Promise me you won't defy me."

"I won't," I mumbled.

"Norton," he began, and then stopped until I looked at him. "I'm warning you. There are ways we can test your theory, but this is not one of them."

"I understand you, Tallent," I said, but I knew he was wrong. There was no other way to test my theory. And if he refused to help me, I would have to do so on my own.

There was a certain brief period every night when the village seemed to pause in its activities, an hour or two during which the daytime hunters overlapped in sleep with the nighttime hunters, and the fire finally burned low, and the only sounds were the myriad cracks and croaks of the myriad unseen creatures who crept through the woods in the gloom.

It had been a very tense evening, spent first in a silent meal with Tallent and Esme, which was followed by a silent collective journal-writing period and which concluded with a silent unfurling of our mats. Later I would ask myself why I decided I needed to act so quickly, and I suppose there was something rash about it, though I would also argue that I needed to act quickly—both before I lost my nerve and before Tallent realized the inevitability of my actions.

Once I was certain that the villagers were all asleep—their snores seemed to reverberate through the trees—I crept over to Mua. I had stolen Tallent's flashlight from his bag while he was helping bathe the dreamers, though I was determined to use it as little as possible. I had to use it now, however, to find Mua; the group of them slept in a muddle, a jumble of limbs and hair that always looked and smelled faintly unwashed despite their daily ablutions.

I found him lying near Ika'ana, his head resting on Vi'iu's back, one arm flung out over Ivaiva's breasts. Slowly I knelt and shook him awake.

"Mua," I whispered when he at last woke with a grunt, struggling up through layers of sleep. "I need your help." And then I remembered that he could not speak English.

I grabbed a stick and drew the sign of the opa'ivu'eke in the dirt beside us—the circle bisected with the line—and then pointed to myself. "Opa'ivu'eke," I said, to clarify. "Vaka'ina," and then pointed again at myself.

"Ah," he said, and clambered to a sitting position.

One of the useful things about the dreamers' impaired state, I reflected, was how little explication they demanded. Even if we had been able to communicate, Mua would not have asked me why I was waking him so late at night to fetch the opa'ivu'eke, or why I needed it right now. He was becoming a set of reactions born from years of conditioning, and while I could see quite clearly how an abandonment of logic could be a dangerous thing, at the time I was glad for it.

Around the village we walked, past the sighing hogs, past the low purrs and grumbles of the men and women and children, heading toward and then beyond the ninth hut, back into the jungle, which seemed to swallow Mua in a single greedy gulp. There was no light, and for a minute I was unable to move, so seized was I by a cold, irrational fear; I even forgot my flashlight. And then there was Mua tiptoeing back into view to find me, and saying something I could not understand, again and again. I realized then that it was a chant, two phrases that he repeated in a loop, until after a while they ceased to sound like words and became as meaningless as drumbeats, and I felt myself shuffling my feet in pace to its rhythm.

It had been some time, it seemed, since I had walked with such purpose or so far into the jungle, and where I had once seen it as something vital and teeming with busyness, with lives, it now seemed to me dead, a vast graveyard of trees, empty of anything else imaginable. I cannot say why I felt this exactly, other than that it seemed I had already discovered the greatest of its mysteries and anything else it may have yielded would have been thin and meager in comparison.

I followed Mua's voice as he turned right, and abruptly we were in a clearing, a small plateau high above the village; above us was the rest of Ivu'ivu, its towering, impregnable peak. Behind us was the forest, dark and quiet, and before us was a blank drop, the side of the island whooshing down toward an ocean we could not see. I began to walk, hypnotized, closer to the edge, until Mua reached out an arm to stop me. "Ea," he told me—*look*—and I lifted my eyes; there, in front of and above and to either side of me, was the sky, such an unbelievable, fathomless black, its surface scudded with smears of stars, so large and bright that I could see their hard glitter, could feel the icy clouds of dust that surrounded them. There were so many of them that the sky seemed more light than dark, more full than empty.

It had been so long since I had seen the stars, and looking at them, at the great vastness of the sky curved above me like an embrace, I thought of Owen and wondered where he was. Still in Connecticut? Or had he gone somewhere else, as he occasionally threatened to do? And it was then that I found myself crying, and although I tried not to make a noise, it was somehow comforting, as was that distinctive, almost-forgotten taste of tears, as salty and hot as blood in my mouth.

Mua seemed not to be bothered by my tears, and we stood there for a while longer. Above us the stars winked and shone. Then he made a grunt, and we began walking again.

For a moment I was perplexed—had we stopped on this plateau on our first visit to see the opa'ivu'ekes?—and then, abruptly, frightened: where was Mua leading me? But when I turned back and saw the forest, so blackly impenetrable, I knew I had no choice but to follow him.

By the time we reached the final clearing, I was so anxious I was shaking. In the darkness loomed monsters and ghosts, and in what I could not see I saw everything I had ever feared. But then, "Opa'ivu'eke," Mua intoned solemnly, and there before me was the lake, the turtles' air bubbles skimming the surface like pearls. He gestured to the lake with one hand and then stepped back to watch.

For the first time I began to feel that my plan had perhaps not been as well considered as it might have been. While the village had been eating, I had managed to sneak into the palm-storage hut and steal a large woven net, which I had carried uphill draped over my shoulders like a cloak. But as I approached the lake, it occurred to me that I had no idea whether this would be adequate to snare an opa'ivu'eke. Were they fast swimmers? Would they try to bite me? Had there been a weapon I could have stolen easily, I would have, but as it happened, there hadn't, and so I had had to settle for the net. I looked back to Mua as if for advice, but he merely crossed his arms and gazed off into the distance, as if what I was undertaking were a private event and one he had no right to witness.

I need not have worried, however. As I approached the lake's edge, the opa'ivu'ekes seemed to notice me, and as a single unit paddled slowly toward me, their limbs cleaving the water so softly that they sent only the gentlest ruffle across the still surface. Their trust made my mission both easier and more difficult, and as I stood there contemplating which of them to take, I had to unexpectedly and sternly remind myself of the necessity of what I was about to do.

I chose one of the largest of the turtles; I assumed that its size meant it was among the elders of the lot, and I wanted to give the young ones a chance at a long life. All I had to do, it turned out, was reach into the water—cool and so clear that I could see the moon gliding along its mucky bottom—and heft it out. He was quite heavy, and a bit slimy, but not difficult to handle, and the other opa'ivu'ekes reassembled themselves at once to fill the space left by his absence, watching me with their large eyes. Unusually for a turtle, he did not burrow back into his carapace upon human contact but instead waggled his legs a bit, rotating his head, so that it felt like I was holding a large anteater, something shelled and armored but babylike in its defenselessness.

Staggering, I carried the turtle over to the edge of the forest, far enough away from the lake that his companions would not be able to see what I was doing. I was tired from the walk uphill and from the turtle's weight, and I sat down beside him, resting my hand on the back of his shell, and he closed his yellow eyes as if in pleasure, as if I were petting him. For a minute we rested, both of us savoring the air, the hushing of the trees, and the simple, stupid fact of being alive.

Then it was time. I had a penknife in my pocket (also stolen from Tallent) and a roll of large palm leaves (stolen from the palm hut). My plan was to cut away as much meat from the opa'ivu'eke as possible (I didn't know if I would have the strength or, frankly, the nerve to lift away its shell), wrap the pieces in palm leaves, pack them into the net bag, and bury the carapace under some of the forest decay. I'd take everything back downhill and dry the meat in the branches of my tree. I'd eat some myself and record any deleterious effects; the rest I'd take back with me to the States so I could have it more thoroughly tested.

A breeze licked its way between the trees, and as the opa'ivu'eke stretched his neck forward to partake in it, I flicked open the blade and brought it down on his neck. I thought it would be an easy cut, like slicing through warm butter, but his skin was much tougher and more webbed than I had expected, and in the end I had to saw away at it, so that his head separated from his throat by degrees, first nodding to one side, then dangling to the other, until only a last flap of particularly stubborn skin united the two and I had to work the blade between its grooves, flicking it upward until the skin separated with a series of wet, elastic slaps. Except for a sort of soft, slow sigh, like a tire deflating, he made no sound, but his eyes remained open, their pupils shrinking into the irises like splashes of ink in water.

So intently was I concentrating on the laborious work of detaching the turtle's hind leg that I mistook the shout for Mua's and called back (pointlessly, of course) that I was busy and he had to wait. But when I heard him running across the grass toward me, shouting incomprehensibly all the way, I was forced to stop my task and look up, whereupon I saw that it was not Mua racing in my direction but Fa'a.

Stupidly, my first reaction was happiness. Fa'a was here! I had always felt safer around him, and had even, I realized, grown to like him, despite his carefully maintained inscrutability, which did little to conceal the fact that he was growing more disenchanted with our expedition by the day. But I felt—romantically, perhaps—that in my most sorrowful or conflicted moments, Fa'a had been there beside me, as steady and reliable as a tree. I had a vision of him as a shepherd, someone who stood sentry for all of us as we slept or hunted, someone whose eyes scanned the landscape so we would not have to, someone who was there to witness every remarkable event. As the other guides had lost interest and fallen away, bit by bit—they were still among our number, of course, but seemed to spend increasing amounts of the day hunting for vuakas (I was amazed and slightly repulsed by their apparently insatiable appetite for them) and gathering various fruits and seeds and strange growths from the forest floor—Fa'a was always there. Uva and Tu continued to perform their duties with the dreamers, but in a somewhat rote fashion: at the stream, they stood and spoke and laughed with one another while the more impaired of their charges splashed their hands or feet uselessly in the water, unsure of what they had been taken there to do. But when it was Fa'a's turn, he scooped handsful of water over their backs and shook out their brushy hair and murmured back at them when they sighed with contentment. Certainly I respected him; perhaps I even admired him.

But I was very quickly made to adjust my reaction once I saw Fa'a's face and recognized the tenor of his voice. He was shouting, truly shouting, one hand playing worryingly over his spear, the other pointing to the dead opa'ivu'eke, its head—its eyes still open— arranged decorously in the middle of the largest palm leaf, waiting to be wrapped like a gift. He was so angry that his eyes were bulging, and bits of foam, as white as stars, sailed forth from his mouth, and I found myself wanting to laugh.

It was only then that I recalled how reverentially he had chanted when we had encountered the opa'ivu'ekes the last time, and with what awe he had watched the vaka'ina, and so there seemed to be little to do but let him have his rant. I had felt certain Fa'a would never touch me, but suddenly—and I will never know his intentions—he raised his arm with the spear: not threateningly, I will admit, nor even in my direction, but the mere act of his wielding a weapon alarmed me, and I instinctively lifted the turtle's corpse before me, his rounded shell a shield, and thrust it toward Fa'a just at the moment he was leaning in my direction. And it was then, as I was wriggling the turtle in front of me, cowering behind it, that I heard

Fa'a emit a shriek. I looked over the top of the carapace and saw that I had brushed Fa'a's outstretched hand with one of the turtle's dangling forelegs, and in that moment I heard his shouts become keens, and he dropped to his knees on the ground, holding his affected hand before him and wailing.

Had I been a less sensitive person, I surely would have succumbed to laughter. But that was only initially, and soon, as I watched Fa'a bent on the ground, his right hand—his spear-carrying hand—stretched toward the turtle as if in a sacrifice, that I began to sense the sincerity of his despair. His keening quieted to weeping and then to nothing at all, just a constant juddering of his shoulders and back, his face turned to the dirt, his spear abandoned at his side. For once I was glad not to speak U'ivuan, for he believed he was now doomed to become a mo'o kua'au, or that he had doomed someone in his family to it, and nothing I could have said would ever have been able to convince him of the contrary. And so I watched him for a while, in fascination and sympathy, until finally there was nothing left to do but continue my tedious work, bundling the flaccid pieces of the opa'ivu'eke in the satiny palm leaves, the ground beneath me black with its blood.

*

Our trip down was muted and hurried, and by the time I had sent Mua and a stunned, staggering Fa'a back to the group and tied my six packets of turtle flesh to the highest branches of my tree, the air was beginning to lighten and the first of the morning birds were starting to chatter.

We had all, it seemed, resolved to pretend: Tallent that we had not fought, Fa'a that he had not been cursed, I that I had not done what I had needed to without permission or encouragement. Throughout the day I would intermittently be struck by the courage and resolve I had exhibited the previous night, as well as by my resourcefulness, although there was no one with whom I could share my story. I passed Fa'a once—I was on my way to the creek for water; he was just returning—but as I walked toward him he turned away, and I saw the planes of his face slide and lock into one another in an expression of utter unreadability that I never saw him without after that day. I knew then that he would never reveal to the others what he had witnessed that night; to do so would mean having to confront his own stain, his own ruination.

Only Mua seemed to have forgotten everything of our night-time adventure. That afternoon I happened to see Fa'a, both hands wrapped around his spear, his chin propped on its blunt end, staring at him—though whether with envy or pity, I could not say.

Earlier I had sneaked over to my tree and retrieved the packages, and then dug into the ground as deeply as I could, the soft, floury earth as rich and moist as cake, before placing the packages in the hole and covering them with dirt. One, however, I set aside and unwrapped. For several minutes I remained there in a crouch, preparing myself to gag down the wet red flesh of one of the opa'ivu'eke's feet. This, I reminded myself, was why I had disobeyed Tallent and gone to the lake: to taste and swallow, to prove to myself that there was nothing to fear. But instead I found myself paralyzed with my own ambivalence. Not to eat it was to admit that I was frightened, that the impossible was possible after all. And oh, I wanted it to be true, I wanted to be correct, I wanted to know that my discovery was real. And yet I also *didn't* want it to be true—I didn't want everything I had always thought upended, to have certainties and practicalities tossed away like molding fruits. To eat the turtle would be to admit that I was wrong, but it would also be to admit that the world I knew would continue as it had, unruffled and unchanged, its laws unchallenged and unassaulted.

But I couldn't do it. In the decades after, I would recall this moment as if it were a hallucination and remember how close I had come to joining the ranks of the dreamers. What if I had not rewrapped the foot and placed it among the others but had instead allowed my tongue to touch its surface, if I had allowed myself to succumb to the tide-pull illogic of that strange and haunted evening?

That night my dreams were wild and diverse, the ending of one leaking into the beginning of the next. I dreamed I was wandering through the forest, making our uphill climb to the village, and that all the trees had become Ivu'ivuans, their babble filling the woods like birdcall, their feet bleeding into the trees' roots and their hair weaving itself into branches. I dreamed that the chief and I were riding sidesaddle atop a car-sized opa'ivu'eke, who trudged through a dried mudflat landscape denuded of all trees, but faint on the horizon, against a plum-colored sky, was a miniature city of parched cement. I dreamed that I was sitting at a table in a wooden house where the ceiling was trussed with thick-grooved pieces of lumber, with a metal platter before me on which sat a strange pink creature, four-legged and with saggy pooling flesh, which I came to realize was a carapaceless opa'ivu'eke. Across from me was Fa'a, dressed in a pale button-down shirt, his hair trimmed short around his ears, his hand holding out to me a knife and fork, and as I came to understand that I would have to eat the turtle, it twitched its head and opened its eyes and mouth, and its mouth, when it opened it, was the boy's mouth, with his little jagged teeth and his small, bright tongue.

I woke then, to the forest unremarkable around me, and with Esme and Tallent beside me as they should be, and still on Ivu'ivu, in the midst of one of its dense black nights. Nothing around me had changed.

The next morning, Tallent announced that we were leaving.

## V.

It made sense, I knew, and it was inevitable. I had been told that we were to be there for at least four months, or at least some finite amount of time. But still the news came as a shock. First, despite all appearances, there really had been something of a plan all along, and even up here in the village, where governments and technology and clothes and books and schools and hospitals had no place, we were not free from its tentacles. Then there was the shock of time itself, its sudden reappearance and relevance in our lives. Here, time twirled itself into long, spiraling whorls, defying biology and evolution; not even the human body respected it. And yet the definition of time we had to obey was the one determined in the part of the world where people consulted clocks and made and kept appointments, in which time was measured in increments smaller than seasons. It was unsettling to remember that that world existed still, and that as foreign as it was, it was that world that still commanded us, that made our decisions and determined our arrivals and departures. I had the sudden fanciful thought that perhaps the reason the villagers lived so long was that no one had ever thought to tell them they couldn't.

That last week was very crowded: there were final interviews to conduct, final measurements to take, final physical evaluations to make, final drawings of the village to be rendered, final head counts and numbering of the stores in the meat hut, the dried-goods hut, the palm-leaf hut to do. Unpacking my rucksack late at night to make room for the packets of opa'ivu'eke meat—I had managed to cadge some salt from Uva and had cured the parts, which I would pack just before we left—I came across the two dozen needles nestled in their cotton blanketing, and with their smooth, cold glass-and-metal surfaces they felt somehow like curiosities, as if the village were the more advanced culture and these were artifacts, purpose unknown, from some primordial past. I had by that point almost nothing left in my bag; my clothes I had for the most part given away to the village women, who stared perplexed at my jacket and button-down shirts until I demonstrated how they might be ripped and their sections used to bind two pieces of palm rope together, for example, or a sloth's legs to a spear, and the microscope had broken early in our journey, and more recently so too had the thermometer, with whose spooky silver beads of mercury the village children had played, coating them with a powdery fluff of dirt and rolling them into one another until I had collected and removed them.

It had occurred to me belatedly that Sereny must not have thought very much of me at all. The entire medical school, in fact, must not have thought much of me. Had I even been requested? Or had they convinced Tallent or whoever had ill-advisedly given him the funds for this expedition to let me come along? Had I even been wanted? The brief, as I understood it, was that Tallent would search for his mythical lost tribe, and he had, however improbably, found it. But who would have thought that the greater discovery would be mine, and that it would be what it was? There had been no knowing in advance that a scientist would be needed; my presence was the consequence not of luck but of the school trying to get rid of one of its least promising students by sending him off on an absurd mission that was doomed to failure. I was humiliated for not having seen it before, and humiliated that I should have been such a pawn in such a poorly played game. And yet despite this unpleasant revelation, I was determined not to think like Smythe—*I'll show them; I'll prove them wrong*—although I also could not help but project my thoughts into the future, for I knew with certainty that I had found something spectacular, something bound to change science and society forever. I had found nothing less than immortality itself. It sounded so grand to say aloud (and so I didn't), but its import could not be ignored, even with its hovering cloud of fairy dust.

(What did *you* do, Fitch and Brassard? *We injected mice with viruses.* Why, what did *you* do? *I discovered a group of people who never die.*)

It was now critical that I convince Tallent to let us take a few of the dreamers off the island, and to my surprise, he acquiesced without much of an argument. Naturally there was a longish lecture about the dangers of removing native peoples from their context and the extreme unlikelihood that they would ever be able to assimilate back into their society, but his arguments seemed a bit wan, not to mention absurd. Soon, if I was correct, they would have no conception at all of their context anyway, and their society had already rejected them, so why shouldn't we remove them?

"Well," he said at last, lamely, "we should at least ask the permission of the chief."

Not surprisingly, the chief did not seem to care. He even seemed slightly pleased with our proposal, although as I have said, he was quite unemotive in general. And why should he not have been pleased? We were volunteering to take away four useless mo'o kua'aus, and with them gone, there would be four fewer people looking for vuakas and eating manamas, four fewer people who might someday, in their endless perambulations, happen once again upon the village.

Then, "What about the others?" the chief asked.

"What do you mean?" Tallent replied.

"They cannot stay here," the chief said.

Tallent opened his mouth and shut it. There was nothing for him to do. "We will take them away," he said, and the chief nodded.

Then he turned and left. I don't know why—movies, perhaps, or fables—but I had thought there might be some longer leave-taking, an exchange of gifts or perhaps a ceremony, especially given the culture's love of them. But there was none of those things. Just the chief's back receding from us and his hog's hooves scuffing up little bursts of dust behind him. It occurred to me then that there was no ritual for leave-taking because there were no visitors: no one ever arrived, and no one—except the mo'o kua'aus—ever left.

Then I remembered something. "Wait," I told Tallent, "get him back here for a moment," and Tallent called out to the chief, who turned and walked back to us with great reluctance.

"Ke," he said flatly. *What?*

"Ask him," I instructed Tallent, "if he's ever known of anyone who has celebrated his vaka'ina who *hasn't* become a mo'o kua'au?"

He didn't want to answer, I could tell. It wasn't only because he was exhausted by the topic; it was because his answer would be an admission of his own fate. Until this moment he had been able to avoid the question, to imagine—as surely every other sixty-year-old had before him and would after him—that he might be the first: in his daydreams, he was chief forever, eating every few years at a new person's vaka'ina, his wives and children and grandchildren and great-grandchildren following him in a flock, the meathouse never empty, the palm-frond hut constantly replenished. He would grow so old that he would initiate his own great-great-great-great-grandson at his a'ina'ina, so old that he would watch this same boy grow up and initiate *his* grandson. He would grow so old that the little sproutlike shoots of manama trees that fringed the border of the village would grow to maturity and die and be replaced again, so old that someday he would be as old as the gods themselves, so old that one day they would reveal themselves to him, A'aka and Ivu'ivu, and maybe he would one day be a third in their union, and be granted some realm of his own. The stars and rains and winds and waters and sun had their guardians, but maybe something would be assigned to him— the trees, perhaps, or the flowers, or the birds whose claws pinched the branches high above him. These were his daytime envisionings. No wonder he often looked heavy-lidded, sated—he was drugged on them, and they were lovely things, savory and enchanting and easy to indulge in as often as he wanted.

But by night he would have different dreams. Of one day being led into the forest, perhaps so far lost to himself that he would no longer remember that he had once been chief and that he had had a shiveringly awful hog who had followed him everywhere like a retainer. Of his spear being taken from him, perhaps by a grandson he had initiated. Of walking day after day through the forest looking for food, of hearing the calls of birds and monkeys above him and being unable to remember how to catch them, of not even remembering how easy it had once been or, worse, having a half-memory of it tug at the edge of his consciousness, reminding him of what he did not know but almost did. Of discovering a pinkish fruit at his feet, worms Medusa-ing from its scalp, and not remembering that it was for eating and that he had once enjoyed it—had, in fact, been able to consume them by the dozen. Had liked them dried, so that the edges were thin and crispy with crystallized sugar, or mashed into a paste and daubed on a chunk of sloth meat, the sweet slobbering into the salty. Of being alone when he had once led sixty-five others, of day becoming night and then day again but with nothing to mark the passage of time—no ceremonies, no events, no chants or intercourse or hunts, nothing but his own diminishing relevance to himself, which would happen so gently and smoothly that he wouldn't even notice it. It was those dreams that were the real ones, and he knew it. It was why he would yearn for the daylight, when he was in control of his own mind and in control of everything else besides. I saw then the discipline, the courage, it must have taken to have the dreamers in his midst, to know that every one of them was proof of the inevitability of his nighttime visions and the falseness of his daytime ones.

He never answered us but instead walked away. As I have said, to answer would have been to acknowledge what he tried very hard not to. He was sixty o'anas. Soon—not terribly soon, but eventually—his future would arrive, and he would become someone whom even he would not be able to recognize. He didn't need to speak; it was all the answer I needed.

The trip downhill was much faster than our ascent had been, and less wondrous too. Here for the second time were the plains of moss, the clans of cycads, the jewel-bright spiders, the occasional gusts of gnats or butterflies, and the unseen toucans hooting to one another from the unseen treetops. Nearly six months ago it had been a place of mingled delights and horrors, but now it was discovered land, and we were already bored with it. And here again were the dreamers, all tied together with a length of palm-leaf cord we had been reluctantly given from the hut, led by Fa'a and tailed by me or

Esme. Before us walked Tallent, and far ahead of him—so far that we had lost sight of them—Uva and Tu.

We had agreed, Tallent and Esme and Fa'a and I, to abandon the dreamers we could not take with us in the more forestlike part of the jungle, the antechamber to the village. The chief had not specified how far away we had to take them, but Fa'a had suggested at least three days' walk, and as the end of the third day approached, I could feel us all slowing our pace, matching our strides to Eve's stumbling instead of yanking her along as we normally did. Sometimes Fa'a would hum to the dreamers in brief nasal puffs and they would hum back, and although their tones were unpretty, they could sustain a note for an astonishingly long time, until their hums melded with the hums of the forest itself and everything around us seemed to thrum with noise.

Finally the air around us seemed to paint itself gray, as if it had been washed with gouache, and we knew we could avoid it no longer. All of us, including Tallent and the other two guides, who had returned from their advance work, followed Fa'a as he led the dreamers toward an enormous makava tree, the biggest I had ever seen: the six of us together could not encircle it. As Fa'a talked to the dreamers in his kind, quiet way, the other guides lifted their hands out of their palm-rope handcuffs, separating from the group the four we had determined to keep: Eve, of course; Vanu and Mua, because they were father and son; and Ika'ana, both for his extreme age and because he formed a link between Eve and the others.[46] Uva worked a different length of palm around their wrists and led them away, the four of them following him obediently and without question. As nighttime came they grew more pliable than ever, and watching them leave, I could not help but feel a sort of pain at their gentle acquiescence, their old men's shuffling.

Now there were only the others, the four we had chosen to leave

---

[46] Norton later told me that one of his greatest regrets from this period was not also taking Ivaiva and Va'ana with him, and indeed, I had always wondered why he hadn't—they were twins, after all, and would have made for a particularly interesting study. But Norton said that at the time he thought he would be able to successfully corral and control only four subjects, and he decided that it was more valuable to chart the differences between two blood relations of different generations, which meant that the twins by necessity had to be left behind.

behind. Tu and Fa'a took the long length of palm rope and restrung them together like a sad chain of paper dolls, the cord loose on their arms. They sat them down at the base of the tree, their backs against the bark, and then tied one end of the rope—again, very loosely, so loose a sharp tug would have broken it—around one of the low-hanging branches. (The rope was meant to protect them, or so we thought: if they stayed together rather than wandering in their separate directions, we thought they would ... what? Be able to watch one another die instead of dying alone? But at the time it seemed a kindness, although it is difficult now to remember why.) Before them, Tallent and Esme and I placed tiers of food: Spam, slid from its metal containers and placed on palm leaves, kanavas and mana-mas and no'akas. There were those weird fungi Eve liked, and rat-tly portions of things I realized Tallent must have filched from the dried-goods hut, including a small stack of vuakas, which Tu and Fa'a glanced at covetously before turning resolutely away.

When we were finished, we stepped back, and something about seeing them all looking at us, their eyes as large and black and trusting as a sloth's, and the ground at their feet decorated with gifts as if it were Christmas and these were the presents under the tree, wrenched something inside me, and for a moment I was paralyzed by the cruelty of what we were doing.

I think we all must have felt the same way, for although I could not understand him, I could hear the anguish in Fa'a's voice and saw the tenderness with which he laid his hand on each shoulder, gesturing toward the food as he spoke to them. Later Tallent would tell me what he had said: *Don't leave one another. Take care of one another. Eat the food when you get hungry. Stay by this tree. We'll soon return.*

And then we left. "Don't turn around," Tallent warned us, and we all stumbled forward, driven by our desire to move as far away from them as possible, when they suddenly, as a group, began to hum, a fat, buggy drone that sounded mysterious and full of portent, a chant of goodbye, although really it was nothing of the sort, just a sundowning reflex, a bit of echolalia.

We walked later than we ever had that night, so late that soon the only light we had was the red glint of bats' eyes as they flapped noisily above us and the phosphorescent gleam from a flock of hard-shelled beetles that crested above us in a clicking, clackety gaggle, knocking into one another with crisp little *tok*s and careening off branches. It was imperative that we put as much distance between the abandoned and ourselves as we could, but even after our walking became first inconsequential, as we were going so slowly, and then counterproductive (had we been moving in circles? It was impossible to tell), we seemed unable to stop ourselves. In the forest's dark, in the absence of sight, all sounds became magnified, and out of the darkness loomed visions and nightmares. At one point I swore I felt something large and furred skim fleetingly over the top of my head, almost as if the air itself had grown feathers, but when I asked the others if they had felt it too, no one had. I found myself aware, as I had not been in the village, of the woods beyond and what might be living past the tiers and tiers of trees we had not even thought to access. Earlier in the day I had watched as a swarm of moths, so densely clumped that they appeared to be one creature, threw themselves at two kanava trees in a barreling kamikaze mission. But to my surprise they disappeared between the trees, vanishing into what I saw was the barest of fractures between them, an opening so slender I hadn't even seen it. What else had managed to muscle through the trees' barrier? There was the forest we knew, but beyond it perhaps there was a whole other forest, an entirely different eco-system with its own distinct set of birds and mushrooms and fruits and animals. Perhaps there was another set of villages as well, protected by the trees for centuries, whose people lived to be a thousand and never lost their minds, or who died when they were teenagers, or who never had sex with children, or who only did.

I could hear Fa'a and Tallent speaking to each other, and eventually, when Fa'a fell back, I asked Tallent what they'd been saying. "He's upset," said Tallent, and he sounded upset as well. "He says we should never have tied them to the tree."

"But the cord's easy enough for them to break."

"That's what I told him," said Tallent. "But he says he never should have told them to stay. He says they'll never break the cord—they'll just sit there, waiting for us to come back, because we promised we would."

"But won't they forget we said that?"

He sighed. "I explained that to him," he said. "But." He didn't say anything more.

We were quiet for a moment. The ground crunched and squished beneath us.

"So what does he think will happen?" I finally asked.

"He thinks they'll just stay there, not touching the food, waiting for us to return, until they die of starvation."

"Isn't that a bit extreme?" They had, I reminded myself, coped well on their own for years, for decades. And yet a part of me understood Fa'a's distress: now that we had entered the dreamers' lives—now that we had named them as dreamers, now that we had cared for them, now that we considered them ours, something found and given meaning—it was somehow difficult to imagine them capable of living on without us.

He sighed again. "He wants to go back for them. He wants to take them to his village. I told him he couldn't. He said he was a killer."

"Poor Fa'a," I said, although my answer was more reflexive than anything else. He was a good, kind person, and although I thought he was being melodramatic, I appreciated his compassion. In the absence of action, *Poor Fa'a* seemed to be the only thing to say.

"Poor Fa'a," repeated Tallent, his voice low. "Poor Fa'a."

And then we were almost at the end. I had experienced the journey of almost six months before in reverse and was surprised at how familiar the sensations felt, and how friendly too: here I was stumbling over the same slippery crosshatch of roots, and growing heartily tired of the endless march of green, and feeling the wet air press upon me like a water-soaked mattress. Even with the dreamers—who, it must be said, were very good: obedient and placable—we were a day ahead of schedule. The boat would pick us up at midday on Tuesday, and by late afternoon on Sunday we had only another seven hours of walking to go. Once again I was impressed that Tallent had all along been keeping track of time; he even produced from his rucksack a small calendar, and seeing the days ticked off by a pencil mark made our stay on the island feel somehow both longer and more real.

He decided that we would stop early for the night and have an easy amble the next day. On Tuesday morning we would walk the final two hours to the shore, but it wasn't worth going earlier, because that would mean sitting by the shore getting bitten by the mosquitoes that were becoming more and more frequent the closer to water we got. Knowing that we were so near the sea made me jumpy with impatience: how I longed to see something more powerful and unknowable than the jungle or the forest, something whose surface would prickle with light, something that could ferry us away from this place.

That night we ate the last of the Spam, and I remembered the meal of crackers we had had early in our trip and how Tallent had said I would miss their crispness. There were no crackers this time—they had been consumed long before—but their absence made me think of what an imperfect place this island was: above, in the village, there was fire but no water, and here everything sagged and burped water. The trees were swollen with it, the ground was fecund with it, our bodies produced it with such unceasing constancy that everything I owned was silky with moisture. Still, it was a nice penultimate meal on the island, and the food we ate and what we lacked were only incidental. Even the dreamers seemed to realize that something grand and exciting was about to happen, for they smiled their silly smiles and chattered away and at one point Mua even rose to do a funny little half-dance that resembled the one that the women did after the cessation of their menses. Uva and Tu—who had taken advantage of the leisurely day to go vuaka hunting and had returned with a sack that squirmed with so many of them that it resembled nothing so much as a gigantic, bloated manama fruit—were particularly joyful, laughing and talking and showing their pointy teeth, relieved that their time in this impossible place was almost over and that they would soon be home, alive and, even better, with a rich man's haul of monkeys. Only Fa'a remained locked into his fugue state, and as the rest of us clapped our hands and shouted at Mua's dancing, he sat apart from us, staring in turn at each of the dreamers, rubbing his thumb up and down his spear. It was impossible not to intuit what he was thinking: in the dreamers he saw not only his fate but his responsibility. Their presence was an unbearable reminder to him of what he'd done and of what he'd become. When he murmured something to Tallent and left, stalking into the woods beyond, I thought nothing of it, only that he wanted to be alone, away from us. And why would he not want to be alone, to prolong considering the inevitability of his departure? He was returning home a cursed man. What would he say to his family?

I woke the next morning to screams, to Uva and Tu running toward us, shouting at Tallent, startled groups of bugs and birds rising up and screeching away in their wake. "Fa'a!" they were shouting "Fa'a!," followed by something else.

He was up and running after them at once. "One of you, stay behind with the dreamers!" he called back to us, but both Esme and I bolted after him, which I later had to admit was not very wise— they could have wandered off and we might never have seen them again.

We ran, and for once the jungle, as if recognizing our panic, seemed to adjust itself to us. Our feet did not land in the hollows of roots and did not skid over the ankle-breaking rimes of moss but instead floated over every impediment, each footfall landing as cleanly and solidly as if we had been running on lawn, on tarmac.

Before us, in the distance, was a tree, an enormous makava, its branches stretched low and long like an octopus's tentacles, and from one of them hung Fa'a. He had used a length of palm-frond rope, the same we had tied the dreamers with, and made an imperfect noose, so imperfect that when I examined him and felt his neck intact, I realized that he had suffocated and that his death had been a slow and agonizing one.

Uva and Tu were howling, their heads thrown back and their eyes seamed shut, their slabby tongues working muscularly in their mouths. Esme was crying. "Oh," she said. "Oh, Fa'a." Tallent looked exhausted, his face pulling itself down toward the ground, his hands hanging at his sides.

It took all of us to bring him down. Tu climbed up the tree and onto the branch and sawed at the rope with Tallent's knife. Tallent and I caught him as he fell, and we all carried him back, Tallent and Tu on one side, the rest of us on the other, Fa'a a solid, swinging weight between us.

I had not witnessed a death the entire time I had been in the village. A birth, yes—the baby, like any other baby anywhere else in the world, had slid out, snarled with fleshy cord and colored that particular unattractive mauve color that newborns are, as I watched, barely breathing so as not to betray my presence, from behind the hut—but not a death. So I did not know how the Ivu'ivuans would bury their dead, or even if they had many occasions to do so.[47] But the U'ivuans' treatment of their dead would be different from the Ivu'ivuans' anyway, Tallent reminded me. In U'ivu they would take the body to a remote location high in the hills and leave it to be consumed by animals. Then, six months later, they would return and move the bones somewhere secret; only the deceased's family would know the location, and they would never tell for fear that someone else would steal the bones and with them the dead person's spirit.

But here there was no high hill nearby. That afternoon (we had kept Fa'a's death from the dreamers) Tu and Uva took Fa'a away. They were gone for so long that, although we did not voice this fear to one another, I think we were all concerned that they might not return, even though they hated the island, and even though they had left their sack of vuakas behind. By the time they did walk back to us it was daybreak, and the sky was lightening, and we could see small dust-colored insects, their wings webbed and traced with veins so fine and yellow they looked like strands of saffron, clogging the air before and above us.

---

[47] The Ivu'ivuans' method of disposing of and remembering the dead is notable mostly for its brisk efficiency, especially given the enthusiasm and glee with which they commemorate the more mundane passages of life. The dead spend a day on display in the center of the village, lawa'a frills covering their eyes. That night, after dinner has been cooked, they are placed on top of the fire and left to burn overnight. (In his book, Tallent, who witnessed one of these outdoor cremations, gives a wonderfully vivid rendering of the little firecracker bursts that are audible throughout the night as various body parts explode and their contents simmer in the flames.) The next morning the fire is extinguished, the remains are collected, and a relative of the deceased is dispatched to bury them under one of the trees lining the village's rim (each family has a certain number of trees allocated to them for these occasions). Tallent notes that the days surrounding the death are marked not by keening or weeping but instead by a "dignified, almost majestical, sense of quiet and contemplation. The deceased's immediate family continues to go about their daily rituals, but their silence, their lack of chatter in this busy, intimate community, is a ritual in itself, and the other villagers give them peace until the bereaved signal their intention to return to the life of the community. Sometimes this silent mourning takes only days; sometimes it takes months. But it is a remarkable demonstration of being absent in a place so intensely present, of being granted solitude while surrounded by many" (Tallent, *The People in the Trees*, 178).

They were spent, gray-faced. They spoke to Tallent. "They've hidden him somewhere," he reported to us. "They said they'd return in six months to hide his bones." But we knew, all of us, that this would not happen, that Fa'a's body would remain wherever they had left it, to be nibbled away at by ants and bats and birds and beetles until it was picked clean, its bones as white as butter.

In the end, we had spent so long waiting for Tu and Uva that we had to hurry the rest of the way downhill to meet the boat. Tu carried Fa'a's spear, which he would return to his family and which would serve as evidence that he was truly gone. By the time we reached the little shore, where the water lapped so far up onto ground that there was a span of about ten yards that was not quite ocean and not quite land, where you could see the two worlds coming together into one—fish swimming above grass and orchids shimmering beneath the ocean's oily slick—the sun was so high in the sky that for a moment I feared that the boat had already come and gone and we would be trapped here forever, too far from one civilization and unwilling to return to the other. But then we heard a far-off chugging and watched the boat materialize in the distance as a gray-brown smear before it drew closer and solidified into shape. After these months it looked, for all its crudeness, impossibly sophisticated, a creation of a bold and ingenious society. At the prow, the boatman held up his arms, and Tallent waved back to him. I wondered what the boatman would think of his extra passengers, and what the dreamers would think of the boat, and, later, what it would feel like to be on the open water, to have the ocean bouncing away beneath us. With each yard we would be drawn farther away from this place, which was already beginning to feel like a dream, a series of events and meetings that had never happened, and back toward our own society. I asked myself if I was happy about this and was surprised to find that I didn't know that I was.

The boat was now close enough for its driver to see who we had with us, and even from the shore I could see his mouth form itself into an *O*.

"Bring them closer—get ready to board," Tallent told us, already wading out into the shallows to help pull the boat in.

We drew them along, Tu and Uva and Esme and I, each of us holding one of the dreamers' hands. They were reluctant to put their feet into the water, but once they did, they let out small sighs of happiness, although Ika'ana's hand tightened around mine, and I squeezed his back to reassure him.

"Come on," I told him, even though he couldn't understand, and he looked at me trustingly, his eyes mild, and it was difficult to remember that he had once been a warrior and had once carried a spear that he had protected with his life. *Ma'alamakina, ma'ama.*

We walked carefully toward the boat, the last in line. The quilt of rocks beneath us was uneven, and Ika'ana swayed a bit from the effort. I could see the boatman's shaking hands as he touched Eve's wrist and helped heft her up. Behind us, the jungle steamed.

But I didn't look back.

# PART V. THE FIRST CHILD

## I.

What happened next is so well documented that I hardly think it worth much time to tell it yet again. Indeed, a number of books have chronicled the decade following my initial departure from Ivu'ivu much more thoroughly, and in much more exhaustive detail, than I could have done myself, in particular Jeremy Lauerman's *The Immortals: The Discovery That Changed the World*, which focuses mostly on the first three years of my return to the States, and Katharine Hetherington's *An Island Good and Small: Norton Perina and the World He Made*, which takes as its subject the later years of my research in what would come to be called Selene syndrome, and the denouement of which is an almost Talmudic rendering of my receipt of the Nobel Prize. Finally there is Anna Kidd's *Of Stone and Sun and Everything In Between: A Biography of A. Norton Perina*, which, aside from portraying me as something close to godlike, remains my favorite of the trio for its evenhandedness and its author's superior scientific understanding. I sat for many hours of interviews with all three of these authors, and they have presented me and my work faithfully.

However, certain stories from those years remain largely untold, and I would like to use this opportunity to answer some of the mysteries that persist.

The first concerns the fate of the dreamers. Although I left U'ivu the possessor of perhaps one of the greatest scientific discoveries of the twentieth century, I returned to America a virtual leper. I may have been an explorer with a wonderful, an unimaginable find, but to the academic establishment I was merely a researcher without a lab, and therefore an outcast. Back then, however, I was still too young and guileless to properly appreciate the impossibility of my situation; in fact, I fancied myself something of a ronin, ready to serve anyone who might grant me a home. As it turned out, that place was Stanford, where Tallent—who had, in less than six months, been transformed in anthropological circles from a rebel into a genuine hero—managed to hastily secure me a lab and some money, no doubt funneled improperly from some mysterious slush fund.[48] Because my operation was so small, I was made to share techs with a much larger adjoining lab, which of course did not go over well. Mostly, though, my peers didn't know what to make of me: I was too inexperienced to be running my own outfit and yet too worldly to be under anyone's command. It was clear that I was

---

[48] As Norton indicates, the arrangement he enjoyed at Stanford was highly unusual. What is more unusual is that the source of the funding has never been definitively identified, even all these years later. In her book, Katharine Hetherington speculates that there are two possible candidates. The first (and most colorful) is a man named Rufus Gripshaw, a very wealthy and eccentric Stanford alumnus who made his fortune from inventing a vacuum sealer that is now used in numerous food processing plants and who was obsessed with achieving immortality. She speculates that Tallent spoke to the dean of the medical school on Norton's behalf and asked him to approach Gripshaw as a silent patron for Norton's research with the dreamers. Although this is a compelling theory—obviously, Gripshaw had a great personal interest in Norton's project—it assumes that Tallent was much more interested in assisting Norton's work than Norton himself seems to indicate (or indeed ever believed). This is, of course, another case in which Tallent's lack of archived papers and journals makes re-creating history, much less his motives, very frustrating. In the years that were to follow, Norton was never quite certain how Tallent felt about him and his work, and it is easy to imagine that Tallent himself was ambivalent about how, and whether, he wanted to collaborate with Norton. (On the other hand, he had essentially abetted Norton in his plan to bring back the dreamers.)

Besides Gripshaw, Hetherington suggests that Norton was funded out of, as he puts it, "some mysterious slush fund," one bankrolled by a governmental agency interested in developing new drugs. This theory is actually less cloak-and-dagger than it sounds. It was, of course, 1950, barely five years after the end of the war, and at the time a great deal of money was being invested not only in the relatively embryonic field of virology but also in a very early iteration of biowarfare. It is entirely possible that Stanford was one of the universities given a grant to pursue such studies and experiments and found a worthy recipient in Norton. (Katharine Hetherington, *An Island True and Small* [New York: Pantheon, 1992], 205–18)

protected by someone; I had to hope every day that they wouldn't discover that it was the Anthropology Department.

It sounds a silly thing to say—after all, I had not been gone so long—but readjusting to America was more challenging than I had anticipated. I was struck by how sparkly and new everything seemed, by the cars gleaming their bright, artificial colors like saliva-slicked sweets, by the sheer volume and inventiveness of clothing everyone seemed to wear: brogues and hats and suspenders and belts and handbags and clinking bracelets and bouncing strands of pearls—a whole language of sartorial excess when only a pouch and a length of fabric would have sufficed. And I marveled too at how stark, how denuded of plant life, the cities were, just one gray block after another, and where there would have been trees there were instead mouse-colored buildings spilling silent people, all in their layers and layers of elaborate and superfluous costumery.

Inside the lab, however, it was always Ivu'ivu. I had tried to make the transition—from island to mainland, from Stone Age to modern age—as seamless as possible for the dreamers, which meant that I'd had to start drugging them more or less from the moment we had arrived on U'ivu, which had been terrifying, overwhelming, to them. (This was back when you could do such things without ethics boards howling at you, when you could ease a transition that otherwise would have killed with its abruptness and severity.) And I had sedated them, of course, on the plane ride to California (all those hours of checking their pulses, their breathing, of shining a tiny penlight—itself a miracle—into their eyes to watch their pupils contract into beady black pinpricks), and during the car ride to the basement bunker beneath the lab where we kept them for several days while we were assembling what would become their permanent residence, and had woken them only when I had safely ensconced them in their new home: a fifteen-by-fifteen-foot room, windowless so they would not be detected by others, with plain walls and a linoleum floor that had been spread with layers of palm leaves and dotted with buckets of bromeliads and potted trees both approximate (a cycad) and not (a ficus) to what they would remember from Ivu'ivu. At one point I tried to introduce a terrarium with a turtle in it, but I came in one morning to find the turtle with its carapace half torn off, its neck limp, and a clot of bloodied feces coating its tail. They were not violent, the dreamers, but they were increasingly agitated and fearful, and their agitation and fear made them sometimes behave in ways that were foreign to them. It was a delicate balance, their sedation: too much and they became logy and staggery, and it was difficult to discern how much of their incomprehension was due to their mental state and how much was artificially induced; too little and they grew anxious, scratching at the walls and wailing at nothing. The goal was to keep them alert enough that they might notice something curious about their surroundings but disoriented enough that they wouldn't be able to specify what was amiss.

I had assistance in this; I had been assigned a postdoctoral student named Cheolyu Ryu, who was on a visiting scholarship from Seoul. I'm not sure what he'd done wrong to be assigned to me, of all people—other than being a foreigner and, I'm sorry to say, somewhat inscrutable —but he was a great help. He was reluctant to speak English (though when I heard it, his English sounded fine, if heavily accented), but he followed orders closely and without any contradictions and kept fine notes. It was Cheolyu who was responsible for perfecting not only the formula of sedatives we fed the dreamers but the formula of stimuli as well; he knew exactly how much time spent outside their room would upset them and was even eventually able to take them outside the lab entirely for short periods at night, when the electric lights were dimmed and the grass was cool under their feet and the buildings' other occupants—from whom we kept the dreamers' existence—had left for the day. Sometimes I would go with him on these night rambles, each of us holding two of the dreamers' hands, and follow him across the short, well-kept lawns, avoiding the sidewalks and the buildings, waiting as they exploratorily lapped at the bark of a eucalyptus and rubbed their shoulders against a spindly cedar. At these times he reminded me of no one so much as poor Fa'a; they shared the same indulgent patience, the same protective instincts, the ones that made him swerve the dreamers away from concrete and guide them toward a grove of beeches that might as well have been flowers, so little did they resemble manama trees, but were better, I suppose, than nothing.

The dreamers were deteriorating very quickly now. Indeed, they had become more ... well, mo'o kua'au-ish in the first month following our return than they had in the fourteen weeks or so that I had known them on the island. Again, it was impossible to conclude definitively whether this was because of their environment or organic, or whether it was for some other reason entirely—diet, perhaps. Naturally, no manama fruits were available, but with Tallent's help I had re-created as closely as I could an Ivu'ivuan diet. We had substituted veal for sloth meat (though I fear that that parallel was grounded more in sentiment than anything else; my logic, I seem to recall, was that sloths were slow-moving and fatty and gentle and so were calves, and therefore the latter might make an even swap for the former), small rotisseried chickens for the vuakas, and mangoes for the manamas. Back then it was much harder to find mangoes in northern California than it is today, and a significant percentage of the lab's expenses was dedicated to the procurement and purchase of the fruit.

Still, one did not have to be particularly bright to recognize that the culprit was probably the lab itself. The dreamers had gone from wandering the forest—the whole length and width of an island—to being confined in their room, or if not their room, the lab beyond, where they were pricked and poked and swabbed and made to urinate in plastic cups (something they had never seen before) and plucked like birds. I sometimes wondered what the lab represented to them: too much stimulation or not enough? On one hand, there were things that they could not even begin to comprehend—glass, for example, and ceramic countertops, and plastic and metal. But on the other hand, the lab was so arid. It was an albinic landscape, one without any color or sound or smell beyond a chilly metallicism, one with nothing to dazzle and delight an eye that had been dazzled and delighted all its life.

Whatever the reason, they became deader and deader with each day. Not physically; indeed, the only thing that was remarkable about their X-rays, their reflex tests, the substantial quantities of blood we siphoned from their veins each week was how extraordinarily physically healthy they were—their blood pressure admirable, their pulses thudding as softly and unhurriedly as metronomes, their bones unnibbled by osteoporosis. But as if in compensation for their bodies, which, once exposed to food other than manamas and those shingley mushrooms, grew sleeker and plumper, their minds diminished piece by piece. Soon not even Mua could find the energy to make conversation with Tallent when he came by on his twice-weekly visits.

"E, Mua," Tallent would greet him, resting a hand on his shoulder, and Mua, as if from a great depth, would slowly raise first his eyes and then his head to see who was talking to him. He would open his mouth but make no sound. And there they would remain, until finally Tallent would take his hand away and show him the mango he had hidden behind his back. But Mua would only gaze at that too, and at last Tallent would have to cut it and remind him that it was to be eaten and enjoyed, opening his mouth and inserting a fibrous sliver of it, chewing and swallowing until Mua realized that this was something he was still capable of doing.

 

In order to prove my theory—that ingestion of the opa'ivu'eke was responsible for the dreamers' superannuated lives and eventual decline—I had to try to re-create their condition in animals. But owing to various administrative difficulties (that is, the perpetual twin problems of funding and space), I was not able to begin my experiments until the spring of 1951.[49]

---

[49] In the meantime, Norton kept himself busy with a number of extracurricular projects, the most important of which was a paper, published in April 1951 in the *Annals of Herpetology,* in which he identifies the opa'ivu'eke as a previously unknown salt- and freshwater turtle. The paper, while brief, is surprisingly charming; with it, Norton reveals that he too had been taking copious notes on the island, and indeed, his observations of the opa'ivu'eke's (or *Chelonia perinia,* as it is now formally known) activities and behaviors have been cited countless times in the decades since. Aside from producing the satisfaction that comes from discovering and naming a new life form, this paper also laid necessary groundwork for Norton's future paper, the famous "Eternity Claim," which he would publish nearly two years later.

The *Herpetology* paper garnered Norton a great deal of attention in zoological circles, and for a brief time he even considered moving into the field; the only thing that stopped him, as he later realized, was his fundamental lack of passion for reptilia. Not everyone was happy with Norton's report, however; in her memoir, Duff claims that she and Tallent were the true discoverers of the opa'ivu'eke and that credit should be given to them. Even if that could have been proven, however, all scientists know that—fairly or not, although fairness seems somewhat beside the point at this level—it's the person who actually reports the finding to the scientific press who gets the credit for the discovery, not the person who merely makes note of it in his logbooks or journals.

My homemade curing seemed to have worked very well, but I guarded the packets of meat, still wrapped in palm leaves, almost maniacally, storing them first in plastic containers and then in the lab's freezer, the temperature of which I checked daily. I cursed myself for being too cowardly to rip off the creature's shell and save the meat within; now I had only the four legs and head and the flap of tail, and who knew how much turtle the mice would have to consume in order to experience its effect? Who knew how carefully I would have to ration my remains? There was no way of getting *more* opa'ivu'eke; I was committed to the lab, and although Tallent was already planning his return to Ivu'ivu for the summer, I couldn't ask him to get me another—he didn't even know I had this one.

So I was very careful with the amount of turtle I fed the first group of twenty-five mice. I made Cheolyu cut a section of the foreleg into twenty-five snippets, each no larger than a thumbtack. I had to hope that it would be enough. I was working under the assumption that the results would be apparent—or not—from only one feeding; either it would work or it wouldn't. The other twenty-five mice I fed similar-sized portions from a box turtle I had bought from an animal supply company.

The maximum lifespan for a lab mouse is about a year and a half. If my theory was correct, the first group of mice would be alive not only three months from now (I had specified that all fifty be fifteen months old, to best re-create the age at which an Ivu'ivuan would ingest his opa'ivu'eke) but after two years, three years, perhaps even five years. At some point they would begin to behave in a disoriented manner, even as their physical condition remained essentially unchanged. I had also replicated, somewhat prematurely and almost as a lark, the experiment on a second group of one hundred mice, half of whom were fed the opa'ivu'eke, and the other half, the box turtle. These mice, however, were newborns and would essentially come of age in a controlled experimental environment.

The days churned by. Cheolyu took excellent care of the mice, and excellent care as well of the dreamers. I had somehow expected

---

It is unknown what Tallent thought of Norton's report about the opa'ivu'eke. His few existing papers include no mention of it, and Norton has never revealed whether the two of them ever spoke of it.

Tallent to be a more frequent presence in the lab, but aside from his weekly visits—which were spent mostly in the company of the dreamers—I seldom had reason or opportunity to speak with him, and when I was in his presence, I felt more, not less, awkward. After we began the experiment, I was grateful for his brief visits and his apparent lack of interest in what I was doing; explaining my intentions would mean revealing my theft of the opa'ivu'eke. Part of me suspected that Tallent was somehow aware of what I'd done, and another part of me argued that he wouldn't care—we were off the island, back in civilization, and he no longer had any jurisdiction over me. But in the end, neither of those arguments proved compelling enough to convince me, and I found myself making excuses and scuttling away whenever he stopped by. At least he came alone, unaccompanied by Esme, whom I hadn't seen since our return. I knew she was somewhere on campus, doing something or other, but as long as I didn't have to see her or contemplate further her still unresolved (at least to me) relationship with Tallent, I was satisfied.

A life in the lab is a lonely one, especially when you have only one colleague and your position is tenuous and you are sneaking around your suspected benefactor and concealing from him the true nature of your work and you are in the period of your experiment when you are simply waiting for something to happen. Oh, of course there are other things to do—life in a lab is nothing if not busy, with its dozens of essential little chores and tasks to be completed each day, but it is often less than stimulating. Out of desperation I was even driven to try to make small talk with Cheolyu, which became something of its own experiment in absurdist theater. I would say something, and then perhaps five minutes would pass, and he would reply with something that might be considered a response to what I had said . . . but might just as well have been a non sequitur. By that point, it would hardly seem worth the effort and mutual embarrassment to continue the conversation, and both of us would slip into a silence that might be maintained for hours, or days.

However, this period was not a total waste, as I decided to fill the long blank days with a study of U'ivuan. Tallent brought me a primer he and Esme had assembled (most of it handwritten in her strangely bubbly schoolgirl cursive), with a few hundred words and phrases translated into U'ivuan and, where applicable, the Ivu'ivuan dialect.

Unfortunately, even as I was learning their language, the dreamers were forgetting it, and I was left to repeat the words to myself late into the night, their thick glottal clumps fattening the air.

I was surprised, after several weeks of my new routine, to get a letter from Owen. It turned out that he was nearby, teaching freshman English at, of all places, Mills (a situation that he later told me he knew even then was a complete waste).

We made plans to meet for dinner. Owen had a friend with a car and drove down to Palo Alto. Why we decided to remain near campus and not go into San Francisco eludes me now. But my world had by that time shrunk to such a narrow locus—the lab, my on-campus apartment—that it is simply likely I was unable to think beyond its borders.

It felt pleasantly familiar (a strange sensation, after months of aggressive unfamiliarity) to see Owen, although he now had a beard and was fatter than I remembered.

"Hi," he said, holding out his hand.

"Hi," I said, and shook it. "You got fat."

He shrugged and grunted irritatedly. I remembered that he had never had a very good sense of humor. "Let's go."

We had drinks, and I asked him about his work. "Are the students smart?"

"What do you think?" He grunted again. "They're silly girls. They spend most of their time here, actually"—meaning Stanford—"and at Cal, trying to meet husbands." He sighed. "I feel like a cow in a henhouse."

"You mean a fox," I said.

He looked annoyed. "No," he said, "I mean a cow. Cows are herbivores. They eat grass. They're not interested in eating chickens. To them, they're just smelly and stupid birds."

I suppose this was Owen's way of telling me he was homosexual, for we never discussed his preferences again, and yet the next time I saw him, it was in the company of a very young man who laughed nervously at Owen's every weak joke. Many years later, when people began to discuss such topics publicly, I heard him recount to someone how he had "come out" to me. It was clear that he was (still) quite pleased with his cleverness, but hearing it again only reminded me of what a tortured and unsuccessful metaphor it was.

Over dinner, as I half listened to Owen drone on about the college and how much he hated California, and some long explanation about something that seemed to have happened to my winter coat when he had had to use it to put out a fire in his room, I reflected upon how fundamentally naive he was, how small and plebeian his concerns were, and how he never could have endured what I had, and how profoundly changed I now was. I had no disdain for him, however, and indeed, it was soothing to be with someone for whom life was a series of the familiar, whose every problem was solvable, who could find such pleasure in the everyday. It was startling to remember that I had once been one of those people as well. Now, however, I no longer was.

## II.

Of all the emotions to describe in retrospect, happiness is perhaps the most dull, but awe is the most difficult. Years later I would be asked (and asked and asked) how I felt when the fourth month and then the fifth month and then the sixth month passed and the mice I had fed the opa'ivu'eke lived on, burrowing into their shredded-paper caves, spinning vapidly on their wheels, sucking at their cages' water bottles, even as the control group became an ever-vaguer memory, incinerated long ago after they all died, one after the next, in the seventeenth through twentieth months of their lives.

"I was amazed," I would say, and while this was true, it also was not. Although I could not say so until much later (I was still endeavoring back then to be humble, as it was notable displays of humility that won young researchers grants), any initial shock I might have felt was eclipsed by a quiet sense of vindication. As I watched the mice live on and on, I felt no excitement of discovery; in fact, the whole thing seemed a bit anticlimactic. My theory had always made sense to me, and I had never doubted it, but now I would have to go through the necessary (and tedious) steps of proving it to everyone else.

I had the second group of mice (the ones I had procured as pinkies) already started on the regimen, but in July of 1951 I began a third experiment, this time on a group of 200 fifteen-month-old mice. If my theories were correct, the 100 mice who ingested the opa'ivu'eke would live, on median, at least twice as long as their natural lifespan.

While I was watching mice and getting bored stupid with the dreamers, however, Tallent was becoming famous. In October of 1951 (the opa'ivu'eke-eating mice from the first group were by then twenty-three months old and as frisky as ever), he published a report entitled "The 'Lost Tribe' of U'ivu: An Ethnological Study of the Village Peoples of Ivu'ivu" in the *Journal of Ethnography*. A fevered skim of the article revealed page after page of highly pointillist renderings of the tribe's family structures, rites, rituals (not, notably, the a'ina'ina), philosophies, origin myths, taboos, notions of time, and social workings but relatively little—shockingly little—about their extended lifetimes. There was a long section about the opa'ivu'eke, and an excessively granular description of the vaka'ina (so granular that it managed to convey none of the wonder and terror one felt while watching it), and, buried in an endnote, this comment:

> *I have spoken of the tribe's fascination with immortality. Although this is a preoccupation central to the U'ivuans' mythology as well, it would not be overstating the case to call it a subject of obsession among the villagers. Indeed, they believe that the ingestion of the opa'ivu'eke[50]—the turtle devoured during the vaka'ina ritual by those reaching or having surpassed the age of sixty o'anas—confers eternal life. There is, of course, no conclusive scientific proof of these claims, although there is evidence that certain members of the tribe are unusually long-lived.*

Reading this, I felt three things. First, amusement at Tallent's timidity; was it not he who had been so quick to insist that Ika'ana was centuries old? Second, an odd sort of relief at his uncharacteristic circumspection: not only had he not revealed what was fundamentally my discovery, but he had left room for me to enrich and emboss his account with my own. And third—and following those

---

[50] Norton's earlier study about the turtle was of course cited in Tallent's paper.

initial two reactions—a niggling suspicion that Esme, not Tallent, had been responsible not only for the note (its poor delivery, its bland writing) but also for Tallent's apparently newfound wariness.

Fairly or not, I found myself disappointed with Tallent. As I have said, I did not and do not consider anthropologists the most creative and disarming of thinkers—though they do take superlative and meticulous notes—but I had come to admire what I had grown to see as his single-mindedness. But he was also to be my first lesson in the strange phenomenon that besets all of us who travel to strange places and find our own assumptions and lessons proven not just wrong, but opposite. It is very easy to be intellectually brave in such locations, where the academy, one's peers, and the entirety of Western history and religion feel not only irrelevant but misguided. But *unlearning* things is much more difficult than learning them, and even the most courageous of minds will find itself tempted to retreat back into the known at the first opportunity. It is astonishing and a little sad to realize how many discoveries, how many advancements, have been delayed for years, for decades, not because the information was unavailable but because of sheer cowardice, fear of being laughed at, of being ostracized by one's colleagues.

Luckily, I was never limited by such worries or constrained by such fears (being ostracized by my colleagues seemed something to covet, not avoid). And so in 1953, I published a brief postulative paper[51]—really nothing more than an announcement, the medical equivalent of Martin Luther posting his theses on the church's wooden door[52]—in a small, now-defunct journal called the *Annals*

---

[51] Norton Perina, M.D., "Observations on Prolonged Human Longevity Among the Ivu'ivu People," *Annals of Nutritional Epidemiology* (December 1953), vol. 42, 324–28.

[52] Norton's revolutionary paper (commonly known as the "Eternity Claim" paper) was not the only gauntlet thrown down to the mainstream medical and scientific establishment that year. In April, James Watson and Francis Crick had published *their* brief postulative paper in *Nature*, "A Structure for Deoxyribose Nucleic Acid," which first described the double-helical nature of DNA. This, coupled with Norton's discovery, has led numerous scientific historians to identify 1953 as the "year of miracles"—ironically, of course, as miracles were exactly what these scientists strove to disprove with their research.

Although Norton was naturally highly impressed by Watson's scholarship, he was not in general impressed by Watson the man, whom he found far too obsessed with

*of Nutritional Epidemiology.* In it I revealed my findings: not only were a significant percentage of the mice from the first group that had eaten the opa'ivu'eke still alive, but so were the mice from the second and third groups.[53]

It is very difficult for my biographers and for younger scientists to comprehend when I tell them with what ridicule, what scorn, what *hatred* this paper was received. The *Annals of Nutritional Epidemiology* was at best an obscure publication, but somehow my essay seemed to be read by people who would not normally have troubled themselves with such journals, and in the coming months the *Annals* (rather pantingly, I thought) published all manner of letters from various doctors and scientists outraged that this sort of "childish fiction and robust fantasies" should be taking the place of real science, etc., etc. The fellows in the adjoining lab—still bitter at my youth, my space, and my mysterious funding—took to dropping by

---

his pursuit of women (a quest detailed by Watson himself in his memoir *Genes, Girls, and Gamow* [New York: Knopf, 2002]) and his hunger for fame, which continues unabated to this day.

[53] The purpose of Norton's initial three experiments was to prove that the mice who were fed the opa'ivu'eke would, after a single feeding of the turtle, live on median significantly longer than their natural lifespan of eighteen months. Of Group A (the twenty-five fifteen-month-old mice), 81 percent of the animals were still living, making the median survival age in September 1953, when Norton submitted his paper for publication, forty-six months, which meant that their lifespans had been almost trebled. Of Group C, the hundred mice who were also fed the opa'ivu'eke at fifteen months, 79 percent were still alive at forty-one months, which meant their lifespans had increased by 150 percent. The control groups from experiments A and C—that is, the mice who had been fed the box turtle placebo—had a median survival of 17.8 months—in other words, their typical lifespan. Not discussed in Norton's initial paper were the subjects of Group B (the fifty newborn mice fed the opa'ivu'eke in their infancy). All of them were, astonishingly, still alive at the time the paper was written, at thirty-one months old. But because their lifespan had not yet been proven to have been doubled by eating the turtle, Norton decided that publishing their results was still too premature.

The scientific importance of Norton's experiment was twofold. First, he proved that an organism's lifespan could be controlled or manipulated by a foreign element. Second, he established that this extended lifespan—what he termed "imaginable immortality"—could be achieved by the ingestion of this element. In just over two years, he had solved the riddle that has preoccupied every culture since the beginning of time. It is perhaps no wonder, then, that his findings were greeted with such passion and anger, because it is only fear that can provoke such responses.

under the pretense of talking to Cheolyu, whom they'd update with fresh insults about my work that they'd recently overheard from this chemist or that biologist. (The fact that Cheolyu would only gape at them and every now and again blink his small eyes behind his glasses until they triumphantly flounced out seemed not to register with them at all.)

Did any of this bother me? No, it did not. I was certain I was correct—more and more certain, in fact, when, with each passing month, the opa'ivu'eke-fed mice lived on, their little lives stretching out, a thin elastic line, longer and longer—and as I have said, it was not in my nature to listen to the chatter of others, especially others for whom I had no particular regard.

However, I was also not impractical. The one, the only frustrating thing about my paper's less-than-enthusiastic reception was that it would retard my ability to make for myself the kind of life I had decided I wanted. I have spoken before about my fundamental ambivalence about lab life, and this was still true. But if the rhythms of the lab were not necessarily always the most stimulating, the rhythms of my *own* lab were. Being left alone—without oversight, without having to report to anyone, without having to manage someone else's pointless projects—was a glorious freedom, and one I realized very quickly I wanted for myself. I wanted to perform my own experiments. I wanted to write what I wanted, to answer what I wanted, to follow my every passion and curiosity. In order to do that, I would need my own lab. And in order to have my own lab, I would need funding, which meant I also needed to be proven, very quickly, legitimate.

I spent much of my time brooding over this apparently insurmountable problem, gazing at nothing while Cheolyu fed the mice and made notes and dealt with the dreamers (with whom I was working less and less). And then, beginning in late February of 1954, two things happened in quick succession that would change my fate. The first came in the form of a letter from, of all people, Adolphus Sereny. In his short note, Sereny congratulated me on my successful return from U'ivu and—revealing himself a secret herpetologist—my essay on the opa'ivu'eke. More important, though, he admitted himself intrigued by my paper in *Nutritional Epidemiology* and expressed interest in re-creating my experiments. I of course immediately responded. Sereny was a respected scientist with a well-organized lab. If he could successfully replicate my findings (and I had no doubt that he would), it would confer on me an almost instant and absolute acceptance and validity, which would in turn lead to the sort of life and intellectual freedom I craved. Even I could not help but appreciate the irony of my situation: Sereny, who I had thought hated me! I had Cheolyu carefully pack one of the opa'ivu'eke's legs,[54] along with complete copies of my data and detailed instructions on dosing, etc., and sent it off to Cambridge.

The second thing that happened was that the mice from both the first and, to a lesser extent, the third study began demonstrating dramatic signs of mental decay. At this point, the mice from the first group were fifty-one months old and those from the third group forty-six months old. I was not exactly unprepared for this; even as I had readied the paper for publication the previous summer, Cheolyu had noticed that the mice in the first group had been behaving oddly: they would run in tight circles, so quickly and crazily that their feet would tangle up in one another and they would fall onto their backs, kicking their paws in the air and chirping. Or they would press their noses into a corner of the cage and make strange, unrodentlike gulping gestures, opening their little mouths and closing them again and again. They would do this for hours sometimes, their azalea-pink eyes wide open and unblinking. This made sense to me; after all, they had at that point been alive slightly longer than twice their natural lifespan, the same point at which the dreamers had begun to demonstrate their first symptoms of mo'o kua'au-ness. What was truly exciting was the behavior that they were demonstrating as they reached the point at which they would be alive for three times as long as their natural lifespan, or about the equivalent of Eve's age. And indeed, as I had hoped, their deterioration had become suddenly more profound. Seven months before, they had experienced periods of lucidity, when their behavior was still recognizably mouselike: they ran in their wheels, they burrowed in their snowfalls of shred-

---

[54] Norton had used the opa'ivu'eke's left foreleg to feed the mice in the first and second experiments and the right hind leg on the mice in the third experiment. He actually sent Sereny both the remaining legs, the right foreleg and the left hind leg, so that Sereny would be able to replicate the variables as closely as possible. Sereny ended up using the left hind leg in his own experiment.

ded paper, they picked up the pieces of food we gave them with their two front paws and nibbled away. Now, however, the twenty-three mice who remained had lost even those basic behavioral reflexes.

Later I would be asked how and why I had decided not to reveal these findings. But it was hardly a decision that was mine to make. As I have said, no one was exactly clamoring for my thoughts on anything, much less mice with extended lifetimes who were displaying progressive dementia. Even if I had wanted to say something, no one would have listened. However, I must admit that something else—I hate to use such a term as *precognition*, but there it is—also kept me silent. I knew even then that one day soon my discoveries would be legitimized and appreciated for what they were, and that in the mice's behavioral deterioration was not only the next step in the narrative but my next challenge. I had already proven that the opa'ivu'eke could prolong life; now I had to discover how it might do so without delivering in tandem its terrible punishment.

⁂

Never had twenty-four months felt as long as the ones I endured after Sereny began his experiment, which replicated my initial one exactly.[55] And yet now of course I realize that twenty-four months is nothing: two million breaths, a slur of vision-blurred nights, a series of meals eaten and books read. Twenty-four months—exactly the time I will spend in this place—is brief, so brief that its days vanish before one can even record them.

And it is not as if I was not kept informed. Sereny wrote me letters—sometimes long and detailed, sometimes brief and perfunctory—keeping me abreast of the experiment. I made a chart so I could follow its every development, track which mice had died and which seemed sluggish, note how many days, weeks, months they had lived

---

[55] It actually replicated the third of Norton's experiments. On March 14, 1954, Sereny began an experiment in which he fed one hundred mice aged fifteen months a portion of opa'ivu'eke. The control group of one hundred was fed the same species of box turtle that Norton had used. A voluminous and highly technical correspondence specifying the amount of turtle that should be consumed by both groups was exchanged, all of which can be found among Sereny's papers, which are in the possession of Harvard Medical School.

beyond their natural lifespan. Even so, even with Sereny's information and my own endeavorings to discover why the opa'ivu'eke's gift of prolonged youth and life soured so spectacularly and what might be done to reverse it, I felt time pressing against me. Each day passed under the *thunk* of a remorselessly ticking clock, each second in my mind as loud and hollow as a slap. I turned thirty, then thirty-one, and around me my colleagues, all younger,[56] all arguably no more talented than I, hurried toward grand appointments and glory and recognition, while I sat in a lab and waited for the day's packet of mail to thud to the ground before hurrying to it as the mice hurried toward their feed, desperate for a letter from Sereny.

But then, finally, came the day I had been waiting for: in early April of 1956, Sereny sent me a note saying that he was readying his own paper for submission. Eighty-seven percent[57] of his mice that had ingested the opa'ivu'eke were alive at forty months;[58] the control group was long dead. Sereny, being much more respected and distinguished than I, had already spoken to his friend who was the editor of the *Lancet*; the paper would be appearing in the September issue.

Was I to know what kind of reaction Sereny's paper would receive?[59] No, of course not. I suspected, naturally, but it was as if

---

[56] Norton is probably referring to James Watson, who would have been only twenty-seven in 1955.

[57] A slightly better survival rate than Norton's mice, but not necessarily significant, for reasons explained in the following note.

[58] It is not known why Sereny decided to submit his paper when the mice were just forty months instead of waiting for them to reach forty-six months, which was the age of Norton's mice when he submitted his paper.

[59] Adolphus Sereny, "On 'Observations on Prolonged Human Longevity Among the Ivu'ivu People,' by Norton Perina: A Response," *Lancet* 268, no. 6940 (September 1, 1956), 421–28. Interestingly, it was Sereny who ended up naming the Ivu'ivuan village people "the Opa'ivu'eke people of Ivu'ivu." The villagers had no name for themselves—they were simply *u'ivu'ivu*, or "of Ivu'ivu"—and so Sereny's moniker eventually became commonly accepted. It was also Sereny who later named the condition "Selene syndrome." (Sereny had studied classics as an undergraduate and was famous among his students for his love of mythological allusions and references. It was said that in order to succeed in Sereny's classes, it was good to know the difference between the trochlear and the trigeminal, but it was far better to know the difference between Tiryns and Tartarus.)

overnight I had gone from being a pariah to being something of a god: I had become my own opa'ivu'eke, a creator of life and a granter of miracles, someone who had discovered something that made the impossible possible. In those days news did not travel as quickly as it does now, and so in the two weeks or so between the publication of Sereny's paper and the journal reaching its Stateside readers, there was a period of silence; it was almost as if Sereny had not written the paper at all. I had received an early copy of his report—which was quite satisfactory and essentially reiterated everything I had already said or otherwise knew, albeit from a much more trustworthy source—and in the days immediately following its publication, I called him and telegrammed him and wrote to him at what I will admit was an obnoxious rate, demanding to know what kind of reaction he had received and what it might mean for me. Sereny was, I can now see, rather good about the whole thing, and even before the paper had been submitted he had been kind enough to begin introducing me to various people at universities and institutes who might be able to give me some sort of permanent position. I talked, finally, to the head of Stanford's medical school, and to the head of Cal's, and took a trip back east to meet with the Neurology Department at Harvard (Sereny was mysteriously out of the country when I visited and was unable to see me) and assorted others at Johns Hopkins, Rockefeller, Yale, etc. While I was there I stopped to visit Owen, who was fatter and more bearded than ever and now lecturing at Amherst, which was apparently much more to his liking than Mills. We sat on the steps of the English Department building (it was late spring but still bitter cold), drinking tea that tasted as if Owen had left a shard of bark in some hot water and swirled it around a bit, and I watched as Owen watched the parade of undergraduates shuffle by, his eyes narrowed into greedy little slits. He was feeling particularly victorious as his first book of poetry, *The Nautilus Sky*, had just been published by some obscure press[60] to slavering reviews. It was a very low moment for me, feeling him sitting next to me as hot as a radiator with his triumph, while I had nothing to show for my now many years spent in the lab with my silent Oriental assistant

---

[60] Owen Perina, *The Nautilus Sky: Poems* (San Francisco: City Lights, 1956).

except Sereny's promise and his paper, all my hopes suspended somewhere between Cambridge and London.

But after the paper was read! Suddenly the flow of telegrams and letters and telephone calls reversed, and I hurried to the lab to find daily new accolades and inquiries and notes of praise, many of them from the very people who three years before had mocked me (not included in this group were any of my former colleagues from Smythe's lab or my new neighbors, whose visits to Cheolyu abruptly stopped after the *Lancet* article). The only people I might have heard from but did not were Tallent and Esme; they were in Ivu'ivu, where they had been for the past six months—their paper had, I heard, won them an instant new round of funding—and I was glad of this. I was a scientist and in a different field altogether, and there was nothing to be done besides, but I still dreaded the day when I would have to have the inevitable conversation with Tallent about my theft of the opa'ivu'eke.

And then it was almost 1957, and once again events pressed up against one another and all became a flurry. I was in the lab late one night working on answering some of the many letters that were arriving daily when I heard a knock on the door and a tall, bearded man carrying a rattling paper bag walked in.

It took me a few moments to realize that it was Tallent. He had had a beard in Ivu'ivu, of course—I had as well—but it was somehow disorienting to see it trimmed and clean as it was now, not to mention out of context.

"So," he said, after we'd shaken hands and he'd sat down across from me on one of the high stools. "I hear that congratulations are in order."

The beard made it difficult for me to discern his facial expression. I thought I heard—or perhaps I was just being hopeful?—something like amusement in his voice, but I wasn't certain.

I immediately began talking, apparently thinking that if I spoke fast and long enough I might be able to make him—what? forgive me? forget about the turtle?—until he finally held up his hand. "Norton," he said, and I heard something of the old weariness enter his voice, a particular sort of tiredness that he seemed to express only around me, "I had more or less already suspected you did this."

"You're not mad?" I asked him, greatly relieved.

His mouth twitched a bit. "I didn't say that," he said. "You know I don't agree with what you did. But I understand why you did it."

We talked for a while longer then, he asking semi-informed but surprisingly intelligent questions about my work (it seemed that he had read the paper and actually made sense of it).

"Well," he said at last, his voice sad, "it's over for them."

"What do you mean?" I asked him.

"If you're correct, Norton—and even if you're not—then every pharmaceutical company is going to go over there and try to capture those turtles. Not to mention every anthropologist and every bota-nist, herpetologist, you name it. Ivu'ivu as we know it is over."

It seemed unfair to be solely blamed for this, and I said so. Hadn't his own paper exposed the island already? They were already no lon-ger lost.

"Oh, you're correct that I'm to blame as well," he replied. "But my paper revealed nothing but a small group of people, of no real use or consequence to anyone. Certainly of no profit to anyone."[61]

---

[61] In 1993, a much-debated book speculated that not only was Tallent perfectly aware of Norton's theft, but he was aware as well that ingestion of the opa'ivu'eke led both to a superannuated lifespan and to a highly compromised one. In *Nowhere Is an Island: The Man Who Was Paul Tallent* (New York: Faber and Faber), Henry Gombrecht, an American studies professor at Williams, claims that Tallent never announced his findings for fear that the island would be overrun with fortune hunt-ers and scientists. He further claims that once Tallent figured out that Norton had come to the same conclusion, he and Esme plotted to kill him or abandon him on Ivu'ivu, but that Tallent lost his nerve shortly before the deed was to be done. Gom-brecht also claims that Tallent's eventual disappearance was a sort of self-inflicted penance for what he considered his role in the destruction of the island, though in a curious bit of scholarly circumspection, he stops short of speculating whether Tallent killed himself (as many believe) or simply vanished into some small unreachable part of the world.

As efficient and yet dramatic as Gombrecht's theory is, it is very difficult to see where he might have found proof for any of it, given that none of Tallent's personal writings have ever been located. Gombrecht, though (who if nothing else proved himself tenacious in the face of the controversies that erupted after the book's publication), claims to have pages from Tallent's first Ivu'ivu journals that an unnamed source gave to him. However, considering the facts that (1) he has refused to have the papers authenticated, or even to show them to any of his colleagues, and (2) the people who would have had the most ready access to pages from that diary would have been Esme Duff—who died in 1982, when Gombrecht was still in graduate school and unlikely to have cause to be introduced to her—and Norton

He stood and walked to the other side of the table and began to lift various beakers at random, peering into them and placing them back approximately where he'd gotten them. I would have thought an anthropologist, with his avowed fetish for leaving things where he'd found them, would have been a little more conscientious, but I was apparently incorrect in this assumption. "But this," he said, "this is different." He stopped and began fiddling with a stray pipette that Cheolyu hadn't put away. It is amazing and vexing how sloppy and invasive nonscientists are in a lab; to them, the entire space is like a boutique, and our instruments are mere stuff to be handled and fondled and played with like gadgetry. "When we were back this past time—I just returned last week—we were waiting on the shore at U'ivu for the boat to take us to Ivu'ivu when the king's messenger came jogging toward me holding a piece of paper that the king wanted me to see. Who were these people, the king wanted to know, and should he grant them the right to visit the island? And what had I to say about the letter writer's claims about me?

"It was a letter from another anthropologist—someone at Columbia, someone I know. It was written in U'ivuan, but very crudely—he'd obviously had to look up every word and translate the sentences from English literally—but in it he claimed that we were former colleagues and that he had his own journeys he wanted to make in U'ivu. He praised the king—clumsily, as I've said, but deeply—as a great monarch, and said that the West had much to learn from his civilization. And with the king's permission, he'd like to come to the islands so he might educate the West.

"At the end of the letter were, perhaps not surprisingly, a few lines about how my work had portrayed the king and his people as madmen and idiots, and how, thanks to my writings, the rest of the world was laughing at them and, worse, preparing to attack them. He advised the king that if he wanted to protect his people, he should ban me from the islands immediately and make certain I was not able to return."

He put the pipette down and picked up a stack of my correspon-

---

himself, who would surely have volunteered them to a much more respectable and trustworthy academic source had they existed, it is difficult to believe, much less confirm, the veracity of his statements.

dence and started flicking through it unseeingly. "I had thought something like this might happen, but I hadn't thought it would happen so . . . baldly, I guess. I wanted to get on the boat and leave—the guides were already waiting for us on Ivu'ivu—but this was too important to ignore. So I told Esme to go ahead and accompanied the messenger back to the king's palace."

"Was he very angry?" I asked.

"The king is . . . the king is difficult to understand. Conversations with him are full of silences, and you have to learn how to wait through them. I spent the rest of the afternoon and most of the evening there with him. He'll say something, something impossible, like 'Why are you telling people bad things about my country?' and then you have to explain that you're not and that you're being misrepresented, and he just sits there, staring at something you can't quite see, until the silence almost feels torturous, and then his next question—'How long are you staying?'—feels like both a benediction and a test. Are you being approved to go ahead? Is all being forgiven? Or is it purely a factual question? Do you answer, as I did, 'Six months, Your Highness,' or do you humble yourself further and say only, 'As long as Your Highness will have me'?

"In the end he let me go, and I made it to Ivu'ivu only a day later than I'd planned. But before I left, he told me he had received many, many letters from people asking to come to the islands. So far he had not responded to any of them. And was *that* a warning? Or simply a statement of fact?"

"Wait," I said. "How's the mail even getting to them?"

He blinked. "There's an outpost—an unofficial embassy of sorts—in Papeete, on Tahiti. The consul there travels back and forth to Tavaka once a month. All international correspondence is routed to him."

"Oh," I said.

"The point is, Norton," he said, walking about once more, "at some point someone will offer the king something he'll want, and once that happens, the island will no longer be yours or mine, insofar as it is. It'll belong to whoever tempts him most. And then your research will stop, and so will mine."

"But won't he want to protect Ivu'ivu?"

"Not necessarily. The king doesn't care about Ivu'ivu. It's something of an embarrassment to him, and its people are of little consequence to him."

"But what if he realizes it can make him money?"

He shook his head. "The king doesn't care for money. It won't make a difference to him."

And then I thought of something, and the knowledge domed up inside me, frightening in its possibilities. "Tallent," I asked him, "what did *you* offer the king to make him give you access?"[62]

---

[62] This remains one of the lasting mysteries of Paul Tallent's unusually mysterious life. Numerous theories have been postulated, but the two most enduring (if not the most credible) are that Tallent performed sexual favors for the king and that he somehow managed to convince the king that he was a god. The evidence for the former theory is as follows: the king was known for being, in modern terms, bisexual; although he had numerous wives, he also had numerous male lovers. His wives all hewed fairly strictly to the traditional ideal of U'ivuan female beauty—stocky and heavy-hipped, with round, slightly bulging eyes and very black hair—but he was known for being much more catholic in his tastes when it came to his male companions, even going so far as to actively seek out men of diverse appearance (a challenging quest on monoracial U'ivu). A 1986 book by Harriet Maxwell, one of the second-generation anthropologists to study U'ivu, suggests that during his first trip to the islands, in 1947, Tallent became for a brief but potent period the king's primary lover, a sort of treasured oddity in His Highness's collection (it is not known whether Tallent was a practicing homosexual in his daily life, although even if he was, the story, if true, says a great deal about his ambition and determination). Their sexual relationship was not long-lived—although Maxwell posits that Tallent was thereafter compelled to perform sexually for the king on each of his subsequent visits—but he apparently won the king's favor and for many years was the only Westerner allowed unrestricted access to Ivu'ivu.

Eventually, however, Tallent lost his sole rights to the island, in part, Maxwell suggests, because of the very miscalculation that Norton recounts: in the end, it turned out that the king *could* be tempted. Not with money—Tallent was right about that—but with things: the pharmaceutical companies and explorers and various hangers-on that followed were able to purchase access to the island with gifts of planes, boats, refrigerators and other appliances (although electricity was not widely, much less regularly, available on the islands until 1972), and much cheaper flotsam as well. The U'ivu National Museum in Tavaka is full of glass cases of these embarrassing relics—cigarette lighters and record players and cigars and wheeled suitcases, all gifts from scientists and scholars hoping to convince the king to give them access to the wonders of Ivu'ivu. (The most upsetting and cynical gift in the king's collection is a book whose jacket bears an image of the king and the title *His Royal Highness Tui'mai'ele* [sic]: *The Great King of U'ivu.* The book is actually a biography of Abraham Lincoln that has been rejacketed. But the king would not have been able to read English, and it is likely that he would have been flattered, and marveled at how far his renown had spread. The gift is credited to

He turned and stared at me. Once again I thought I saw, under his beard, something like a smile. "I can't tell you, can I?" he said. "Otherwise everyone will know."

I didn't know what to say to this. Did he mean I was a gossip? Or was he making a joke? Why did Tallent always have to be so maddeningly elusive? But before I could formulate my next question, he was walking toward the room where we kept the dreamers, shaking the paper bag over his shoulder at me. "Dried hunonos, fresh from Ivu'ivu," he said. "A special treat."

❄

Tallent's visit disturbed me more than I thought, more than it should have. He had been angry about the dreamers. "Norton, what happened to them?" he demanded after trying and failing to excite them with the hunonos, which not so long before would have inspired fits of salivating and anticipatory teeth-clacking, and before I had a chance to answer, he said, "Mua doesn't even speak anymore. Eve won't even stand up! And they're obese—what on earth

<hr />

"an American scientist from New York, USA, 1964," by which point pharmaceutical companies were swarming throughout Ivu'ivu on the hunt for the opa'ivu'eke.) (*The Disappearing Island: The Mysterious Life of Paul Tallent*).

The second theory, that Tallent convinced the king that he was a god, comes courtesy of another second-generation U'ivuan scholar, Antony Flaglon. In a 1990 paper for the *Annals of Anthropology*, Flaglon relates a tale supposedly told to him by one of the king's adviser's sons, who claims that his father saw Tallent "leaning over His Highness and 'chanting in a deep and sonorous voice' while His Highness lay back against his cushions, mouth open with enchantment." Aside from the use of the word *sonorous* (which seems not at all the sort of language an illiterate U'ivuan might employ, the king's adviser or no), there are reasons to be suspicious of this tale. For one—as Flaglon notes—Tallent was raised in a Catholic orphanage, and it is most likely that he was performing some liturgical chants for the king's amusement, with no apparent aim of bewitchment. For another, there is of course no such thing as bewitchment. More importantly, Flaglon was apparently unable to find any other of the king's intimates, including his children and other members of the court, to confirm the adviser's son's statement (*Annals of Anthropology*, vol. 48, no. 570, 134–43). (Interestingly, Flaglon's paper inspired a new round of advocacy for the first theory, with yet another of the second-generation scholars—this one a professor at McGill named Horace Grey Hosmer—speculating that what the adviser actually saw was Tallent seducing the king as a prelude to beginning some sort of ecstatic sexual orgy ["Far from U'ivu, a Mysterious Life Gets Reexamined Once Again," *New York Times*, March 27, 1991].)

have you been feeding them?" I will admit now that I had not been spending anywhere near the amount of time with the dreamers that I ought to have, but at the time I mostly thought it very unjust that Tallent should be holding me responsible for their decline. Would he have been able to do any better in such an environment? (I thought briefly of the dreamers we had left behind tied to the manama tree; were they in better health, livelier, than the ones we had taken with us? Were they even alive?)

He left in a fury, and I found myself abruptly devastated. Of course it was ridiculous; I had moved far past the point where I needed Tallent's help, much less his approval, not to mention the fact (I had to remind myself) that I didn't even much respect his field of study. And yet I did crave from him something he seemed unwilling or unable to give.

However, this did not stop the elation I experienced when I heard shortly thereafter that I was to return to Ivu'ivu. Along with bestowing on me instant and permanent legitimacy, Sereny's paper had the added benefit (or, if you asked Tallent, detraction) of making every medical school in the country eager to send its own research team to Ivu'ivu, this time for the sole purpose of retrieving as many turtles as possible and bringing them back to its laboratories. Although I had nowhere near official or permanent status at the university—a fact I made sure to remind the president of at every opportunity—I was, as the school's "honored guest," being respectfully asked to go on Stanford's behalf. I would be accompanied, I was told, by someone I knew well: Tallent. And, unfortunately, Esme.

I wasn't quite sure how to react to this news. My attraction to Tallent, my desire to be near him when even I could see that the feeling was not mutual, was something that had grown out of my control: I thought of it as a gigantic mushroom, puffy and mis-shapen and tumorous, ploofing out into strange and fantastic for-mations. I also feared, from our last interaction, that he must have been made to agree to this arrangement somehow and that it would not be a welcome pairing for him. (Less conflicted were my feelings for Esme, but when I asked the president if it was wholly necessary that she should go, he frowned and looked confused and I hurriedly decided to drop the matter.)

And so a month later there I was, deplaning in U'ivu on the

same bumpy, makeshift ersatz polo field, mounting the same ridiculous little horse (or one just like it), and being led by a man, Pava, who could have been Tu's or Uva's clone, so similar was he in appearance to them. But this time, instead of going straight to the fetid shack and from there to the boat, I was taken to Tavaka to meet the king. I was, naturally, excited about this, just as much about seeing Tavaka as I was about seeing the king.

Decades later I would be in Valparaiso, Chile, for a conference and would be standing in the hotel's lounge, looking out the window. In front of me was the port, where crayon-colored storage containers were stacked one atop another as easily as child's bricks by a Jurassic crane, and around me was the neatly inverted ziggurat of the city, the tiers of houses and buildings forming tidy geometric steps as they ascended into the woolly wet gray of the sky. I had never been to Valparaiso, but the scene was somehow familiar to me, like a place I had experienced before. But it was not until much later that day, when I was sitting through yet another endless speech, that I realized why I had recognized it: it was because this was what I had hoped Tavaka might look like.

Of course it was a ridiculous idea. Valparaiso is a busy port city that moves thousands of tons of cargo, whereas to call Tavaka a hub of any kind would have been to stretch the truth until it snapped and split in two. But at the time—for all my worldliness, I was, you will remember, still quite untraveled—it seemed to make sense: Tavaka was the capital of an island and would somehow reflect its position.

Needless to say, it did not. In fact, the most striking thing about Tavaka was how much it resembled the village. Here was the same basic layout—rings of houses surrounding an unpaved town circle—and here were hogs (albeit smaller and more petlike) trotting untethered around the houses, and children (half clothed) wandering about as well, calling to one another and falling down and giggling and crying and generally doing all the things that children do everywhere. The houses were sturdier and more sophisticated—simple structures made of wood, with doors (but no locks) and thatched palm-leaf roofs—and there were more of them, but from a distance it could have and in fact did pass for Ivu'ivu. The essential differences here were the presence of the sea, whose waves licked the same stretch of flat sand again and again and which was only about fifty yards or so from the farthest ring of houses, and the king's palace, which sat approximately where the ninth hut would have been, and the fact that this town was surrounded not by forest but by large squares of tilled land, the deep brown of its loam stitched with bright green fists of young crops. There was jungle nearby, of course, but it had been thinned so aggressively that you could see straight through it to the mountains, whose tops were covered with a crust of wildly tangled trees.

I had at the very least expected something grander from the king's palace, and while it is true that it was significantly larger than the other structures—about seven times the size of a standard house—and raised slightly above the others, its architecture was consistent with the others', and it was by no means particularly kingly. Over its door hung an opa'ivu'eke carapace, handsome but not nearly as beautiful as the one in the ninth hut had been, and draped over it a braided swag of leafy vines, which gave off a lemony, peppery scent as I walked beneath it. As I did, I noticed that the turtle's shell was cracked in one section and that it had been repaired with little butterflies made from wood.

I was surprised by how pleasant it was inside. The house was arranged something like a Japanese temple, just one long, deep, low-ceilinged room, with two small antechambers at either end, the doorways to which were concealed with woven-palm mats. There was no privacy here, and yet there was no sound either. Where were the wives and their numerous children? Where was the king? Also resembling a Japanese temple were the floors, which were covered as well with palm mats. On the far wall, the one facing the entrance, hung a second opa'ivu'eke shell, this one much larger than the one outside. I could tell from the depth of its color and the way the plates had faded and softened at their edges that it was very old, and probably very treasured as well; in the gloom it was little more than a shadow if you were looking at it straight on, but if you moved just a few inches to the right or the left, you could see the plasticky gleam it made as it reflected the sunlight.

Then there was a stirring from the antechamber on the left, and here, suddenly, was the king. Upon his appearance, Pava scurried backward roachily in a crouch that was half bow over the lip of the doorframe and out of sight.

The first thing I thought was that he was far less impressive than the chief had been. He had a pleasant enough face, if such a thing could be said of the U'ivuans—a wide, amused mouth and very round, very dark eyes, like those of a marmoset. His hair was spotted with white and tied into a frizzy tumbleweed, and around his waist he wore a sort of triangular flap of lustrous satiny cloth that I later saw was actually thousands of crimson and black feathers woven into a zagging pattern. The only exceptional things about him were, first, the beautiful crown he wore, an exuberant wreath of what I recognized were lawa'a ferns and through which was threaded some of the citrusy vine that adorned his doorway—which reminded me of the a'ina'ina—and second, his spear, which was very long, at least nine feet, and slender, swelling into a large white tip. Even from a distance I could see that the spear was elaborately carved with shapes of opa'ivu'ekes, and its base was etched with a series of whorls that Tallent later told me were meant to represent waves.

There was only one man with him, one who was skinny and very brown and wore around his waist a leather pouch made of what seemed to be boar skin, and around whose head was a single loop of the vine. He waited until the chief had sat down cross-legged before me and then nodded at me before sitting as well.

"I am translator," he said.

In subsequent years I would be asked and reasked about this interview with the king, as if he were the last unicorn and I the last to see him alive. And each time I would have to send my inquisitors away disappointed, for the truth is that the conversation with the king was rather banal. (Later, when I was to meet other monarchs of other countries, I would realize that the dullness of the conversation had perhaps less to do with Tuimai'ele's capabilities in particular and more to do with the position itself.) He asked if I liked U'ivu and I said yes. He asked what in particular I liked about U'ivu and I, savvy enough at least to know not to reference Ivu'ivu, said I liked the beautiful trees and flowers and his lovely house. He nodded. I thought then, fleetingly, that I might have an opportunity to turn the conversation toward the opa'ivu'eke carapace, but as anyone who has met a head of state knows, trying to introduce any topic of interest— which, as a general rule, they seem not to want to discuss—is next to impossible if one wants to maintain good relations. He said he understood that I worked with Tallent, and I, not knowing what he had been told, replied with great caution: Yes, I worked with Tallent. Yes, he was a good man. Yes, he loved U'ivu very much.

And then it was over. The king, who had not smiled once but whose large, toady mouth made it appear as if he had been grinning throughout, gave a firm and somehow conclusive nod, and the translator gave a subtle flick of his fingers at me, and I crawled backward and out in the same rounded, beetley squat my guide had adopted. Outside, I found Pava at once—he had been leaning against a manama tree and staring intently at the door—and when he saw me, he gave a wide grin that I was left to interpret as I followed him. Were there some people who, upon meeting the king, never emerged? Clearly I had passed some sort of crucial test, but of what—and what punishment I had apparently eluded—I couldn't guess.

He led me toward one of the huts closest to the beach and stopped and called out. I heard a rustling from inside, and then the door pushed open and a woman emerged to stand before me, blinking in the light. Behind her I could see the inside of the house, which was dark and whose circumference was rimmed with things: palm-leaf mats and no'aka half-shells stacked one inside the other like bowls; a collection of bamboo poles; a series of woven baskets, their lids askew. Like Pava, the woman wore a single piece of useless clothing, one that seemed to evade altogether the purpose of clothes; in her case it was a long necklace strung with what looked like hog's teeth, which drooped beneath but did not conceal her teats. Two children—one a boy of maybe eleven (he could not have been much more, for he was spearless), the other a girl of about nine—came out and stood beside her, not touching her, and what was notable about them was their silence, their watchfulness. A few yards from us, a group of children ran by in a noisy flock, but these two did not watch them go, only raised their eyes to me.

Pava was looking at me expectantly, as if I should know them, and when I said nothing, only looked at them and then at him, his expression changed to one of impatience.

"Who are they?" I asked him in U'ivuan.

"Fa'a no ohala," he replied, surprised. *Fa'a's family.*

I was startled and irritated and confused. Why had I been brought here? Was it possible—but no, it wasn't—that I had asked to meet them?

And so I began my second strange interview of the day. I asked questions and the woman, Fa'a's widow, answered them, so briefly and dully that I would later wonder if she might be mentally impaired in some way. All the while, my discomfort was overshadowed by a sort of bright rage. Why was I being made to feel guilty about this, to meet Fa'a's family, to see their sad hut (what I had seen as a disciplined, well-ordered space now struck me as a poor one, bereft of belongings and color and busyness), when I had had nothing to do with his death, which had been, after all, years ago? Had Tallent been subjected to the same meeting? What did they want? Money? Goods?

Any respect I had managed to earn from Pava after my successful encounter with the king quickly dissolved, and after some minutes of this—he looking between the two of us in growing incredulity—he interrupted and spoke at length to Fa'a's widow, so quickly that I was unable to comprehend. He seemed to be half lecturing, half pleading with her, but I was unable to tell which, for she never lifted her head to look at him. The two children stepped closer to her, but neither looked up. I noticed too for the first time how their skin had a dusty cast, as if they'd been rolled in talc, and how the other children, running past them, did so without even acknowledging their presence. From behind the hut strolled two women, carrying baskets and talking loudly, and although they walked within inches of Fa'a's hut, neither of them thought to greet the widow or even to look in her direction. It was impossible to feel completely physically isolated from the others—they all inhabited such a small space, after all— but clearly the rest of the villagers had done their best to exclude Fa'a's family from their society. Even the hut's location, pushed back as it was to the far perimeter of the circle, seemed freighted with meaning; the only place its inhabitants could go from here was the sea. I looked toward the water and saw, perfectly framed between Fa'a's house and its neighbor, the conical mass of Ivu'ivu; this view would be the family's daily reminder of where their husband and father had gone and been lost and the answer, as I would later guess, to their ostracism.[63]

Finally, seeing that he was unable to convince the woman to do as he'd hoped, Pava grabbed the boy by the arm and shoved him toward me. "Do you want him?" he asked me.

"What?" I asked. Naturally, I was shocked. "No, no, of course not!"

He pushed the boy back toward his mother (who was still looking at her feet) and this time pinched the girl around her skinny arm. "This one, then."

"I don't know what you've been told," I said to Pava, "but I don't want either of these children."

"But she cannot keep them," Pava told me.

"Well, I can't keep them either!"

I was expecting him to argue with me further, but instead he turned and spoke to Fa'a's widow once more—a long, diarrhetic stream of words out of which I could pluck only a few unhelpful

---

[63] Fa'a was the third son in a well-respected clan of wild boar hunters who were known throughout Tavaka for their generosity and bravery. But so strong was the U'ivuans' distrust of Ivu'ivu that his extended journey there—in the company of three ho'oalas, no less—greatly damaged his and his family's reputation. When it was revealed that he had died on the island, his family (although not, significantly, his wife) denounced and later disowned him. Norton later told me that he heard whisperings among the Tavakans about Fa'a's suspected fate: that he had been eaten by the Ivu'ivuans (a persistent fable), that he had become one of them, and, most damningly, that he had become the very thing that he had gone to search for, that not-human, not-beast hybrid that roved the island still—a mo'o kua'au.

It is unlikely that Fa'a would have confided in Uva and Tu that he had, however accidentally, come into contact with an opa'ivu'eke; the taboo was simply too powerful. But it *is* likely that they somehow contrived a story that rendered them unwilling participants in Fa'a's scheme and therefore blameless. At any rate, they joined the rest of the family in excluding Fa'a's wife and children, although they reportedly did give them gifts of food and supplies on an occasional basis.

The fate of Fa'a's wife and children remains unknown. Because all U'ivuans share a single family name—in this case, all three of them would have been Utuimai'ele, or "Of Tuimai'ele," because they were all born during that king's reign—Norton would later find them impossible to track down. Given their elusiveness, he would conjecture that they might eventually have been forced to disown Fa'a as their husband and father in order to reenter society, or, alternatively, that they decided to undergo conversion at the hands of the Christian missionaries who would come to dominate island life in the following decade.

terms: *you, Fa'a, children, no,* etc.—and then looked back at me. "Let's go," he said, and began strolling out of the village.

As I trailed him, I fretted and seethed. What was that encounter supposed to mean, and how was I to interpret it? The lesson, clearly, was that Fa'a's death had left his family in a state of penury, for which I was somehow being blamed (though surely the blame belonged equally, if not more, to Tallent—had the children first been offered to him?). Or was that the lesson? And did such a thing as penury even exist here? I had always assumed from the way the village on Ivu'ivu had been run, days and people tumbling into one another with no apparent laws or nuance, that U'ivu too was governed by a sort of lax, unevolved version of socialism, in which everything was shared and no one save the king had anything more exceptional than anyone else. Why, then, were things so difficult for Fa'a's family? And more importantly, and troubling as well, why was I being offered his children, of all things? Surely it would be more feasible to ask me to procure goods (although I would have had little idea of how to go about doing that either, as I had no notion of U'ivuan money or how to get it) or, at the very least, food? Somewhere inside me, a small fern of fear unfurled: had Fa'a seen me with the boy in the woods and formed some sort of impression of me, one that he had passed on to the others? But I could not think that way. The old wearying sensation of being on these islands was returning to me, the one in which I felt I was forever being asked questions I couldn't understand, locked into my end of a one-sided, inexplicable exchange in which all my responses were incorrect.

A week later—or more?—I was back at Tallent's camp, in the same—or was it?—scrub of forest just on the edge of the village. This time my guide uphill had been not a U'ivuan but an actual Ivu'ivuan, a man I remembered from my last visit here, only because he had a terrible cleft palate that made him look as if his lower face had been gnawed on by a beast and then spat up and reassembled. Of course, this did not make him much of a conversationalist, first because he was not given to talking anyway, and second because everything he said was so garbled and slurpy-sounding that he may as well have been speaking underwater.

It had been clear to me from the rapidity with which Uva and Tu had left us to hurry back to their families upon our last return to U'ivu that they would not soon or willingly make another trip to Ivu'ivu, but I missed them and their good-natured ways. The new guide, however—I could not tell if his name was Uo or Uvu—was a wonderful naturalist, and although he could not speak intelligibly, I soon grew to admire and appreciate his ability to spot the smallest of wonders in the forest, which he would either bring to me or point out for my enjoyment. One day he brought me a scarlet petal as small as a chickpea, which upon examination I realized was an orchid, scaled down until it was impossibly tiny, its lip a pale, unearthly gray. When he saw that I liked it, Uo beckoned me to a kanava tree a few yards off our path, and I saw that a small lake of them was painting the jungle floor a vibrant, bloody crimson. But what I loved most was their scent, one that mingled sweetness and decay at once and filled one's nostrils so completely that its very memory lingered for hours afterward.

With Uo I saw much of what had eluded me the last time, and since I was no longer as frightened, nor as anxious to reach our ultimate destination, I was able to examine everything more closely. And this time I did what I ought to have done when I had first had the opportunity: when Uo brought me a creature that I assumed was an armadillo but later saw was a monstrous beetle, its carapace jointed into a hundred flexible plates that rippled and shifted upon one another as it wriggled in his hands, I made drawings and took notes and measurements. I pressed between my notebook pages the round, gingkolike leaves that grew in staggered tiers on a spindly golden-trunked tree I'd not noticed before, the ones that changed color from green at their base to purple at their tips, the space in between filled by a strange, unnameable shade that made me think of dragons' scales. I found a nest of plum-black lizard eggs the size of avocados whose stippled shells reminded me of leather and which peeled off in thick, supple pieces like an orange's skin. (Inside, I was surprised to see the fetal lizards covered in a strange, cottony fuzz, one that began disintegrating as soon as the embryonic fluid was drained.)[64]

---

[64] Norton later compiled many of these illustrations and descriptions into a book called *The Painted Sea: A Naturalist's Guide to Ivu'ivu* (New York: W. W. Norton,

Therefore, it was something of a disappointment when our journey was at last over and I was deposited by Uo among my own people at our camp. Tallent was not even there to greet me when I arrived. Instead there was only Esme, who I am sorry to say had not improved in appearance or temperament in the intervening seven years. She did not look pleased to see me.

"Norton," she said.

"Esme," I said. And that was it.

For all of Tallent's fears about the island being overrun by various competitors and mercenaries, there was only one addition to our group, a minky little man named Johan Meyers, who was a mycologist from Berkeley. He was one of those people you meet and are instantly weary of, mostly because of his globular eyes and his rapid blink (he was very nearsighted) and his dreadful stammer, which was not helped by his insistence on narrating every small thing he encountered. I once made the mistake of going mushroom-hunting with him, and had to endure many hours of his dull prattle: "And now here we see—what is this?—oh, it's a sort of fungus that grows in these stepped formations on this manama tree. Consistency very soft, almost velvety, tipped with what appears to be a very gentle fur, almost like that of a fly, but here powdery instead of coarse, and almost silvery in color," etc., etc. Like most mycologists, Meyers was deeply boring and interested in only one thing: fungi. A dinosaur could have gone crashing through the forest inches before him and it's doubtful he would have lifted his eyes from the puddle of snail-shaped mushrooms that he'd discovered growing at the base of a particularly mature lawa'a fern. He had absolutely no time for turtles or people, much less very old ones, and indeed had the useful ability to simply stop listening when the talk turned to such subjects, drifting off instead into a self-induced trance in which the whole world was remade as various fungal mutations. You always knew when this

---

1972). He is in fact credited with discovering both the orchid (*Miltonia perinia*) and the insect, a relation of the staghorn beetle (*Draco perinia*). Excellent examples of the latter are on view at the American Museum of Natural History and the Smithsonian Institution, but botanists have been unable to create ideal situations for the orchid to thrive anywhere but in the upper Amazon region of Brazil and in the Wai'ale'ale Valley of Kauai, Hawaii.

was happening, for his little mouth took on a sort of lightness and his eyes, behind their glass slabs, became moist and ecstatic. I often envied him those moments.

I hoped to accomplish three things while on my visit. The first was to gauge the chief's mental health (he would be only sixty-seven, and his adviser seventy, and so this was more of a checkup than anything else; I wasn't expecting any mental degradation yet). The second was to ascertain whether anyone else had celebrated their vaka'ina, and if so to begin a file on them. And the third—and primary—goal was to secure at least two opa'ivu'ekes, which I intended to take back alive to the States. I had a little less than a month to do this; on the twenty-eighth day, Uo would guide me back down-island, where I would be met by the boatman and taken back to U'ivu, where the pilot would meet me in the field at daybreak of the thirty-seventh day. If I missed him, I would have to wait until Tallent and Esme left the island, which would not be for another nine weeks after that.

One of the few nice things about revisiting a place that no one ever visits and where nothing ever changes is that one can skip all the introductions and reintroductions and simply reinsert oneself into the current of local life. By the fourth day, I had found the chief and had a brief audience with him. I am fairly certain he recognized me, but he seemed neither particularly surprised nor gratified by my presence. He did not seem to appreciate that I could now speak to him in his language, or the improbability of my reappearance in his life. But I did get from him the answer I wanted: no, no one else had celebrated their vaka'ina. As for the other question—that of his mental acuity—I had to make certain deductions. I could not, after all, give him any tests to measure it without offending him, but I left him feeling quite confident that no diminishment had yet begun.

The acquisition of opa'ivu'ekes was both more and less difficult than I'd anticipated. Happily, I did not have to go through the charade of pretending not to be interested in the turtle; without having to have an actual conversation about the matter, Tallent and I seemed to have reached some unspoken détente: he knew I was here for the opa'ivu'eke and had decided not to mention it if I did not. At any rate, I saw far less of him and Esme than I'd anticipated—their research was about the Ivu'ivuans' family structure and society, things that did not much concern me, and they spent most of their days conducting interviews with the various villagers.

Less happy, however, was my lack of a guide to the lake of turtles. The one thing Tallent had forbidden me to do was ask any of the villagers how to find my way back up that winding path to the plateau; to do so, he told me, would cause such grave offense we'd be lucky to escape with our lives. In later years I would reflect on Tallent's constant threats of the Ivu'ivuans' violence and wonder how much of it was exaggerated to make me behave in a way that he thought I ought, and how much of it was real and based on actual experience. Certainly I knew from the way that I'd seen the villagers kill their catch that they were skilled with their spears and unafraid to use them, but I never, in all my time in the village, saw one man turn his weapon against another. Was it because there was no need to, or was it because they were fundamentally incapable of such brutality? I was never to know.

Naturally, I was not eager to make a stumbling, hapless nighttime exploration to the lake, and so I spent my days venturing farther and farther up the path, trying uselessly to remember what looked familiar and what did not. I began each journey by tying a string around the base of the manama tree behind the ninth hut and concluded each path by tying the other end of the string at its natural end. I had foolishly never considered that the path might prong off in so many directions, but the only thing that saved me from becoming completely frustrated was that each of the routes I unsuccessfully pursued had finished in a dead end: one against a glossy grove of yellow bamboo that was so tightly packed I couldn't even squeeze my finger between them, another against a smooth blank edifice of putty-colored rock. Yet somewhere, somewhere high above me, was that snaking, illogical path that led to that improbable field and its lake with its gulping wide-eyed turtles.[65]

Those were my days, then. But in the evenings I thought about

---

[65] Tallent had in fact made a map of the route to the turtle lake on their first excursion to it with Mua, but Norton was too intimidated to ask to borrow it—although he did tell me that he rummaged through Tallent's bag one night when he was asleep but was unable to find it. Unfortunately, this map is now lost to scholars, along with Tallent's other papers.

the dreamers. It was difficult not to, especially when I was alone and in the forest; I kept expecting that one day I would turn and there, standing before that tree or slumped against that rock, one of them would be. Perhaps it would be someone I knew, one of the ones we had left with their god's offerings of Spam and hunonos, or perhaps it would be one I had never seen before, a twin of Mua or Ika'ana. They might be single or in a group, sentient or not, terrifying in the moment or not. Sometimes in certain late-afternoon light, when the air around me seemed to shimmer and sag with millions of gold particles, I was almost certain that I saw one of them, a shadow of hair making a thundercloud against a curtain of trees, or heard one of their footfalls crunching the rug of dead leaves behind me. But when I looked, there was nothing, and I would have to remind myself that even if I did encounter one, I was fully capable of overpowering him, and that at any rate they would mean me no harm.

One day I was headed back from yet another fruitless search for the lake when I came around a large kanava tree and found myself suddenly in front of the boy, the one whose a'ina'ina I had witnessed, the one I had encountered in the woods that night. He was of course no longer a boy—he would have been about seventeen by the Western calendar—and when I cried out in surprise, he looked back at me with a flat, level gaze, one that made me feel silly for being so expressive.

I must admit that I had been looking for him since I'd arrived, albeit not very hard. Normally, it would not have been difficult to find him, but it was the peak of hunting season, the time of year when the biggest game—monkeys and sloths and the wild boars you sometimes heard thundering through the woods—were slaughtered and skinned, and many of the young men who otherwise would have spent their days lounging about the village were gone in shifts, making abrupt reappearances at odd hours of the night and then vanishing again before the rest of the villagers woke.

He had grown up well; he was a man. In one hand he clutched his spear, and his other hand rested on his hog, which was as mean-eyed and mud-flecked as all the other men's hogs. But still I knew it was he: in adulthood he had the same somehow noble, well-composed face, the same lift to his chin, the same calm eyes. He would be married now, I imagined, and perhaps have a child of his own. Had his days as someone who lurked in the forest at night or embraced other boys under a tree ended, then? Or if I crept my way through the dark that night, my arms aloft as before, would I find myself being led to him once again, standing still and silent, waiting for me to happen upon him?

I could think of so much I wanted to say to him, and yet in the moment nothing would come forth, and so in the end I only nodded at him. After a long pause, he nodded back, and then turned and made his silent way off the path and into an uncharted part of the forest, his hog swaggering alongside him. In seconds he was gone, the thin trees he'd pushed aside to make room for him slapping back into place at once, erasing his presence completely.

I stood there watching the place where he'd disappeared. Had he remembered me? It seemed impossible that he hadn't. And yet the interaction had the strange effect of making me doubt that I had actually ever met him before. That night in the forest, when I had crashed through the underbrush with my hands stretched out before me, running until I encountered him, had been one of the loneliest and most desperate moments I had had on Ivu'ivu. When I had found him, I had been so grateful—not just because of the kindness he had shown me, but because it seemed as if he had been planted there to remind me of my own presence, my own realness. I often felt this way on Ivu'ivu, as if I were floating away from myself, my atoms rearranging themselves so that they were no more permanent or tangible than sunlight, so that the more time I spent there, the less certain I was of my own existence. I could have been lost that night in the forest. But I hadn't been. He had found me.

One afternoon I took a break from my scheming and turtle-searching and, for lack of anything better to do, followed Tallent and Esme for a bit as they made their rounds through the village. (Meyers had invited me to go look at some doubtless fascinating fungal fringe he'd discovered a short way downhill, but I had declined.)

However, watching Tallent and Esme sit at the edge of the village and scribble away in their notebooks was not much more interesting. After a while, Esme marched off to harass the poor woman who was guarding the meat hut, and I sat next to Tallent in silence, he scribbling, I staring at the small, busy lives before me, trying to see in the older children those whom I might have known as babies.

I was thinking about the lake of turtles and all the paths I might still have to explore when a toddler bobbled up to me, holding a piece of grass in her hand. She was probably a little over a year, unusually fat for an Ivu'ivuan, and had a sort of solemnity about her that reminded me of the boy, to whom my thoughts returned again and again.

"Hello," I said to her. "What's that you have?"

She stared. I have never found it difficult, as some do, to speak to children. All one has to do is pretend that they're some kind of intelligent farm animal: a pig, perhaps, or a horse. In fact, one should be much more intimidated by the prospect of speaking to a horse, since they can often be quite quick-witted and possessed of a great disdain for those they feel are not worthy of their attention.

At any rate, we had a nice exchange, the baby and I, which ended with her giving me the grass (and I thanking her) and then her bungling away. Somewhere in the middle of this interaction I became aware that Tallent had stopped writing and was watching us, and as she left, he said, "You're very good with children."

"Oh," I said, surprised. It had never occurred to me that there might be two different categories of people—those who were good with children and those who were not—and that I might be in the former group.

"Do you want children of your own?" Tallent asked.

This was even more surprising. You must remember that in the fifties, people, especially men, did not ask one another if they wanted children. It was assumed that you would have them, and liking them or not had very little bearing on the matter. It was simply something you did: you got married, you got a job, you had children. You might have a single child or many, your wife might be beautiful or not, your job dull or exceptional, but those were the only variations. So, "I don't know," I said. "I've never thought about it." And I hadn't.

"Mmm," said Tallent. "I think you will."

I found his confidence irritating. He had a certain talent for being able to make me feel like a creature from a book he had studied, who was doomed to fulfill a certain destiny whose shape only he knew.

"Do you?" I shot back at him.

He paused then and was thoughtful, which I hadn't expected. "I don't think so," he said at last.

"Why not?"

"It just isn't for me," he said, and smiled—not at me, but at something in the distance, as if at something or someone he recognized. I followed his gaze, fearful that he might be regarding Esme, but when I looked, there was no one there, just the square, empty for once but for the fire, the air around it blurring oilily in the heat.

It was not until the twenty-sixth day that I finally made my way back to the lake of turtles. There they were, paddling toward me, as friendly and gently inquisitive as cows, and there I was, lifting two of the smaller ones, each about the size of a large dinner plate, out of the water and putting them into the punched-hole cardboard carrying boxes I had brought with me.

The way down was not difficult, but it was slow. I had thought about how I might successfully mark my path but had concluded that there was no way of doing so without letting others benefit from it. I could not risk, say, nailing stakes into the earth or scratching symbols on trees without reasonably expecting that some future seeker (though at the time I wasn't wholly convinced there would be as many as Tallent had predicted) would find and follow them himself. So in the end I had to resort to sketching a highly detailed map, marking each turn and change of direction not by landmark—for indeed, the tree I might recognize as a sapling today would be something unrecognizable two or three years from now—but by the approximate distance that separated each one from the next. And of course I had to keep putting the turtles down to make another notation and then picking them up again.

Once I had reached the manama tree at the back of the ninth hut, I crouched behind it and waited for the last of the light to leave the sky; Esme and Tallent had, on this trip or the previous one, finally been invited to join the dinnertime feasts by the fire, and they could spend hours there without looking around them. Meyers generally spent his evenings back at the camp, dusting his precious fungi with one of the many stiff-bristled brushes he had brought and breathing humidly through his mouth. I crept around the back of the storage houses and toward my old tree, where I piled small branches and handfuls of moss on top of the boxes to conceal their presence. I had brought with me some turtle-food pellets I'd bought at an animal supply store back in California, and when I placed some before the opa'ivu'ekes, they stared at them for a moment or two before eating them and I sat back, relieved.

Later, herpetologists would write papers detailing the species' many unusual traits and characteristics, but all neglected to mention the one I found most appealing and singular about them, which was how they could project an almost canine friendliness combined with a feline centeredness. After eating, they padded about me for a few minutes, and when I stroked their carapaces, they did not retreat or take offense but merely shut their eyes and enjoyed it, much as their predecessor had done all those years before.

As I sat there with them, my thoughts turned to that conversation I'd had with Tallent about children. Over the past two weeks, some of the only comfort (and certainly the only amusement) I'd found had been with the village's children. I would encounter them playing on the borders of the village as I slumped back to the camp from yet another unsuccessful day of hunting for the lake of turtles, and after watching them, I began to see games and playacting emerge from what I'd previously been able to view as only a chaotic ruckus. They had one trick they especially enjoyed performing, in which two children would face each other, each with a bit of plant husk balanced on a finger. Then they'd twirl them around faster and faster, and whoever managed to find just the right speed so the husk remained on his finger would win.

There was one child in particular whom I particularly enjoyed speaking with and watching. He was maybe seven or eight, and in his stillness and attentiveness he reminded me somewhat of the boy. He wasn't a social outcast or anything of the sort, but he did seem apart from the others; when they played throwing games, or chased one another around the village, or dared one another to go another foot and then yet another past the manama tree behind the ninth hut, shrieking with fear and triumph as they ran back downhill, he would instead watch, a finger at the edge of his mouth and a worried expression on his face. I was moved by this frown of his, which was so adult and sad and somehow wise on a person so young. As he grew to know me and trust me, he would sometimes place a small hand on my arm or sit next to me and press his body against mine, and I would find myself babbling on to him, telling him about my life and the lab and Owen, none of which he could understand and all of which he listened to quietly, as if my words were a warm rain, so comforting that he felt no need to seek shelter.

One very hot afternoon, after his peers had gone galloping off toward the other end of the village, I realized that the boy had fallen asleep against me. I had been hoping to make one final sally uphill to look for the lake before the day passed, but something—maybe the deep contentedness of his breath—stopped me from moving, and I instead maintained my position and let him sleep. *I could have a child like this,* I thought. And then, *But I do not want a wife.* It was an impossibility, and even here, so far from home and its leaden social demands, I could not think of a way in which I might have one and yet not the other. I did not know a great deal about women then, but even my limited exposure to them had taught me that they were simply not for me. A wife! What would I discuss with her? I imagined days sitting around a plain white table and sawing away at a piece of meat burned crisp as toast, hearing the clop of her shoes as she walked across a shining linoleum floor, her hectoring conversations about money or the children or my job; I saw myself silent, listening to her drone on about her day and the laundry and whom she had seen at the store and what they had said. And then I also saw a different set of images: me lifting a sleep-heavy child and placing him in a bed, me teaching him about insects, or the two of us hunting beetles or butterflies together, visiting the sea together for the first time.

But that night, awake on my mat, what I mostly thought of was the heat of that young body next to mine, the smallness of his hand. I felt both as if they were still upon me, and then mourned for what I had never had and what I probably would never have a chance to have again.

## III.

Nothing had changed; everything had. Back at the lab, the mice were still alive (dopier and less mouselike than ever; they had developed a new habit of falling on their sides and kicking and screeching, apparently unaware of how to flip back onto their feet, that was fascinating and alarming to witness), as were the dreamers. I showed them the opa'ivu'ekes in the hopes of extracting some sort of reaction, but they merely blinked at them and then ignored them.

But those—and Cheolyu, of course—were the only things that remained from the life I had left not six weeks before. And here marks the beginning (although I was not to recognize it until much later) of my new life, and of a sustained period of time that was marked by both horrors and wonders. Every day, it seemed, so many things happened at once that it is very difficult for me to chart the events of the next few years in any linear fashion. What I can say, however, was that Tallent was proven correct.

It took me some time to realize that I was in a race, one that I was simultaneously unaware of entering yet had also begun. I heard through Sereny that this pharmacologist was trying desperately to get to Ivu'ivu, and that physiologist too. There was no question of Sereny himself going; he was too old, he said, and not eager to make such an arduous trip. But he was in the minority. Every day brought new letters—some beseeching, some sly, some vaguely threatening, some opaque—to both me and him, all asking for further information, trying to inquire what I planned to do with the information I had already acquired, or more or less announcing the writer's intention to best me at my own research. It says much about my innocence that none of this worried me, at least initially; in fact, I was a little giddy about it all—I even found it amusing. Part of this misguided confidence, I suppose, came from my trust in the king, in his apparent unwillingness to let anyone but Tallent (and those associated with him) onto the island. And then I also felt that since it had taken me so many days to find the lake of turtles—I, who had been there twice before—it would surely demand many weeks of frustrating stops and starts for the few people who might someday be allowed to set foot on Ivu'ivu. Certainly they could not ask for help in their mission; the Ivu'ivuans' (not to mention the U'ivuans') taboo against disturbing the turtles' peace was too great.

By this time everyone had surmised that the secret lay with the opa'ivu'eke. Eternal life! It was no wonder that schools and companies were willing to spend anything, do anything, to get to the island first. It was no wonder that they thought I was working on isolating the element myself. But I knew what they did not, and so it was easy to remain silent in the face of their questioning and suspicions: I knew that this form of eternal life was horribly compromised. I knew that if it were to be pursued, a solution, an antidote, would have to be found first.

It did not take Sereny long, however, to discern that something was amiss. "You're not telling me something," he accused me in one of our increasingly frequent phone conversations.

I am not skilled at playing the ignoramus, and never have been. Still, "What do you mean?" I asked stupidly.

"There's something wrong with those mice," he said, and gave me a full description of his mice's deteriorating conditions. (A full 79 percent of his were still alive. I had retained 61 percent of mine from the third experiment,[66] although my oldest batch, from the first group, were now ninety months to his group's fifty-three months.) I was excited to hear that their symptoms matched those of mine almost exactly.

And so I was forced to tell him how what we'd observed in our mice was merely a replica of what I had first seen in the dreamers. He listened with growing astonishment as I told him of what I had encountered on Ivu'ivu and of the state—and alleged age—of those I had brought back with me.

"Norton," he said at last, "this is ... this is incredible." But it was not, for proof existed only a few yards away from me, in the small fake Ivu'ivu I had created. We talked for a while about how I might be able to prove my theory on humans, and the impossibility of doing so; no one would be willing to undergo such a risk. Sereny asked if I might be able to perform the experiment on some Ivu'ivuans, whom I could later bring back with me to the States,

---

[66] The hundred that had been raised from the age of fifteen months.

and I had to remind him that it might take decades for the turtles' effects to become apparent; even if we could find subjects in their forties or fifties, we might be waiting another forty or fifty years—at least—for them to manifest any symptoms. No, I told him, the more important and pressing matter was to find an antidote, one that counteracted the turtle's effects.

"And have you spoken to anyone else about this?" Sereny asked. His voice was mild, but I had learned never to trust a rival who feigns a lack of interest or ambition or who pretends to be engaged only in an intellectual exchange for purely academic reasons. Therefore, I was somewhat triumphant (although I did my best to keep it out of my voice) to inform Sereny that I had submitted a paper announcing the mice's decline to the *Annals of Nutritional Epidemiology* just before I left and that it had been (of course) accepted for publication.

"Ah," said Sereny after a long silence, and I could not tell if he was angry or disappointed or both. At any rate, he was not happy. "Well, Norton," he said, "I hope you know what you're doing." He got off the phone quite quickly after that.

Of course I did not know what I was doing. I had sent the paper to the journal in something of a panic, trapped as I was between two unfortunate outcomes. If I waited too long, Sereny would no doubt make his own conclusions about the mice and write his own paper. His would have been much more speculative in nature, but it wouldn't have mattered—he would still be first, and anything I might write later would be seen as a furtherance of his discovery, not my own. But if I published too early, then I would alert the various buzzards circling the island and my work that there was a serious problem with their plans to bottle and sell eternal life. The opa'ivu'ekes would become more hunted than ever, and I would be racing against the others to solve the very problem that they would know nothing of had I not told them of it. It was one bad choice or the other. Either way, I would have no one to blame but myself.

And then, as many others after me would later recount, things got very bad. On my next trip to Ivu'ivu, about eight months later, things remained the same: this time it was only me, my visit preceded by another brief, unilluminating interview with the king. This was the last time I would be granted an audience with him, although I did not know it then. In fact, there would be many things about that visit that in retrospect would be for the last time: the last time I would be the only Westerner on Ivu'ivu, much less in the village; the last time I would be able to make my way unmolested to the lake of turtles, see its surface scummed with their air bubbles, be able to watch them drift so trustingly and peaceably toward me; the last time I would feel that the villagers would pay no heed to their visitor and that a foreign presence would not interrupt even the smallest of their routines. It would be the last time I would see them make and store food in the way they had doubtless been doing for centuries, the last time they would have a diet free from tinned meats and packaged biscuits and cans of sugary cubed fruit, the last time that I would see them wholly naked and be able to watch the switch of the women's breasts as they bent over a hill of seedpods or hear the light slap of the men's genitals against their thighs as they strolled back from a late-night hunt.

But on that visit I knew none of this, and I remember thinking—somewhat smugly, somewhat with relief—that Tallent had been wrong after all, that changes, if they came here, would be halting and incremental but not life-altering. I had already noticed that the bases of several of the trees were wrapped with red twine, and that small areas around them had been staked with thin lengths of rope, and that little placards with Latin names in an indecipherable hand had been affixed to the trees: Meyers's work, of course. If this was the sort of change that would come to the island, I thought, then it was nothing to worry about. I was able to visit the turtles again (my map proved itself useful) and even sought out the young friend I had made the last time, who willingly followed me on my walks deeper and deeper into the forest. On hot afternoons we napped there, and in the early mornings we explored (I found numerous clusters of fungi that would have made Meyers frantic with desire and made some shavings and drawings to take back to him). I saw the chief and Uo and Lawa'eke and many others I had grown to recognize by sight, if not by name.

Later I would ask myself if I had perhaps subconsciously timed this visit to coincide with my next paper's publication,[67] so that I might be able to avoid having to think about the consequences that would arise from it. I do not believe this to be true, although many others do, and I cannot dissuade them from that opinion. What I do know is that by the time I returned to Stanford six weeks later (two more opa'ivu'ekes accompanying me), the scientific world was in an uproar. Accusations were made, counterpapers were being written, the *Annals* was being sent more letters than it had received about any other paper it had ever published. The news of my two discoveries had even infiltrated the popular press, and I was interviewed by writers from both the *Times* and *Time*. It was around then too that Tallent ceased further contact with me, although I was never to know why. Was it because he felt (as others later would) that I had finally, conclusively, doomed the island? Was it because I had ruined the lovely dreamy image of a never-dying people? Was it simply because I had achieved a level of fame that he had not? Cheolyu told me that while I was gone, someone had tried to break in to our labs; he had arrived one morning to find the lock scored with scratch marks and the bottom of the door origamied into a deep pleat. He thought it was another scientist or perhaps a pharmacological team, and while I agreed with him outwardly, part of me wondered whether it might have been Tallent, although again, I could only guess at his motives: To destroy my evidence? To liberate the dreamers? In the months that followed, I tried every way I knew to speak to Tallent—I wrote him letters, I called him, I waited for hours outside his office and then outside his shockingly bleak apartment building. I begged the provost and the dean to intervene. I even tried to speak to Esme. I was like a lovesick girl. I did not even know what I might say to Tallent when I reestablished contact. I only knew that I needed to see him, to gain from him some sort of absolution. The discoveries were mine, as I had to keep reminding myself, but were it not for Tallent, there would be no discoveries to have been made in the first

---

[67] "Mental Deterioration Observed Among Subjects After Having Consumed the Opa'ivu'eke Turtle of Ivu'ivu," *Annals of Nutritional Epidemiology* (January 1958), vol. 47, 259–72.

place. (*And were it not for you*, a small voice in my head said when I heard that the first team of pharmacologists, a group from Pfizer, had convinced the king to allow them entry, *the island would still be safe*.)

All I can say is this: I *did* try. I did what I thought was best. Today I am often torn, when telling this part of the story, between making apologies and not. I did not go to the island, as so many later did, to make money, or to try to convince one group of people to live and eat and believe as I did. I went for adventure, and with the pure hope of exploration. I did not go to destroy a people or a country, as I am so often accused of doing, as if such things are ever as frequent or intentional as assumed. Did I, however, end up doing so? It is not for me to decide. I did what any scientist would have done. And if I had to—even knowing what would become of Ivu'ivu and all its people—I would probably do so again.

Well, that is not wholly true: I *would* do so again. I would not even have to consider it for a moment.

Two years later, then: I had my own lab in the Virology Department at the National Institutes of Health, where I would serve for the rest of my career. Cheolyu had returned to Korea, where he would eventually run his own lab at Seoul National University. I still had the dreamers under my care, although I saw less and less of them. They were forever supervised by those running various tests on them: bloodwork and physical and mental and reflex exams.[68] The institute had converted a spare lab into a very nice, snug space and outfitted it with trees and a leafy floor, and they were given attendants to help wash and clothe them, because although the space was windowless—we didn't want such a foreign view, of the trees' bare black limbs, to worry or distress them—the lab could be chilly at night and it wasn't practical for them to go naked. We had also

---

[68] For at least a decade after their arrival in the States, the dreamers continued to manifest (physically, at least) the reflexes and health one would typically associate with a sixty-year-old. In later years their cholesterol levels, heart rate, lung capacity, and bone density would worsen dramatically, which Norton attributed to their compromised diet and lack of physical activity. However, without access to a control group on Ivu'ivu, this is impossible to conclude definitively. (For further explication, see note 74.)

slowly converted them to a Western diet, and there was much to learn there about the effects of weaning a primitive group of people off a fully hunted-and-foraged diet and putting them on a more processed one. I am sorry to say that they were nearly insensate by this point, and the first time I saw Mua in a wheelchair being pushed back to their sleeping quarters after a day of tests—his head lolling back stupidly, his arms arranged slackly in his lap, his eyes open but skidding about—I felt a pang, remembering how quickly and purposefully he had once walked through the forest, how he had stretched his short legs into splits in order to straddle the enormous tree roots that calved from the ground. It was necessary, this work, and their decline was inevitable, but I still sentimentally wished it could have gone better for them.[69]

The opa'ivu'ekes had not fared much better, and I admit now that I had underestimated how important their context was to their survival and well-being. There were many failed attempts to encourage them to mate, and still more to make them adhere to a regular diet. It occurred to me (belatedly) that I had never thought to properly investigate exactly what the opa'ivu'ekes ate, and so much time was lost in trying to find the right combination of food—the closest we got was a mix of sardines and various lettuces and fiddleheads—that would both tempt them and help them maintain their equilibrium. But as time went by they grew steadily more listless, and finally we killed the two older ones—one we preserved,[70] one we dissected— and concentrated our efforts on the younger ones, although the results were not encouraging.

I was more and more away from the lab, giving lectures here and there, writing papers, and so on, and therefore it was not until the end of 1961 that I was able to make my next visit to Ivu'ivu. Stories had reached me from different sources about how the number of researchers on the island at any time now surpassed the population

---

[69] The move to NIH marked the end of another chapter as well. In the month before Norton left Stanford, the remaining mice from the first group of his initial experiment died, at the age of 120 months. Group C expired shortly after the move to NIH, as did the pinkies from Group B, all around the ages of 118 to 121 months—more than six times their natural lifespan.

[70] This specimen is still at NIH and can be viewed by special request.

of villagers themselves, about how a small settlement of tents had gone up for the roving brigades of Pfizer and Lilly scientists who traveled to and fro on their own planes and own motorized boats and who glared at one another across their self-imposed demarcation lines, each group determined to beat the other, about how swaths of the jungle had been trampled and cleared and the lives of animals and plants disrupted. Meyers called me from Cal one night, his stammer worse than ever; he had just returned from the island, he said, and described a scene that sounded like something out of a hellish version of Brueghel: a filthy village square, dirt-smeared and fetid, and choking black fires and people everywhere.

I hoped Meyers might be exaggerating—I did not consider him wholly reliable on non-fungus-related matters—but it was with some trepidation and even reluctance that I set out on my journey. Now that I was a government employee, there was no waiting about for a transport to the island on which I might be able to beg a spot, and I sat in my seat at the back of the tiny plane, waiting for the jouncy landing that greeted one's arrival on U'ivu. But to my surprise, our touchdown was smooth, silken almost, and when I stepped out of the plane, I saw the first major change: a runway, albeit just a length of perfectly planed dirt, but with all the bumps and stones and bits of shrubbery I remembered from the past removed. Indeed, the whole field had been razed and was now just a great acreage of emptiness: no grass, no little white flowers, just dirt so flat and clean it looked swept. I could feel something shift deep inside me: the first stirrings of dread.

I was met by a guide, one I'd not had before. He could have been anyone, but he spoke a little English, and he was wearing a sarong in dull mustard below a white man's undershirt that was far too long for him. His hair was cut, cropped close around his ears. He led me not to a horse but to an orange-rusted jalopy, a Frankenstein of a car, cut and soldered from many pieces and makes, of which he was very proud, and drove me haltingly over to the dock, where a new deck had been clumsily built. There stood the boatman—the one from my original trip all those years ago, who pretended now, as ever, not to know me—but his vessel was, if not new, newer at least, and fitted with a proper motor that roared and belched as we bounced across the sea. And then, in half the time as before, there was Ivu'ivu, but as we rounded the corner to pull into the lagoon, another shock: the jungle had been pruned back so far that there was now a real beach, a scoop of mucky gray sand, the greenery forming an untidy hairline to its rear. On the sand was a beaming man, waving his arms at me as the boat dredged itself up onto shore.

"No-ton! No-ton!" said the man, and I realized with a start that it was Uva, though not the Uva of my memory.[71] This Uva was wearing pants—khakis, far too large for him—and a real button-down shirt, albeit one that had obviously been washed and rewashed and patched with runnels of stitches so dense they looked like scar tissue. His hair, like the boatman's and the guide's, had been hacked away at as well, and the bone had been removed from his nose, though on either side of his nostrils he carried a dark brown stain where the holes had closed over and healed.

"How you?" asked Uva, smiling proudly, and this—his newly acquired English, and his pride in it—made my skin prickle for some reason, and the enormity of the island's changes loomed large and clear in my mind.

Everywhere were differences. A real path had been dozed uphill, and although we still had to traverse it by foot, Uva now pulled my supplies in a wheeled cart. He was not used to wearing so much clothing and sweated copiously. At one point he fumblingly unbuttoned his shirt partway, and when I took off my own to encourage him, he gazed at my nakedness longingly before turning away and buttoning back up: you could almost see the determination in his face, his new dedication to being fully clad. *But why?* I wanted to ask. One of the things the Ivu'ivuans had gotten right, after all, was their adherence to their own nudity; in such humidity, clothes were not only foolish but ill-advised.

As we went, I could not help but study the treescape around me, trying to map the developments. Was it quieter than it had been last time, less filled with birdcall and monkey screech and insect flutter? Were there fewer manama trees and less fruit on the ground? Did the kanava trees seem less grimed with vuaka shit than they had before? Did that moss always look so trodden, or had someone recently walked across it? Was the passage between that stand of

---

[71] Uva would have been about fifty-two at the time.

palm trees always so forgiving, or had it been widened recently by hand? Was that a white card, a botanist's label, affixed to that orchid, or was it in fact a butterfly, its wings folded into a flat square?

We smelled and heard the village before we saw it, but the smells were ones I recognized from the States, not from here, and the sounds were not of Ivu'ivu either. There was the tart, burned tang of bacon frying, and the hiss of a slosh of grease sliding against a hot pan. There were men's voices, all speaking English, and the bright, aggressive scent of laundry detergent, and the *ching* of metal pinging against stone.

And then we were upon them, their neat clean tents and their laundry—stretched-out T-shirts and cotton pants, all the same linty color—draped over the low manama branches, and the fire over which one of them held aloft with a pair of metal tongs a can of baked beans, whose contents burbled diarrhetically over the rim.

I introduced myself—I couldn't not—and learned that they were the Pfizer group; the Lilly group was apparently to the right of the village, although about the same distance removed. They were respectful, they were hostile, they were surprised; I could see them regarding me with envy, for while they spent their days trying to develop drugs and cold creams, I was doing real work, and they knew I was their superior. And yet they had all the resources—it was clear, from my single rucksack resting in Uva's cart, that I did not—and it was already clear that the ones who had the resources would win. This is always true in science. It was true even then. I excused myself as soon as I could.

But it was when we reached the edge of the village that the horror, the severity, of the island's transformation really assaulted me. The huts were the same, as were the dirt floor's well-drawn boundaries, but those were the only things that had remained as I remembered. Lanced on a stick over the fire was a cube of Spam sweating lardy drops into the flames, and an already roasted block of it sat nearby, its heat wilting and curling the palm leaf on which it rested. And a few feet off, a group of men hovered over a third brick, squeezing off pieces of it with their fingers and feeding their hogs a bite for every two or three they took. But somehow the worst thing was the clothesline that had been stretched between two manama trees on the left side of the village; the line had been made using some of the twisted palm-leaf rope—a precious rope, a rope meant for repairs and hauling and hog-leashing—and draped all across it was a junky selection of used clothes: yellowed undershirts and torn-pocketed trousers and plain, prim, long-sleeved cotton dresses that would have been useless in America, much less in tropical Ivu'ivu. And all around me the villagers went on their way in clothes, sometimes worn correctly and sometimes not, but always worn in earnest and with real effort—which was in many ways the most alarming thing of all, for it meant that it was not a lark, not a game, but that somehow they had been convinced that this was a habit worth adopting, a necessary adaptation. But who had told them so, and why had they believed them?

I found myself walking toward the ninth hut. To one side, two of the pharmacists were kicking a soccer ball to each other and laughing as some of the village children—some in shirts so big that they resembled kimonos, the fabric of the arms sailing as they jumped and ran—joined in. Inside, the hut was as I remembered it: silent and cool and somehow somber. I was relieved, momentarily. But then I thought, was it *too* unchanged? There was something about it that felt *dusty* almost, and I found myself absurdly studying the dirt floor for signs of neglect. It was as if in the context of such enveloping changes, the ninth hut's sameness made it appear less, not more, relevant. It was clear that what had once been—from dress to food to even the children's play—was no longer valued, and the fact that no one had thought to update the hut with some recognition of the new world that had been visited upon them made me fear that it remained not as a symbol of something cherished but as a relic of something outgrown.

Later I would realize that what had taken me weeks to find had taken teams of researchers only days. Later I would hurry uphill toward the lake—the path now an abandoned parade route, all staked with yards of fluttering bright red tape strung from tree to tree—and run crazily toward the two scientists (these from a German outfit that had set up camp some distance from the Lilly group) lifting a large opa'ivu'eke from the lake, the turtle's limbs pinwheeling in fear. Later, after they had left, I would lean over the edge of the lake, its once-clean border made mucky with the stamped-sole imprints of a dozen men's boots, and see only five heads break the surface of the water, and as long as I waited, they would not come to me but would only hover in the center of the pond, and I would have to try to stop myself from howling. Later I would learn (from one of those same German pharmacologists) that Tallent was missing, and had been missing for at least two weeks: he had been on the island alone, without Esme, and had met only some of them. And then one day he was gone. It had taken them a while—two days? three?—to notice his absence, but once they had, they had ventured into the forest in small groups and then sent their guides in after them. But they could find no evidence of him. He had carried only a knapsack, which he had taken with him, and although they had searched, they had been unable to find anywhere that he might have disturbed the jungle: no fields of moss bearing the ghost impressions of his feet, no scattered manama seeds, no smudges of earth and stick where once a fire might have burned.

And then I knew—*this* was the worst thing of all. Worse than the turtles, who had learned not to trust the new humans too late and were now much reduced in number. Worse than seeing the boy, my young friend who had slept leaning against me just a short while before and who seeing me now turned from me, his too-long pant legs sweeping behind him like a bride's gown. I could not believe, could not accept, the fact that Tallent might be gone from me, from us, forever. By day I spoke to everyone I could—Ivu'ivuans, the pharmacologists—asking them for information. The latter group, seeing that it distracted me from getting in their way, indulged me, but they had such little information, such frustratingly little information, that many days I wished I had never asked. How had he seemed in the days before his disappearance? Fine, they said, but because they had not known him (and, I had to admit to myself, neither had I), they could not say whether his behavior was normal or not. He was calm and contemplative and kept to himself. What had he been researching? What had they seen him observe? They didn't know, they said; he spoke sometimes to members of the village, but most of the time he was observing them, writing in his notebook, writing by himself. Had he spoken to any one villager in particular? No, they didn't think so. Had he looked—and here I had to stop until

I was certain I wanted to know the answer—unkempt, or seemed ill or illogical or delusional? No, they said. No, no.

By night I looked for him, taking meandering, meaningless walks through the jungle. They were useless walks, for I never went too far and I never called his name, just swung my flashlight before me in arcs, the flat disk of light skittering across the various surfaces it encountered, illuminating bark here, leaves there, ground there, in jittery sequence. I do not think I seriously thought I'd find him. But on those walks I always remembered how I had first encountered Mua, stepping out of the shadows of the jungle like a nightmare come to life, and I suppose some part of me felt that it might happen again, that one night I'd move the flashlight just an inch to the right and there, centered in its beam, would be Tallent, his beard obscuring his expression, saying, "Well, Norton, what brings you here?"

It was very rare, but every other year or so the villagers would lose someone to the forest: a hunter, usually young and inexperienced, would venture deep into the trees on his own and never return. Sometimes he would be lost forever. The Ivu'ivuans had a saying for such events—"Ka ololu mumua ko," *The jungle devoured him*. The odd thing was that they would never consider that the disappeared person had died; he was simply away, unable to find his way home but alive all the same, trying and trying and trying to return to the village.

Many theories have since been proposed about Tallent's disappearance. He had gone to find more dreamers. He had followed a dreamer into the forest. He had gone mad. He had found another, more secret society and gone to live among them. He had discovered something glorious. He had discovered something terrible. He had been murdered by the villagers and taken away at night. He had become obsessed with a species of flower he had found. He had run away with one of the village women, one of the village men (preposterous, as no one from the village was missing). He had yearned to escape civilization and had gone to found his own. He had escaped from the island in secret and was living under an assumed identity in Hawaii, teaching at the university there. He had killed himself. He was alive still. He knew exactly where he was going. He had no idea where he was going.

I cannot claim to know what happened to him. But I think about him often, more often than I think anyone would expect. When he vanished, I am afraid I have to admit, something I had once had vanished as well: the ability to care as intensely, one might diagnose it, but something else as well. I wonder sometimes, if he had remained in our world, how I might be different, how I might ultimately have found satisfaction other than in the ways I eventually did. And I suppose that if I were made to come to a conclusion, I would have to say that I too think that the jungle devoured him, and that somewhere he walks through it still. Indeed, I sometimes see him, very gaunt now and pale, having spent years and years under the dark canopy of trees, lifting his face to the small droplets of sunshine that the deepest part of the forest allows to penetrate. I never see him in the company of others but rather wandering in the forest alone, his clothes now mere scraps, decorations, a piece of bamboo for a walking stick, his beard scraping his rib cage. I wonder, has he eaten a bit of turtle to stay alive? Does he sing, or talk to himself, for company? Does he remember me? Did he ever find his way back to the village, and did he perhaps visit it once a year or so, standing hidden behind a tree, watching it change so profoundly that after a certain point he never returned?

In my imaginings I sometimes call out to him, and sometimes he turns, and his eyes are bright and luminous and starved, and I am in those moments breathless, at the rapaciousness of his hunger and the keenness of his searching, and I am unable to say anything but stare at him, until he silently, with one thin and darkened hand clutching at his stick, turns back away from me—and is gone.

## IV.

Well, what more is there for me to say on this matter? You know, we all know, what happened next. There were endings, but none of them were happy. Whenever I am asked, I cannot help but be brisk when relating what followed, for it is too difficult for me to make the story into what it ought to be: a saga in itself, a long death that spirals down slowly to the ground.

It was an end full of ironies, as such sad and bad endings often are. Shall I tell you of how the pharmacists and neuroscientists and biologists hurried home with their carrier bags heavy with turtles, and how test after test proved what I already knew and had already tried to tell them: that the mice (and later the rats, the rabbits, the dogs, the monkeys, the who knows what else—there were rumors, but none were ever definitively proven) lived double, treble, quadruple their natural lives, but all of them, every one of the survivors, went slowly but irreversibly and horribly mad? The mice kicking and mewling; the cats, their mouths fixed open into soundless yawps, beating themselves against their cages; the dogs tearing out their own eyes with their paws; the monkeys, the closest to us in temperament and sensibility, who chattered and chattered until one day they chattered no more, and whose eyes grew so blank and unfocused one could look in them and see anything one might wish reflected in them: the sea, the clouds, a lake of turtles.

Shall I tell you of how by the time telomeres were discovered, and then by the time genetic sequencing became sophisticated enough to conjecture exactly how the opa'ivu'eke was affecting normal telomerase, there were no more opa'ivu'ekes to be studied?[72] Shall I tell

---

[72] Norton had proven incontrovertibly that the consumption of the opa'ivu'eke would grant its subject an impossibly extended lifespan. What he did not know—nor indeed did anyone else—was how. This was not Norton's fault; the difficulty was that the science simply did not exist even to give a name to the problem, much less to provide its solution. You must remember that what we now know as the study of genetics is a very, very immature field; as Norton notes, by the time the science was available to theorize that the opa'ivu'eke prolonged an organism's life by inactivating telomerase, it was too late. (Simply stated, telomerase is the naturally occurring enzyme that degrades telomeres and thereby limits each cell's number of divisions; in the absence of telomerase, cells become "immortal" and the person ceases to age. What is theorized is that while the opa'ivu'eke stopped the action of telomerase in most of the body's cells, it for some reason failed to cease the process in certain parts of the brain. This is why, although the body and certain parts of the mind—especially the part governing hearing and gross motor skills—remained remarkably intact, the parts of the brain that control fine motor skills, sight, and reason were not similarly affected.)

This, however, is the story of science. A man discovers something. He doesn't know what it is or what it's for or what it might solve, but he knows he has unearthed another piece of a puzzle whose entire shape and picture and form he can only guess. He spends the rest of his life trying to find that next piece, but because he doesn't even know what he's looking for, it is very hard work and he is unlikely to find a solution. Then comes a man from the next generation. He sees the piece of the puzzle that has been found and he finds the next. So now there are two pieces. And then there are three, and four, and five. But at no point, no matter how many pieces there are, is any one man ever able to say he knows what the puzzle's ultimate shape will reveal. When he thinks he is working toward a picture of a horse, he will suddenly

you how the lake had long been scooped clean, and although in the 1970s a group of a dozen scientists went back to dredge it and then walked the length of the river, its entire reach from the top of the island to its bottom, they never found another opa'ivu'eke? Shall I tell you of the recriminations, the desperation, the bemoaning of years wasted, the millions of dollars spent, the agony of knowing how close we were to eternal life and how it once again eluded us, all dreams of godliness turned into water glugging down a wide-mouthed drain? Shall I tell you of the disbelief, the plans that were made and then had to be scrapped for age-retarding drugs, for anti-aging skin creams, for elixirs to restore male potency? Shall I tell you of Pfizer's sorrow, of Lilly's dismay, of Johnson and Johnson's agony, of Merck's rage? Shall I tell you of the years of feckless, fruitless, desperate attempts to re-create the effect using every sort of turtle on the planet? Of months waiting for the mice to continue beyond their natural lifespan, and then, upon watching them die, beginning anew with a fresh batch, and a new Hawaiian sea turtle, a new leatherback turtle, a new Galápagos tortoise? Shall I tell you about trying to re-create the effect using every animal, every plant, every fungus, that could be harvested from Ivu'ivu? The sloths, the hogs, the spiders, the vuakas, the toucans, the parrots, the hunonos, the manamas, the kanavas, the weird lizardlike things, the fuzzy gourds, the palm leaves, the seedpods—shall I tell you how the island was stripped of everything, whole forests razed, whole fields of mushrooms and orchids and ferns picked like fat red strawberries and shiny green lettuces and loaded onto the helicopters that were now able to land directly on the island because so many trees had been felled that there was open space aplenty?

Shall I tell you what happened to the chief, how in the early 1970s he was lured to the United States by Johns Hopkins, where he was presumably stuck and measured and leeched of fluids every

---

find a fish's fin and realize he's been wrong all along. Then he thinks he's trying to build an image of a fish, but the next piece that slots into place will be a bird's wing lifted in flight. To be a scientist is to learn to live all one's life with questions that will never be answered, with the knowledge that one was too early or too late, with the anguish of not having been able to guess at the solution that, once presented, seems so obvious that one can only curse oneself for not seeing what one ought to have, if only one had looked in a slightly different direction.

day, and may be still, for no one, no one, has ever heard of him or mentioned him again? Shall I tell you about Lawa'eke, who around that time simply disappeared and was never found again? (Shall I tell you how Pfizer accused Lilly of kidnapping him, and how Lilly blamed the University of Minnesota, and how the University of Minnesota blamed the University of Hamburg, and how the University of Hamburg blamed Merck, and how Merck said nothing?) Shall I tell you of the reports of other dreamers being found, stumbling, disoriented, through open plains that had once been forests, blinking in the sudden unfiltered light? Shall I tell you how there were rumors that there were dozens of them, scores of them, hundreds of them, but that I never saw them for myself—that there were stories that they were divvied up like candies by the pharmaceutical companies and flown away to live their lives in sterile labs, where they may be living still, punctured with needles, their arms sprouting tangles of IVs, their legs harvested for scrapings of skin, of muscle, of bone?[73] Shall I tell you how in 1966, when the first institutional review boards monitoring the use of human subjects in research projects was established, I nearly lost my dreamers, and by 1975— after Willowbrook, after Tuskegee, after the birth of the National Commission for the Protection of Human Subjects of Biomedical and Behavioral Research—I had lost them for good?[74]

---

[73] For years Norton petitioned the various pharmaceutical companies that were thought to have imported mo'o kua'aus to their labs for news of the four dreamers— Ivaiva, Va'ana, Ukavi, and Vi'iu—he had left behind. Perhaps not surprisingly, he was disappointed time and again, and today it is unknown whether the dreamers he was forced to abandon were captured or eluded their fate by either hiding (which seems unlikely) or dying (for which one can only hope, for their sakes).

Norton also continued to inquire about Tallent, but no one could or would admit to having encountered him. And for as much forest as was cleared on Ivu'ivu, there was more than enough so that Tallent in theory might have survived their aggressive explorations.

[74] Norton is here referring to two of modern science's more notorious and less fortunate human research projects. Willowbrook State School was a home for around six thousand mentally retarded children on Staten Island. Between 1963 and 1966, children were infected with hepatitis A so researchers could better study the effects of the disease. Naturally, when this became public knowledge there was a great public upset and the experiment had to be abandoned. Tuskegee, the better known of the cases, was an ambitious four-decades-long (1932–1972) project in which poor black sharecroppers in Alabama infected with syphilis were studied but were not offered

penicillin, even long after that drug became the standard treatment for the condition.

Contemporary legislation and guidelines (not to mention bioethics as we know them) governing human experimentation are a direct result of the Tuskegee scandal. Although the NIH had established the Office of Protection for Research Subjects in 1966, it was not until eight years later that the review board that Norton mentions was established and was given real oversight and power.

In 1975 the commissioners paid a visit to Norton's lab to observe for themselves the dreamers' treatment. It is still unknown why they decided to focus on this very small population of subjects when far worse abuses were being committed against subjects in other labs, but one can only imagine that they were encouraged to do so by one of Norton's numerous enemies. Although the visit is often depicted as a "raid," I can tell you authoritatively that it was nothing of the sort. After a few of these site visits, however, the commissioners decided that the dreamers would be more comfortable living in a more social environment, and in October 1975 they were moved to the Thornhedge Retirement Community in Frederick, Maryland.

Not surprisingly, the transplant was not a success. Even though the dreamers were by this stage fairly noncognizant of their surroundings, they were at times still sensate enough to be alarmed and frightened by their new environment and missed one another's company (at NIH they had all lived together in one large room). These radical and cruel changes—to their surroundings, their diet, and their caretakers—disoriented them greatly, and their decline worsened. In February 1976, Norton petitioned the commission to reverse its ruling on the grounds of the dreamers' clear and obvious mental anguish and distress.

During that appeal, the news of the dreamers' existence—which had until that point remained, remarkably, relatively quiet—somehow broke in the mainstream press. Three months later, in June 1976, the dreamers were the subjects of an attempted abduction by a radical native Hawaiian sovereignty rights group that called itself HAWIKA (Hawaiians Avenging White Imperialism, Killing in Anger). The group, which promised to "fight [against what exactly was never specified] on behalf of all native Micro- and Melanesian peoples," managed to, in its words, "liberate" both Mua and Ika'ana before its members were apprehended by the home's security guards as they were in the process of trying to hoist Vanu's wheelchair into their van. It was later discovered that one of HAWIKA's members, a man named Paiea McNamee, had been working undercover at Thornhedge as an orderly for the previous two months. McNamee and his three accomplices were sentenced to prison, and the dreamers were restored to their rooms at the facility.

Upon learning of my long professional and personal relationship with Norton, people invariably have many questions, and one of the first things they always ask about is the dreamers: are they alive still, and what became of them? The answer to the first question is yes: all of them are still living. Eve is 299 years old (this is working from the assumption that she was no younger than 250 when she left the island; it's certainly possible that she could be even older than this). Ika'ana is 225. Vanu is 180. Mua is 153. (And remember, these ages are calculated by the U'ivuan calendar. By the Western calendar, all of them are older still.)

Unfortunately, and as Norton notes in his narrative, their physical decline was both rapid and severe. All of them are exceedingly physically weak, and all lack many basic motor skills. They are capable of walking but reluctant to do so. Ika'ana is almost completely blind. They rarely speak, and rarely respond when spoken to. Their reflexes have degraded as well, and they are slow to respond to most stimuli. The one thing they do still take pleasure in is food: after gaining rapid amounts of weight on an institutional diet, they were in 1985 begun on a new nutritional regimen that more closely echoed their traditional fare. Although they failed to lose much weight—an unreasonable expectation, given how sedentary they now are— they did appear to relish the tastes of mango and what they must have perceived as hunono (actually, earthworms procured from an animal supply company). The great tragedy of the dreamers' state, however, is that we will never know for certain how much of their physical disintegration was due to extreme age and how much was due to their changed environment. One must assume, however, that the environmental factor is the most important one here, as all of them began to display similar diminishments at the same time despite the extreme differences in their ages. (I should add that I am, alas, excepting Eve from all of the above-mentioned pleasures and abilities, however limited; two years ago, her caretakers noticed that her pupils were remaining fixed even in response to the brightest lights, and further tests have proved her to be effectively brain-dead. Her lung function, however, remains that of a woman a fraction of her estimated age.)

After the HAWIKA incident, Norton fought very hard to have the dreamers returned to his care. But although the commission rejected his appeal, the dreamers were moved the following year to a secure facility. The place, whose name I cannot divulge for obvious reasons, is actually the gerontology unit of a well-known maximum-security federal prison, and there the dreamers have been reunited and live in their own self-contained wing. Although the facility is too far from Bethesda for Norton to make regular visits, it is close to a respected medical research hospital, and Norton was able to advise a group of gerontologists and neurologists there who make frequent trips to study and observe the dreamers.

The second question I am always asked is whether I think Norton is responsible for the dreamers' fate. This was for many years a more complicated matter for me. By the time I met the dreamers, in 1972, they already bore much more of a resemblance to the creatures they are today than to the ones Norton encountered in 1950. So I cannot say that I mourn the people they once were. On the other hand, the differences I saw in them between 1975, when the commission removed them, and 1977, when I was next allowed to visit, were quite appalling. When I first met them, they still possessed a little life, a little energy: one might stroke Eve's hand, and she might respond with a purr, and one could imagine that it was a sound of contentment and that the lolling of her head against her wheelchair's pillow was a gentle swoon of pleasure. In 1977 she would do nothing at all. Her head would be tipped back, her forehead strapped to the cushion to keep it from dropping forward, and she would be completely silent. Her hand was as cold as stone. One had the feeling one was touching something made of clay and hair, not something human at all.

It was such a shocking and unpleasant experience that I can only imagine now how difficult, how devastating, it must have been for Norton, who had known them when they were much more vibrant beings, ones still capable of speech and movement

Shall I tell you of the scores of people (Sereny, Esme, the entire Stanford University Anthropology Department, *Harper's Magazine*) who made me their enemy, who accused me of, variously, withholding the truth, distorting the truth, ruining a civilization, and ruining mankind's hopes?[75] Shall I tell you how bad followed bad to Ivu'ivu, how after the pharmacists flew out for the last time, they were replaced with fleets of missionaries, who were this time able to accomplish what their predecessors could not? Shall I tell you of the hundreds who were converted, how the remaining villagers on Ivu'ivu, their forests denuded and trampled and shorn, were taken over to U'ivu in boatloads to live in a tin-and-wood village on the eastern side of the island built by a particularly energetic group of Mormons from Provo?[76] Shall I tell you how, when one of those

---

and even endowed with their own small sensory gifts. But still—and I will admit it, shamefully—at the time I was angry with him and held him responsible. For years I thought (but kept to myself) that he should have found some better way to take care of them, even that he should have found some way to return them to Ivu'ivu. But these were childish, uninformed opinions, and I eventually grew out of them.

The fact remains: Norton did as much as he could for the dreamers for as long as he could. He did far more than he was ethically or legally required to do for them. He tried to make every provision for their comfort and well-being. They were never hurt under his supervision, or ill-treated, or starved. He was, indeed, a pioneer in human experimentation, and under very difficult circumstances. For anyone to suggest anything less reveals not only a grave misunderstanding of his efforts but is scurrilous in the extreme.

[75] Esme Duff was particularly vicious and unrelenting in her assaults on Norton, whom she perplexingly but unwaveringly held responsible for Tallent's disappearance. After Tallent vanished, she remained at Stanford as a lecturer but never earned tenure. She never married, and committed suicide in 1982 at the age of sixty-two.

[76] So thorough was the various pharmaceutical companies' and universities' removal of the mo'o kua'aus who were allegedly discovered on Ivu'ivu that it is thought highly unlikely that any of them were actually ever transplanted to U'ivu. Naturally, both of the aforementioned parties had their own reasons for not allowing any of the dreamers to migrate there, but it is also highly unlikely that the U'ivuans—given the mythology and fear surrounding the mo'o kua'au—wanted any of them in their midst. (Later several of the pharmaceutical companies would claim that they took the dreamers who were discovered back to the States for their own protection, because they would surely be ill-treated or ostracized if they were displaced to U'ivu.) Consequently, the dreamers, as well as the vaka'ina ceremony, remain as exotic and incredible on U'ivu as they do in the States—perhaps even more so: a particularly vivid ghost story, never to be definitively disproved.

transplanted villagers—the chief's proxy—tried to initiate the a'ina'ina ceremony, he was put into jail (a structure that had never existed until then, the U'ivuan king preferring more straightforward punishments such as abandoning the miscreant or casting him out to sea)? Shall I tell you how it was rumored that after Ivu'ivu had been picked clean of its wonders and exhausted of all its plants and fungi and flowers and animals and was left with only its beauty and mystery, the United States military—no, the French; no, the Japanese—was using it to test nuclear warheads? Shall I tell you how the king's son, Crown Prince Tui'uvo'uvo, now the king himself, was whispered to be a puppet of some foreign military and how he took to strutting about U'ivu in an epaulet-trimmed wool jacket that he wore atop a sarong, his face vivid with sweat? Shall I tell you how there are really no new stories in cases like these: how the men turned to alcohol, how the women neglected their handiwork, how they all grew fatter and coarser and lazier, how the missionaries plucked them from their houses as easily as one would pick an overripe apple from a branch? Shall I tell you of the venereal diseases that seemed to come from nowhere but, once introduced, never left? Shall I tell you how I witnessed these things myself, how I kept returning and returning, long after the grant money had disappeared, long after people had lost interest, long after the island had gone from being an Eden to becoming what it was, what it is: just another Micronesian ruin, once so full of hope, now somehow distasteful and embarrassing, like a beautiful woman who has grown fleshy and sparse-haired and mustached?

Shall I tell you of how in the end the only person with whom I could chart the island's changes—each, inevitably, an insult—was Meyers, the only other person who, like me, kept stubbornly going back, first with funding and then with his own money? Shall I tell you of one day in the spring of 1968 when we were walking through Tavaka (now a miserable, cluttered little town and renamed Tui'uvo, after the new king) and two small children—one a boy, one a girl, obviously siblings, the boy about five (or so I thought at the time) and watchful, the girl around three and giggly—began following us around? Shall I tell you of how Meyers and I bought them manamas, speared on a stick and rolled in grainy sugar, that were being sold by a deflated-looking woman from her tin-tabled stall, and watched as they devoured them, the sugar stubbling their faces like beards? Shall I tell you how day after day they trailed us, as close as hens, and after we had returned from an exhausting, depressing trip to Ivu'ivu (coming back in the boat, which now had such a powerful motor that its nose heaved up from the water at a terrifying angle before smacking back down into it, we had avoided looking at one another, for to look would be to see our own sadness mirrored), they were there waiting for us, crouching on the dock like bookends? Shall I tell you how, after asking person after person who cared for these children—the girl Makala, the boy Muiva—and receiving nonanswers, or no answers at all, Meyers and I, almost as a whim, an impulse acquisition, took them back to the States with us?

Shall I tell you how Muiva was my first child, although of course I did not think of him at the time as my first, simply as my only, and my own? And how even after I learned that he was not five but seven, and even after I learned how much I had to teach him—how to eat, how to use the toilet, how to speak English; he was not unlike Eve in certain ways—I loved him anyway? Shall I tell you of what a sweet boy he was and what joy he brought me, and how the dream I had had on Ivu'ivu of carrying a sleeping child to bed was just as satisfying as I had hoped it might be, so satisfying in fact that I began to want to repeat it again and again? Shall I tell you of how I began to adopt other children—how once I began to pay attention, I found there were dozens, scores, who were parentless or as good as, their parents were so useless, so lost to alcohol and God—initially only boys, because I thought I could relate to them more easily, but then girls as well? Shall I tell you how Uva's son brought me his own toddler, a two-year-old named Vaia, and asked me to take him with me? Shall I tell you of how when Meyers died in 1977, after a very quick bout with stomach cancer, I took Makala into my house as my sixteenth child, and, I thought, my last? Shall I tell you of how I was wrong, and then wrong again, and with each trip I made back to U'ivu—a biannual event that I had learned to dread even as I had accepted that it was inevitable—I would find myself returning with another child? Shall I tell you how I always looked for those two boys—now men, now undoubtedly with boys of their own—who were lost to me, the one from the a'ina'ina and the one who would lean against me and doze, and how I searched for and hoped for something of them in every new child I collected, how I wanted to see the same steadiness in their eyes, feel the same trust as they leaned against me? Shall I tell you how with each new child I acquired, I would irrationally think, *This is the one. This is the one who will make me happy. This is the one who will complete my life. This is the one who will be able to repay me for years of looking.*

Shall I tell you how I was always wrong—eighteen, nineteen, twenty times wrong—and how although I was always wrong, I didn't stop, I couldn't stop, I was searching, searching, searching.

Or shall I perhaps tell you of a trip I made in 1980, the trip that, although I was not to know it, would eventually destroy my life?

By this time I had twenty-six children in my care—more than I needed, of course, and more than I wanted. By now the public perception of my extravagant collection had altered considerably and in certain quarters had become yet another measure of my monstrousness. When I first began accumulating my children, I was of course treated as something of a hero—an odd hero perhaps, barely on the right side of eccentricity, but a hero nonetheless. I was a single man, I was a noted scientist, and yet here I was, opening my house (an eight-bedroom Colonial just outside town that I had bought with some of my inheritance) to these undernourished and primitive orphans, whose pitiable state was compounded by their being dark-skinned and flat-nosed and completely uneducated.

I would estimate that my heroism ran out after I brought back my ninth child. Suddenly, as if a bulletin had gone out to the brayers and opinion-sharers and women of the world generally—for it was women who seemed to have the strongest feelings about my personal doings, as women often do—I was an object of suspicion. Why did I need all those children? Why did I have all these children and not a wife? What exactly was I trying to do? There was something unhealthy about it all, wasn't there? The suspicions never morphed into outright accusations, but I could feel them there, held just under the tongue like a dissolving cube of sugar. I am convinced that even Mrs. Tomlinson, a local woman I had engaged to serve as a house-keeper-cum-nanny (I hired her on the basis of her looks alone: she was dense and sturdy and florid, a Dickensian scullery maid grown up and out and come to life in modern-day Maryland), who liked to ostentatiously share with me the many times she had defended me to her girlfriends and sisters-in-law, doubtless shared her theories with those same girlfriends and sisters-in-law: *Well, what* does *he need with all those children, after all?* (At the time they were easy to dismiss, but in retrospect, I would agree with them: there was something fevered and grotesque, alarming even, about the rate at which I adopted these children.)

And then in 1974 I won my Nobel and once again I was the hero, my "miscalculations" (as the *Times* characterized my apparent failing of the dreamers; in the same article I was also blamed in a roundabout way for Tallent's disappearance and the destruction of Ivu'ivu) balanced against my obvious humanitarian inclinations, the one-man charity show I was running with as much color and élan as P. T. Barnum. In the months of interviews that followed, I was asked about the island, the dreamers, Tallent, and the turtles (and to a lesser extent about my work and its implications), but mostly I was asked about my children: Could I pose with them? Had they had a hard time adjusting? Did I have any favorite stories about them? They were always looking for these stories, anecdotes about the children's adorableness, and I never had any to provide: they were children, after all, and their store of adorableness was rather shallow. Again and again I was asked why I had adopted them, a question I found difficult to answer. The truth would be distasteful, and the lies—because I wanted to help the less fortunate; because I loved their company—seemed laughably simplistic and banal. But to my surprise, the interviewers all jotted down my responses without question, and later I would read my own words back to myself in their papers or magazines and see myself called "a loving papa" or "a doting father" and marvel.

On U'ivu, my Nobel made no difference; there, I was the white man who came twice a year and on whom all sorts of unwanted children could be foisted. It was one of the central ironies of the place that the very people who had enabled me to discover immortality were so far from immortal themselves. Uva had died in 1965, at the age of fifty-six; Tu had died shortly after. Some of their children—Uva's son, who had pressed his child on me; Tu's daughter, whose twin sons were now in my care—were dead as well, their brief life-spans hurried to a premature close by alcohol.

I had the strange sense sometimes as I walked through Tui'uvo, its thoroughfares wide tracks of footstep-engraved mud, its boundaries stacked with the debris of long-abandoned and improbable projects—here a sagging sack of concrete, slit down the middle and dribbling silt that was once meant to built a roadway; there a pyramid of orange-rusted rebar bound together with frayed lengths of palm-leaf rope—that I had landed in the wrong place, and that somewhere on the other side of the island lay the capital as I had known it. What *was* this town, with its increasing number of beggars (I always wondered whom they were begging from, as no one in the town had any money and the foreign visitors who had once descended here in great busy flocks were long gone, a decade gone, never to return) burning small, sullen fires by the road's edge, and the slumping shacks, the palm leaf freckled with dark dots of mold? The only new structure was the king's residence, with its long, ugly façade of cement, its surface perforated by small glassless windows. The king had run out of money before he could complete its painting or roofing, and so the whitewash stopped abruptly halfway through, and the entire thing was crowned with a flat top of layered palm leaves; they were new, at least, but the effect was curiously like a toupee, because no one in the village remembered quite how to knit together a roof that would be both protective and elegant.

I stayed where I always did, in the second grandest and only other cement building in town, a six-room inn in which I was always the only guest. In my room was an approximation of a bed (an ancient iron bed frame, a large muslin pouch half stuffed with crunchy bits of palm husk for a mattress) and a crucifix, made from bamboo and easily the prettiest thing in town, hanging on the wall. The inn was near the water, and from its roof, where I ate my dinner of Spam and chunks of boiled sweet potato, I would watch the sky turn so dark that eventually Ivu'ivu would seem to disintegrate into the night, its bulk receding into the black. No one was allowed to travel there any longer, on penalty of death; the king was rumored to be convinced that someday the scientists and the money would return and was planning to offer it to them for a huge ransom when they did. In the meantime, though, it was the property of whichever government had paid him for its use. But then I heard other rumors as well: that on the far side of Ivu'ivu was a team of scientists (from where, no one could say) who were scouring the island's underwater caves for any remaining opa'ivu'ekes, or that the king was using the island as a penal colony, where the punished would live the rest of their lives in near isolation. And sometimes I thought, *There too is Tallent*, and I would picture him, his face lifted to the sun, moving uphill through a mist of ivoried butterflies.

Because I had grown to realize that I made these trips as a form of self-punishment, I never spared myself anything. I sought out the most depressing sights: the squalor of the town, of course, and the contrasting tidiness of the missionary camp on the north side of the island, where the jungle had been so eradicated that you often felt like you were in Montana. Here there was a different kind of awfulness: no alcohol, no begging, no fires, but U'ivuans working as messengers, and farmhands, and housemaids, and always smiling, smiling, smiling. But the worst thing was that none of the U'ivuan men who worked for the missionaries had their spears; they had given them up to become Christians, and the sight of them without their spears was somehow obscene, as if they were missing their heads. Even the most destitute, the most unrecognizable of men in Tui'uvo kept their spears; often it was the only thing they had.

I went to Iva'a'aka, where once were great fields of vegetables and groves of trees, destroyed long ago when Lilly bought rights to the land to begin a turtle breeding farm. Now the lake it had created was a brackish swamp, its water as black and thick as petroleum, the earth around it foul and greasy with poison, the air ahum with the ever-present tornadoes of flies drawn to the smell of death. The few seasonal workers from U'ivu who lived there stood guard over this sewagey mess, their eyes fixed on the horizon, waiting for the plane that would bring their employers back.

It was an island of waiters, where once waiting had been a foreign concept. This had never been a culture obsessed with the past, and why should it have been? Nothing ever changed. But now that everything had, all its inhabitants could think about was what they had lost. And so they remained frozen in their vigilance, toggling between hope and despair, waiting for their world to be restored.

It was my last day and I was leaving for the field to catch my flight. As always, I had packed sample boxes to secrete and protect any interesting clippings I might encounter, and as had been the case for the past several years, I left with them empty.

As always, I walked down the main street—stickier than ever with mud after a sudden rainfall—through a phalanx of out-stretched hands, the corps of U'ivuans appearing suddenly and mutely before me, ready to take whatever I might have to give them. I had grown used to this as well and was prepared with pocketsful of things I thought they might use: not money, but dried scraps of mango, handkerchiefs (which they could use to clean their spears or diaper their babies), nuts, and penknives for the ones who seemed particularly pitiable.

At the field I waited. Some company—Merck, I had heard—had, in a last burst of investor's optimism, paid to have a runway constructed but had abandoned it before its completion, and so it, like much of the island, was left half finished and half not, of less use to anyone in this state than it had been before. Now weeds and tiny, furry trees thrust through the tarmac, buckling the surface into a series of blackened soufflés.

A man came slowly toward me. For whatever reason, very few islanders lingered about the field—maybe from habit, since it had once been the king's hunting grounds, or maybe from fear, as they did not like the airplanes—and I watched him, fanning myself in the heat, as he approached. As he drew nearer, I saw at once that he was Ivu'ivuan. You could always distinguish the Ivu'ivuans: they were slightly smaller than the U'ivuans, and darker, and something about them seemed permanently nonplussed, disoriented, no matter how long they had lived on their new island.

This man was older, maybe in his early forties, and seemed more defeated than most; his spear was gouged at its tip, and its shaft was thorny with splinters. He wore a sarong that had once perhaps been dark blue, and I could smell the alcohol sweating off him, as sweet as rotting roses. But for all that, he was oddly confident, and when he beckoned me, I found myself following him.

On the edge of the field was a clutch of ragged and dispirited-looking guava trees, and the man pointed to a bundle of cloths, as colorless as his sarong, secreted between them. When I did not move to collect them, he gave them a kick with his toe and the cloths turned over and I saw that it was a child. The man barked a command and the child stood. He wore only a T-shirt, one more holes and rips than actual fabric, and his hair was so magnificently snarled that I remember thinking, almost reflexively, that I would have to shave it off and begin anew.

But then I remembered myself and told the man that I didn't need any more children.

The man gaped at me in apparent disbelief. I had said no to parents before, of course—especially when the children were noticeably deformed—but they usually accepted my rejection quietly, resignedly, and nodded at me before returning to their perch at the edge of the road. But this man, it appeared, would be different. I must take the child, he told me, and then when I refused, he repeated it again: I must take him. I didn't want the child, I told him. I had no more room for children.

"But he is such a small boy!" he told me, and then, when he saw me unmoved, his tone changed and he became placating: Would I not please take the child? He knew I was a rich man, and a good man. He even knew my name. "No-ton," he said. "No-ton, please take the child."

The child had his head bent this entire time, and now the man pushed him toward me. "You take him!" he wailed, and then he repeated the same words, this time in a shout, because the plane was swooping overhead, its propellers whirring noisily, readying for its landing.

I turned and began walking toward the plane, and the man followed me, yanking the boy behind him. "He will do anything you want! Anything! You can do anything with him!" The man was yelling now, and something about his voice, its fury mingled with desperation, made me turn and look at him more closely. And there, for just a second—and it really was that brief—I suddenly thought I recognized him. His jawline was fluffed from too much alcohol, his eyes were as yellow as suet, but there, in the lift of his chin, in his still slender arms attached to the puff of his torso like a spider's legs, was there not the boy from the a'ina'ina, the one who had held his head so erect and steady, the one who had let his hands skim over me like insects' wings?

And then, before I knew it, I found myself reaching my arms forward, and the man, with a groan of relief, shoving the boy—still mute, still with his head bowed—into them. The plane's door was opening, its stairs louvering down, and as I trotted toward them, I could hear the man again, calling after me.

"What do you want now?" I shouted back at him over the din of the engine. "I'm taking him with me!"

"You must give me something for him!"

Even in my haste to leave, I found myself slightly outraged at this—first he was imploring me to take the child from him, and now he was asking for payment? "I don't have anything," I told him.

"Please! No-ton! Anything! I must have something for him!"

So I dug into my pockets, setting the boy down on the ground in order to do so, until I found my last penknife, which I gave to him along with a fistful of pistachios. He snatched them from my hand and trotted away, his spear held above his shoulder in apparent triumph. He never turned around to look at the boy. Suddenly I felt very sorry for him; he had not wanted the boy, but the boy was also his only possession, his only thing to sell or trade.

From the plane, the pilot waved—he had already gathered my bags, and now it was time for me to come aboard. "Come," I said to the child in U'ivuan, and when he didn't follow me, only stood there staring at his feet, I was made to march back and pick him up. His shirt was glazed with oil and faintly slick to the touch, and his breath on my cheek was hot and unpleasantly yeasty. But he clung to my neck with his arm and turned his face into my shoulder as I climbed the stairs.

I sat at the window and watched the island shrink beneath me. The child had not let go of my neck. Later he would urinate on me, and I would spend the rest of the flight to Hawaii sitting in his waste. I didn't like him, but I felt pity for him, which is often the first step toward liking anyone. I was fifty-six, I was going home, I had another child. I felt only exhaustion. This trip, I swore, would be my last, my very last.

The child fell asleep and I set him down on the floor on a blanket. *Another one*, I thought, dully. *Another one to name, and feed, and clothe, and raise.*

In Honolulu, I shook the pilot's hand and thanked him. He had been the copilot on my previous flight from U'ivu, and he told me he was French but had been raised and was still based in Papeete, so he might see me again if I ever flew this route again. His name was Victor, he said.

A good name, I thought, somewhere over California. It was very late; I had been traveling for many hours; I was very tired. Certainly good enough for a boy without a name. Later, much later, I would reflect on how this child I had acquired and named so thoughtlessly should turn out to become the most important of creatures, how he would upset my life and the lives of others beyond recognition.

But back then, of course, I could not have predicted it. Outside my little shell of a window I could see the bank of clouds plumping beneath us. Beside me, the boy—Victor, now—slept. And finally, I closed my eyes as well, and slipped into a sleep without dreams.

# PART VI. VICTOR

### I.

He was difficult from the beginning. *Difficult* is such a useful, vague word, but in this situation its lack of specificity is intentional. This is because almost everything about Victor—every interaction, every exchange, every rite of childhood—seemed particularly fraught, and even the basic facts about him that should have been easy to ascertain became the subjects of labyrinthine explorations and investigations. There are children who make life difficult for themselves through their bad behavior or lack of personality or common sense, and there are others for whom—through genetics or circumstances—life is already difficult. It should be said that although Victor eventually became a member of the former category, he began life with me as a member of the latter.

Take, for instance, his age. It was no surprise to me that Victor's father (or whoever he was) did not know or care how old his child was. The first time I was able to hold him and regard him closely—to scrutinize the smeary eyes, the distended stomach, the scrubby scab of dirty hair, the colonies of glistening, plump lice, each as fat and slick as a grain of buttered rice—I guessed him to be six or so, although an early childhood of malnourishment and disease gave him the appearance of a three-year-old. Upon returning to Bethesda, I took him to see the children's pediatrician, Alan Shapiro, who thought, after examining him and taking into account his obviously stunted growth, that he might be as old as seven or as young as four. Guessing the age of these children is an imperfect art, one I had long ago ceased fretting over too much. Indeed, it is usually beneficial to shave as many months off these children's lives as one is realistically able to; it gives them a year or two to adjust to the work of being a developing American child and eases their burden to thrive and succeed. (Call it a sort of developmental affirmative action, if you will.) So after a sort of lazy, halfhearted debate, Shapiro and I came to an understanding, and on Victor's medical files (and all official records thereafter) we listed August 13, 1976, as his birthday, August 13 being, of course, the day I found him. I had entered Shapiro's office with a mystery of a child; I went home with a certified four-year-old.

Nineteen eighty, the year Victor entered my household, was unusual for two reasons. For one, there had never been as many children living in the house at one time as there were that year. For another, it turned out to be one of those years in which the population of children fell fairly neatly into two distinct generations. At one end was a gaggle of eighteen-year-olds—Muti, Megan, Gunter, Lani, Lei, Terrence, Karl, and Edith, I believe—all of whom would be leaving for college, followed closely by another group of older adolescents (sixteen- and seventeen-year-olds, primarily, with a few slightly younger ones, including Ella, who was twelve at the time, and Abby, who was eleven, tossed in). But the next oldest children to follow them, Isolde and William—the children who would be Victor's primary peers—were only six. Altogether, there were some twenty-two children living in the house that year. Most of my memories of that time are sensory rather than anecdotal ones—the lugubrious, looping strains of the rock music the teenagers would play hour after hour; the sickly, fruity stench of the alcohol they filched from somewhere; the various sartorial failures that paraded past me in the mornings. In the evenings the girls talked on the phone and the boys stayed in their rooms and, I am sure, masturbated. At times I was certain that several of them were having sexual relations with one another, but it seemed too exhausting a topic even to begin to address. They all spent a great deal of time fighting, and watching television, and loudly declaring how relieved they would be to finally leave the house and go to college and be on their own (with, of course, ample financial assistance from me). Needless to say, I spent as much time as possible abroad, attending conferences, giving lectures. Returning from the airport, I always half expected to turn the corner and find the house a pile of rubble, with all of them waiting impatiently and crossly for me to come home so they could leap on me with their demands and complaints and needs.

I wonder what Victor must have thought the first time he saw the house and met the strange, populous collection of children whom he would now be expected—if only legally—to regard as his brothers and sisters. I am certain it must have been overwhelming for him; I myself had a difficult time keeping track of the faces that walked by me every morning, asked me for money, thrust report cards and petty injuries in front of my face. At one point one of the older children had even brought a friend of his home to live with us for a week to see if I'd notice an extra setting at the table, an extra permission slip to sign. Naturally, I didn't notice at all (my time and thoughts being occupied with a multitude of things), and when the prank was finally revealed to me, amid much hilarity, I laughed as well, and shook the hand of the interloper, an angular, handsome boy whose skin was the purplish black of figs. In the mornings children would literally fly past me, leaping off the middle of the flight of stairs toward the front door, or trooping out the back door in dense flanks, clasping hockey and lacrosse sticks and baseball bats like weaponry, like the spears they would once have taken everywhere. (Sometimes I would watch them marching together, their blunt, unfriendly, planar faces brailled with acne, and think involuntarily of Captain Cook's cloaked advice that I had chosen in my youth to disregard— *The fierceness of the Wevooans makes the crew uneasy*—and shudder, because was I any more equipped to live with these people who had so unsettled the explorer's brave crew, who knew more and had seen more than I ever would?)

I do admit that I had trouble remembering everyone's name. I would call for the girl I thought was Lani and in her place would appear someone I had always thought was Megan (that is, if anyone heeded my call at all). Sometimes this was not my failure but an intentional bit of trickery; they would try to play games like this—one person standing in for another, trying to confuse me— but quickly learned not to do this after I began playing some games of my own: giving money to the person who answered my call, for example, or requesting that he or she complete a particularly odious chore. Squabbles would break out, confessions would be made, mistaken and deliberately confused identities would be righted. It was this generation of children who had instituted the prohibition against, as they said, "infants" at the dinner table, which meant that Isolde and William (and thereafter everyone younger than seven) were consigned to the "baby table," a squat, white-laminated wooden toy of a thing that was used primarily for quick, slapdash breakfasts eaten in the kitchen, to take their evening meal with Mrs. Tomlinson an hour before everyone else ate. There was, of course, much crying and screeching from Isolde and William over this decision and an equal amount of not quite logical but self-righteous screaming from the elders ("Majority rules! Majority rules!" shrieked Fred, one of the sixteen-year-olds, who was studying the Constitution in high school; you could always ascertain their school syllabus by observing the realpolitik they tried to apply to various household regulations), but in the end the amendment was passed. Even I had to admit it was an inspired solution; at any rate, it made dinnertime less of a spectacle than it had been.

Into this household, then, came Victor, whom I introduced to them on a weekend evening when poor weather had kept everyone indoors. He did not make a very good impression on them. The older children gawped at him silently for a long moment. The more polite ones gave him nervous, useless smiles; a few of them reached out to touch him and then withdrew their hands quickly, as if Victor might leap out of my arms and gobble them whole. Isolde and William stood in the doorway and stared. Victor, for his part, turned his face into my shoulder and remained completely silent. After I had had Mrs. Tomlinson take him away, they began pecking at me with questions.

"What's wrong with him?"

"Why does he look like that?"

"Is he sick? Why is he that color?"

"How old is he?"

Hearing their reactions upon the introduction of a new child always amused me. How quickly they forgot what *they* had looked like when they had arrived in this country! They came, most of them, accompanied only by lice and disease and wearing scraps of filthy cotton that could only aspire to be called proper clothing. The nature of their infections varied from cholera to dysentery to gangrene to conjunctivitis to malaria, as did the rate of their recovery, but they were all malnourished and undersized and (it must be said) notably unattractive, with large, pulsing, delicate heads and curled, flaccid limbs; they looked like oversized fetuses, things born too unformed and monstrous to be allowed among humans, mistakes never meant to be seen.

"You should be embarrassed," I told them. "Don't you think you looked like that, Megan, when you first came? Or you, Owen?" I was always made to rebuke them in this way after their initial reaction to a new child: the older ones would be ashamed, the younger ones defiant.

But this time they were unmoved. "We didn't look like *that*," they chorused.

And they were not, it must be said, entirely incorrect. I have commented earlier on the depravity of Victor's previous situation, the physical shock one felt upon seeing him. But here, if I am to be honest, I must also say that one was not merely astonished when regarding him but rather repelled. I have, over my years, been privileged to see some of the worst ravages disease can wreak on the human body, and while Victor was not—not by a very long measure—one of the most *impressively* diseased specimens I had encountered, he was certainly one of the most pitiable. Not because it was clear that he possessed a great natural beauty or native attractiveness that had been deadened or distorted by his illnesses, but rather because of the *thoroughness* of the infections. Indeed, nothing that I could see or feel had managed to escape the marks of disease—no part of him appeared healthy. Looking at him, I felt, not for the first time, a sort of admiration for the multitude of viruses and bacteria, the distinct and creative marks they had left on even the smallest, most forgettable parts of his body, how they had mapped his skin with furrows of hot, bubbling welts, each capped with a snowy peak of pus, how they had moved across the whites of his eyes, leaving them as yellow as fat and secreting a mysterious slime that was as thick as wax. Various bacteria appeared to have successfully conquered even the most inconsequential parts of his anatomy: even his toe- and fingernails were as opaque as bone, the tips ossified into jagged arrowheads. Every orifice wept liquids, some thin and rust-colored that bore the sharp, steely stench of menstrual blood, others clear and jellylike that oozed to the surface only reluctantly. He was fascinating, a home to thousands of visitors. Shapiro and I spent a few pleasant afternoons examining him, naming the diseases we could (ringworm, conjunctivitis, eczema) and arguing over the ones we could not. It was a great, thrilling puzzle, and Victor—who sat quietly, breathing adenoidally through his mouth as Shapiro and I poked and prodded and ran our fingers over his body—was, I must say, very patient. But of course most of his infections, no matter how alarming or intimidating in appearance, were in fact quite treatable, and after his nightly bath I would settle him in my lap, rub cream into his sores, and give him antibiotics secreted in a plug of honey cake. Over the days I'd watch his skin smooth as a crunchy scab of blisters that had annexed his inner thigh slowly dissolved, like salt disintegrating into a dark puddle of liquid. So while his initial appearance was unsettling, it was certainly not permanent, and in fact easily rectified. No, the greater problem with Victor was his almost complete lack of socialization, his fundamental—and the word is intentional—savagery. For very shortly after I acquired Victor, I realized that I was going to have to teach him how to be a human.

There are people—even otherwise logical and clear-minded people—who believe that we are born with a predisposition to behave as, well, humans. That is, that we are born with a certain set of desires or tendencies—the tendency, say, to be sociable with others, or to share with others, or to communicate with others. (These are also the people who believe in such concepts as good and evil and enjoy debating whether man is one or the other.) But although this is a pretty notion, it is fundamentally untrue. For proof, one need look no further than my own children, and especially Victor, who seemed to have little understanding of what it meant to behave like a human being. His body fulfilled its basic needs, of course—he ate, he slept, he defecated—but he was not, it appeared, capable of doing anything else. To begin with, he was almost wholly unemotive. Once, as an experiment, I pricked the sole of his foot lightly with a pin, and although he twitched his head, he remained mute, and his blank, dumb look did not change. I devised other tests as well. At mealtimes he would open his mouth, eat whatever was placed within (he had no idea even how to feed himself; if I set a plate in front of him, he would only gaze at it fixedly, as if it were some precious thing he had been assigned to guard), his jaws opening and closing with a steady rhythm, his teeth coming together with an exaggerated, steely tap. Once I slipped into a spoonful of cooked carrots a small square of newsprint, which he imperturbably chewed away at until I reached into his mouth and retrieved the pulpy mash of inky paper. In these moments I would look at his face and be able to see only Eve's echoed back to me, and his presence would seem a punishment, and a reminder of how I would never escape what I had seen and been and done on that island. At night he would be placed in his bed, but by morning either Mrs. Tomlinson or I (or William, with whom he shared a small knuckle of a room on the third floor, under the sloping eaves of the attic) would find him curled into a knot in the corner of the room, dark and silent and still, clutching his genitals with his hands.

There were other, less tidy puzzles as well. It became clear that he was obsessed with his feces; he would leave woody lengths of them on the carpets, in the yard, on the table. The strange thing was that he did not seem unfamiliar with the toilet itself; Mrs. Tomlinson reported to me that upon his introduction to it, he had pressed the lever with a manual dexterity and confidence that had yet to manifest itself in any other noticeable way and had watched the water swirl away. One night I watched him leave his bedroom and walk toward the bathroom, only to stop a few feet from it, almost lazily undo the strings of his pajama pants, and squat directly above the hallway carpet's centerpiece, a large faded fuchsia rose. He had in the previous day or so acquired a facial expression that he interchanged (often, and for no discernible reason) with his usual automaton's gaze: a ghastly facsimile of a smile, in which he spread his long mouth into a wide crescent and revealed his few dust-colored teeth. When I called out his name, he turned to me unhurriedly and gave me this smile. Even after I smacked him across his bottom and groin, he continued to smile, as if his facial muscles had seized themselves into a rictus from which they could not relax.

It seems foolish to admit this now, but at the time I allowed myself to be surprised by Victor's behavior. He had been so quiet, so defeated when I discovered him that I mistook his wanness for a certain promise of tractability, a willingness to learn and be taught. The fact that he initially had little discernible personality of his own only assured me that my job with him would be easy; I would instill in him the properties I had always wished to bestow on my children—he would be inquisitive, and polite, and obedient, and reasonable. But over his first month I came to see that he was more stubborn and altogether less pliable than I had assumed; indeed, his very impassivity began to seem a sort of spiky defiance. I began to think of him, with his masklike mien and terrible smile and graceless, stiff-limbed walk, as a golem, something I had unfairly and unreasonably awakened and let loose to totter through my household, wrecking it with its inhuman, robotic, indecipherable movements, its impulses ungovernable by man. Indeed, he was difficult not because the problems that he presented were so insurmountable but simply because I was unsure how to go about addressing them. I had had other children who were monstrous—Muti, during her first month in the house, had tried to kill the cat by gouging out its eyes with a pair of chopsticks; Terrence had torn the head off one of the older children's gerbils with his pointy little teeth (*that* had caused quite an uproar)—but I had at least understood them. They had liked screaming and shrieking and throwing loud, sustained fits. Moreover, they were excited to be screamed back at, to have someone with whom to engage. Such episodes were, of course, wearisome, and frequently messy, but they were at least the beginnings of conversations, or at the very least of exchanges.

But such interactions seemed to have no effect on Victor. Over the months I tried approaching and then punishing him in every way I could. I praised him and cursed at him. I kissed him and hit him. I gave him extra portions of pasta (he seemed particularly fond of various carbohydrates, unlike the others, who had craved meat) and withheld food entirely. I sang to him and slapped his face, murmured nonsense into his ear and pulled his hair, but he remained spectacularly indifferent to my various attentions, only sat grinning like a skull.

After several months I grew to regret ever bringing him home with me. The various infections that had written themselves on his skin had vanished (and indeed, he was pronounced by Shapiro to be in excellent health), but the transformation from a sick child to a well one was not as dramatic as I had expected. Some of the children, after making inauspicious first impressions, revealed themselves to be delightful creatures: their skin smoothed and their cheeks became fat and shiny, and their peculiar, rootlike hair grew in thick and faintly sweet-smelling, like mesquite wood. The restoration of good health (if, that is, he had ever been in good health to begin with) to Victor revealed no such pleasant surprises. He did not become a gleaming-eyed boy with an infectious laugh and a steady, focused gaze. Indeed, he was, once healthy, much what he had been before: neither a winning nor an attractive child, he remained stubbornly unlikely to inspire any feelings of affection or endearment, even from those in whom such emotions were expected.

Eventually it became clear to me that Victor was not the sort of child with whom a behavioral threshold could be reached and crossed. Rather, his socialization would be a long and tedious process, full of infinitesimal, unnoticeable bits of progress and lengthy, discouraging periods of regression. I spent an evening watching him, taking note of what he did and did not know, what he might be easily taught, what bad habits I might have to break first. He had, predictably, no language—although when forced or suitably inspired, he would let loose a series of terse, simian grunts—but he seemed to be able to understand timbres. A rebuke conveyed in a tone that cracked the air like a slap would still him, and a voice pitched to a high register, singy and false, seemed to comfort him. But in general he seemed to have learned not to react to things at all; hence the frightening, inappropriate smile, the weird, frozen blankness.

It was the smile that bothered me most. I offered twenty dollars to the first child who could teach Victor to successfully mimic acceptable facial reactions, and for several nights after they spent their evenings in the living room ringed around him. They tickled him, told him jokes (which he of course could not understand), danced about him, funneled cake bits into their mouths, making expressions of delight. Naturally, though, there was no response from him, and after a week or less the children lost interest and returned to their aforementioned after-dinner activities. Still, I did not think the week a waste, for I had seen him turning his veiny head from one eagerly beaming child to another, his mouth slightly open, as if curious to learn the rules of some complex and bewildering game, one whose skillful mastery would determine his ultimate happiness. I'm not sure, then, that he understood this consciously or not—or that he would even have known how to begin to comprehend the idea of happiness—but he seemed, after a period of many weeks, to consciously devote himself to his studies. A few months later, I found him watching a talk show on television one morning. It took me some minutes to realize that he was looking at the newscasters' faces, their bright, clownish smiles. After a while he stood and padded over to the hallway bathroom. I followed, silent as a specter, and stood for a very long time, watching him pull his mouth into odd and imperfect expressions of joy, gazing at himself in the mirror as if trying to memorize the exact angle at which his lips should curve upward, puzzling over the many muscles that such an apparently simple gesture seemed to require.

By the next year he had learned first how to approximate and then how to truly engage in appropriate human behavior. Although he never became a particularly captivating child, he managed to do well enough for himself: he grew, and ate, and acquired language and apparently genuine human emotions. On a more mundane level, he learned how to use the bathroom correctly, and how to eat with a fork and spoon, and how to tie his shoes. It was also revealed that he had certain easily indulged interests; he was very fond of simple mechanisms—anything that involved pulleys or levers fascinated him—and he could spend literally hours playing with the old dumbwaiter outside the kitchen, watching the box silently glide up on its twirled, shiny ropes and then lowering it back to the basement again, where it would come creaking into sight like some archaic spacecraft. Eventually he was sent to school, where he learned to read and write and even made a few friends.

After a few years he was, in every respect that mattered or was noticeable, a perfectly average boy, one who smiled and frowned and raged and laughed. His transformation had occurred so slowly, and over such a long period of time, that I was able to recognize it only long after it had ended. Indeed, I began to think of his initial years in the house as his sort of chrysalis phase—I could remember (and would, often) the child he had been when I discovered him, but I soon found that it was very difficult to recall exactly how he had metamorphosed into what sat before me at the dinner table or behind me in the car, eating or chattering or merely watching the scenery slide by. The future I imagined for him, when I did so at all, was remarkable only for its haziness: he would, I suppose, go to high school, then perhaps college, would find a job (and I was unable to imagine what that might be, whether he would be a tradesman or perhaps work in an office in a white shirt, a tie wrapped around his throat, his diction perfect and deracinated), would marry and have a family. I would see him and worry over him less and less frequently until he became as pleasantly remote as a memory.

And really, that should have been the end of my story with Victor. Over the months his problems began to seem less exciting, less mysterious, less *vivid*, than they had at first. For one, there were new children, who would prove challenging in different, more understandable ways. A year after I adopted Victor, I added to my family another child, a boy, whom I named Whitney. He, like Victor, was underfed and undersocialized, but unlike Victor, he was wild—a screecher and a tantrumer. In other words, he was easy to discipline and swift to improve. Still, after Whitney, I decided to take a break from adopting children. (It is curious to me now that I thought of my decision in exactly those terms: I would, I resolved, *take a break* from children, but I was somehow unable or unwilling to admit the truth: that I had long ceased to derive that joy I so desired from a new child's arrival, that I should simply stop adding them to my life.)

Consequently, those years, between, say, 1982 and 1985, were very pleasant ones for me. A batch of the children went away to college, and suddenly the house was empty (or at least emptier than it had been in a long time), and I was able to travel, often and for extended periods, both to places I'd long wanted to go and to places I hadn't visited in years. One weekend I left the children at home under Mrs. Lansing (after more than fifteen years of tending to my children, Mrs. Tomlinson decided to retire, giving me the telephone number of her sister-in-law, a similarly capable woman named JoAnne Lansing, before she did) and went to see Owen at Bard, where he had just begun teaching. We spent a very nice few days together, Owen and

I, as well as a boy[77]—one of his students, I believe—whom he was dating at the time.

But in 1986 I was seized by—what? A sort of boredom, I suppose, or else a madness (or was it simply my old yearning?), and traveled once more to U'ivu, where I spent a few listless days trekking over the island and charting its ongoing decline. And when I returned to Maryland, I found myself doing so with a set of twins, Jared and Drew, as well as a girl, Kerry. Suddenly my life once again seemed to elude my grasp, and three years later I was almost horrified to find myself with an entire new generation of children; it was almost as if they had multiplied one night when I was asleep. Indeed, it seemed a far more plausible explanation than the truth: that I had, for some inexplicable set of reasons I could not quite articulate to myself, repopulated my life with a dozen new existences, all of whom I would have to witness trundling through the multitudinous steps of childhood, adolescence, and adulthood. I began to wonder seriously whether I had something of a tic. How was it, I thought, that I found myself now with *more* children, when only a few years before I had been anxiously waiting for the house to empty of them so that my life, alone, unburdened, might finally begin anew? Why was I incapable of stopping? What was I hoping each new one might provide me that the previous thirty-odd had not? What was it that I wanted?

## II.

In retrospect—when it is so easy to blame oneself for everything that has gone wrong—I realize that I should not have been so complacent about, so accepting of, Victor's apparent maturation without first finding a way to properly control him, a way of exerting my authority that he would understand and respect. But something had changed. Once I would have wanted to discover why Victor behaved the way he did, but that was no longer true; by the time he had begun to behave appropriately, I was merely relieved that he had learned to be manageable and that he had left certain behavior behind. I began to realize that I was bored, or rather, that I had lost my taste for the whole occupation of child-raising. I was no longer interested

---

[77] Actually a twenty-two-year-old man who was enrolled in graduate school at Syracuse University.

in solving the formerly intriguing puzzles of my children's psyches. I no longer cared why one shrieked hysterically when confronted with coffeepots or why another cowered at the sight of the orange juice in its sweating, frosted bottle. Before, I would have spent many contented days mulling over the (usually unhappy) possible events and narratives that had resulted in such reactions; I often thought of them as bright, snappy little mindbenders, rubber bands to mentally stretch and tease when I was taking a break from the real work that filled my day. And such petty quandaries were in their own way immensely fulfilling, for they satisfied much of what I considered the romance of child-rearing: that it *should* at times be puzzling and elusive and problematic, that each child was a being who could be understood and, if need be, led in one direction or another. Indeed, when I had adopted Muiva, in 1968, the prospect of raising a child had seemed both tantalizing and rich with wonder: to have as one's charge something both knowable and not, at once predictable and full of startling surprises, seemed to promise unimaginable adventure, dozens of daily revelations wrought in miniature.

And for many years, for decades even, it had. But then (again, in creeping stages I would not recognize until they were long past) things began, inevitably, to change. For one thing, I found myself growing old. In 1984 I turned sixty, and the lab threw me a small birthday party, something that, given my frequent and sustained absences, I had been able to avoid every year previously. Still, it was not so awful. Two of the institute's emeritus professors came, both offering me ironic congratulations (they were both past eighty, after all), and there was a Lady Baltimore cake with buttercream frosting and some not terrible brandylike liquor that one of the more refined fellows had been developing in his idle time.[78] One of the techs wove around the desks with a camera, taking pictures of the festivities, and I found myself, unexpectedly, having an enjoyable time.

The next week, a plain brown envelope was left on my desk, and inside it was a picture of a man whom I at first could not identify.

---

[78] In the lab, of course. There is invariably a gourmand—or, if one is being less charitable, a budding alcoholic—among the staff of any lab who spends his leisure time developing various liquors in the beakers and decanting them at impromptu office parties. Some of these brews are actually quite respectable.

He looked familiar, and for an instant I wondered if he was someone I had encountered not long before and liked despite myself: he
had a slant of marrow-colored hair, a simpering smile, and huge,
bready hands, each finger as yeasty as a rolled pastry. But of course
the picture was of me, and I stared at it, teetering between dismay
and a sort of clinical curiosity, for some minutes. I had never had the
inclination or the freedom to spend a great deal of time considering
my appearance, but there was, I realized, something obscene and
horrific about my girth, the rind of fat that had grown around my
midsection, about the way my lips appeared thickened and oddly
mauve, the way the folds of fat at my neck lay in heavy pleats as if I
were some clumsy, flightless bird. What was most striking to me was
the apparent absence of any bone structure at all; indeed, it looked as
if I had been fashioned from a soft block of sweating lard. Age—and
the thought of aging—had never particularly upset me, but I was
depressed upon seeing that picture and contemplating the decay of
my body and my knowledge of its apparently disgusting appearance.
Of course I had noticed that I was growing old, that memories were
no longer as crisp as they had been, that I found myself breathing
through my mouth after mounting the stairs to my room, that my
sleeping patterns had grown erratic. But it was not until I saw that
picture that I was able to understand how stealthy and cruel age's
progress was, how noticeable and irreversible the decay. *Oh god,* I
thought, *there will be another fifteen or twenty years of this, and every
year will grow worse.* Suddenly the thought of my life, its relentless
march forward, seemed almost unbearably oppressive. And I could
not forget that were I somewhere else, I would have been feted not
with cake but with an opa'ivu'eke of my own, and I imagined myself
at the fire's edge, Tallent beside me, the turtle's mounded back being
slowly dragged into view, moving ever closer to me.

I suppose, though, that I was lucky in other ways. In 1989, when
I turned sixty-five, I should have, according to various governmental
regulations and so forth, been asked to retire, or at least accepted the
position of director emeritus. Such a demotion would have left me
somewhat emasculated but still able to participate in the daily life of
the lab. But to my surprise, there was no letter from some bureaucrat
reminding me of the imminent diminishment of responsibilities
and inviting my retirement. I was, it seemed, an exception. Not that

it would have bothered me terribly had I been asked to adhere to the rules. By that time, after all (as had been the case for some years), I scarcely needed NIH's name or association to support me; had they insisted on holding me to the same standards they did everyone else, I simply would have accepted one of the offers from Johns Hopkins or Georgetown that were extended to me annually. If I am to be honest, I would not have minded going to a private institution elsewhere, but of course my movements were restricted by the children and the care I was obligated to provide for them.

But whereas a few years before I would have been quite accepting of this fact—I had, after all, adopted them of my own free will, fully conscious that I had chosen the responsibility—I had come to feel inexplicably and unfairly resentful, as if I should somehow be exempted from the tedious selflessness of parenthood. For a period shortly after it became clear that I was not to be asked to vacate my position at the lab, I found myself at dinner glaring at the children, all of them forking great quantities of food into their mouths with a greed and vigor that struck me as repellent. As I have said, I knew even then that I was being unreasonable—they were, after all, healthy American children with healthy American appetites, appetites that I had created and encouraged—but still, the sight of their enthusiastic consumption (and all they seemed to do, in the end, was consume and consume) invoked in me something close to anger. Things that had normally been merely dull (their constant questions, their numerous demands, their lack of perspective) or even charming became over those years almost unbearable. I had experienced these feelings before, and sometimes for quite prolonged periods, but I had always been able in the end to resume my usual, basically affectionate feelings before the children were able to notice my temporary distaste for them. No matter what they may say now, their mental health was of some importance to me, and I did not think it fair for them to feel apologetic or indebted to me or responsible for my moods. Not, I should add, that there was ever any danger of that.

Such then was my state of mind in 1989, when there began to unfold a chain of events that has led me to my present state. I have spent many months mentally replaying the circumstances I am about to relate, wondering what I might have done differently, wondering if I could have foreseen the path of my destruction. In some moments I found myself thinking that perhaps there was something inexorable about the way events unfolded, as if my life—which had begun to seem something not my own but rather something into which I found myself blindly toppling—was indeed something *living*, that existed without my knowledge but that pulled me along in its strong, insistent undertow.

But after many months of consideration, I find I still lack an adequate explanation for what happened, as well as for any way I might have prevented it. Indeed, such is my continued bewilderment at the velocity and ferocity with which my life was changed that I have found that contemplating the events of that year becomes tolerable only when I consider them as things that happened long ago and to someone else—some series of misfortunes and tragedies that befell someone I once admired and had read about in a dusty book in a grand, stone-floored library somewhere far away, where there was no sound, no light, no movement but for my own breath, and my fingers clumsily turning the rough-cut pages.

Soon after realizing that I was to be mysteriously spared from the government's knife and would be allowed to continue life much as before, I was forced to admit to myself that I had been—secretly, so secretly I had not quite allowed myself to believe it—longing for some sort of excuse to curtail my professional activities.

I was tired. It sounds such a plain and ordinary thing to say, but it is true. I was now at an age when one often finds more pleasure in reflecting on one's past triumphs—which, along with mistakes, I had in great number, of course—than in plotting future ones. I sometimes wondered if in continuing to present myself at the lab, in continuing my lecturing, in continuing my searching, I was somehow defying the natural arc of human life: early life is made for exploring, and middle life is made for reaping the benefits of that exploration. But should I not, in my sixties, simply *stop*? Should not the next few decades be spent keeping myself from future problems and troubles (and, yes, from future successes)? Was there a finite number of accomplishments one person might be granted in his life, and if so, hadn't I surely reached my quota?

And then I would think I was being ridiculous, and lazy, and impractical as well, for what would I do without my work? Would I sit at home and help Mrs. Lansing raise the children and vacuum the floors? Would I become (as I inevitably would) one of those emeritus professors with which the institute seemed particularly well stocked, the sort who take to making impromptu visits to their old labs, embarrassing and irritating everyone with their doddering and countless questions about what everyone is working on and incessant stories of what they did twenty, thirty, forty years ago, back when people cared? Sometimes a few of them would come over to my lab, and although there would invariably be some banter about my advanced age and when I was going to leave all these headaches behind and move on, I could see always the greed in their eyes as they flickered across the room and the way that they caressed even the most everyday objects—a beaker, a flask, the fabric cover of one of the pistachio-green journals in which we wrote our notes—and know that they envied me and regretted ever having left.

"What are you doing with yourself these days?" I'd always ask politely, even after I had long discerned that the question was not a kindness but a small cruelty. *Oh, this and that,* would be the answer, and although the replies were always long ones, they were in the end old men who could not conceal what their lives had become: days abuzz with little flecks of industry, trips with the wife to the grocery store, hours spent reading scientific journals that they had once allowed to accumulate in the corner of the lab in a large sliding heap, back when they were scientists themselves and too busy with their own studies to worry about reading someone else's.[79]

---

[79] Much of Norton's work throughout the 1980s concentrated on the Karée people, a small tribe (its total population was less than six hundred) who live in northern Brazil off a particularly narrow and treacherous Amazonian tributary. The Karée were encountered in 1978 by a botanist from the University of California, Santa Cruz, named Lucien Feeney, who stumbled on their society by accident while searching for a rare fern (*Microsorum coccinella*) that he speculated was an early cousin of the modern palm tree and that had been harvested to near extinction throughout the rest of the basin some two hundred years prior. When he observed the tribe, Feeney knew that there was something strange about them, but he was unable to determine what, exactly, made them unique. Upon his return to Santa Cruz, he contacted Norton through an acquaintance at Johns Hopkins, and Norton made his first visit to the tribe shortly thereafter (I accompanied him on this trip as well as subsequent ones). Tests and other fieldwork revealed that the Karée experienced an unusually delayed

So I could not leave. But I did begin spending more time at home. Not because I wanted to be at home, necessarily, but because it was either being there or being in the lab, and I was finding that I could no longer be at the lab indefinitely. Sundays, for example, I used to spend all day there; by the time I got home it would be dark and the children long to bed. But I began to come home earlier and earlier, until I was there more of the afternoon than not.

One Sunday found me at home particularly early. Victor had been given an assignment for history class in which he had to re-create a seed cake that the early American settlers ate and that involved large quantities of millet and cornmeal and rye. The assignment was due the next day and he had to make enough for everyone in the class to try a slice, and naturally, he did not think to share this information with me until lunchtime.

I suppose he was expecting me to do the assignment myself (and why would I have? I wanted to ask him, for I did not think I had a reputation among the children as someone who would take responsibility for their failings), but I commanded him to the kitchen and

---

adolescence; indeed, neither boys nor girls displayed any signs of secondary sex organs until, on average, the age of twenty-five. The puberty that followed was an intense and brutal eighteen-month ordeal that culminated in marriage. After, their biological lives proceeded as normal, which meant that the women had a relatively brief two decades of fertility before undergoing menopause. As a result, there was a great urgency to have as many children as possible, and many of the Karée women died as a result of excessive pregnancies and collectively experienced a remarkably high rate of gynecological complications.

In an echo of the Opa'ivu'eke people, the cause of this abnormality was originally attributed to an endemic rodent (*Hydrochoerus feenius*) that all Karée children grow up eating (it was favored for its succulent, sweetish meat). This was of course highly exciting, especially given Norton's earlier groundbreaking work, but later studies revealed that the culprit was not in fact an external element but something specific to the Karée's biology. Nevertheless, Norton tried to bring back a number of the Karée to his lab for further study but was prevented from doing so by the National Commission for the Protection of Human Subjects of Biomedical and Behavioral Research, which had kept him under unnaturally strict surveillance ever since he had appealed the removal of the dreamers in 1976. Various political struggles forced Norton to abort his work with the Karée in 1990, and today it is Harvard University that maintains a satellite lab—and therefore controls which scientists might be granted access—on the tribe's land. Norton, understandably, remains bitter about how these events unfolded, which is probably why he fails to mention his work with the Karée in this account. Those interested can find an evenhanded rendering of the situation in Anna Kidd's excellent *Of Stone and Sun and Everything In-Between.*

ordered him to start mixing the ingredients, none of which we had, of course, which necessitated a hurried trip to the store before it closed for the day.

We worked in silence, mostly. He was restless, quite literally jumpy, hopping from foot to foot in a manner that I found very distracting but that I would later realize was a sort of warmup, a prelude to a fight to which I had not known I was invited. "Now you have to roll out the dough," I told him, and when he didn't respond—he was staring, mouth slightly open, at apparently nothing more interesting than a fat squirrel crouched on an apple tree branch outside—I snapped at him. "Victor! The dough! Victor!" And he turned back to me, scraped the dough out of its bowl, and slammed it onto the counter with a wet *thwack*.

"You're getting it everywhere, Victor," I said to him, and then, when he once again didn't respond, "Victor! I am talking to you!"

Again silence. And then, "Why was I named Victor?"

"I told you," I said. "I named you for the pilot who took us away from U'ivu when I was adopting you."

"But why him?"

They always wanted to know, my children, why they had been given this name or that. They were fond of self-mythologizing, and I think they all hoped that there might be some heroic story behind their naming, that they alone might be imbued with a special significance, that I might have secreted some message to them in my choice that they would one day understand and appreciate. The truth, however, was that I had usually simply named them after people I had encountered on my journeys to and from retrieving them: they were named after check-in counter clerks at airports and managers at hotels, customs agents and bellhops, pilots and stewardesses, seatmates and waitresses, unknown State Department functionaries who had cleared their entries and familiar immigration officials who had waved at me as I advanced toward them, holding the hand of a new charge. What could I do? I had long ago exhausted the names of friends and colleagues, and by the late 1970s the children were arriving so quickly that contriving imaginative names for them hardly seemed an essential concern.

"Why not?" I asked him. "It's a good name."

"Victor is a stupid name," said Victor.

"Don't act like a child," I told him. "Victor is a fine name. And anyway, it's the name you have, so you must learn to live with it."

"I *am* a child," said Victor. "And I hate the name Victor."

"You weren't listening to me," I replied. "I told you not to *act* like a child. Being a child in and of itself doesn't obligate you to behave like one. And I never said you had to *like* the name Victor—go ahead and hate it all you wish. I only said you had to learn to live with it."

He had no response to this but a sulky silence, and I found myself weary of him.

And then I asked the question no parent should. "What would you like to be called instead?"

Of course he had an answer prepared.

"Vi," he said triumphantly.

Sometimes I really don't understand what came over me. Why had I provided him such an opportunity? But occasionally, after years upon years of these conversations, one forgets oneself and makes regrettable errors.

"Vie?" I asked him. I wasn't sure I'd heard correctly. It reminded me of the time Sonia[80] came home with her beautiful woolly hair chopped off at the ears and dyed with white streaks. As a parent, I was always ready to let my children "express themselves," or whatever the excuse for bad behavior is nowadays, but I do have limits. What child psychiatrists and liberal-minded teachers refuse to acknowledge is that most children have no taste and indeed tend toward the tacky. Just as it is a parent's responsibility to instruct his children in the matter of manners, ethics, and morality, so it is to give them some sort of aesthetic and cultural education, so they don't grow into vulgar adults, the sort who contrive new and needlessly complicated ways to spell their names and consider the plotlines of recently viewed television comedies appropriate dinnertime conversation. "As in to vie for a new position? Or to vie among your siblings for a new way to irritate me?"

But he wasn't provoked even by that. "V-I," he explained, as if to a slow child. I had heard him use the same tone with Giselle, one of the toddlers.

---

[80] Sonia Alice Perina, arrived 1970. She now goes by the name SoAP and is a performance poet and artist of some renown in New York.

"Vi," I repeated. It still didn't make any sense, and I told him so. "Really, Victor," I said, "if you feel that strongly about changing your name, I suppose we can discuss it, but couldn't you pick something less ridiculous? Why not go by your middle name?" Victor's middle name is Owen.[81]

"No," said Victor briskly. "That's a stupid name too. I won't have some white man's name."

And at this I was surprised, and turned around just in time to see him smile. He was triumphant that he had gotten me to react, and I cursed myself silently. "What are you talking about?"

"Have you ever noticed," asked Victor, "that all of us have white men's names? All of us. It's so *false*. You're trying to whitewash us, make us forget who we are and where we come from."

And once again I found myself turning and looking at him. *I gave you a name because you were nameless when I found you*, I thought. *A dog. Less than a dog.* It took some effort not to say this, and had I been more perturbed, I might not have been able to stop myself.

Where did they learn these things? Victor was very wrong if he thought he was the first child of mine to experience this false revelation and then accuse me, haughty with outrage. "Came from," I corrected him. "And really, Victor, this is too boring a conversation. You sound like some reactionary, and reactionaries are never noted for their originality." He had by this time sewn his mouth into a long, thin seam and was looking at me with something like hate in his eyes. "And if we're to speak of contrivances," I told him, "then the name Vi is one of the most preposterous I've heard. Vi is no more a U'ivuan name than Victor is!"

(Still, the minute I heard that absurd name, I knew how he had conjured it: the *vuh* sound, its short, clipped monosyllabism, gave it

---

[81] Norton had named previous children Owen. There was Owen Ambrose (arrived ca. 1969), Owen Edmund (arrived ca. 1969), and Richard Owen (arrived ca. 1971). By 1986 or so, around which time Norton was busy adopting what was to be his final generation of children, Owen had become the de facto middle name regardless of gender: I clearly remember, besides Victor, a Giselle Owen, a Percy Owen (there was also a Percival Owen in an earlier generation), a Drew Owen, a Jared Owen, and a Grace Owen. Whether this was a result of Norton's forgetfulness or distraction or was in fact a sort of homage to his brother was never clear.

a faint whiff of the South Pacific, albeit in only the most reductive and affected way. Over the years my children have created all sorts of names they believe allude to their native country and culture: Va, Vo, Vi, Ve, Vu; though Micronesian in intent, they usually wind up sounding rather Vietnamese.)

Victor opened his mouth and then closed it; he was, after all, still a child, and he knew I was correct. And then, in a gesture that reminded me so much of the boy's I felt chilled, he raised his chin unnaturally high and lowered his lashes, so it appeared that he was looking down at me, though I was much taller than he. "I don't care," he said (a child's last defense). "Vi at least sounds more U'ivuan than Victor." And with that, he turned and left the room.

"Victor!" I called after him, more irritated than angry. He had left half the dishes in the sink undone, and there were still mountains of dough to shape and mold. "Victor! Come back here!" But he didn't, and I had to finish rolling the dough myself, straining my shoulders against it as if I were kneading flesh.

※

Still, I was not unduly worried. Say what you will about me as a parent, but you must admit that I have never demanded gratitude from my children, have never demanded that they thank me or behave well simply because I saved them. Indeed, I sometimes thought they would probably have been just as happy, if not happier, back in U'ivu, albeit with stomachs ballooned with malnutrition. And at any rate, most of them recognized at one point or another (usually in their twenties, or when they had children of their own) the opportunities I had provided them, after which they came to me tearfully, sweetly apologizing for their behavior and for the terrible things they had shouted at me over the years, and then confessed (sheepishly, but a little proudly as well) that they had long considered me a colonialist, a eugenicist, and an enemy of native cultures (the terms *Hitlerian, white man's privilege,* and *racial holocaust* usually made an appearance). And then it was my turn to pat them on the back and kiss them on the cheek and thank them sincerely for their maturity, and to let them know that their gratitude was more than I had ever expected but I was of course happy to receive it.

I always knew when this exchange must be had. After years of truculent behavior (glaring at me across the dinner table—I had one of them ask me what right I had to sit at the head; ostentatiously opening books whose covers bore the image of Che Guevara or Malcolm X; challenging my supposed political leanings), they would one day appear unexpectedly at the house, usually at a mealtime— they all seemed to think I enjoyed surprise visits as much as they did—and over lunch or dinner they would evince a sudden interest in my work, ask about my health, and bark at the other children for their poor manners. After, they would insist on doing the dishes, joyfully stacking the plates in the cupboard and heaving great nostalgic sighs. Then they would enter my study with a cup of my favorite tea and tremulously ask if I had a minute to speak to them, as there was something on their mind they needed to discuss.

*Oh god,* I always thought (they seemed always to want to have these discussions when I was at my busiest and most preoccupied), but of course I turned to them and said gently, "Yes, my dear. You can always talk to me about anything."

And then it was always the same. Tears, confessions, self-recriminations. The pattern never varied. You'd think the script had been passed down from child to child. Perhaps it had.

It was almost a rite of passage for them. After joining the household, there is a brief, pure period in which they love me, as touching for its intensity as for its brevity. Then there are years (sometimes decades) of hatred and resentment. Finally they are able to realize what beasts they were and what their lives might have been had I not adopted them and are overcome by a simple, powerful gratitude, which they feel they must share. I had always been slightly amused by this, but nothing more. Happy that they had matured, of course, but not terribly surprised. Children enjoy these sorts of rituals, the palpable (though of course contrived) sensation that they are physically or emotionally leaving behind one imagined stage in their lives and traveling to another. And really, they were not as far from their native culture as they knew; in U'ivu their adulthood would have been celebrated with feasts and ceremonies, and I suppose their confessions and carefully prepared speeches were in their way a ceremony of their own.

So Victor's little prank was nothing I had not experienced before; after all, it was not the first time a child of mine had yelled at me, passionate with the fiery resolve of the young. But Victor proved to be more determined and stubborn than most. This was not exactly surprising—such qualities had always served him well, had indeed saved him when he was a toddler and starving and had only his inexplicable tenacity to hold him to life.

At dinner that night (with an extra loaf of the bread I had had to finish making on the table), he ate hungrily, helping himself to an enormous second serving of spaghetti, over which he slopped an extreme quantity of sauce.

"That's enough," I told him, but he pretended not to hear me, didn't look up.

To my left and right, Kerry and Ella (who had shown up unexpectedly for dinner; I knew I would soon be in my study, patting her on the back and murmuring words of comfort at her) were discussing Ella's college's lacrosse team. Next to them sat the twins, Jared and Drew, and then Isolde and William, Grace and Frances, Jane and Whitney, and finally, at the foot of the table, Victor.

There are always many times during the day when you must wonder, do I step into the fray of the argument now? Or do I wait until later? Raising a large number of children is actually not unlike running a lab. Do you challenge your renowned colleague in front of the juniors? Or do you wait until the two of you are alone to ask him to justify his opinion or conclusions? It is not only or always a matter of exerting your power; as heady as that can be, you must never forget that cordial relationships must be maintained above all else. It is, if possible, always preferable to address the person at fault in private; public humiliation makes people angry, then vengeful, and if they are even a little intelligent, that can be a very dangerous thing. I had to be circumspect at work; I did not want to have to be so in my own home. So I did not rebuke Victor when he ignored me. But when I looked at him, mechanically stabbing his fork into his mess of noodles (bloodied with sauce and looking like a shredded mound of raw flesh), something in me broke and I seethed.

But I remained calm. "Victor," I called to him, "will you please pass me the salad?" All of the food—the pasta, the sauce, the bread, the fish, and the salad, which he had of course not touched—had somehow migrated to his end of the table.

He did not look up, kept chewing. I could see the powerful veins at his temples throbbing grotesquely.

*Oh god,* I thought, more weary than anything else. Still, I did not raise my voice. Around me the children continued talking: Kerry to Ella, Jared to Drew, Isolde to Grace, Frances to Jane, Whitney to William. Only Victor was silent, chewing, chewing. "Victor," I said, a little more sharply but not angrily. "The salad, please."

Still nothing. But now Grace, who was seven and who had just weeks before graduated from eating with the babies, and who had been exceedingly careful, with all her best manners on display, gave me a quick worried look and reached her arms out for the bowl of salad.

"No, darling," I told her. "It is too heavy." She was a worried, solicitous child, Grace, and was often just as likely to cause a horrible mess in her attempts to help. "Victor," I said. "Please pass me the salad. Now."

By this time the other children had noted my tone and were looking between Victor and me, watching to see what might happen. Why, I wondered, must everything become a show? Why were they always so eager to become spectators? And still Victor said nothing, only stared at his plate and chewed and chewed.

But I kept on. "Victor!" Nothing. "Victor!" Nothing. *"Victor!"* His name had begun to feel strange in my mouth, and for a second, hearing it aloud in its two parts, like a plastic egg cracked in half— Vic. Tor.—I thought, *He's right. It* is *a ridiculous name.* But that soon passed, and I was flooded with anger once more.

And then I heard Grace's hoarse little voice, the sound of which always made me wince. "It's Vi, Papa. Victor's called Vi now."

Here I must admit that I was flabbergasted, momentarily struck speechless. "What's this, darling?" I asked her.

"Vi," she repeated. "He told us last week." I saw the twins nod in agreement. I avoided looking at Victor but knew he was smiling his stupid, smug smile, the one that made me want to smack him as hard as I could and keep smacking him until his eyes became shiny with tears and his face grew ugly with misery.

But of course I did not. "Is that so?" I asked sternly, looking around at the table, watching the children lower their eyes.

Only Whitney met my gaze. "Yeah," he said. He was twelve and already busy hating me, but he had always been a fast learner. "If you were around more often, you might know that." He looked over at Victor eagerly, as if expecting to be praised for his loyalty and complicity, but Victor (and here I had to look at him) stared straight at me, grinning significantly.

Silence would perhaps have perplexed me, but children can never resist the sound of their own voices, and Victor was no exception. "From now on, I'm only answering to Vi," he announced, still staring at me. "Not Victor. Not Vic. Not Tor"—the twins giggled at this—"nothing but Vi. Everyone got it?"

"Oh, *Victor*," scoffed Ella, "you're so immature. Stop acting like such a child."

But Ella's scorn seemed only to glance off him. And besides, he didn't care what the other children thought of him; Victor never did. The point with Victor—it was always the point—was to infuriate me, to make me engage in his games.

"Victor," I began, taking a breath, and he raised his chin, readying for his fight. The other children were watching me eagerly; even Ella could not resist slipping back into the outlines of her old teenage self: she pretended to be dismissive, but she too was awaiting a juicy brawl. And then suddenly it occurred to me: *Victor is thirteen. I am sixty-five. I am too old and too accomplished to be arguing with this ridiculous boy.* "Fine," I told him. "That's fine. You can have your sisters and brothers call you that moronic name if you choose. It is only your dignity. Do you hear that, children? No Victor."

The children looked from me to Victor, and I could see at once that he was disappointed. Who knew what scrap-iron ammunition he had stored in his arsenal, what books he had read to prepare for our duel, which arguments he was eager to make, which theatrics he had anticipated employing? There is no one more disappointed than the pugilist whose sparring partner forfeits the fight.

I stood, and as I pushed my chair back, its legs made a sharp screeching noise against the floor. "I'm going to my study now," I said. "Isolde, you wash. Whitney, you dry."

"I'll do it, Papa," said Ella sweetly, over Isolde's and Whitney's complaints.

"Fine," I said, and turned to leave the room. When I was at the door, though, I stopped and spoke to the empty hallway. "This is the last minute I'll waste on this topic," I said, loudly and clearly so the entire room of children would hear me. "But Victor, don't expect me to call you by your new name. From now on I shall think of you as my No-Name Boy, like a stray dog, all right? But no more Victor, I promise you that. Goodnight, Ella, Kerry, Jared, Drew, Jane, Isolde, Whitney, William, Frances, Grace. Goodnight, Boy."

I didn't have to turn around to see what was happening in the silence; the children's anxious, excited expressions, their eyes gleeful with anticipation, and Victor's chin thrust high in the air, the inscrutable expression in his dark hooded eyes.

I realized in the days that followed that Victor had decided to think he had won a sizable victory against me. Unfortunately, this feeling was shared by some of the younger and more impressionable children; although they did not wish to be humiliated by me as Victor had been, they would engage in games they thought provocative, such as calling Victor Vi in my presence before glancing at me quickly and giggling nervously. I would smile beatifically or ignore them, and they would giggle again, all of which served only to severely undermine the seriousness of Victor's intent. He would only scowl and turn down his mouth. But soon they too tired of this game.

When there was need to use his name, I continued to call him Boy, but mostly I did not call him anything at all. In his confusion, he seemed to have become resigned to the name, mostly, I believe, because he could not find a good argument with which to counter it. As long as I did not call him Victor—and, true to my word, I ceased to do so at once, thinking carefully before I spoke to him—he would come when I called, grudgingly and slowly and in fact very much like a dog. (One could always tell which children were squabbling or dissatisfied with him, for they too would call him Boy; to his friends and supporters, though, he was Vi.)

After a few months, this became quite normal. In fact, many unusual things eventually become normal in a large family, in which a gift for consistent adaptation, not cleverness, is often the best means to survival. Indeed, for a longish stretch of time, life remained locked in its unexciting rhythms: the children went to school and played and fought and ate. Children detested me and others returned to profess their newly discovered love for me. I went to the lab and gave speeches and wrote and published. It was a contented time for all of us.

Thanksgiving arrived, and a dozen or so of the older children returned to the house with their spouses and children, their bags fat with presents for the current generation: dresses and soccer balls and motorized cars and trinkets from the mall that the children seized in a frenzy as if they had never seen toys before in their lives. That year we had twenty-six of the children at Thanksgiving dinner, as well as eight spouses and eleven grandchildren. Of course they could not all stay with me, even tripled up in the rooms, but they all seemed to spend a great deal of time idling about the house, and I was glad when the holiday was over and they returned to their normal lives and I was able to enjoy the brief week of quiet before it was time to prepare for the Christmas holidays, when the entire production would repeat itself, albeit with many more people. Still, I was eager for Christmas that year, as Owen and his current companion, a thirty-seven-year-old sculptor named Xerxes (whose real name, he had once accidentally revealed, was Shawn Ferdlee—Ferdlee!—Jones), were coming to visit.

The month between Thanksgiving and Christmas is always one of the most unpleasant in the year, and that year was a particularly difficult one. It had always been that there were in the house at least two or three older children to manage the younger ones' holiday shopping and gift wrapping, and to buy and decorate the Christmas tree the children insisted on, and then to supervise the cleaning and some of the cooking. As it happened, though, that year the oldest children still living at home were Isolde and William, who were both fifteen and therefore not of much use: neither of them knew how to drive, and both of them were still too young to exert any sort of authority over their siblings. The college and graduate students too were of little use; they generally made their appearance the weekend before Christmas, lugging with them garbage bags full of reeking laundry and preferring to spend their time squashed into the sofa, idly flicking through the television channels and sprinkling their dinnertime pronouncements with bits of atrociously accented but confidently delivered German or Spanish and brushing the little ones aside impatiently. Finally I called Ella, who was at university in Washington, and asked if she could come home for the weekend and, as I said vaguely, help out.

"Oh, I'd love to, Papa," Ella lied, "but . . ." And then she detailed a quantity of schoolwork she would have been lucky to complete in three years, much less three weeks. Apparently the brief period of intense, heartfelt gratitude, which often translated directly into compliance, that Ella had experienced after her lachrymose confession had come to an end, without my having benefited from it in the slightest.

*These children of mine,* I thought, and not for the first time. But as usual I was uncertain how I dared end my thought.

And so in the end I was forced to complete the majority of the work on my own. Mrs. Lansing had picked, of all times, the first week in December as the date to have her hysterectomy, which meant that my time at home was quickly filled with all sorts of dreary errands and tasks: I drove to the dreadful mall in Bethesda; I spent thousands of dollars on crackly silver foil wrapping paper, and plastic robots that, with a touch of a button, fired little plastic torpedoes from their arms, and yellow-haired baby dolls with bubbling eruptions of lace at their cloth throats, and scraps of dresses made from shiny, slippery fabrics that smelled of cooked vinyl. There were other errands and chores too, of course—I made heaps of cookie dough, most of which I ended up shaping myself, late at night, dousing the cookies with lashings of glittery colored sugar before burning them in the oven; I had the housecleaner, Mrs. Ma, come three times a week instead of twice, but not an hour after she had left found the house littered with debris and the walls waxy with smears of crayon. I think it is enough to say that I resented spending my time on the many conversations and tasks I was forced to have and do in a day. I was quickly and continually reminded of the wisdom of spending the month occupied with work and conferences (as I had every year previously), and I passed most days wondering why I had chosen to subject myself to such inanities and irritations.

I suppose part of the reason I stayed home was in anticipation of Owen, whom I was very excited to see; in November we had made up after a significant argument we had had the previous July, and there were moments during the intervening months when I had missed him so purely and profoundly that my chest would feel empty and cavernous. Then there was the fact that of late I had begun to feel very old and very alone, as well as exhausted, and I craved the companionship of someone who had known me earlier in my life, when I was unfettered and the only responsibilities facing me were my own. Sometimes I would look at Eloise, the youngest child, and feel a sort of despair. *Oh god*, I would think, *what have I been playing at?* In those moments I would suddenly see myself as a fraud, a charlatan whose joke had gone too far without his even realizing it. I would look at the children clustered around the table, eating and eating and eating, and suddenly find the scene both repulsive and unnatural. It was not the first time I had been struck by the fundamental absurdity, the excess, of the situation I had brought on myself, but it *was* the first time such feelings had been accompanied by such pure, unfiltered despair.

And then there was another, troubling development, as recently I had found my thoughts returning, again and again, to the boy, and how I had felt when I was with him, and how fervently I had hoped and tried to recapture that sensation, to make that joy part of my daily life—*that* was why I had brought them here. *That* was what I had wanted from them. And yet with each one, the feeling of pleasure I craved was ever-briefer, more elusive, more difficult to conjure, and I was lonelier and lonelier, and finally they were evidence only of my losses, of my unanswerable sorrows. Sometimes I wondered—had I adopted them to punish myself? And if so, for what? For Ivu'ivu? For Tallent? It was not a happy speculation, but it was at least logical in its way. Surely I have done this to myself for a reason, I would think; surely this is not for nothing; surely this is not just a folly; surely I have not imprisoned myself with these children as I had once been imprisoned by their parents and uncles and grandfathers, in a place that had taken from me everything I had loved. In these moments, I would watch the children dispassionately, almost as if they were monkeys in a lab and I would be able to leave them at the end of the day.

But of course there was no leaving them. I sometimes had dreams in which I was a traveler stranded in a land densely populated by strange, unknowable creatures. I had a notebook with me in which I recorded the sights I had seen during my travels, but the creatures were hard to describe, and harder still to draw. They were not pleasing, but neither were they beastly. They looked similar, but each had some feature that distinguished him from his brother: one had a great beak, massive and hard and cruel, the pale pink of milky blood, another a set of mud-colored wings that when lifted revealed a gorgeous riot of scarlets and lilacs. They were essentially benign, but sometimes one would jump on my face without provocation, its clumsy claws gripping at my nose, my eyeglasses, and squawk. Their home—which was in one direction a thickly bubbling swamp, in another impregnable forest, its endless columns of trees vanishing into an eggy mist, in another a parched stretch of livid orange dirt— was no less strange or understandable. But what was most notable about the landscape (which was beset with strange cycads, from which hung clumps of bananalike fruits, grossly swollen and smelling of sugar and peat) was its sounds: the air was thick with whoops and cackles and purrs and hoots, all of them so loud that the sounds seemed almost tactile and seemed, like invisible creatures, to fall from the sky and creep upward from underneath the tall, striped grasses. Sometimes I felt I could almost distinguish the calls and wondered how the creatures were able to separate one sound from another amid the din. And then I noticed that the creatures had no ears; they were making noises simply to feel the vibrations in their gleaming, scaly throats, to feel their frightening, imperturbable land echo with their sounds.

I experienced this dream often enough to become resigned to it. Initially its exoticism, its mystery, scared and thrilled me and left me full of awe. But later I found myself simply eager for my time there to be over. In the dream I would find a rock, furred with a soft fungus the color of eggplants, and sit quietly and wait to be transported elsewhere, out of this land whose mysteries had long since failed to move me with wonder. Above me, an unkindness of ravens, the only animal I could identify, flew in tight, swooping, mournful arcs. They flew back and forth, back and forth, their eyes glinting, sharp and beady, but although I listened closely, they never made a sound.

## III.

By the time Christmas Eve arrived, I was so eager for the holiday to be over that I had, the day before, accepted a last-minute invitation to a conference at Stockholm University that began on the thirty-first and lasted until the fifth of the new year.

It had been an awful week. The day before, I had had a conversation with Owen that had degenerated into a shouting match. Over the years, Owen—despite not having any children of his own—had come to determine that he was far more of an authority on them than I was, given his years of service educating undergraduates on the oeuvres of Whitman, Cavafy, and Proust. Even then, when we were old men, Owen's naïveté continued to astound me: after his infrequent visits, he would call to tell me that he had interpreted the children's complaints to him about the tidy and disciplined household I ran as "cries for help," as if I were a despot running a small slave state and he were a crusading United Nations envoy who had been sent to bear witness to their lives of misery and injustice. I did not care for Owen's behaving as an anthropologist in my own house, and I told him so. Still, he persisted, dispensing unwanted advice and even less wanted admonishments about a practice—the successful ferrying of children into adulthood—that I had been engaged in for more than thirty years and he for none.

That Christmas, however, he called, full of a degree of disapproval and self-righteousness unusual even for him, to inform me that Abby, one of the college-age students, had turned up in the lobby of his and Xerxes's building in New York, "scared and desperate" (his portrait of her distress was near Victorian in its piteousness), claiming that I'd thrown her out of the house. Yes, I told Owen, I *had* been forced to ask Abby to leave the house, where she had been squatting for much of the fall, because she had insisted on smoking marijuana in her bedroom, which I had asked her repeatedly not to do. Owen, unsurprisingly, thought this appalling and inhumane on my part. I normally did not engage with Owen's provocations, but in that moment I could not stop myself, and the fight quickly expanded in scope to cover my apparent decades' worth of parental shortcomings. To this day I cannot account for his sudden ire. Was it born of boredom, or the elderly's tendency to involve themselves in matters in which they are not wanted or needed? Or was it—as I sometimes thought, as much as I shrank from it—inspired by a sort of jealousy, something that I always sensed roiled just beneath Owen's consciousness, sometimes cresting, sometimes receding, but ever-simmering, its boil growing louder and hotter with each year, with each approbation that was given me, with each child I sent sailing into the world's slipstream? I had everything, after all, and he had only Xerxes and his thin books of poetry and a life lived mostly within New York State.

At any rate, the talk did not end well, and at its end he announced that he (along with Xerxes, whom I had been curious to meet, and Abby, whom for all I cared he could keep for as long as he wanted, if he thought he could do a better job than I) would be staying in New York for the holiday. "I'll send the children their presents," Owen snapped before hanging up the phone, and as dismayed and angry as I felt, I remember also registering his comment with some bitter relief: Owen could always be counted on for superior gifts, which the children awaited every year.

That night, after everyone had gone to their rooms, I ventured down to the living room with a large plastic filing box Mrs. Lansing had prepared for me shortly after Thanksgiving. Downstairs, dozens of stockings, each with a child's name on it, hung from every surface—the children had even taken down the pictures from the walls and hung their stockings from the hooks. The room looked like the result of an insane person's obscure and dedicated obsession.

Mrs. Lansing had written me specific instructions: each stocking was to receive from the box a ball of chocolate wrapped in foil that was stippled like an orange's skin; a rectangle of peppermint candy; a milky round of glycerine soap, in the middle of which floated a plastic toy (a dinosaur, a butterfly, a pig, a shark); a tiny spiral notebook with a tinier, blunt-nosed pencil; and a handful of the salty honeycomb candies I so enjoyed. In addition there was a wrapped toy for each of the thirteen children still living at home; for the adults and college students, there were envelopes containing checks. All of these I distributed—in the stockings, under the tree (awesome and horrible, it towered in the corner, covered with ornaments that had been made in school with construction paper and glitter and clotty gobs of glue that looked like tatters of litter, its hard white lights winking gaudily), taking care that every stocking had been filled. When I was finished, I sat down and ate some chewy and under-baked chocolate-chip cookies the youngest children had made and left near the fireplace earlier that night and returned the cup of milk to its plastic jug. I thought suddenly of my conversation with Tallent, his sly certainty that I'd find myself with children. Had he perhaps known what my life would be before I did? I had the sensation that I was being watched, or observed, really, and I turned, thinking for a moment I might see him peering out at me from behind the high-boy, his pencil gliding across the page as he stared at me, a specimen who had grown into exactly what he had expected. But there was no one there, and I was embarrassed, and relieved, and then embar-rassed anew to be relieved.

I was tired but not yet ready to sleep. Indeed, I felt itchy with impatience and disappointment. I had been brooding over my recent fight with Owen and found myself wondering idly whether I should not just call him up and apologize. *Listen, Owen,* I'd say. *I'm sorry. We oughtn't fight. We are both old men.* Five years before, I would not have dreamed of having such a conversation with him. But now our arguments, which had once seemed exciting and bracing, vibrant colorful displays of will and opinion, were enervating and tiresome. Perhaps I should simply call him and assume the blame, I thought. He would be momentarily triumphant, and it would be irritating. But, I thought, I had already written my own story for history, and it would not include the details of my spats with Owen: who began it, who ended it, who won, who lost.

Through the kitchen door I could see the moon, seeping a thin yellow light like pus. I stepped outside, and above me the sky was smeary with thin rubbings of cloud and spangled with bright white stars. I don't know how long I stood there, watching my breath leav-ing my mouth in ghostly streams, still holding one of the children's unsuccessful fat cookies in my cold fat hand. I could leave, I thought. I could pack a small bag and get into my car and drive away. I would take a plane to a European city, any city, and live there. Any uni-versity would accept me enthusiastically, with no questions. It was a perfect time; the older children were home, would take care of the younger ones, would figure out whom to call. The youngest children—little Eloise, Giselle, Jack—might, I thought, be adopted by the elders. The others, I assumed, would go into foster care, which would be regrettable. Although perhaps their association with me would find them adoptive families; I would be glad of that. But of course this plan would not do, no matter how logical it seemed to me.

It was now quite late, for the night was very dark and silent, and I was eager to return to my study. I would sleep, perhaps, for a few hours, and then the children would wake and I would find myself marching through another day. But when I turned the handle of the door to go back inside, it would not budge.

Almost immediately my mouth became rich with the flavors—old blood, brackish water, metal—of fear, and then anger. The door did not lock automatically; it had to be locked purposefully from the inside. I pounded on the door, slapping my palm against the square panes of glass. "Hello!" I cried, absurdly. "Hello! Let me in!"

And then I saw someone skittering out of the darkness. His torso was hidden by shadows and so I could see only his legs; for a moment, I fancied that it was not one of the children but rather an imp, a wicked sprite who darted through darkened houses, searching for its other half.

But of course I knew who it was. "Victor!" I called, as loudly as I dared, smacking the glass. To go around to the front door I would have to have been able to somehow straddle the wooden gate that separated the front from the back yard, which was not only taller than I but could be unlocked only from the front side (why? I wondered). I had no other options, no options but Victor. Screaming for help? It would not do to have the neighbors discovering me, the great scientist, in his bathrobe and slippers, locked out of his house and commanding one of his children to let him back in! (The other children I imagined upstairs, slouched into positions of unearned indolence, their round dark ears cupped with foam-fattened headphones, their poor fragile eardrums assaulted by thumping basslines, drumbeats, horns.) There was only Victor, only Victor. "Boy! Open the door this instant!"

The legs stopped then, a few feet from me. "Boy," I hissed. "Open the door right now. Do it now." I was about to threaten him, but then I realized how weak and pathetic it sounded: I was the one outside in the cold, with only my bathrobe for cover. He was inside, in the house, in *my* house. In the windowpanes I could see the reflection of the tree, its lights blinking meaninglessly. On and off, on and off. "Victor!"

And then he came suddenly very close to the glass, and I am sorry to say I took a short step backward, which he of course noticed. He smiled, and for a moment, with his fierce grin and sharp, bright, pointed teeth and his dark eyes—so moth-dark that it was difficult to determine where the pupil met the iris—he looked like a demon, and I was frightened of him.

"My name," he said, and I could hear him through the glass, "is Vi!"

"Victor," I said slowly, in a tone I knew was frightening, "you are to open this door right now. Then you are to go to bed. If you do not open this door right now, I will beat you so hard that you will be unrecognizable." To myself I thought, *I will anyway, whether he opens the door now or five minutes from now.*

But he just tilted his head and stared at me. Nor did he drop his ferocious smile, which stretched his mouth into a long, thin, evil-looking shape, like the blade of a scythe. It was, I realized, the same awful smile I thought I had rid him of all those years before, and I felt a shiver run through me. "I would have," he said, in a voice that was meant to mimic my own. "But you called me Victor. After you said you would not."

I knew he was not finished. "Victor!" I hit the door again. "Victor, you animal!"

But he was not shaken. "And so," he continued, "I'm afraid that makes you a liar. And what is it that you've always taught us about lying? That it is a degradation of one's integrity. But I don't believe that. I believe that it damages the person you lied to as much as the person who told the lie. And so I am going to punish you." He took a step back, so his face was lost again to shadows. Still, I could hear his voice. "I'm afraid," he said, in that cold voice, "that I will have to leave you there to think about what you have done." Another step back, so I could see him only from his chest down. And now his voice was fainter too. "It's never too late"—another step back; only his waist and legs were visible—"to learn a lesson." Another step back. "Papa." The word felt like no more than a whisper. And then he turned, and I could see the whites of his soles as he walked away from me.

I realized then that I had remained frozen during the last part of Victor's speech, and suddenly I saw my reflection in the glass: my palm, crepey and lined, scratching against the door, my mouth gaping and mute, my eyes startled and wide with the helpless confusion of the elderly. *My god*, I thought. *My god. Who is he? Who is this child I have living in my house?* I thought again of how I had found him, curled on the ground, covered with a layer of soot so dense it was like a pelt. Like an animal, I had thought, and had been outraged. But now I thought it again. *Like an animal.* And my outrage, though no less real, was not directed at his circumstances but at myself. I should have left him, I thought. It was never my place to try to save something that no one else had wanted.

But I continued to call. "Victor!" I shouted, as loudly as I could. I clawed at the door. "Victor! Victor!" I continued to bang against the door and call for minutes, hours. "Victor!" While upstairs, I knew, he lay curled up in the bed I had given him, in the room I had given him, and slept.

It was Gregory, one of the adult children, who found me the next morning, slumped against the doorframe. It seemed as if I had eventually succumbed to sleep, and when I was awoken by his cry, I was made to experience anew both the indignity of my situation and my physical dishevelment—a long sparkling floss of saliva stretched from lip to chin, and once inside, I began to shake with such ferocity that I could hear my teeth clicking against one another like castanets.

"Papa, what were you doing outside?" he asked me. I assumed he had already opened his envelope, for he was particularly solicitous, scurrying around me, handing me his cup of coffee, draping a blanket around my shoulders.

"What time is it?" I asked him, and my voice was hoarse; the words scraped against my throat.

"Eight," he said.

Eight. How long had I been outside in the cold? Five hours? Six? Only anger, the taste of it hot in my mouth like blood, had kept me from freezing.

Gregory led me through the kitchen and into the living room, where I saw that all the children had gathered and were busy palming handfuls of candy into their mouths, laughing and talking and fighting.

"Look who I found outside," Gregory announced loudly (he had always craved attention), and the others looked. And then at once there was a great sound, not unlike the sound of a flock of large birds rising from the beach, and a good many of them (the older and the very young ones only; the adolescents merely gazed at me stupidly) came charging at me, their arms open and expressions of great, elaborate pity wrought on their faces.

"Papa, we were looking for you!"

"Where were you?"

"Are you shaking?"

"You're so cold!"

"I didn't get as many candies as Jared did."

But I wasn't listening; instead, I looked among them for Victor. But he wasn't there.

And then suddenly he came whooping into the room, holding high in one hand a couple of batteries and tucked under his other arm the remote-controlled car that he had begged for and that I had bought and wrapped for him not a week before. "I've got them!" he was shouting, sliding across the carpet to land near Jack. "It'll work now." He had not yet seen me.

*That little beast*, I thought. *That wretched monster.* I wished fervently that he was dead, or that I might be able to kill him.

"Victor," I said, and I kept my voice icy. "Victor."

Naturally, he did not look up.

"Victor!"

There was no response. But by now a sort of murmuring, wondering disapproval was wending its way through the room. The adults, some of whom were not familiar with the battle that had been fought (and surrendered) over Victor's name change, scowled openly at him. "Answer Papa when he talks to you, Victor," I heard someone say, and a tiny voice, a girl's, responding, "It's Vi now."

Then I was walking over to him. "Stand up," I commanded him. "Stand up." He looked down, his mouth disobedient and wide and flat and ugly as a sand dab's, and would not. I grabbed him by his arm and brought him to his feet. He was only a few inches shorter than I, but scrawny, and I could feel the sharp, complicated bones of his elbow underneath my hands. And then I hit him, in the face, as hard as I could. His head jerked backward, then snapped forward. I hit him again. Both times I used the flat of my palm, and after, my hand stung in the same needley way it had when I had been slapping the glass, yelling after him. "How dare you?" I asked him, keeping my voice low and awful. "How *dare* you, you beastly insect, you thing, you *nothing*. How *dare* you come down here, partake in my kindness, my generosity. How dare you open the gifts you've done nothing to deserve but that I bought you—I *bought* you—out of kindness?

"Do you know," I heard myself continue, "why I took you in? I took you in because I pitied you. Because you were less than a human, less than a child. Your father would have sold you to me for a piece of rotting fruit. I could have done to you anything I wished. I could have taken you with me and kept you chained in the basement and no one would have known or cared. I could have sold you to a man who would first have mutilated you and then chopped you into bits for pigs' feed. There are people who would have done this, too, and your father was perfectly willing to sell you to any of them. It only happened that he sold you to me first.

"You are nothing. I gave you meaning. I gave you a life. And this is how you behave?" I slapped him again. A thin rivulet of dark blood began to creep from his nostril.

Around me the room had of course gone utterly silent. I knew that if I looked, I would see them as still as marble, their mouths slightly open, their arms full of the gifts I had given them.

I bent, still holding his arm, and picked up his toy car, his stocking heavy with candy, and flung them at the nearest child, who was too stunned to squeal in delight. "Toys are not for animals," I told him. "And you are less than one. Now go. Get out of my sight. I don't want to see you." I dropped his arm then, and he stood, slightly swaying, before turning and walking toward the staircase.

"No," I called after him. "Animals stay in the basement. Downstairs."

He turned again, still rocking a bit, and looked at me, directly at me. For a second a strange smile seemed to move over his mouth, but then I realized that it was one of confusion and fear, not triumph, and allowed myself to relax. And then, without a word, he turned again, and we watched him walk out of the living room, and through the kitchen, and then down the stairs to the basement, the door latching shut quietly behind him. I walked over, locked the door after him, and slipped the key into my bathrobe pocket. Behind me the room was still, as toneless and suspended as a scene in a picture.

The day was ruined, of course. The older children left soon after, waving vaguely in my direction and thanking me with a carefulness that I found embarrassing. The younger children cleaned up the living room without my having to ask and sneaked upstairs with their new toys and clothes. We usually ate together on Christmas, but that day I went instead to my study, and then to my bedroom, where I slept. When I woke, late that afternoon, I could hear the children creeping about downstairs, fixing themselves plates of food.

I stayed in my room all night long. Around me the house settled into a fur-thick silence. It occurred to me late that night, as I lay awake, that Victor had meant for me to die outside, to freeze against my own door at my own house.

*Oh,* I thought, and shivered. I had had children who had despised me before, had loathed me in fact, whose eyes were animated and had shone with hatred. But I had never had one who had tried to kill me, who had detested me so much that he would try to facilitate my end. Realizing this was somewhat perversely reassuring, for I was now aware what he was capable of, and it would be my new task to sort out how best to control him. I would not, I decided, be frightened of my own child. I could not.

The next morning, before the sun rose, I went downstairs to the kitchen and prepared two plates of food. On each I folded slices of turkey, a few sharp triangles of cheese, rolls crunchy with nuts, a spoonful of olives glistening with oil, and a mound of buttery lettuce. I set one of the plates in front of my seat at the kitchen table. Then I unlocked the door to the basement and placed the other at the top of the stairs.

I had half expected to find him sitting there, ready to spring into my face like a feral cat, but instead the basement was dark, the stairs vanishing into the black, and completely silent. Indeed, I could hear nothing, no breath, no sound. "Victor," I called into the dark silence, "I have left you some food." I paused, uncertain how to continue. "I will leave you more later today," I finally announced. I wanted to say something else, something declarative, but could not think of what it might be. And so in the end I simply closed the door behind me, locked it, and sat down to enjoy my meal.

At the end of the day, before I went to bed, I unlocked the door again to leave him another plate. But the one I had left him that morning was still there, its contents untouched, the edges of the turkey browning and curling like old parchment paper. I said nothing, though, merely placed the new plate down next to the first.

When, three days later, I opened the door for good, there were eight plates, each full of moldering food, completely undisturbed but for a single fly that moved dozily from one plate to another, complacent in the face of such unspoiled variety. "Victor," I called into the blackness, "I am leaving for work now. Please clean this up after you leave." Once again I hesitated, unsure what else to say. And then I left, leaving the door ajar behind me.

That day at work I found it difficult to concentrate: What would greet me that night? Whenever the phone rang, I flinched, certain that this would be the time one of the techs would come and fetch me, his eyes wide, to tell me that the police, the fire department, the hospital, was on the line for me. I had a vision of driving home, the sky above me dark with swirling clouds, and then I would realize that it was not clouds I saw but smoke, and I would follow it home to see my house burned to cinders, the lawn transformed into a volcanic sprawl, the children standing on the edge of the curb in a weeping clutch, Victor nowhere to be found.

But when I went home that evening, although the door to the basement remained open, the plates were gone. Later, I saw them cleaned and stacked in a neat pile on the counter, almost glowing in the white pool made by the overhead light.[82]

After that, the situation with Victor became, if not easier, then at least more predictable. Indeed, there is hardly anything more worth saying on the matter. He never became what I suppose one would call an exemplary, or even a good, child, but neither did he slide

---

[82] There is a section following this that I have, as an editor, elected to excise.

into delinquency, as I was certain he would. Instead, he spent the next five years in my house merely existing, at once both present and not. During the children's monthly movie nights, he would lie on his stomach, slightly separate from the group, and eat popcorn in the same distracted, vacant way he now did everything, staring at the screen without reacting. Sometimes after the rest of the children had laughed at something he might chuckle too, but it would always be a beat too late, and no one would understand why he was laughing. Nor, I think, would he. He became a set of social reflexes, many of them misapplied just enough to make him sometimes seem very strange, a person for whom time was measured on a different scale. He would look at me with those flat eyes, but where once had been challenge and obstinance now there was nothing, just a dull black like a shallow puddle of oily water.

If I am guilty of anything, I suppose, it is the fact that I was secretly quite contented with Victor's new state. And yet I knew too that it was not healthy, that it was not something I should desire for one of my children. But I could not help myself. He had been so horrible for so long that I almost allowed myself to believe that this was in fact who Victor had been before he had been seized by the furies of adolescence, before he had been transformed into a defiant, willful, uncontrollable creature, as different from the toddler I remembered as a beast was to a human. And besides, he was not a zombie; he took pleasure from many things in life: he competed with his high school's track and field team, for instance, and joined the school choir. (Listening to them sing at a concert, I could distinguish his flat, toneless tenor from the others' and wondered why he had not been dismissed.) His grades were mediocre, but he had never been a stellar student. Still, I told him—as I told all the children—that I would gladly send him to the best college that would accept him, and when that proved to be Towson State, I wrote the first tuition check straightaway and bought him a brushed-steel watch, just as I had done for both William and Isolde two years before when they had graduated from high school. Later I helped him pack his clothes and books and various knickknacks into boxes and garbage bags and left him at his dormitory room with his new sheets and towels Mrs. Lansing had bought him. After that I saw him less frequently, although of course he was always welcome in the house. Like the other children, he liked college, or rather I assumed he did, for I never heard from him. Really, only the bill from the bursar's office and the intermittent report cards (which told me that his major was something called sports ideology and that he was making Cs and, in a couple of classes, Bs) told me that he was still where I pictured him, attending classes or not, reading or not, perhaps going to parties or sleeping with pretty girls, the sort who found his elusive national origin exciting. At times I found myself wondering idly, as I had not done with the other children, what he had done the previous night or what he was doing at that moment. I pictured him in class, his legs stretched out in front of him, throwing back his head on his long neck and yawning, his mouth opening wide to reveal his fleshy salmon tongue and his white, white teeth, each topped with a tiny, pricey porcelain cap.

One day during the spring of Victor's sophomore year of college, I was sitting at home in the garden. It was a beautiful, damp day, the kind of early-spring day in which everything becomes, as if at once, a hundred unnameable shades of startling green, and I was gazing at the trees, their new leaves so tender and young and light that they were as translucent and resplendent as if fashioned from thin sheets of gold. I had come home early from work because I had been suffering from an intestinal flu, and my head felt cottony, my saliva tangy with bile. But I remember feeling grateful to be at home and in my garden, with the world quiet around me.

I was in such a state of enchantment that I did not even hear the knocking on the door, did not hear the doorbell's insistent chime. So when the two men came through the back door to the garden, I was surprised, and quickly stood. One was black and one was white, one older, one younger. "Who are you?" I asked them.

The young white one answered me with a question. "Abraham Norton Perina?"

What could I do? I nodded.

"Detective Matthew Banville, Montgomery County Police Department," said the man, and coughed, as if embarrassed. "I'm afraid, Dr. Perina, we have some questions we need to ask you down at the station."

Above me a butterfly, the first of the season, had suddenly appeared, flapping its clean white wings near my face in such a frenzy that I thought for a moment it was trying to beat out a warning, a message only I would be able to understand.

But there was nothing. And when I turned back to the men, they were still there, waiting for me silently, their faces stern and blank and dispassionate—not the kind of faces I was used to seeing at all.

"I need to get my pills," I was finally able to say, and Detective Banville looked at the other, who nodded, and the three of us walked into the house together. They let me go into the bathroom by myself, and I stood in front of the mirror for a long moment, staring at my face and wondering what was going to happen to me. I realized then that I had not asked them on what grounds I was going to be questioned. *I have done nothing,* I told my reflection, which stared back at me blandly. *I will ask them why they are here,* I thought, *and it will be nothing and this will be over and it will be as if it had never happened.* So I did go out to ask them, but as you know, it was not nothing, I was not let go, and my life, as it was, was forever changed. And had I known then how profoundly difficult things were soon to become, I think I would have endeavored to remain in the bathroom for much longer, staring at my face as if for answers, while outside the men waited, and the earth twirled lazily on.

# PART VII. AFTER

Now begins a very upsetting and difficult time of my life, on which I would rather not (but suppose, in the interest of honesty, must) dwell, if only briefly.

I have to admit that I remember very little of the initial interrogation and rather less of the arrest, which is strange, for I recall feeling extraordinarily alert and almost painfully engaged in the activity at hand (which was, unfortunately, a recounting of the events leading to my undoing). I remember looking about me at the colors and shapes sharpening and deepening in tone and line before my eyes, and finding the world oppressive, with its needlessly aggressive colors and strange objects and harsh, jangling sounds. Sometimes I would have to take my glasses off simply so the world would smudge and recede for a moment and cease to seem so relentlessly present tense. In particular, I remember waiting in an interrogation room at the police station, and even in the blandness of that space—the dreary, dimpled sea-gray brick walls, the stone-gray floors, the gray aluminum table with its silvery filaments like threads in silk—I felt attacked, as if the gray itself might gather into a great wave and drown me under its weight.

So. What can I say about the accusations, the investigation, the articles, the trial? What can I say about the institute placing me on administrative leave (after assuring me that I had its full support), about the quotes from unnamed personnel that began appearing in the articles in the *New York Times*, the *Washington Post*, the *Wall Street Journal*? What can I say about how my remaining children were taken from me, how I was denied access to Victor, how when

I showed up at his dorm room—I wanted only to talk to him, and he had not returned my calls or my letters—I was arrested like a criminal, even though I had every right to speak to him? It was my money that had paid for the room he hid in, laughing at me, and my money that had brought him here to begin with.

But although all of these things were awful, unbearable, the worst moments were not when I learned of my rapidly diminishing rights—each day seemed to bring a new betrayal, a new humiliation, a new insult—but when I learned of Owen's involvement: how after Victor had called him one night, it had been *he* who had urged him to speak to the police, *he* who had helped him find a lawyer, *he* who wrote the checks to his college after I no longer would. My own brother, my twin, my constant, choosing a child over me. I could not fathom it, cannot fathom it still.

Then there were more details. Victor had become friends with Xerxes, Owen's companion (how, I wanted to know—for did not that relationship, between a grown man and a college-age boy, seem suspicious in itself?), and it was Xerxes who had presented Victor's accusation to Owen, and Xerxes, presumably, who had convinced Owen of its veracity. This information I learned in shreds—an unhelpful piece here, an upsetting bit there—from the few children who had decided that they would believe me, the man who had paid for and raised them for these many years, over Victor. I was happy for their loyalty, of course, but there were very few of them, very few—far fewer than I would have assumed or expected—and at times I found myself outraged that I should even have to be grateful to them at all, that I should have to consider exceptional what should have been the only proper response.

In the end, though, it is not Xerxes whom I blame but Owen. "Who *are* you?" I asked him in my last conversation with him, one of the few we'd had between my arraignment and my trial, after which we never spoke again.

"Who are *you*?" he hissed before hanging up.

That was a bad day, one of the worst. On that day I crashed about my house looking for something to irrationally break, someone to irrationally kick. This was during the period when I was imprisoned in my own house, my occasional fantasy ironically having come to life: there were no children, no sounds, none of their possessions and odors and noises, although every now and again I would come upon one of their toys or an item of their clothing—a domino, which I mistook for a square of chocolate; a sock frilled with lace and ripped at the heel—that had been dropped in the state's haste to remove them from my oversight. For the first time in many decades, the bathtub drains were not clogged with deposits of their boiled-wool hair and the windows were not smeared into vellumy greasiness from the imprints of their many hands. I had always felt that the house seemed to vibrate, just subtly, as if a ghost train were making its rounds far beneath the bedrock, but with the children gone, I realized that that trembling was the collective presence of so many lives being lived in one place—what I had sensed was the shivering of speakers as a guitar was plugged into an amplifier, the crashes made from jumping from the top of a bunk bed onto the thinly car-peted floors, the tremor of a huddle of boys shoving and grabbing one another on their way to the bathroom in the morning. *Poor house!* I thought, and at moments I would find myself stroking one of its white-painted doorframes as if I were petting a horse's nose: gently, slowly, trying to soothe it back to calmness.

In those days I was convinced that nothing would befall me. I certainly did not think there was any good chance I would go to prison. For were not any mistakes I may have made with my chil-dren far overruled by the very fact of their existence? Later, during the trial, the lawyers would show the jury a family picture, with some of the younger children's faces blotted out with gray thumb-prints, but even so you could see that they were well dressed, that the lawn behind them was an electric, almost assaultive green, that their skin against it shone like polished rosewood. One of the faceless children—I think it might have been Grace, as a very young girl—was holding a popsicle, her arm flung out in an expression of obvious joy, the popsicle staining the inside of her wrist a merry crimson. I wished then that I had documented what they had been before I had saved them, back when they were as skinny as dogs and their skin the dusty chalk of rubble, back when it would never have occurred to them to make such a carefree gesture, back when they never would have let food melt away because they knew that there was always more, always another they could retrieve from the freezer. I thought often of Victor and of his special patheticness, and at night when I lay awake in bed, the only noise the refrigerator cycling through its monklike drone, I would wonder what my life would be like now if I had done as I ought and simply turned away from the man and boarded the plane, leaving Victor behind to live his tiny life.

But as it turned out, of course, I was wrong. I overestimated how much my magnanimity would mean. In the end it meant nothing—not in the face of the charges, at least. Against the charges, my Nobel could have been a plastic trophy I won for bowling, so little did it matter.

I saw Owen one last time. It was the day Victor came to testify against me. On that day the courtroom was quiet, and as I watched him walk to the stand, I felt, despite myself, a flash of something resembling pride: Who was this lean, handsome boy? He was wearing a suit I had not seen before and later assumed Owen must have purchased for him, and as he sat in the box, I could see on his left wrist the watch I had bought him. For a second I thought it might be a sign—surely he hadn't worn it thoughtlessly? Surely he could not feel its weight on his arm and fail to think of me, and consequently of what he might be doing to me?

He put on a good show, Victor did, and as he spoke—his answers brief and intelligible, his voice low, his eye contact with the prosecutor steady—I saw that I had raised him well. He was a monster, of course, but I had socialized him, I had taught him how to conduct himself, I had given him everything he needed to ruin me. After he stepped down, he looked in my direction and smiled, a beautiful smile full of expensive white teeth, and as I was deciding what he could mean by this, I realized he was looking not at me but past me, and I turned to see who could be the recipient of Victor's signal and saw Owen, sitting in the spectators' seats just a few feet behind me. He was next to Xerxes and smiling back at Victor like an idiot or a conspirator, and then his gaze shifted and he was looking at me, and in that moment, before his face could react and recompose itself into a glare, he was smiling at me, my onetime joy echoed in him, a mirror of my own past happiness.

That night my lawyer came to meet with me. "Change your plea," he urged me, but I would not.

"I don't care," he said after I'd explained to him why it was so unjust, why it was so unfair, and then he stopped himself and began again, his voice gentler. "The jury doesn't care, Norton," he said. "I'm telling you to change your plea."

But I didn't, and we know what happened next.

⁂

I have been told more times than I can tally how lucky I am: for the brevity of my sentence, for the fact that I have been placed in isolation, for my placement in this prison, which is considered one of the "better ones." I sometimes feel that I am a cretin who has been miraculously admitted into a top-tier school and is never to be allowed to forget my odd good fortune.

Now my days here are almost at an end. In my more optimistic moods, I tell myself that this place will soon be just another of the many I have occupied and left: Lindon, Hamilton, Harvard, Stanford, NIH, the house in Bethesda. But in my more sober state, I realize that this is not so: all of those places (with the exception of Lindon) are destinations I aspired to and won entry to, each one researched and chosen, each one a place where I took and took what I needed in order to move on to the next. They were all places I wanted and dreamed of, and when I was ready to leave each, I did.

This place, however, is the opposite: I was made to come here, and I will leave it only when they have decided they are done with me.

I consider myself fortunate always to have had very vivid dreams. Once, when I was a young man, I expressed this to Owen, and he said that my dreams were wild and improbable and bright-spangled because my mind in its conscious state was not; he said that no person could live without wonder and that my dreams were my mind's way of correcting my own literalness, of coloring my life with something of the fantastic. He meant it partly humorously, of course, but he was also serious, and we began a lazy sort of argument, one pitting the scientist's intellectual rigor against the poet's self-indulgence.

But since I have been here, I have had no dreams. They have disappeared exactly when I yearn for them, when I need them to fill my waking hours with their peacock extravagance. And in their absence I have begun to return more and more frequently to Ivu'ivu, which is, oddly, the place that this place resembles the most. Not in appearance, of course, but in its implacability, in its capture of me:

it will decide when it is through with me, and apparently it isn't yet satiated.

And so I spend my days allowing my mind to flit among a flickering film reel of images: I see the vuaka, its fur glimmering in the soft air as if lit by stars, and the peachy pink of the manama fruit. I see the fire smoldering beneath a charred creature, its skin slubbing off in jigsawed patches. I see the tornado of birds shrilling above a kanava tree and the opa'ivu'eke's rising head breaking the horizon line of the lake. I see the boy, his hands as bright as flowers in the dark night, moving over my chest as if he were washing off my sadness, as if it were something that clung to my body like a scum. And of course I see Tallent, walking through the trees still, his movements as silent as a sloth's, his long hair painting his back a river of gold and wood. Sometimes when I fall asleep in the middle of the day, dozing despite my best efforts to wait until the lights clunk off and I know it is night, I imagine myself walking alongside him. In these moments I have never left Ivu'ivu, and the two of us are companions, wandering the island together, and although it is small, it feels limitless, as if we could walk its forests and hills for centuries and never find its boundaries. Above us is the sun. Around us is the ocean. But we never see them. The only things we see are the trees and the moss, the monkeys and the flowers, the ropes of vines and the scuff of bark. Somewhere on the island is a place where we can rest. Somewhere on the island is a place where we belong, where we will lie down next to each other and know we will never have to look again. But until we find it we are searchers, two figures moving through a landscape while outside and around us the world is born and lives and dies and the stars burn themselves slowly into darkness.

*A. Norton Perina*
*December 1999*

**January 13, 2000**
**Renowned Scientist, Recently Paroled, Is Missing**
BY ASSOCIATED PRESS

*Bethesda, Md.—Dr. Abraham Norton Perina, the Nobel Prize–winning scientist who was recently released from the Frederick Correctional Facility, is missing.*

*Dr. Perina was convicted on two counts of sexual assault in 1997 and sentenced to twenty-four months in jail; he was released in January. Earlier this month he failed to report to his parole officer. Now county police report that Perina's home has been vacated and that none of his former colleagues have been in communication with him since before his release.*

*Compounding the mystery is the simultaneous disappearance of Dr. Ronald Kubodera of Palo Alto, California, Perina's longtime colleague and friend. At the end of last year, Perina reportedly transferred most of his assets to Dr. Kubodera, who was a scientist in Perina's lab for many years and was most recently a professor at Stanford University. The university reported Dr. Kubodera missing on January 3, after he had failed to report for classes for two days. His apartment has apparently been abandoned.*

*Perina, 76, won the Nobel Prize for Medicine in 1974 for his identification of Selene syndrome, an acquired condition that granted its victims extended lifespans while causing their mental decay. He was equally well known in Bethesda for his adoption of 43 children from U'ivu, the Micronesian country where the condition was first observed by Dr. Perina in 1950.*

*"We are determined to locate Dr. Perina," said a spokesperson for the Montgomery County Police Department. "Anyone with any tips as to his whereabouts should call the police immediately."*

# EPILOGUE

We have traveled far, Norton and I. I do not mean this in some vulgar, sentimental way but literally: we have traveled far. But I am afraid that is almost all I can say on the matter.[85]

What else? I can tell you that the air here is overwhelming, so full of scents that I sometimes cannot stand it and must retreat indoors, and that there has been no rain for the past ten days. In the kitchen, Norton likes great shaggy arrangements of flowers, so I spend a few mornings a week with P., our gardener, gathering armfuls of molting flowering plants, the names of which I still do not know. One is a stalky stem at the end of which is a bonnet-shaped cluster of individual buds, each as yellow as a Japanese pickled radish. Another is a branch from a tree, bristling with tiny flowers shaped like cracked pistachio shells. And still another seems to be a succulent of some sort, with thick, viscous leaves and stiff, turretlike petals. P. helps me cut them down, and I put them in a large glass jar; the sight of them never fails to delight Norton. We are very happy here, the two of us.

Sometimes, though, I will admit, I miss the life I left behind. I think often of my lab and my colleagues, and occasionally, of my children, whom I know I will never see again. There are times when

---

[85] I know the reader is probably wondering how we have managed to successfully avoid detection. All I can say on the matter is that such things can, under the right circumstances, be arranged without too much trouble.

Also, I would like to apologize in advance for the regrettable coyness of this epilogue. I loathe it myself but am sure the reader will understand that anything more candid could lead to unpleasant consequences.

I wish I could speak again to people from my past, or when I crave my old life and wonder whether I have made the correct decision. But these moments never last long, for I am always able to search out Norton—the reason I am here, after all—for a conversation, and listening to him talk reminds me that my decision, while perhaps one with its own set of imperfect realities, was the correct one. And at any rate, I am convinced that these feelings will diminish with time.

When I first came here, I yearned for information, for news, about the life I had left behind. Actually, I yearned for news of any kind. I could not help seeing my new life through the lens of my old. The second day here, I wondered, *What are they saying about me back home? What are they saying about Norton? What must they think?* I'd imagine my phone at the lab ringing, my mailbox stuffed with envelopes and pieces of paper. I had written a few notes before leaving, but kept my missives to a minimum: one to my ex-wife, explaining that I had left some money for the children in an account I had established at my bank, and since I would not be returning, they would be her responsibility; one to my sister, thanking her for her many kindnesses over the years; and one to the president of the university that did not say much of anything at all. I began (and rebegan) letters to my two children but was unable to find words to express what I needed to (and in truth was unable to determine exactly what it was I hoped to articulate), so I eventually gave up. Their mother, I know, will be able to tell them something convincing; she was always better at that than I.

Although these cravings have lessened, they do sometimes reappear, often at night, while I am trying to sleep. The first time it happened I thought I was hungry—after all, I had not eaten dinner. Careful not to wake Norton, I ventured down to the kitchen, where I stood in front of the open refrigerator, examining the dishes that M., P.'s wife and our part-time cook, had left there that morning. I sat down at the table with a plate of boiled chicken, cubes of cheese bathed in olive oil, and buttered zucchini and ate until the sun rose, after which I was violently ill. This gluttony unfortunately repeated itself several more times before I realized that my cravings were not for food but for something far away and unattainable. Understanding this, I am certain, will make withstanding these episodes easier, and at any rate, I fully expect them to disappear entirely with time. Any new life, no matter how long dreamed of and desired, demands a period of adjustment.

My story—Norton's story—is almost over, but I have two more things to share with you; one will follow the other, and it is not necessary to read them. Our story could end here, and it would be, I hope, as satisfying a conclusion for you as it is for the two of us.

There is one—entry, I suppose, of Norton's writing that I have withheld throughout this story, and I must admit that I am including it now with great ambivalence. I am not sure at all whether it is the correct thing to do. I am also cynical enough, I suppose, to understand that although it should not make a difference, it may. Therefore I can say only that I hope that it will stand as a curious little footnote (for that, really, is what it is; the story is no more or less without it) and that the many qualities that have been displayed to their best effect in Norton's writings—his wit, his intelligence, his passion and compassion—will be the things the reader remembers from this account, will be the things that define him in history. But after great consideration, I have chosen to include this fragment for no reason other than I think it remarkable for its awkward expressions of tenderness, for its openheartedness, for its proud expressions of love and its admissions of fallibility. It reminds us that love, at least the sort of pure love that so few of us will admit to feeling, is a complicated, dark, violent thing, an agreement not to be entered into lightly. One can disagree with Norton's opinions on the matter and still think him a whole, and a good, human being. At least this is what I hope, though it is ultimately for the reader to decide for himself; I have already made my decision, long ago.

The second thing I have to share with you—for I am as frustrated as you that I am not able to share more details of my life here, though discretion is of course a matter of necessity, not whim—is what happened that day, one year ago almost exactly, when I went to retrieve Norton from prison. It was a day that I had been awaiting for some time, and I had flown to Bethesda several days in advance in anticipation. For those three days I was able to think of little else but Norton. When Norton had first suggested his plan to me in a rare phone conversation, I had replied cautiously, even warily, but a few hours later I knew: of course this is what I would do. I had been waiting for it my entire adult life, after all, and could not find any misgiving serious enough to keep me from doing what I knew I would never regret. After all, I have always been loyal to Norton. I saw no reason that I should abandon that instinct now.

Finally, after three days of wandering around the town, with its expensive little boutiques crowded with useless bric-a-brac I couldn't imagine anyone ever buying (designer olive oils and vinegars; woven-rush baskets shaped like ceramic vases and ceramic vases glazed to look like woven-rush baskets), I drove to the Frederick Correctional Facility to collect Norton. I had run a few errands at his request: to the store, to fetch some supplies I knew he would need, and to his accountant and his lawyer. His lawyer met me with an expression I could not interpret and silently handed me the materials that Norton had asked me to retrieve. I had not seen him since the hearing, and we spoke only a few words. I did not visit the lab—indeed, did not desire to see anyone from our old lives.

At the facility I was frisked and made to walk through the metal detectors twice. I had left my bag, as well as the one I had packed for Norton, in the car. I was directed to a window where I signed several documents, and then made to wait in an evil-smelling concrete room. I watched the second hand of the clock tick past the minutes and waited. I had waited so long, I did not mind.

After two hours or so, an officer came into the little room to tell me that owing to a bureaucratic mistake, Norton had been processed earlier that morning and was apparently waiting for me at his lawyer's office. Of course I put up a ruckus, not because I was particularly annoyed for my own sake but because I hated the idea of Norton leaving without anyone to greet him and somehow finding his way to his lawyer's office by himself, all his belongings in tow. But then the guard told me that the lawyer had come to fetch Norton himself (a detail, may I add, that he might have told me when I visited his office) and that the entire process had gone smoothly. Still, I continued (simply out of my own velocity, I suspect) to berate the officer, who remained irritatingly serene and entirely unapologetic. Finally, sensing that the guard was of limited intellectual capabilities as well as apparently immovable, I was defeated. It was beginning to occur to me that it was the last time I would ever have to visit the prison, any prison, and I was suddenly anxious to leave.

At that very moment, I knew, Norton would be sitting with his lawyer, listening to him drone on about his parole and his obligations. He would nod, by all appearances be in total agreement: *Yes, yes, of course.* Of course he would submit to an outpatient program for committed pedophiles. Of course he would agree to see a psychiatrist. Of course he would agree to respect the terms of the restraining order Victor had requested. Nothing was too much, nothing was too constraining; he wanted to show he was a reformed man, wanted to be as accommodating as possible. He would sign documents, agree to meeting times and responsibilities that would, in a matter of hours and as long as we were careful, lose meaning. The lawyer, who had become strangely distant after losing Norton's case, would be condescending, but Norton would not mind; the charade would almost be over, and he would be feeling generous.

I was in a hurry. I know I have said that I was determined to be patient, having waited so long, but then, knowing that Norton was so close, that our new life together was about to begin, I was nervous and, for the first time in very many years, excited. I waited impatiently as I was patted down by an officer, and then finally there were only a hundred or so yards of hallway and a short drive left before I would see Norton once more. We would have a night together in a hotel, and then the next day we would be gone, and all of this—the years, our careers, our families, the trial, the humiliation—would be forgotten. Ahead of us lay something shining and clean and so new that I could not quite see it. And then I was walking down the hallway toward the exit, my heart beating faster with each step, and it was all I could do to keep myself from flinging open the doors, from running down the prison's steps and shouting, an unformed, squawking syllable of noise. Norton was waiting; soon I would see him. What would he want to do first, in his new free life?

Outside, as I approached my car, a flock of crows that had been congregating on its roof rose at once, a flapping, screeching rustle of black, and for a second I wanted to laugh. They seemed glorious, scattering into the toneless sky, which was as white and grainy as silt: I felt as if I could have seen forever.

*Ronald Kubodera*
*December 2000*

# POSTSCRIPT

*(This is the missing fragment from Norton's account of his difficulties with Victor, from page 339.)*

I would like to tell you that things became markedly easier after this episode, but they did not. Or rather, they both did and did not. In the days immediately following his release from the basement, it is true, Victor seemed willing to admit defeat: he was quiet and obedient and lowered his eyes shyly, almost flirtatiously, when he passed me in the hallways. Indeed, what was most noticeable about him was his new quietness. Victor had never been a particularly noisy child, but neither could he be called taciturn; he, like the others, liked to hear himself talk and make all sorts of pronouncements. He had been, I suppose, social, and soon after ceased to be.

I do not wish to give the impression, though, that he became a recluse after his punishment. Rather, he seemed to mature somewhat; there were no more curls of the lip when I asked him to do the dishes on a night other than his usual one, no more scowls when I instructed him to do his homework, no more heavy sighs when I reminded him to use his manners or modulate his voice or when I corrected his grammar. Instead there was a sort of blankness, an absence, almost as if he had been given a sort of benign, bloodless lobotomy. Still, he was not an automaton; he continued to do the things the other children did—fight, play, talk, argue, laugh. He never cried, but he had never cried. It was something I had always respected about him.

And I too played my part. He was a proud boy, and I understood that and could be sympathetic to it. So I never reminded him of his humiliation, never used his behavior as a lesson to the others. And I never called him Victor again. I wanted him to maintain his dignity.

But then, after a month or so of this new calm, he once again became beastly. He skipped school and lied about it. He pushed Drew down a flight of stairs and broke his wrist. He shaved—carefully, and with great artistry—an extremely vulgar word into the plush fur of our neighbors' cat. I walked into the room he shared with William one night and caught him doing this. For a minute, though, I could only stare at the tender way one arm encircled the cat while in his right hand, the razor—*my* razor—purred through the soft landscape of the animal's hair. He was murmuring to it in a low comforting way, but what was most startling when he finally turned was his expression: in his flat eyes were the expected defiance and rage but also a sort of genuine bewilderment, as if he were unable to stop himself from misbehaving, as if his hand, moving silkily through the cat's fur, was manipulated by demons over which he had no control.

After that, relations between us once again grew sour and dark. At dinner he would shout at me without provocation, hurl terrible accusations my way. Of course I was not hurt by them, but I was growing weary of these fights, of hitting him, of thinking of new ways to punish him, to force him into obedience. I dreamed one night that Victor was a particularly large and aggressive spider, with tough, sinewy legs and cruelly glittering red eyes. For some reason I was trying to guide him into a small and flimsy woven basket. I tried tricking him, forcing him, and even enticing him with a smudge of grainy honey, but he escaped me again and again, and I woke up with my hands, still in fists, sticky with sweat and frustration.

And then suddenly, just when I was about to throw him into the street or to have him institutionalized (such things are not as difficult as one might think if one knows the right people), he would improve, become compliant and almost meek, would seem once again to recede. But I soon grew to fear and mistrust these periods of fake calm most of all, for it meant that he was conjuring something particularly nasty; he would wait for me to be soothed into complacence and then, when I was fat and sleepy and unaware, would come flying at me, his inexplicable rage as sharp and dangerous as talons. At these times I wondered if he might be ill in some way, although really Victor's fury was too purposeful, too controlled, to be attributable to mental disease; rather, it was part of a concerted campaign to make me—what? Kill him? Kill myself? Even today I am not sure what it was he was hoping to make me do. Perhaps it was merely a game for him, a series of feints and withdrawals, each time more serious and potentially dangerous than the previous one. Naturally, I was able to dispense with him rather quickly; after all, I was the adult, and smarter and stronger besides, and he the child. But he was also a boy, and indefatigable, and had hours and hours in which to perfect his cunning, in which to sharpen his mischief as cleanly and carefully as another would whittle a blade.

One night I came home late from the lab and found on the floor of my study a neat little hill of shards. Stepping closer, I found it to be the ruins of a large crystal bowl that Owen had given me when I had won the Nobel. The crystal had been heavy and as pure as water, saturated with color, liquid lozenges of aqua and green the color of serpents. The bowl was one of the few gifts Owen had given me, and one of the most meaningful, for it had originally been his. Seeing it one day at his apartment, I had exclaimed over it and held it wonderingly to the light, watching the reflections of color it made slide around the room in circles. Owen had snatched it out of my hands, screeching that I would break it, and an argument had begun. But then that year a package, huge and bulky and wrapped in layers of brown butcher paper, had arrived, and inside, wrapped in cloth and tied with waxed red twine inside a wooden crate, was the bowl, as perfect and weighty and jewel-bright as I remembered it.

And now it had been destroyed. Victor—for I knew it was he—had pounded its lovely fluted base to smithereens, so all that remained was a fine pile of sharply glinting dust. The sides of the bowl had been broken into large, uneven pieces, and each had been scratched (with a stone, perhaps) so deeply that the lines seemed like decorations, inexpertly rendered etchings in glass. Underneath the remains of the bowl was a note, printed awkwardly on my stationery: "Oops."

I stood with some difficulty and stared at the bowl for many long minutes, listening to the clock ticking its uncaring tock. And then I turned and walked down the hallway to the staircase, where I paused again, waiting for nothing, and up to his room. At the doorway, which was ajar, I stopped and watched him breathing. William was spending the weekend at a friend's house, and Victor was sleeping in his bed (he had always been convinced that William had the better bed). I watched him breathe for what seemed like a very long time. He was sleeping on his back, his arms above his head, and his pajama top was unbuttoned at the bottom, so I could see a band of his dark, satiny skin, the sad protruding whorl of his navel. *Oh, Victor,* I thought, *what am I to do with you?*

I took a step into the room and closed the door behind me. The shutters were open, and I could see an edge of the moon framed in the corner of the window, its sallow light filtered by the curtains. Many thoughts spun through my mind, one following another, as I sat down on William's bed next to Victor's feet, but I do not think I would be able to articulate them now. Or perhaps even then; it was a torrent, a dark tumult of arms and legs of thoughts, a hideous, sticky confusion of fused body parts and howls, something one finds only in nightmares.

I stood and picked the pillow off Victor's bed and sat back down again. For minutes—I'm not sure how long—I held the pillow in my lap and watched him breathe in and out, in and out. I remembered again how I had found him at the field, how his body had been covered with oozing sores, how he had been too weak and exhausted to cry. I noticed a faint sickle-shaped scar just above the bone of his ankle. It glowed there, white against the wood of his skin, like a cartoonish smile, and I all at once felt very sad for him and overcome with emotion. I began to rub his ankle softly, caressing it with my thumb and index finger, and in his sleep he moved and smiled and gave a little sigh.

And then I was climbing on top of him and pressing the pillow against his mouth. His eyes, when he opened them and saw me above him, were bright and clear with fury, and then, as I pulled down his pants, with confusion and fright. I felt him begin to shout, although the pillow muffled the noise, and his voice sounded very far away, like a faint, fading echo.

"Shh," I told him. "It's all right." And then I was stroking his face with my other hand, cooing to him as I sometimes did with the babies. He struggled beneath me, tried to scratch my face, but I was stronger and heavier than he and was able to force his legs apart with my knee even as I caught his arms with my free hand, pressed down hard against the inside of his elbows.

As I forced myself into him—such a feeling: of relief, of hunger, of such a pure simple joy that I cannot adequately describe it—I felt once again that delicious flood of anger. "You broke my bowl," I whispered, absurdly, into his ear. "The bowl that my brother gave me. You beast. You little monster. You animal." Faintly I could hear his moans, and then, as I pushed harder, his sharp little yelps. I wondered if he felt as I did, as if my very insides were being scooped out and held aloft, the harsh, cold wind rushing through the cavity of my poor, filthy body, cleansing it and carrying away its impurities, scattering them to the night air.

I had been with many boys over the years, a few of them, I am not ashamed to admit, my own: beautiful Guy, with his long eyelashes and curls the exact shade of copper of his skin; Terrence, with his eloquent arms and legs and ink-drop spatterings of moles; Muiva, my first and in many ways favorite child. I had loved those boys, loved their beauty, their dreamy, resigned compliance. They were lovely, and I was a man who appreciated their loveliness, who taught them that it was their gift, their gift to bestow upon others. But I had never come to one with the same sort of anger, of rage, of terrible love and hate, with which I came to Victor. And he, for his part, never stopped struggling, even when I came to him the next night, and then the night after that, and many more nights after, whispering that I would punish him, that I would break him, that I would force him to behave. And then after, when I lay exhausted atop him, I would find myself uttering words of love and longing and making him promises I had never made before, my voice sloppy with tears. Later, when he accused me, I was shocked. For I loved him, you see, loved him despite everything. At the trial I would say that I had given him exactly what I gave my other children—money, a home, an education. But really what I thought was, *I have given him more than I have given anyone else. I have given him what I always yearned to give.* That moonlit night in William's bed, with him squirming under me, I knew what he had been trying to provoke from me, and that night I gave it to him, gave it to him without hesitation. For this is what I whispered to him before I left the room, as the sky outside began to lighten. "Vi," I told him, the pillow still over his mouth so he would have to listen to me, "I love you. I give you my heart."

# APPENDIX

*1924*: Norton Perina born in Lindon, Indiana

*1933*: Mother dies

*December 1945*: Sybil dies

*1946*: Father dies

*May 1946*: Graduates from Hamilton College

*June 1950*: Graduates from Harvard Medical School

*June 21, 1950*: Lands in Ivu'ivu (end of lili'uaka)

*Late November 1950*: Returns home from Ivu'ivu; begins work in a lab at Stanford University

*Spring 1951*: Begins first experiments with opa'ivu'eke. Group A consists of 50 mice of 15 months of age; 50 percent are given the opa'ivu'eke; the other 50 percent are the control group. Group B consists of 100 newborn mice (50 percent control, 50 percent given the opa'ivu'eke).

*April 1951*: Publishes paper on the opa'ivu'eke in the *Annals of Herpetology*

*July 1951*: Begins third experiment. Group C consists of 200 mice of 15 months of age; 50 percent are given the opa'ivu'eke; the other 50 percent are the control group.

*December 1953*: Publishes paper in the *Annals of Nutritional Epidemiology* (the so-called "Eternity Claim" paper)

*March 1954*: Adolphus Sereny begins his experiment replicating Group C of Perina's experiments

*April 1956*: Sereny readies his paper for publication

*September 1956*: Sereny's paper is published in the *Lancet*

*February 1957*: Returns to Ivu'ivu

*May 1957*: Discloses to Sereny the mice's deterioration

*January 1958*: Returns to Ivu'ivu. Publishes paper discussing subsequent mental deterioration from consumption of opa'ivu'eke in the *Annals of Nutritional Epidemiology.*

*February 1958*: Returns to Stanford; ceases contact with Paul Tallent

*1960*: Runs own lab at National Institutes of Health

*End of 1961*: Returns to Ivu'ivu; Tallent disappears

*1968*: Adopts first child, Muiva Perina

*1970*: Ronald Kubodera begins work in Perina's lab at NIH

*1974*: Wins Nobel Prize in Medicine

*August 13, 1980*: Adopts Victor Owen Perina

*March 1995*: Arrested

*December 1997*: Sentenced to 24 months in prison

*February 1998*: Begins serving sentence at the Frederick Correctional Facility

*GLOSSARY OF SELECTED U'IVUAN WORDS*

Note: Vowels in U'ivuan are pronounced as they would be in Japanese or Spanish.

*E*: Yes, or general greeting (hello, good morning, etc.)

*Ea*: Look (used as a command)

*Eke*: Animal

*Eva*: What is it?

*Hawana*: Many

*He*: I am (precedes an adjective)

*Ho'oala*: White man

*Ka'aka'a*: A now outlawed medicinal practice

*Kanava*: A tree; relation of the manama. Home of the vuaka

*Ke*: What? (Used as a response)

*Lawa'a*: A large fern resembling a Monstera

*Lili'aka*: Literally, "small sun"; equivalent to our summer and considered the most pleasant season (100 days)

*Lili'ika*: The Ivu'ivuan siesta; begins directly after the midday meal and lasts through most of the afternoon. On U'ivu, lili'ika was banned by King Tuima'ele in 1930, under the missionaries' influence.

*Lili'uaka*: Literally, "small rain," equivalent to our spring (100 days)

*Ma*: When preceding a word and followed by a glottal stop, an honorific (see below). Literally means "my" or "mine."

*Ma'alamakina*: The traditional U'ivuan spear all males are given upon reaching fourteen o'anas

*Makava*: A tree that used to grow on U'ivu and now mostly grows on Ivu'ivu

*Male'e*: Hut

*Manama*: A tree with an edible fruit resembling a mango

*Moa*: Food

*Mo'o*: Without

*No'aka*: A coconutlike fruit; its shells are used as bowls by the islanders; more commonly known on U'ivu as *uka moa*, or "hog food"

*O'ana*: The U'ivuan year; 400 days

*Ola'alu*: The prehistoric U'ivuan hieroglyphic alphabet; rarely used in modern times

*Tava*: A cloth resembling kapa made from pounding palm leaves into a fiber

*U'aka*: The hottest season, equivalent to our autumn (100 days)

*'Uaka*: The traditional wet season, equivalent to our winter; lasts for 100 days

*Uka*: Hog

*Umaku*: Sloth fat; used as a lubricant and a polish

*Vuaka*: A primitive micromonkey; considered a delicacy. Hunted to near extinction on U'ivu

# ACKNOWLEDGMENTS

My great thanks to Norman Hindley and Robert E. Hosmer for their early faith; to Fundacion Valparaiso and the New York Foundation for the Arts for their gifts of time and money; to Kaja Perina for her wit and good name; to David Ebershoff for his counsel and forbearance; to John McElwee for his humor and assistance; to Ravi Mirchandani for his charm and passion; to Jim Baker, Klara Glowczewska, and—especially—Kerry Lauerman for being delighted for me (even when I didn't know how to be); and to Stephen Morrison for his comfort, constancy, excellent matchmaking skills, and beloved friendship.

I am so very grateful to everyone at Doubleday for their enthusiasm and care, in particular to Bill Thomas, to the smart, soothing, and hypercompetent Hannah Wood, and, most of all, to Gerry Howard for his advocacy and large-spiritedness, and for being the kind of editor who offers his engagement and intelligence with such grace and selflessness.

To the lovely and steadfast Anna Stein O'Sullivan, who believed from the start and whose opinion and advice I always treasure, my forever gratitude, respect, and affection. To Andrew Kidd, who saved me at a crucial moment and without whose brilliant editorial discernment and enduring support I would have been lost, my profound thanks.

I owe everything to Jared Hohlt, my first and favorite reader (and all-around superior human being), for his kindness, intelligence, patience, wisdom, and dear presence—but I hope he'll settle for my inexpressible and unquantifiable love, thanks, trust, and apologies. Everyone should be so lucky to have such a friend.

And, finally, for all the qualities and generosities listed above, as well as their irreverence and taste, my deepest thanks to my parents, Ron and Susan. My father, in particular, has not only always encouraged but often abetted my every confabulation. For that, and for many other reasons besides, this book is dedicated to him.

# picador.com

blog
videos
interviews
extracts